The
Death of Valdez

Michael Seirton

First published in Great Britain in 2022 by STA BOOKS

ISBN 978-0-9933957-7-2

Copyright Michael Seirton © 2021

A CIP catalogue record for this title is available from the British Library.
This novel is entirely a work of fiction. Names, characters, businesses, organisations, places, and events are eiter the product of the author's imagination or used fictitiously, and any resemblance to actual persons, living or dead, is purely coincidental.

I dedicate this book to my wonderful mother,

The lovely, Irene Chambers 1916 – 2019

my lifelong friend and companion, without whose
unshakeable belief in my creative ability, I would never have
had the courage to attempt a third, yet seemingly impossible
career as an author

God bless you Mam, for every treasured moment we have
shared together, here in Netherseale, in Marlow, India and in
Hollywood

I pray that you are at peace, tending the gardens in heaven.
Your loving son, Michael xxx

3

Acknowledgements

With special thanks
Primarily to my agent, Fiona Spencer Thomas,
for her continuing support, and for getting the first novel
published in this unpredictable series.

Many thanks to my editor, Ian Howe,
For his careful editing and understanding of these important
characters, abandoned in an unthinkable situation.

Thanks also, to Joss Marsh for her earlier, editorial notes.

Chapter One
Archie Westbrook

When Archie staggered clear of the river, deep in the Amazonian rainforest, there was no sign of his rescuer except for a few long strands of copper hair caught up in the holster of his revolver. He had no idea who the incredible swimmer was but blessed him again as he found his badly injured friend Rolly, pulled just clear of the logs at the water's edge where their saviour must have left him. It was an incredible feat, given the mass of uprooted trees piled up in this section of the river. It was clear the man had risked life and limb, diving through a narrow opening to where Archie had been trapped by the turbulent floodwaters, seconds from drowning. Yet, miraculously, thanks to this unknown rescuer, he had survived.

With every ounce of strength he had left, Archie Westbrook hauled his friend clear of the riverbank and away from the ubiquitous black caiman. He cursed himself for his failure to prevent Rolly from being trapped by the crushing weight of the trees when their boat capsized.

Barely able to look at Rolly's shattered legs and crushed pelvis and knowing they had barely any time before the flooded river would surge again, Archie dragged the injured man as high up the bank as he could. It was clear, even had there been a hospital nearby, that Rolly would never recover from such dreadful injuries. Even so, he felt he needed to do something, anything to help ease his childhood friend's pain. His first thought was to get him back upriver somehow, if the boat could be salvaged. Otherwise he knew Rolly would be dead before they could reach the nearest village, not that he even had any idea where to find a settlement in the dense forest.

"Drink this, Rolly," Archie said, easing his friend up as gently as he could and tilting the hip flask against his gasping mouth.

"Aghhh! For pity's sake, Archie, lay me back down!" Rolly screamed, pushing the flask away.

"I have nothing to ease the pain, Rolly. All I have is whisky."

"Then save it for yourself and put me out of this misery. Shoot me, Archie. For God's sake do it," he gasped before screaming again.

"You can't ask me to do that, Rolly," Archie said hesitantly. Yet he knew that the exposed, shattered bone and the flow of blood that was impossible to stem, meant that it was only a matter of time. Archie had only three bullets remaining in his revolver and, once any predatory animals got the scent of blood, there would be little chance of keeping them at bay.

"If you ever cared for me, Archie, then do this. I'm begging you!" he shrieked, writhing in agony and smashing the flask from Archie's hand. "In the name of Christ... Archie, help me you bastard. You would not let an animal suffer like this."

"I would do anything for you, Rolly, but not this."

"You must... I would do it for you if you asked." Rolly screamed again before he mercifully fell into a state of unconsciousness.

Tearing his shirt into shreds, Archie packed the material against the severed artery while he applied tourniquets to the splintered thighs. Searching through his backpack, he found what remained of his medical kit; miraculously a phial of morphine was undamaged and, while the syringe had a bent needle, it was just about useable. With Rolly on the verge of regaining consciousness, Archie straightened the needle as best he could and injected the morphine into his friend's arm, only then allowing himself to deliberate on what to do next.

Having only a hunting knife and no saw, it would have been impossible to remove the crushed legs before he recovered. The only alternative was to bind up the limbs with splints, hastily improvised with saplings, which he then

6

lashed up tightly with vine. Archie had barely completed the task when Rolly began to wake. Fortunately the morphine was beginning to work, although not well enough.

"Holy mother of God, Archie, what are you waiting for? Shoot me. You will never get back alive with me in this state," he pleaded.

"I am not leaving without you, Rolly. There must be a village close by with a tribal shaman who might help."

"Bollocks, Archie. My legs are useless and my spine is crushed. It's only a matter of time before some predator finds us. I don't want my life to end in the jaws of one of those bloody caiman. It must be by your hand, and soon."

"You can't ask me to do this. It is not Christian."

"And you think allowing me to suffer like this is? If our friendship ever meant anything to you, do it now, before the morphine wears off." The stains on the bandaging around his thighs, already crimson, were spreading, his fingers clawing at the air with desperation.

"Are you really sure about this, Rolly?" Archie said, checking the remaining bullets in the revolver.

"I am; only promise me that you will continue with the search for your friends, otherwise my life will have counted for nothing."

"Then I promise you this faithfully," Archie said, and he squeezed the trigger before he had time to change his mind.

It took Archie a full day before he'd buried the body deep in the earth, covering it with a mound of stones. To mark the burial place, he fashioned a crucifix from a shattered plank caught up in the debris, and on it carved an image of Rolly's old dog, with which they had grown up on his father's estate in Ireland.

After the burial, he again examined the long strands of bronzed copper hair trapped in his gun holster during the underwater struggle, the only clue to his rescuer's identity. Archie carefully removed each one and plaited them into a neckband, knotting it around his neck for good luck. He had no intention of ever taking it off.

It took three more days before Archie finally left the area, having salvaged whatever food he could retrieve from the wreckage, to make his way back to the port of Apalla on foot. He was now more determined than ever to locate the missing family who had disappeared without trace almost two years earlier. It was doubtful that any member of the aristocratic English family could have survived in such a remote region of the Amazonian rainforest without help. His only hope was that perhaps they had located the absentee parent, Lord Oliver Saint Hubes. He would not give up the search, not only because of the promise he had made to his childhood friend but for his own peace of mind.

After journeying overland for a week on foot, being almost crushed by an anaconda and escaping a jaguar which he killed with his last bullet, Archie finally made contact with a small, friendly tribe, with whom he traded his hunting knife, a shaving mirror and a hurricane lamp for the loan of a dugout canoe, along with Tark, a sturdy paddle-man.

Eventually, after three weeks of arduous paddling, they reached the small port of Karaka. From there, Archie got passage on a steamer bound for Apalla at the mouth of the Amazon, the last known whereabouts of the missing family. From here he planned to make a return trip with more information as soon as the floodwaters had subsided.

He had met the family he was seeking for less than ten days at his grandmother's plantation in Pernambuco but the mother, Lady Claudia, had grown up with his father Rufus on neighbouring ancestral estates in southern Ireland until they were separated by their feuding parents in their late teens. Soon after, she had married Lord Oliver, a charismatic and handsome man with an eye for a beautiful woman who had investments in a research facility at the Hospital for Tropical Diseases in London. It was there that Lady Marguerite, their eldest daughter was born, a talented watercolourist who, if she had survived, would now be twenty-eight.

8

Her sister Rosamund, he calculated, would by now be almost eighteen and two years earlier was already showing signs of becoming an elegant beauty like her mother. The last member of the family was Sir Geoffrey who, although just as handsome as his younger sister at barely eleven months older, was undoubtedly the most annoying teenager Archie had ever met. It filled him with dread to imagine how a sensitive and talented musician like Geoffrey, not to mention his refined mother and sisters, could possibly have survived in an uncharted area of the rainforest. Archie damned their father for forcing them to make the perilous journey from England, solely so that Lady Claudia could locate and finally divorce him.

Before he set off again, Archie sent a telegram to his grandmother, Lady Harriet Drummond, informing her that he was safe but would be unable to return to the plantation for at least six months. He chose not to mention anything about the death of Rolly until he was able to tell her in person but he did write to Rolly's mother, who had been a cook on his late father's estate in southern Ireland. Once the messages were dispatched, he went directly back to the shipping office to seek out any additional information on the family's last known destination.

"I gave the other clerk all the relevant details," Archie said, waiting for the man to finish eating.

"Who are you again?"

"Archie Westbrook. The information concerns the Lady Claudia Saint Hubes and her three adult children, who docked here in the summer of 1909."

"And what would such a lady and her party be doing here, this far away from the city?" the man asked, waving off a swarm of flies that were buzzing around him.

"Why they were here is irrelevant. My question is, can you help me or not?"

"Probably not. I know of no one by that name."

"Surely there must be something in your records?" Archie persisted.

"Only the shipping movements are kept in this office. Nothing is recorded on either freight or passenger information. All documentation is collected by head office at the end of each month. If not I would be buried alive in paperwork and ledgers, as you can see by this lot." The clerk indicated shelves crammed with ledgers and boxes balanced on filing cabinets piled high with damp and curling paperwork.

"There must be some way of finding out what happened to them."

"Someone might remember if it was two weeks ago but not after two years."

"There has to be some record of passengers. The previous clerk said he would look into it."

"That was a year ago. If you had bothered to come back here again after you asked, then maybe Sanchez might have been able to help but, as I have already explained, he is long gone from here and I cannot help you now… sir," the clerk said.

"Then what about the shipping agent in charge before him? Emile de Costa was the name my grandmother remembered. I passed his name on to Señor Sanchez," Archie said with growing exasperation. "Surely there is a contact address for him? You must keep records on your own staff, for heaven's sake?"

The clerk, clearly frustrated, lifted down an armful of ledgers, which he went through grudgingly until he came across the relevant entry.

"There is some paperwork in here about an Emile de Costa," he said, removing a folded note. "The register here states that he was only engaged by the company in a temporary capacity, sir."

"Might that paperwork you have be connected with the Saint Hubes family or the shipping agent?"

10

"It could be, if this note is what Sanchez tracked down."

"Might I take a look?" Archie asked.

"I cannot allow that, sir, it is against company policy but what I can tell you is that the de Costas' house in Apalla was sold at auction well over a year ago. Beyond that, there was no other contact address." He refolded the note and replaced it in the ledger.

"And that's it?" Archie asked. With no other lead to follow, his hopes of tracing the family seemed to be at a dead end.

"Would that be all?" the clerk asked, poking his teeth with the point of a pencil.

"Not quite," Archie said. "I do have one last question. Perhaps you might have information on what other vessels were in this port when the ocean liner *Lugansa* sailed for England during the period in question."

"I am a clerk, sir, not a miracle worker!" the man retorted, wafting away the flies that were buzzing around the remnants of his food.

"It would hardly need a miracle to check the exact date the *Lugansa* was docked here in the summer of 1909, now would it?"

"And what exactly would that achieve... sir?" he asked, staring at Archie as though he was insane. "Surely it would be more sensible to get the date of departure, if you need to locate these people?" The man wiped the pencil on his grubby linen jacket.

"That would be pointless, since the family never arrived in England. Once I have the relevant docking information it can be cross-referenced to the vessels that were here at the same time and what ports they might have docked at along the Amazon."

"I cannot do that right now. If that will be all, there is important company business I must attend to," the clerk said dismissively.

"Very well, but I am not done yet. I will come back again tomorrow and every day after that until I get the information I require." Archie held out a silver English crown temptingly between his fingers. "Once I get what I require, this will be yours. However, if you are able to have that information ready for my return, this amount will be doubled."

"I will do my very best to oblige, sir," the clerk said, eyeing the coin greedily.

"Expect me here at seven in the morning," Archie called back as he walked out.

After a restless night, Archie entered the shipping office as the clock struck seven. Laid out on the previously cluttered counter were three worn shipping ledgers, already open at the relevant pages. In the first was the shipping log with a date when the *Lugansa* had docked at the port of Apalla. In another, he found nothing except for a shallow-draught steamer loaded with animal hides. In the final ledger, there was reference to a paddle steamer that was due to dock at the small port of Karaka, the very port from which Archie had recently returned. Beyond that, the steamer had been due to call in at the port of Coyacuche, before making the return trip.

Armed with this new information Archie handed over two silver crowns to the clerk and made a reservation for travel on the following day to the port of Karaka on a mailboat. Rolly had made endless enquiries at that same port when they first began their search, and he doubted there would be any new clues to follow up after another lapse of time. But he was now intent on chartering a steamer and captain to search the smaller tributaries.

Once Archie arrived in Karaka the search could begin in earnest but, having had no luck at the shipping office, he decided to call in at some of the drinking houses to try and discover more information.

12

"What I am looking for is the captain of a shallow-draught boat, who is both honest and reliable, and prepared to navigate some of the lesser-known tributaries if that is where the search leads us," Archie asked of the bartender at the third tavern he'd entered that morning.

"That no easy want, señor," the barman said, scratching his beard.

"I do not see why. There must be twenty steamers moored along this stretch of water."

"Boat is no problem, señor."

"Then what is?" Archie asked.

"Captain the problem, if you asking for honest," he said, shaking his head.

"Surely there must be someone trustworthy you could recommend?" Archie glanced around the room for a possible contender.

"Maybe you like Captain Papas, most of time him honest. He try be good Catholic," the barman said reluctantly.

"Which one is he?" Archie asked, scanning the dimly lit room.

"Captain Giorgio, in back room, he sleeping from hangover," the barman explained.

"You cannot seriously be recommending a drunk?" Archie said.

"Captain Giorgio... sometime he drink much but not all time, señor."

"I need someone I can trust with my life in a difficult situation. I am not looking to charter a boat for hunting. I am on a mission to locate a missing family. A drunk would not be reliable," Archie said, his distinctive brogue becoming more pronounced as his concern grew.

"But señor... you Irishman, I think; you drink plenty, no?"

"On occasion, yes I might, but not when I need a clear head."

"Captain Papas would never risk damage boat, señor. Giorgio care more for that old wreck than he do for wife." The barman smiled broadly. "He only drink much when whoring, him fine after sleep."

"You seem to know a lot about this man. Is he a regular?"

"Si señor, he my father." The barman smiled again. "Captain Giorgio, him speaking much good Inglesi, better than me."

"That is a plus, since my knowledge of Spanish is not good. What about his navigational skills?"

"He know backwater tributaries better than most. Juanita, my wife, she no like Giorgio on dry land but on river, she say him much good captain."

"She trusts him then?"

"Only for navigate boat, not as good Catholic."

"Then it is fortunate I am not looking to be converted, just for a boat with a trustworthy captain."

"Then Captain Giorgio is man señor need."

Even though his son seemed confident that Captain Giorgio was the right choice, Archie had his doubts. The bartender was well into his thirties, which meant that his father must be close to sixty. However, the man's English was a lot better than he was expecting and he had even recognised Archie's Irish accent. If his father's linguistic, observational and navigational skills were similar then, drunk or not, the man would probably suit Archie's needs very well.

On first impressions, Captain Giorgio Papas was a likeable rogue, though as he rarely had a flask of whisky very far from his reach Archie wondered if his decision-making might come into question later. But the captain was clearly well aware of the dangers of venturing down the uncharted tributaries and seemed generally cautious. In the light of what had happened to Rolly, Giorgio was a suitable choice and because of his good grasp of English, Archie soon began to relax in his company.

"Where do you want to begin this search, Señor Archie?" Captain Giorgio asked.

"I was thinking that perhaps one of these branches here might be an option, after we call in at Coyacuche," Archie said, consulting the captain's detailed, hand-drawn map.

"Coyacuche... that is music to the ears of an old river dog and, since we are docking there, what interests me is what a fine gentleman such as you will think of our town of whores without giving into temptation," Giorgio laughed.

"Trust me, Giorgio. I am not suggesting we dock there to sample the pleasures of the flesh. I am only interested in getting information that will help the search." Archie hoped his words would put an end to further tales of the captain's sexual exploits. However, the town's unsavoury reputation gave him good reason to wonder how an upright English family would have reacted to such a place, if indeed they had docked there. How might the impressionable, barely eighteen-year-old Geoffrey have coped with the inevitable attention his extraordinary good looks would have attracted from the predatory madams of Coyacuche?

"How old are you, Señor Archie?" Giorgio asked unexpectedly.

"I will be twenty-six next month. Why do you ask?"

"I ask merely out of curiosity, because most men in my acquaintance with wives back home would be like dogs on heat, straining at their leash once we docked at that port."

"All men are not the same, Giorgio. Some have moral standards, which your son and I apparently share."

"Please tell me you are not a virgin at your age, señor!" Giorgio spluttered, laughing uproariously.

"No I am not. I have a son." Archie responded swiftly to the jibe, regretting it instantly.

"Why no wedding band if you are married?"

"There would be no point since I am not but it is my intention to be in the not-too-distant future. It was my father's dying wish that I should produce a legitimate heir."

"I see by that smile, señor, you already have someone in mind."

"If she is still alive, then yes I do," Archie said, before focusing his attention on Giorgio's chart.

From Karaka, the journey to Coyacuche took three days. Thanks to Giorgio's navigational skills they avoided two potentially serious accidents with larger vessels on route, and Archie knew he had made the right decision.

"Señor Archie!" Captain Giorgio called suddenly, pointing towards the far bank. A Spanish galleon sat wedged high on a rocky outcrop, just a few feet above the height of the most recent flood. The ancient vessel must have been at least 300 years old, but its presence here confirmed what Archie had read about a similarly disastrous flood centuries earlier, when in 1568 a monstrous tidal wave had uprooted acres of the ancient forest and devastated the area.

"It is hard to believe that a ship of that age could still be intact," Archie commented.

"Built to last, I suppose, unlike this rust-bucket of mine."

"Even so, exposed to this awful humidity, why has it has not rotted away by now."

"Probably because it has been well taken care of," Giorgio snorted, emptying some tobacco out of a pouch before rolling a cigarette between his nicotine-stained fingers.

"Who would want to?" Archie asked. "It would be impossible to refloat."

"Not if the owner is living there."

"What the hell is he, a privateer?" Archie asked with amazement.

"Who can say for certain? Although, with his reputation for collecting fine works of art, he might well be something like that."

The port of Coyacuche was a modest-sized town, built partially into a hillside, with a cluster of makeshift shacks of varying sizes and shapes close to the water's edge. Here the floodwater had deposited mounds of stinking refuse that was not carried away with the current when the water level receded. There had been considerable flood damage to the docking area where some reconstruction was now under way. On higher ground, away from the docks, there was a large warehouse at the edge of the town, surrounded by run-down taverns and whorehouses. It had been a fashionable district at one time, with cobbled streets lined by once elegant buildings, most of which were in various states of crumbling decay, leaving only fragments of the architectural detail evident on the imposing facades.

In one of the streets closest to the dock, a number of enticing young women lounged provocatively outside the houses, receiving attention from the recently disembarked crew of a cargo steamer. What most of the men failed to notice was the haggard faces of older women peering through the windows, or the toothless hags pegging out sheets in side alleys, women who would be brought in later in dimly lit rooms to swell the ranks whenever trade became too brisk or the customers were too drunk to care.

Surprisingly, although Captain Giorgio seemed well known to some of the brothel madams, he never once entered any of their buildings during the first two days of their stopover, instead spending much of his time questioning women who were willing to talk without the incentive of money.

"Would it not be useful to at least pay them something, Giorgio?" Archie asked.

"If they think they will get paid for information, they could make up any wild tale to make it worth my while and none of it would be true."

On the third night, however, Giorgio didn't return to the boat until well into the following afternoon, barely able to walk in a straight line and reeking of booze. Once he had clambered on board, he promptly stumbled over a coil of rope, fell and went to sleep where he lay.

"Wake up, you old reprobate, we have things to do." Archie prodded the sleeping man with his boot but it was clear the captain would wake when he felt like it and not before. Now Archie understood why his son had dumped him in the back room of the bar until he sobered up.

What ran through his mind as he waited was that, after such a long period, there was little hope of finding anyone in these remote regions who might offer up any clue about what route the family had taken. On the other hand, there could be more hope of tracking the movements of the father, Lord Oliver. If, as Archie had been informed, he had been out there for four years conducting experimental research into cures for tropical diseases, the Englishman must have left a trail. Supplies of tinned food, clothing and medical equipment would have to be collected from a small port or trading post nearby and, if he could locate it, that would provide him with the location of his base camp.

Frustratingly, Captain Giorgio did not emerge from his hangover until the following afternoon.

"And about time too, what the hell were you thinking? I am not paying good money for you to go whoring all night and then turning up here pissed as a parrot and needing a day to sleep it off."

"Señor, I very bad, I know this, but I still working."

"Like hell you are."

"I need go now, señor but Giorgio come back with information. This I promise," the captain said, tucking a grubby shirt into his trousers and splashing water on his face from a barrel, all the time smiling broadly.

"If you do not… then you will be out of a job when you get back and I will continue this search on my own. Do not imagine that I am unable to navigate this old boat of yours on my own, because I can."

"I understand, señor. It was never my intention to seek out a woman on this trip, but my abstinence ended at Madame Dresden's establishment where I gave in to temptation and sampled the delights on offer. Which I must confess was most educational… even for an old river dog like myself."

18

"I am not interested in hearing any more gory details of your exploits, Giorgio."

"Then you might be interested to know that, after taking part in a gratifyingly and most educational experience in the art of sexual contortion, I received some important information that relates to our search," he said, obviously pleased by Archie's shocked reaction to his teasing.

"You actually got information about the family in a place like that? Did any of this involve a young boy named Geoffrey?"

"What is this name again, señor?"

"Sir Geoffrey is the son of the missing family."

"There was no mention of a son, señor, only that Don Oliver was a regular at Madame Dresden's house until two years ago. They say this man, he much handsome and... athletic." Giorgio laughed, pouring out a generous measure of whisky into a tin mug. "Señor, I think you need drink this."

"Was there any mention of where he was based?" Archie asked, draining the mug in a single draught before handing it back for a refill.

"No, except he was awaiting deliveries of medical supplies to a trading post."

"Where would that be?"

"All they say, señor, is the region is remote, up one of the tributaries ahead." He gestured the hopelessness of the search with open hands.

"Was anything else mentioned?"

"A Jesuit priest was mentioned as a friend of Don Oliver, they played chess."

"It is hard to believe that someone who frequented a place like this would maintain a friendship with any man of God."

"Madame Dresden is many things, Señor Archie but a liar she is not. She say this priest is Americano."

"Well, then His Lordship must be seeking redemption."

"I think not. This priest might preach about God but he also takes comfort in a woman's flesh... like me." He laughed again.

"And is probably more in need of forgiveness than most of his flock. However, if this priest is a frequent visitor to the base camp, then his mission could be nearby and, with luck, maybe the trading post too." Archie examined the map carefully but could find no trace of either.

"I will ask around the docks, Señor Archie."

"Perhaps, but not tonight; just find out what you can at first light. At least the crews of the working boats should be sober enough to think clearly at that hour."

It was barely daybreak when Giorgio got the information they needed from an animal trader. Although the man knew a Jesuit mission existed, he couldn't say exactly where it was located other than that he knew it was close to the Paputa Falls, which the Captain was able to pinpoint on the map.

Two hours later, Captain Giorgio steered the steamer slowly along the riverbank, while Archie stood on the prow, checking each of the narrow offshoots and overgrown tributaries until they approached the one they had marked.

"Damnation!" Archie exclaimed. "This must have been where Rolly and I went wrong. If only we had taken the next river, then he might still be alive."

"An easy mistake, Señor Archie; sometimes even I get confused," Giorgio reassured him, shielding his eyes from the sun reflecting off the water. Swinging the wheel hard over, he narrowly avoided the build-up of trees and roots torn up by the floodwaters and was able to manoeuvre the rusting steamer through without any difficulty.

The deeper they were able to penetrate over the following days, the more disturbing the aftermath of the flood devastation became. In a rocky canyon the pressure of dammed-up floodwater had eventually broken through a blockade of uprooted trees and boulders, carrying the debris on a monstrous surge of pressurised water, bursting the banks as it raged overland, felling acres of ancient trees in hundreds, crushing, killing and wrecking all that stood in its path.

Even after three months, the aftermath of the flood was still a terrifying spectacle. There had been plenty of flood damage on the route that he and Rolly had taken before but that was nothing compared to the scale of what was confronting him now as the steamer chugged through miles of shattered forest. The bleached bones of animals and humans were caught up and dangling among the shattered trees. The sickening images worsened the further they travelled and it was hard to imagine how even one member of the missing family could have survived the devastation.

"I knew the flooding was brutal, but nothing like this," Archie said when they dropped anchor.

"Do you want to continue, Señor Archie, or turn back?"

"I can't go back now," Archie insisted but Giorgio seemed doubtful.

"It is not possible Inglesi people could survive, señor. Not even mystic River People could survive this."

"Who are they?"

"I no speak of tribes living by rivers, Señor Archie. River People are different. They ancient mystics, like these," Giorgio said, indicating the few magnificent trees that had survived the flood.

"How come I have never heard of these mystics before?"

"Only a few have survived, señor. Local tribes fear their magic. It is told some of them can transfer thoughts but the special ones transmit images. Many were hunted down and sacrificed as witches by the Portuguese and Spanish invaders."

"Who did this mystic cleansing? The conquistadores?"

"No, señor, having them sacrificed was encouraged amongst the native tribes."

"But what would induce local inhabitants to kill off an indigenous race?"

"Western goods were the temptation. They were offered in exchange for proof of execution. The more mystics killed, the better was the selection of goods."

"What proof could the authorities have asked for?"

"They demanded the head, plus the right hand and foot of the mystic. Nothing less would qualify."

"That is absolutely disgusting!" Archie exclaimed.

"To the invaders, the native population was an inconvenience. Their own methods were equally as brutal."

"But why request those specific items?" Archie asked.

"Because this race all have red/gold hair, the same as that band you wear," Giorgio said, indicating the plaited cord around Archie's neck.

"You seem very confident about this?"

"I am, señor. I am one of the few with the good fortune to see one close up." Seeing that Archie wasn't convinced, he elaborated. "They have scales like a fish and webbed fingers and toes." He fanned out his fingers.

"Then if they are born with this abnormality, that probably enables them all to swim exceptionally well, does it not?"

"Si, señor, like fish."

"Then if you have seen one, there must have been a few survivors."

"The few that escaped used their powers to blend into the forest and were barely heard of again. I saw for myself how they can also stay underwater for the longest time but no one on God's Earth could swim fast enough to escape this." Giorgio indicated the piled-up flood debris around them.

"So you are convinced this race still exists?" Archie said.

"The one I see was many years ago in a still lagoon, when three dolphin fins headed towards my boat. When they stopped a few feet away, a pair of adult dolphins leapt clear of the water, twisting up and over, followed a heartbeat later by a red-haired boy, maybe seven or eight years old, paired with a young dolphin, executing perfectly the same movements as the adults."

"But why do you think this boy was one of that mystic race?"

"He must have been, señor. Once he re-entered the water after the leap, he never resurfaced again, even though I watched the dolphins' fins cross the lagoon until they disappeared. The boy never once came up for air."

"Where was this place?"

"It is not far from here. No tribesmen go there because of the strong currents."

"Could you have been mistaken about the boy's heritage?"

"No, Señor Archie. This boy was no native, not with that hair and his pale skin."

"How long ago would that have been?"

"It was maybe thirteen... fourteen years ago, señor."

"And the boy never resurfaced?"

"No, señor, he did not and I watched every section of that water for over an hour." He opened a bottle of whisky and poured some into a tin mug. "You want, señor?"

"No thanks," Archie said thoughtfully. "Are you certain this boy did the same back-flip as the dolphins?"

"Si, señor."

"So by now that boy would be aged around twenty?"

"Why, Señor Archie, did you see him too?" Giorgio asked, pouring another generous slug of whisky into the tin mug.

"I am not sure who or what I saw, Giorgio. What I do know for certain is that, when Rolly and I were thrown off our boat moments before it was crushed by that tidal wave of logs, an exceptional swimmer saved my life. He tried to save my friend too, under the most difficult conditions imaginable."

"All men and boys on this river are taught to swim before they can walk, señor."

"I am aware of that, but this man was different. He swam like an otter underwater and displayed such strength and power. To have been carried along against that tremendous undercurrent was almost unreal." Archie fingered the plaited band around his neck. "I remember that he took hold of my face as I was fighting for breath, planted his mouth firmly on mine and forced a huge amount of oxygen into my lungs. His skin was tinged with green. Without it, I would never have survived. It stopped me struggling and allowed him to get me free from that whirlpool. We must have been trapped beneath the surface for God knows how long, until he dragged me clear of the logs and we surfaced near the bank."

"What else do you remember about him?"

"He was a little younger than me and his hair was gold and copper and it seemed to glow underwater."

"Did he speak once you resurfaced, señor?" Giorgio asked.

"Maybe, I cannot tell. Everything was a blur in those few moments." Archie tried desperately to recollect his thoughts, all the while toying with the woven neckband. "All I have are these strands of hair that got caught up in my gun holster."

"Was he alone?" Giorgio asked, staring enviously at the woven band around Archie's neck.

"I am not exactly sure."

"You saw another of them?"

"I did not see anything, Giorgio. It is what I might have heard that is puzzling. There was a young woman with him." Although Archie clearly remembered the sound of the girl's voice, he was still confused by what she had said.

"What language did she speak, señor? Was it Spanish or Portuguese?"

"She spoke in English, calling me by my own name. Which means that I probably imagined the whole thing."

"Not if you have some of the swimmer's hair, señor. What did she say?"

Archie remembered clearly what the girl had said in that sweet, gentle voice that would be etched forever into his memory.

"Archie… my dear cousin, you must wake… only you can find them."

"Who are you?" he recalled asking as he regained consciousness but seeing only the blurred shape of a girl kneeling against him.

"You know who I am, Archie. Please find them before it is too late. Tell Jeffy I am safe," the girl had said and that was the very last thing he remembered before blacking out again.

"Señor Archie? Why you no say what you remember?" Captain Giorgio persisted. Archie wished that he had never mentioned anything at all; even though it might all have been a dream it seemed too personal to repeat to anyone.

Chapter Two
Dangerous Waters

It had been raining heavily during the night, and a dense mist hung over the water, obliterating the forest on either side of the river and making navigation almost impossible.

"Señor Archie, look out ahead for any sign of rocks in the water. This is a treacherous section," Giorgio instructed.

"I can't see much through this mist. Would it be more prudent to drop anchor and wait until it lifts?"

"That would be unwise, señor. Tribes in this region hate anyone with pale skin. They use poison darts to stop them getting too close to the bank." He kept the boat in the centre of the river. "With my mixed heritage it is no problem but you would be a target."

Confronting them in the middle of the river as the boat rounded the bend was a small island, which from that angle gave the impression of a giant lizard's head, rising up through the mist.

"We should moor up here," Giorgio said, cutting the engine.

"Is it safe?" Archie asked, before jumping onto a ledge of rock.

"No tribesman would come here. They believe this place is haunted." He threw a line to Archie, which he tied securely to a dead tree.

"There is a cave here," Archie said and was about to investigate until the captain stopped him.

"This place is a sacred area, señor. We should not go inside. We can wait out here until the mist has cleared." He indicated the animal and human skulls that were hung at regular intervals around the entrance. Just inside, there was a figure-of-eight shape made from stones. Here, among the remains of a fire, was a charred human skull.

Once the mist had cleared, the flood damage became increasingly apparent the further inland they went. On the banks most of the ancient trees had been shattered or uprooted, and once again Giorgio asked if Archie had second thoughts about continuing.

"We cannot turn back, not now," Archie said, despite the awful devastation. "But why would such a force of nature destroy only a section of the forest, but not all of it?"

"This section of river flows through a narrow canyon from a mountainous region up ahead where the damming must have occurred. Once released, a vast amount of water would create mudslides, carrying along rocks and felling trees. It would be impossible for anyone to have survived something like this."

"Unless they reached higher ground before the dam burst, or sought refuge at the Jesuit mission, assuming the place exists."

"I am told that it does, señor. Just pray it was built away from the flood path."

After two further days of travel, they moored up for the night at the entrance to a tributary beyond which the captain had never ventured.

"How do you rate our chances of getting down there without mishap? It seems barely wide enough to get through," Archie said, scratching his chin irritably.

"With that growth of beard, Señor Archie, it is hard to believe you are the same Irishman I set off with." Captain Giorgio laughed and poured out another generous measure of whisky.

"Shaving is hardly a priority on this trip. So what is your plan?" Archie grumbled, staring at the map.

"I need to avoid any strong currents that could drag us on towards the Paputa Falls, otherwise we could be carried past the opening. It is narrow, but possible to navigate, but not until daylight," Giorgio replied.

The following morning it was soon apparent this section of the journey would be the most difficult, since there was barely a tree still standing. With no tree cover to protect him from sunstroke, Archie wore a battered hat which he jammed over a torn piece of cloth to cover his neck. Throughout the day, Archie had to repel the constant mosquito attacks, covering his mouth and nose with a handkerchief against the rising stench from the slime deposited by the flood. On many occasions, the combined strength of both men was needed to move clumps of debris by dragging it clear with boathooks or prodding the object away with the blunt end, so as not to risk life and limb with the ever-present threat from the black caiman and swarms of red-bellied piranha lurking beneath the surface.

At the end of two days of relentless slog forcing a slow passage through the seemingly endless debris, without warning, the floating blockade began to ease off and they could make steadier progress as the channel widened out.

"Finally our prospects look good, Señor Archie," Captain Giorgio said, consulting his chart. "Not too far ahead, there should be a junction of rivers where any trading post would surely have been constructed."

It was a prospect that was timely for Archie since, for the past hour, the neckband of hair had become increasingly uncomfortable and he had twice almost lost his balance in his effort to loosen or remove it.

"Come back in the shade, señor," Giorgio called from the wheelhouse, shielding his eyes from the glare. "The channel should be clear from now on."

"Are we any closer to where the priest might be found?" Archie asked when they had moored up against a cliff face, taking advantage of the cooling shelter.

"This area is marked down as Guava. If the mission is anywhere, it should be here."

As they chugged around the next bend Archie was immediately on his feet, pointing at a building perched on the edge of a cliff ahead. Soon after, the boat was securely moored to a tree stump while Archie and the captain clambered over slime-covered rocks and debris, finally reaching their objective almost half an hour later.

"Any priest would need a helping hand from the Almighty to reach this place," Giorgio grumbled, mopping sweat from his face.

"Unlike us, he would have the advantage of having God on his side if ever he chose to reach the mission this way, instead of taking the road," Archie said, lending a hand to help the older man up the final section.

"What road, señor?" Captain Giorgio gasped, catching his breath as they reached the top, his eyes wide as he stared at the well-trodden track leading down to the river's edge. "Why you not show Giorgio this before we climb, señor?"

"Because, like you, Giorgio, I have only just seen it," Archie said, barely focusing on the narrow trail leading up from what remained of the forest as his attention was now captivated by a life-size, woven figure overlooking the river from a rocky shelf, just a few feet above them.

When they reached the platform, Archie was able to examine the workmanship of the figure in much greater detail. The simple beauty of the woven shape was overwhelming. The partially unfurled wings and leaning body of the creature gave it the appearance that it was preparing to launch into flight out over the river. For once, even Captain Giorgio seemed lost for words as they inspected the six-foot image of the winged creature, intricately crafted from a mesh of finely beaten silver.

"I have never seen the like of this anywhere; how about you, Giorgio?" Archie said, removing the hat to fan his flushed face, opening the neck of his shirt as far as it would go and dabbing the sweat beading on the back of his neck with his handkerchief.

"Not until now!" the captain said, staring not at the woven figure but at the exposed area between Archie's shoulder blades.

"Why are you staring at me as if you have seen a ghost?"

"This tattoo you have, señor, it must have been copied from this... this figure. Whoever did this on your back must also have been here."

Archie was about to correct the captain's mistake when it struck him that the wings and body shape of the figure were indeed so clearly identical to his birthmark and he had some difficulty in covering up how shocked he really was. What was also troubling him was remembering another fragment from his semi-conscious state after being rescued from drowning: that the girl who had called him her cousin had been resting her cold hand on the birthmark when he awoke.

"Señor Archie... can you hear me?" Captain Giorgio asked, shaking him by the arm.

"Sorry. I must get out of this sun," Archie said, self-consciously buttoning up his shirt.

Compared to the intense heat outside, the coolness of the air in the spartan interior of the mission came as a blessing. More of a shock was the basic nature of the facilities provided for whatever congregation the preacher had been able to attract. What passed for seating were regimented lines of roughly sawn planks, supported on packing crates. The pulpit was the remains of a dugout canoe, with a top made from a thin slab of rock, on which incongruously sat a huge Bible.

Against the back wall there was a battered oak table draped with a plain piece of sailcloth. Positioned on this were two very large brass candlesticks. Hanging above them, and in contrast to everything else in the mission, was a magnificent crucifix, intricately woven from strands of beaten copper, recognisably by the same hand that had fashioned the winged figure outside.

"What a strange set-up this is," Archie commented, looking around for any sign of the priest. "Listen... can you hear that?"

"Hear what?"

"There it is again. An infant, wailing with some distress." Archie paused, trying to establish where the sound was coming from.

"Where is it señor? Outside?"

"No, most definitely not, the sound is too muffled." Archie was alerted by the clanking of metal and the bleating of a goat from behind one of the two doors on opposite sides of the altar.

"Take a look through there, while I try this one," Archie said. He carefully opened the door, only to be confronted by a girl of mixed race, maybe ten years old, glaring at him with intense blue eyes. She was carrying a battered galvanised bucket containing a small amount of milk. Behind her, two goats were tethered in a makeshift stall at the far end of a corridor, but there was no sign of the wailing infant.

"Who is you?" the girl demanded as she pushed past him, dropping the bucket with a loud crash. Her bare feet skidding on the spilt milk, she failed to reach Captain Giorgio before he thrust open the other door to reveal a long, dark corridor, down which the infant's lusty wailing became instantly louder before the girl slammed the door in his face.

"What the hell!" he blustered as the girl positioned herself fiercely between him and the closed door, barring his way and glaring at him with those piercing blue eyes.

"You go away!" she screeched. She was less than half the size of either man but clearly determined not to allow either of them to enter. "Master, him no like 'ere, you make much angry."

"We mean no offence," Archie tried to reassure her. "We heard a child crying."

"Him need sleep. You go. No stay." She flapped her tiny hands anxiously towards the entrance.

"Once we have spoken with the priest, then we will be on our way," Archie said, distracted once again by the uncomfortable heat that seemed to be coming from the band around his neck. "Can you please bring him to speak with me?"

"Him no here, now you go!" she said, determinedly pushing Archie and then the captain in the small of their backs.

"You can stop that game, missy," Giorgio growled, yanking her hand forcibly.

"Be careful, Giorgio, you could hurt her."

"And I will if she carries on like this; this girl needs to be put in her place… Where is the priest, girl?" Giorgio demanded, shaking her roughly by the arm.

"You will not get any answers from her by rough treatment," Archie remonstrated, forcibly removing the captain's grip and placing himself between them. "We mean you no harm, señorita. Just tell me where I can find the priest."

"Him gone… Master, he no back – two moons full," she said. "You go… no stay."

"We cannot wait here for two months, señor!" complained Giorgio.

"There's no need. I can leave him a note."

"Unless this titless guard dog destroys it the moment we are out of sight," Giorgio protested.

"I doubt that. The priest is not far away," Archie said. He had noticed a pair of blood-spattered sandals leaning against the pulpit as well as some recently washed strips of bloodstained linen, hung out to dry on a rope hooked between the pulpit and the crucifix. "From the state of those bandages I'm sure if he wanted to speak with us, he would have come out by now."

"Should we not try and find him, señor?"

"Not if it means the girl will get in trouble. He obviously intimidates her, otherwise she would not look so damned terrified. We can forget talking with this priest, at least for now and make our way to the trading post; it must be nearby judging by these packing crates he uses for seating. If we have no luck there, we can always come back."

"What if the priest is in need of our help?"

"I doubt that very much; he is being well tended by the girl." Archie wondered what the relationship was between the priest and the girl with the startling blue eyes. Combined with the sound of a wailing child, it gave him good reason to believe that, as the Captain had suggested, the religious morality this American Jesuit preached to his congregation would be some way down the priest's own personal agenda. Using his Irish charm to calm the girl before they set off, Archie questioned her about the location of the trading post and got more information than he expected. He left a brief note stating they were searching for a missing English family and would call back again if their mission was unsuccessful. Rather than use his family name of Westbrook, he chose instead to sign the paper using his title as the Earl of Glendower, which he hoped might carry more weight with a renegade American priest.

"Did you notice that big mule in the makeshift lean-to?" Archie asked as they made their way down the footpath.

"Si, Señor Archie. There was also a boy watching us leave."

"I saw him too. He had the same blue eyes as the girl." As soon as they were away from the building Archie noticed that the heat from his woven neckband seemed to ease, and the sensation had gone completely by the time the steamer chugged out of sight of the mission.

It was approaching dusk when the trading post came into view at the intersection of five rivers. Here, like the mission at Guava, the main building had also been constructed on high, rocky ground, but because of its reliance on river trade it was easily accessible via three levels of staging, all interconnected by steps leading down to the dock.

Only three of the shattered supports for the dock were left standing and all but one level of the upper staging had been wrecked completely. There was some evidence of minimal rebuilding work on another dock where a few dugout canoes were tied up to the mooring posts, leaving barely enough space for Captain Giorgio to manoeuvre the steamer close enough to moor for the night.

"The owners were damned lucky it was built on high ground," Giorgio said.

"And it's fortunate for us there is someone still occupying the place," Archie added, seeing two hurricane lamps alight inside the structure. "With so much of the staging gone, I'm not sure how we can get up there."

"It would be unwise to go up at night, señor. We should wait until daylight, when we can see who is there. No point taking any chances in the dark."

The captain explained that the traders might not be the legitimate owners of the post and could be a threat to any foreigner with white skin. Also, as he and Archie were there not to trade but only for information, negotiations could prove difficult.

"If they are a band of cut-throats, it is good if we stay here until daylight and you should sleep while you can," Giorgio said, reaching for a half-empty bottle of whisky.

"What about you?"

"I am used to going without much sleep. I will keep watch on deck with Bella for company," Captain Giorgio said, holding up a rifle.

"Then I will catch up on some rest," Archie said, "but only if you promise to wake me in two hours."

In less than an hour, Archie awoke with a start at the sound of a man's screams. He was on his feet immediately as the first shot rang out and on the deck in moments brandishing his revolver. On the landing stage a few feet away from the boat lay a dead caiman with a man's arm hanging out of its mouth. Backed up against the staging was the arm's previous owner, screaming as blood spurted from the ragged remains of his missing limb.

"We must help him, Giorgio!" Archie called out, preparing to get off the boat until the captain prevented him.

"No, señor, he was not alone," Giorgio said, motioning into the shadows with the rifle cocked before shouting, "You there, drop the machete… Do it now!"

Within seconds, not one but two machetes were tossed onto the staging.

"I will count to three for the other, or I will start firing!" the captain growled menacingly.

Moments later a vicious-looking meat cleaver skidded across the deck, then two natives and a man of mixed race stepped cautiously out from the shadows.

"Keep them occupied, Giorgio, while I see to this injured man." Archie leapt out of the boat before the captain could object.

Archie had barely applied a tourniquet to the remains of the man's arm when he became aware of another shadowy figure who had crept up behind him stealthily and was about to slit his throat with a hunting knife. Archie instinctively spun around and shot him between the eyes without a moment's hesitation.

"Forget about waiting until morning; I think we need to pay the trading post a visit now," Captain Giorgio said, lashing the three men together and forcing them ahead of him up the temporary stairs, leaving Archie to follow with the one-armed tribesman.

"What about the man I shot?" Archie asked, uncertain what to do.

"Leave him. The caiman will have got rid of him by the time we get back."

Once they reached the top, at first it appeared that no one was inside the sprawling building, a structure thatched with layers of palm fronds that must have housed countless reptiles and spiders. However none of them could have appeared more venomous than the owner, who now appeared in the doorway as they approached, surrounded by a group of muscular bodyguards.

"Why you here, white men?" she asked suspiciously. "You have Americano goods for trade with Misqualla?"

"Are you the owner?" Archie asked, removing his hat in deference.

"Si… this belong Misqualla," she said grandly, making a theatrically sweeping gesture with an armful of jangling bracelets.

It was obvious that Misqualla had been instrumental in the attack at the dock, despite her denials, with a toss of her turbaned head that revealed the single sapphire earring she wore. It was impossible to mistake such a remarkable piece of antique jewellery as the one that now dangled from the large earlobe of the proprietor, one of a pair that Archie immediately recognised as having belonged to the mother of the missing family.

Although she professed to know little of the English language, it was clear that Misqualla understood the spoken word very well, seeing how alert her eyes became when Archie quietly mentioned to the captain that he was convinced he had identified the jewel that she wore.

After a short and heated exchange in Spanish, Archie and the captain set off from the building with two bottles of whisky, two reasonably clean lengths of calico to replace the grubby sheets on his cabin bunk and the all-important information as to which branch of the river would eventually bring them down to Lord Oliver's research compound.

"Did that woman say if any of the family might be there?" Archie asked tentatively.

"I did ask but she refused to answer, probably because I told her you recognised that earring. She would give me no information as to how she came by it or why she only had one but with that collection of misfits protecting her, I decided against asking more."

By now they had reached the lower dock where, although the dead caiman was still there, the severed arm had gone, as too had the body of the dead native.

"It would be wise to keep that pistol handy, señor, in case there are more of the bitch's scavengers lying in wait up ahead."

"If that compound is somewhere along here, I doubt if any of it could have been left standing," the Captain said, reducing speed to negotiate another threatening pile of debris projecting out from a sharp bend of the river. "Look, señor? What is that over there?" He shaded his eyes from the reflected glare on the river.

Jammed on a lower bough of a shattered tree was a snapped-off section of handrail from a colonial-style veranda. Immediately above this, impaled on another jagged bough, were the remains of something that it took Archie a few moments to make out.

"A grand piano, I think," he said, barely able to focus on or believe the grim tableau that was confronting them on the opposite bank. The shattered remains of the magnificent instrument had been crushed almost beyond recognition, having been harpooned by the jagged bough of a tree. Still more disconcerting, dangling from the branches were the macabre remains of a human skeleton, bleached white by the sun after every fragment of flesh had been picked clean by an army of soldier ants. What remained was unidentifiable as either male or female.

Further on there was more evidence of domestic wreckage caught up amongst the shattered trees. Two veranda chairs were marooned high up and a large bookcase had been upended in the slime, doors broken and glass shattered. Strewn around and pulped were the remains of what had once been a large collection of books and ledgers. Among them were the remnants of shredded curtains and clothing. Snagged on boughs and bushes they fluttered in the wind, an ominous sign of former human habitation.

"There is nothing you can do for anyone now, señor. No one could have survived this," Giorgio observed grimly.

"Perhaps not, but at least I can search for any remains and offer them a decent Christian burial." Archie gripped tightly onto the steamer's rail, his face as white as his knuckles as the captain cut the engine and steered the boat into a shaded area where he dropped anchor.

"This seems a safe place to rest up. You can decide later if you want to continue."

They moored until the following morning. After another hour of chugging upriver, as the steamer rounded a bend, the remains of what had once been a small dock confronted them.

"These posts seem sturdy enough to moor the boat securely," Archie called from the staging as he started tying up. He had barely secured the rope around the upright when he stopped abruptly to examine an area near the top. A bullet was lodged deep in the bleached wood. What had at first appeared to be natural colour striations in the timber was in fact the ingrained remains of a huge patch of dried blood.

"This has all the hallmarks of an execution," Captain Giorgio said, examining the stains engrained into the planking surrounding the post.

"Surely not," Archie protested.

"I witnessed something like this as a young man and I can assure you, señor, you do not forget images like these in a lifetime. Something bad happened here."

After following what remained of a track for only a short distance, they were confronted by the decaying carcass of a large black caiman. Although the reptile had been shot neatly between the eyes, bizarrely it had also been impaled on a shattered tree trunk with what remained of a primitive spear. The spear had pierced clean through the upper section of the creature's gaping jaw, driven with astonishing force by a ruthless, upward thrust. It would have required nerves of steel for anyone to stare into those jaws of death before ramming that spear through the roof of the creature's mouth. Unsure where this fearless native might be at this moment, they proceeded with extreme caution towards what little remained of a once decent-sized compound.

From the moment Archie had stepped on to the dock, he had felt the plaited cord around his neck begin to get warm and, the further he went, the hotter it became. Here in the lower area, only partial sections of the framework of the structures remained. The gaunt, jagged fragments might have been in a desolate warzone, rearing up through piles of slime-covered wreckage.

By Archie's estimation, there had been five cabins. One of these had been much larger and grander in style than the others and a remaining section of the shattered wrap-around veranda confirmed that the grand piano would most certainly have come from there too.

Added to the rear of this structure was evidence of an extension and the medical equipment littered around indicated this area was used for Lord Oliver's research. Of all the buildings in the compound, only one had escaped destruction since it sat higher up and apart from the others on the edge of a cliff. This would have been accessed by steps but, since the lower sections were missing, Archie and the captain had to seek an alternative route.

At the base of the makeshift steps was the carcass of a bright emerald-green boa constrictor, at least thirteen feet long and with a partially severed head. There was no sign of decay or of any carnivorous activity on the remains, so Archie guessed the reptile had been thrown down from the upper level, where it had become piled up on the rotting carcasses of two butchered caiman. Both of these had been trapped by weighted fishing nets. One had been speared and the other, although it had clearly been partially mauled by some fearsome creature, had died from the accurately placed stabs of a hunting knife.

"Whoever did this has no sense of fear, Señor Archie," Giorgio said in a hushed tone as they made their way out of the compound and climbed the difficult slope towards the remaining cabin.

"I agree. The hunter must have been close enough to feel its rancid breath on his face to have been able to kill the creature like that. It was probably the same hunter that speared the first caiman against the tree." Archie paused to catch his breath as they neared the top.

Although smaller than the other structures on the lower level, this building had been equipped with a narrow veranda. Here there was some evidence of a woman's occupancy: a recently washed underslip was draped over the railing to dry. The garment was torn, with patches of washed-out blood. Clustered around the porch was a mass of unidentifiable plants, each of them carefully potted up into hand-woven baskets as if for transportation.

"Señor… you should take care," the Captain said, his rifle held in readiness.

"For God's sake, put that damned thing down, Giorgio."

"But señor, we need this for our protection."

"Not from whoever lives here. We are the intruders, Captain, not them."

Attached to the side of this cabin was a fair-sized storage area, combined with an empty stable. Since there was no evidence of anyone either here or in the area around the buildings, it was clear they were on their own.

"What say we take a look inside? There might be something to tell us more about the woman living here," Archie said, stepping onto the veranda.

"What if they come back, señor?"

"I am not suggesting that we remain here for any length of time, only that we take a look."

At one end of the veranda was a handcrafted crib, which still bore the remnants of dried river slime trapped in sections of the intricate carving that would have been almost impossible to wipe clean. Disturbingly, there was an offering of a single spray of orchids where the infant had once lain.

Cautiously, Archie stepped inside the interior, followed closely by the captain.

"What the hell?" Archie muttered, his eyes fixed on the framed pencil drawing of a clean-shaven young man, smiling and relaxed, that hung on the wall above a narrow bed.

"Señor, what is this?" Captain Giorgio asked.

"Not what, Captain, but who," Archie said, scratching his beard.

"You know this man, señor? Is he the one you seek?"

"There would be no point, since I see this face looking back at me from the mirror every day. It is a drawing of me, Giorgio, without the beard. God alone knows how it was done, or when. I have no knowledge of this portrait at all!"

"This face is very handsome, señor. It would attract a lot of attention if it was hanging in my son's bar. We should take it with us, Señor Archie." The captain was just about to take the drawing down when Archie stopped him.

"Leave that where it is, Giorgio; it belongs to whoever lives here. Why would there be a drawing of me, here, in this godforsaken place."

"Whatever the reason, señor, even if you were shagging this woman, she would never think you were the same man in this picture. No one could recognise you from this drawing beneath that beard," Giorgio laughed.

"What the hell is wrong with you, talking that way at a time like this?" Archie snapped. He wished, not for the first time, that he had focused more energy in his selection of a companion for the search.

"There is nothing wrong with me, señor. I have much experience in these matters, as any of my wives would tell you," the captain blustered.

"Wives? How many were there?"

"As a good Catholic, only one was in the eyes of God, but how many others is hard to say, not accurately anyway."

"There is more than one person living here," Archie said, cutting him short as he noticed two spears leaning against the wall next to a straw mattress that had been raised off the floor on three tea chests. There was a piece of stained sailcloth, draped over a rope line as a privacy screen between the two beds. "Did you notice the crib outside?"

There was no time for an answer, for at that very moment Archie caught sight of a figure that had appeared through the bushes without making a sound. He was a barbaric-looking creature, with a lean, muscular body, visible through the ragged remains of a threadbare waistcoat. He was horrifically scarred and he held in one of his mutilated, clawlike hands a spear, perfectly balanced, poised in readiness. At the man's side was a battle-scarred wolfhound, equally as alert and wary as its owner, as if they had both sensed they were not alone.

"Is he from the missing family?" the Captain whispered.

"Impossible. This savage looks about my age. The father would be much older. His son was barely eighteen when we met and scared of his own shadow. You saw the butchered reptiles below. This is clearly a seasoned killer, so don't take any chances."

"Not if you hand me the rifle, señor."

A few feet away the weapon was leaning against the veranda railing too far for either of them to reach undetected. As Archie moved towards the gun, it was clear the mysterious figure was aware he was being watched, as too was the hound, which now bared its ferocious teeth and emitted a low, threatening growl, its hackles raised like spikes.

"Too late, the man has seen us," Archie said, and stepped outside where he could be seen clearly.

"Señor, do not go any further towards them, otherwise that animal will tear you to pieces!"

"If I do not go now, we will both be dead anyway," Archie said, aware the spear was poised in readiness to hurl at him.

"You will not stand a chance on your own, señor."

"We will be fine once he sees that I am no threat," Archie reassured him, emerging from the gloom on to the veranda. "Leave this to me and please... just stay where you are."

"Do what you like... at the first opportunity, I will shoot the bastard," Giorgio hissed.

"Do not do anything, otherwise we are both done for," Archie insisted. He spoke more calmly than he felt, confronted by the prospect of his own imminent death and strangely conscious of how man and dog seemed to move together, synchronised with perfect coordination like a lethal killing machine.

"Use your pistol, you crazy Irishman and kill them both," Giorgio whispered, inching his way closer to the rifle.

"If I make one false move that hound will tear my throat out. The best weapon I have is to show no fear." Archie boldly stepped into the clearing where the savage could watch his every movement, knowing full well that he would be dead in seconds if he made a single mistake.

"That might be your choice, but not mine," Giorgio hissed.

Archie continued moving slowly towards them, trying but failing to stare down the scarred hound that snarled back through bared teeth, poised as if spring-loaded in preparation to attack at the first command. Even in that life-threatening situation, he realised with a shock that the creature had at some time been domesticated, as evidenced by the broad collar around its neck.

This was no leather collar, however, but was made up from many layers of fine copper strands woven into an extraordinary mesh that must have taken hours of painstaking work to produce. Clearly, this was a feat that would have been an impossible task for the savage to accomplish with such mutilated hands. To anyone else it might have appeared the collar was reflecting the intense sunlight but Archie knew instinctively this collar had been worked from lengths of copper-like hair, just as his own had been. It was clear the hair did not belong to the bronzed savage whose own, long and matted beneath his woven headgear, was bleached almost white by the sun, making Archie wonder if he might have been an albino, or a throwback from Nordic parentage. The savage, he now realised, wore an intricately woven, gold-mesh armlet, almost identical to the collar on the hound.

The makeshift hat, plaited from palm fronds, that was crammed on his head made it difficult to see all of his face but it was the gruesome mutilation of both of his hands that caused Archie to shudder.

Not once during Archie's cautious approach was there the slightest tremble of the deadly spear aimed directly at his heart. Nor was there any sign of mercy in that intense stare with not a word spoken from the grim set mouth.

"I mean you no harm," Archie said, indicating the plaited band around his own neck and doing his best to appear calm.

At that moment he became aware of the knife sheathed in the man's belt. The hasp of the silver and bone-handled hunting knife was unmistakable. With that burst of recognition Archie's caution instantly left him.

"How did you get hold of my knife, you heathen bastard?" Archie challenged in a fury, now heedless of the spear that remained levelled at his heart. His temper was up and he was fully prepared to strangle the hound with his bare hands if it launched at him.

"Move, señor... I need him in my sights," Giorgio cried, reaching for the rifle.

"Answer me, you bloody moron, where did you get it?"

Even now the man said nothing, only narrowing his eyes as they shifted towards the Captain on the steps of the veranda.

"If there is a tongue in your head, then bloody well answer me! That's my knife you have on your belt, so where the hell did you get it?" Archie demanded. "Where are that boy and his family?" he challenged, his natural Irish brogue clearer than ever in his uncontrollable fury.

"Señor, move... I can take him down from here," Captain Giorgio called, shouldering the rifle in preparation to take the shot.

"Keep out of this, damn you. I want answers!" Archie shouted back angrily, without taking his eyes off the wild man for a second.

In response to Archie's threatening attitude, the wolfhound crouched in preparation to launch its attack. What the

Irishman wasn't expecting was for the savage to place a mutilated hand on the beast's neck, restraining it.

"Bog Boy, stay!" the wild figure commanded.

"Bog Boy? Who the hell are you?" Archie asked in astonishment, trying his utmost to examine the face beneath the brim of the woven hat. "Why the devil did you call him that? Tell me why, damn it!" he shouted, taking a step back, amazed to hear the irritating nickname and remembering who had given it to him.

"Archie?" the savage muttered, resolutely keeping the spear balanced in readiness as he offered the hunting knife by the blade.

"You know me?"

"Get clear, Irishman, now. I have him in my sights!" the captain cried, clicking off the safety catch and squeezing the trigger at the very moment Archie stepped deliberately into the line of fire.

"For God's sake no… I know him," Archie gasped, reeling forward from the force of the bullet. "Jeffy…?"

Screaming with rage, the savage hurled his spear with absolute precision, impaling Captain Giorgio's forearm firmly against the upright post of the veranda, sending the rifle clattering to the ground amid manic howls of pain and fear as the ferocious wolfhound sprang forward to attack.

Chapter Three
Departure

The music room floor was littered with sheets of discarded scores, pages of partially finished work and piles of books. Geoffrey Saint Hubes was attempting to cram even more books into an already overloaded tin trunk.

"Geoffrey, you must stop this at once!" Lady Marguerite, his older sister, protested, struggling to pick up some of his unfinished compositions because of her great bulk. "You are packing far too much. Mother has specifically asked you not to, yet you ignore everyone as usual. For heaven's sake, we will be home again in less than three months."

"So what...?" he retorted, raking his fingers irritably through an unruly mass of fair hair before exchanging a large book for a slimmer volume, allowing him to close the lid. "Besides, what about these clandestine excursions of yours."

"What excursions?" she blustered.

"When you sneak out of the house before anyone else is out of bed. Are you having a romantic liaison?" Geoffrey asked, his voice echoing around the grand music room.

"What on earth put such a ridiculous idea into that... that empty head of yours?"

"It is not at all ridiculous. You creep out of the house before dawn and come back looking like hell, sometimes with mud splattered along the hem of your skirt. Even Rose commented on that and she notices nothing, except her reflection or a new frock." He snapped down the catches on the trunk.

"I paint watercolours, like I have always done. What is so secretive about that?"

"Pull the other one, Maggs. I might be ten years younger than you but do not take me for a fool. No one can paint in the dark."

"Do not keep calling me Maggs. You make me sound like a pet dog instead of your sister," she snapped, clearly unnerved by the interrogation.

"You are evading the issue, Maggs. I can tell when you are lying. What are you really up to? Is it that gardener chap, whatever his name is?"

"I cannot believe you do not know Frank by his name and for your information we occasionally talk about his eldest son in the Merchant Navy. I thought it might be useful to get what information I could on South America."

"What good would that do? We only dock there for a week at the most, before the liner continues up the coast to the mouth of the Amazon River and then returns home," he said, repacking a few loose pages of sheet music. "If you are going to come up with a lie, then you need to do better than that. If you have been up to no good with old Frank in his potting shed, then take my advice and find someone a bit younger than him. That crumpled wreck is old enough to be your grandfather."

"Do you have to be so vulgar? I am not having an affair with anyone. I do wonder how a young gentleman could suggest such a thing."

"This is 1909, for pity's sake, not the middle of the last century. I will be eighteen next week, not eight and do not imagine for a moment that I spend all my time practising the violin. Five hours a day is enough for anyone, even me. Every now and then, I read through some of Pa's racy novels that he hid in the library. They used to be out of reach on the top shelf but not any more now I am taller." He grinned more broadly at her shocked reaction.

"Father keeps books on filth in here? How could you lower yourself to his level by reading anything so tawdry? It will be a road to your own ruination and eternal damnation, just like him, if you persist."

"Strewth… they are only books."

"Father's… and they should be destroyed, not read."

"Why do you dislike him so much?" Geoffrey retorted, checking the padding around his violin case.

"You would not understand," she snapped.

"Maybe I would if you did not keep everything to yourself. Father's been gone for the past four years and I can barely remember what he looks like, so why continue this grudge against him, particularly if you are willing to travel halfway around the world to see him. Why do that, if you dislike him so much?"

"You know exactly why. I shall be accompanying Mother. She will not admit to being unwell but she and I cannot allow her to travel that distance alone."

"You are making that up. There is nothing wrong with Mother; I would know if there was. Besides, she would not be alone without you there, because I will be going."

"If you had taken my advice, you would be swotting for a place at the Royal Academy of Music, instead of insisting on travelling across the Atlantic with us. It is not too late to change your mind."

"You know perfectly well I will not. The Reverend Brice assures me that my playing is up to the Academy's requirement and my latest composition would pass muster for any entrance exam. After all, he should know better than anyone. He tutored there for eight years before he found religion."

"Regardless of that... Mother needs a woman's company," Marguerite protested.

"She has Rose."

"Rosamund is barely seventeen and the only reason she is accompanying us there is because her looks are attracting too much, well, male attention."

"Of course Rose could cope. Mother was already married at her age," Geoffrey said, bringing an abrupt end to the discussion.

Because they would be crossing the Atlantic on Geoffrey's eighteenth birthday, his mother had arranged a garden party the following day, which would also serve as a farewell gathering in the grounds of the estate.

On what promised to be a beautiful day, the marquee and bandstand had already been erected. The reflections of silver and crystal glittered on the starched white linen of the long buffet table. Crisp tablecloths fluttered in the warmth of a summer's breeze, glasses clinked amid guffaws of laughter as servants bustled to and fro. A string quintet played a selection of requests, none of which appealed to Geoffrey's classical ear and he managed to sidle away from the crowd without being noticed either by the Hon Felicity Brown or more particularly by her domineering mother, seeking out prey for an advantageous marriage.

Rosamund too had been under attack from a stream of would-be suitors but, aided by her mother, was able to slip away on some pretext. In contrast, the bulky figure of Marguerite attracted no one except for a woman of similar age wearing an ugly dress, who was offering his sister a couple of old, rat-eared books.

Other than Rosamund, it was only his mother, Lady Claudia, who caused a stir wherever she went in the crowd, elegantly but simply attired in a dress of Honiton lace and wearing their grandmother's dangling sapphire earrings, which shone like frozen ice in the final rays of the sun.

The wind began to pick up and within moments the storm broke in earnest. In the general panic to shelter from the downpour, only Rosamund remained outside, on an upper level of the terraced gardens. Geoffrey watched transfixed as the fashion-conscious young woman was transformed into the girl he cared about more than any other, removing her elegant shoes and stockings before twirling around barefoot on the wet grass, her slender arms arcing above her upturned face like a graceful flamenco dancer, her Parisian silk gown drenched and clinging to her sylph-like body.

As if sensing she was being watched, she looked across at her brother and smiled, adapting her movements into the rain dance they had devised as children while beckoning him over.

After the briefest hesitation he kicked away his shoes and tugged off his socks before he ran laughing towards her, dumping his blazer on the way and pulling his loosened tie over his head.

Rosamund handed him two of the four garden canes she had retrieved from the flower beds. Holding a stick in each hand, they twirled around in the rain, grinning as they clacked the sticks together in their version of a tribal rain dance, never missing a beat or fumbling their make-believe swords, both of them moving as if to a ritualistic, instinctive rhythm.

By morning, the rain had given way to a clear sky. Dappled sunlight filtered through the avenue of ancient oaks lining the long drive until the convoy of three horse-drawn carriages emerged through the gatehouse and rumbled into the lane, bound for the town of Ashbourne and the railway station. Travelling in the first carriage were Geoffrey and his two sisters. Lady Claudia occupied the second with Florence Taylor, her maid. In the third were Geoffrey's valet and the chaperone and maid to Rosamund. Strapped on to the rear of this carriage was a considerable amount of hand luggage, for their overnight stay at the Grand Northern Hotel in Liverpool. The main bulk of the luggage required for the voyage had been sent on ahead to the Canada Dock.

Just before they reached the gatehouse, Geoffrey hung his head out of the window for a final glance back at Waterlilies, their ancestral home. He could easily understand his elder sister's obsession with painting the property. The manor house had been altered many times over the centuries from a fortification built at the time of the Crusades by a French ancestor of his mother's from the Angevin line. It was ideally situated on high ground with an idyllic view over a vast area of parkland that blended into the surrounding countryside. Bordering the Derbyshire Dales, the estate incorporated three tenanted farms, a working mill dating back to the Middle Ages and the ruins of a cloistered abbey, adjacent to an Elizabethan dower house.

"The old house must look perfect in this light," Marguerite mused.

"It does," Geoffrey said, as their carriage lurched into the lane to the clatter of hooves and the house disappeared from view.

The family had barely reached the platform when the locomotive chugged noisily to a grinding halt, hissing steam as the couplings clattered between the jolting carriages, and belching clouds of acrid smoke over the waiting passengers.

His mother, elder sister and the staff and luggage were soon safely on board but Geoffrey and Rosamund remained on the platform, gathering up the spilled contents of her vanity case after the catch had broken.

"Be quick, for God's sake," Geoffrey urged, seeing a young porter limping awkwardly towards them.

"I will not be bullied, Geoffrey. I am not leaving anything behind. The train can wait a while longer," Rosamund said, looking up with astonishment as he climbed into the carriage without her.

"Do what the hell you like, you generally do anyway!" Geoffrey retorted, shuddering as the porter reached his sister.

"Allow me to assist you, my lady," he said, swiftly gathering together the remaining items before assisting her into the compartment.

"Liam… I barely recognised you, not in that uniform."

"I expect I will grow into it; it belonged to an older porter who handed it on," he said, flushing scarlet.

"I must tell Mama you are working here!" Rosamund said.

"There is really no need, Rose. It was Lady Claudia who arranged this job for me," Liam said, lowering his voice with embarrassment as the lady in question got up from her seat to speak with him.

"Liam, how are you settling in?"

"Very well, Milady."

"Tell me, Liam, how is your mother managing since the tragedy?"

"Well enough, Milady. With the pay I bring home we manage better than most. She will always be indebted for the support you gave us in the months after the fire."

"To lose a child under such horrific circumstances would be hard enough for any mother but for your father to have perished in the blaze trying to save her must have been unbearable. My contribution of an empty cottage was the least I could do." She lowered the veil from her hat as the stationmaster approached the carriage and caught hold of the young man's arm.

"You know the rules about conversing with passengers, son. It isn't allowed," he said, closing the door and snapping the brass catch securely into the retainer. Stepping back from the carriage, he blew shrilly on a whistle, waved a green flag at the engine and disappeared in a cloud of smoke as the carriages lurched forward.

"Promise you will come to the house and see me on our return," Rosamund called out of the window.

"Why do you bother with someone like that?" Geoffrey said moodily.

"Like what?" she challenged.

"Deformed!"

"You can be so insensitive at times, Jeffy. You know perfectly well that Lord Byron had a club foot too. He also boxed and wrote verse; it did not make him any less of a man. You have a book of his poetry in your room."

"Byron was a man of breeding and great intelligence. You cannot compare him to that ruffian, who Father forbade you to spend any more time with," Geoffrey said, unable to admit that he was actually terrified of seeing anyone with even the slightest deformity.

"Liam could not help having one leg shorter than the other. Fortunately it did not prevent him from learning to swim. Otherwise he might easily have drowned when Papa made him clear those weeds from the edge of the lake. It took weeks."

"I know nothing about that, and nor do I care."

Changing trains at Crewe was a living nightmare. Belching smoke was blown on a bitter wind as they avoided scurrying passengers being offloaded from trains, desperate not to miss their connections. Marguerite couldn't be persuaded to change platforms using the stairs to the raised walkway because of her fear of heights. Instead, Geoffrey's valet assisted her into a service lift along with their luggage, from where he escorted her through a tunnel underneath the tracks.

The hotel in Liverpool was a grim, uninspiring building, blackened with soot and glistening with damp in the dim streetlights. At Reception, Geoffrey noticed his mother taking two red pills from a medicine bottle in her Gladstone bag and wondered if his mother really was not as well as he'd imagined. He was pondering on this at dinner when Rose asked an unexpected question.

"Mother… who was that awful woman who called to see you last week?"

"Mrs King is an acquaintance of your father's. Her late husband had been financing your father's research and, now recently widowed, she is collecting his outstanding debts. Among her other demands," Lady Claudia added, pushing aside her uneaten food.

"What other demands?" Geoffrey asked. "What could Father owe her late husband's estate, apart from money?"

"Nothing that cannot be resolved once I have spoken with your father. Her demands were as fabricated as you might expect from her theatrical background," Lady Claudia said. "But, erring on the side of caution, I had documents drawn up by our solicitor that must be signed by your father, to avoid any unpleasantness later."

"Is that what Forsythe delivered in person yesterday? There was quite a bundle," Geoffrey said, wanting more information.

"Estate matters in need of his signature. There is no need for concern."

"Which estate would that be? Derbyshire, Ireland, or the one in Brittany?"

"Actually it involves all three properties, but mainly Derbyshire. Because of recent events, it is clear that your inheritance must be made legally watertight for you and your sisters to inherit what is rightfully yours. I do this as a precaution."

"Against what exactly?"

"Should anything happen to me… unexpectedly and your father then remarries an unprincipled woman, problems might well ensue. It is essential to have my wishes on each of your inheritances well documented and that cannot happen unless they have all been signed, making them legally binding."

"But why travel such a distance just to have him sign this paperwork?" Rosamund asked. "He will come back to England when he has completed this research, so why not wait until then? Besides, surely he would inherit by law anyway?"

"Normally he would but this is more complicated. You must know your father was penniless when we married. His own father's estate had been sold off to cover his gambling debts. All he possessed was a derelict castle and a title. It was stated in our marriage contract that my father's ancestral estates would be handed down only to his direct descendants," Lady Claudia said wearily.

"Then why bother making this trip at all, if that's been secured?"

"It is the amount of your father's inheritance that is open for negotiation and, now, if you will excuse me, I must retire to my rooms and rest before my headache gets any worse." She reached for a glass and swallowed two more of the bright red pills.

Geoffrey barely slept on a flock mattress that he could have sworn had been stuffed with rocks. He then had to share a bathroom with two other guests on the same floor, both of whom came at separate times to hammer on the door, demanding access to the lavatory, which he deliberately ignored.

Waiting for his mother and Rosamund to join them at breakfast, Geoffrey soon tired of exchanging information on the inadequate furnishings in their accommodation with his elder sister, being more interested in the two books Marguerite had been reading.

"What have you got there?" Geoffrey asked, grabbing one of them before she could stop him.

"Do you never say please?" she snapped with annoyance.

"Why on earth have you brought these along?" Geoffrey laughed, scanning through the dog-eared book, some of its copperplate engravings still protected by sheets of fine tissue paper. "*Lost Tribes of the Rainforest*? It is unlikely we will see any of those in Pernambuco. Where did you get this from, Grandpa's library?"

"These volumes were a gift from Violet Dobson."

"Am I supposed to know who that is? Is she one of mother's society friends from London?"

"Not in the least. Violet owns the bookshop in Ashbourne."

"Not that rat-infested junk shop down by the canal?" he smirked, now opening the other volume with undisguised interest.

"It might be a little run-down but it is a bookshop nevertheless, and a very good one too!"

"I would not be seen dead in that dump. Mother would have a fit if she knows you go there by choice," Geoffrey said, carefully turning the ageing pages of the second book.

"Mother knows of the arrangement I have with the bookshop," Marguerite said.

"What arrangement?"

"Miss Dobson has asked to see my watercolours of flora and fauna on our return. The arrangement is that a publisher friend of hers might be interested in printing a short run of my illustrations for publication."

"And have you met this Dobson woman's so-called contact?"

"Actually no, but Violet assures me his interest is genuine."

"Even so... it is a stretch of the imagination to think anyone would consider the risk of publishing works by an unknown artist, not unless he has actually seen what you can do."

"He has been most complimentary on some watercolours Violet has in safe keeping. The offer *is* genuine, and I have accepted the commission."

"Why have you never said anything about this before?"

"That is probably because you never asked."

"How would I know what to ask? I'm not a bloody mind reader," Geoffrey snapped.

"Do you have to swear so much, Geoffrey? It really is most unbecoming in any young gentleman."

"Only a prude like you would think so. And for what it is worth, I am sure that woman is having you on. No publisher in their right mind would deal with a shop like that. Not unless he was as mad as a turnip," he laughed. Yet he had to admit that his sister's work was extraordinary.

"Then you might be surprised to learn that book collectors from all over the British Isles visit her shop. Judging by their age, these two volumes are probably very valuable."

"You cannot know that," he said, examining the second tattered volume, titled *The Uncharted Tributaries of the Amazon*. His grin faded. "Good lord... this must be the rare edition by Grifka."

"Have you heard of it?"

"I came across a reference to this when I did a bit of research on the Amazon basin in Grandfather's library; in that book they referred to this volume as a lost work."

"Then perhaps you would do well to alter your opinion of Violet Dobson," she bristled.

Chapter Four
High Seas

The transatlantic crossing was aboard the *Lugansa*, an elegant liner of the Trident Fleet, boarding at the Canada Dock. She was a magnificent vessel, awesome in her towering domination over the other ocean-going vessels in the dock. Because of their status, the family would normally have been among the first passengers to board. As it was, his mother and Rosamund went on ahead, leaving Geoffrey and her maid Florence to assist a reluctant Marguerite up the gangway. With the help of one of the ship's officers they eventually got her standing on the deck.

"I would assume that your mother has no head for heights," the officer said with a smile. "Nigel Beresford, Lord Geoffrey, the ship's doctor. If you so wish, I can prescribe something to help this agitation when she is due to disembark."

"For your information, Beresford, the lady you are referring to is my elder sister. The lady approaching is my mother," Geoffrey said tersely as they helped Marguerite into a deck lounger.

"I offer my sincere apologies," Beresford said uncomfortably.

"Thank you for your kindness, sir, in assisting my daughter; she suffers badly from vertigo. Lady Saint Hubes," she said grandly, offering her gloved hand.

"Nigel Beresford, milady, the ship's doctor. If I can be of service during the voyage, I would be happy to be of assistance. If you don't think me too forward, milady, I wondered if you were aware that Lady Drummond is also a passenger on board the *Lugansa* today. With the dowager's knowledge of Pernambuco society, she would be an excellent source of information on what the city might have to offer, for both relaxation and entertainment."

"Lady *Harriet* Drummond?" Lady Claudia asked, with obvious interest.

"You are acquainted with her ladyship, milady?"

"Only by reputation," she responded, with a surprising flush of colour to her cheek. "I look forward to making her acquaintance. Thank you again, Dr Beresford, you have been most kind."

After adjusting to the restricted proportions of their accommodation, the family gathered beneath the sparkling chandeliers in the grand dining salon, turning heads as they were guided to their table. Lady Claudia was resplendent in a gown of the finest Nottingham lace, emphasising the youthfulness of her figure., Unlike many others among the glittering array of female diners her inherent grace was accentuated by the sparseness of her adornment. The sapphire earrings, pendants of the darkest blue, shimmered with every movement as she walked arm in arm with Rosamund, herself attracting the attention of young and older gentlemen alike, until she was seated beside her mother.

Geoffrey also made heads turn, something he deliberately chose to ignore as he arrived late with his elder sister, a ballooning, shapeless figure who glided between the tables like a brown galleon in full sail.

When Geoffrey went out on deck in the afternoon the following day, he was pleasantly surprised to find Marguerite there already. Bundled up in a shawl against the strong wind, the first impression of his sister was of a brown bear, gripping tightly on to the handrail as the liner channelled a route through the grey, choppy waters of the Atlantic.

"You are the last person I expected to find out on deck in this wind, Maggs."

"It is too claustrophobic to remain in the cabin. How could anyone stand sailing any distance in tiny boats, bobbing up and down like a cork?"

"I guess sailors do not have a choice. They do what they have to."

"Well fortunately our passage is calm enough, even on this rough water. You would have to shoot me first before I set sail on anything smaller than this," she said grimly.

"There will not be much chance of that!" Geoffrey said, turning up the collar on his jacket "but I did overhear an officer say on the way up here that we are heading into stormy weather and probably bad, judging by his expression. Even so, a liner of this size is big enough to cope with any storm."

"I pray you are right. Geoffrey, you really must get out of this wind, your hands are blue with cold. Why are you not wearing gloves to protect them?"

"There seemed no need to pack any. Montreal is supposedly hot at this time of year, and we only dock there to take on more passengers. After that we are sailing to South America, unless you have forgotten?" he laughed. "Have you any idea why Mother takes so many of those red pills? You must know something; she talks more freely to you than to anyone else."

"Mother has not been herself since the Chelsea Flower Show but she has said nothing to me either."

"Then we must both keep an eye on her."

For a time they stood together in silence, looking at the ever-darkening sky above the cresting waves in the distance, comforted by the vast size of the liner.

"You might want to take a look through these before the storm breaks," Geoffrey said, handing her a set of photographs from the garden party. "There is a lovely portrait of Mother amongst them but keep them safe. I want that one framed when we get home." He steadied himself against the sudden roll of the ship. Feeling unexpectedly queasy on his way back, he made a bolt for the toilet in his room. Overnight, the rolling motion of the ship increased and it was impossible for Geoffrey to get any rest. When his bedside cabinet smashed into the cabin wall after a sickening lurch he yanked on his dressing gown and, fearing for the safety of his mother without her maid in attendance, cautiously made his way along the corridor, gripping the polished brass handrail. Nearby a waiter's tray had become tightly wedged amid the broken fronds of a once graceful palm, the damaged leaves glistening with shards of broken glass and dripping champagne. Speared onto the jagged leg of a shattered chair was a panel of beaded fringe ripped off an evening gown, just a few feet from his mother's door which was swinging back and forth ominously with the motion of the ship.

Geoffrey found her on the floor, lying against the bed, soaked with water from an upturned vase of flowers, oblivious to the broken stems scattered over her. There was vomit and spots of blood on her sodden nightdress. She was groaning and semi-conscious but ,even so, finding his mother in a state of undress, he did his best to avert his gaze as he struggled to lift her into a more comfortable position.

"Mother… can you hear me?" he asked, as insecure as any child and uncertain as to what to do before she responded weakly.

"Ask your sister to help. You should not see me like this," she said, failing to pull the bedcover around her shoulders.

"I will get Rose. Her cabin is closer," he said, with more assurance than he felt.

With strength born of desperation, Geoffrey burst open the locked door of Rosamund's cabin, only to discover his sister just as distressed and seasick as his mother. She lay spread-eagled, fully dressed, over the crumpled coverlet from her bed, retching with every lurch of the liner.

"Jeffy… I need Mama," she groaned tearfully. Unable to help, he supported himself on the edge of her dressing table where the surface was cleared of everything, the shattered, silver-topped bottles and jars rolling aimlessly on the floor against his feet.

"I cannot do that, Rose; Mother is too ill herself. I will try to reach the lower deck and get Florence to help. It might take a while, because she must attend Mother first." He staggered across the room to the door, forcing himself to ignore the overwhelming feeling of nausea.

He quickly realised that, because of the violent motions of the liner, it would not only have been impossible to reach Florence Taylor's cabin on the lower deck, it would also have been useless, recalling that the maid too had been suffering from seasickness. Instead he made his way unsteadily along the corridor to Marguerite's quarters.

His sister was lying face down, drenched with perfume from an upturned bottle which was glugging out what remained of the contents. A settling cloud of face powder from a shattered bowl was layering her dark hair with grey. It was clear she had received a crack on the head from hitting the cabin floor after tumbling out of bed.

"Get up, Maggs, for God's sake… Mother needs you. She will not allow me to do anything," Geoffrey pleaded, wondering if he would have the strength to lift her to her feet.

"Leave me alone… can you not see that I am ill?" she cried, struggling to right herself. "I cannot help anyone, even Mother. Get Florence, she will know what to do."

"Mother was asking for you, not her maid. For God's sake, pull yourself together and go there now!"

"I cannot be seen in public like this. Ask Rosamund to help. I will come along once I am presentable." She tried to steady herself, spreading her hands on the floor.

"This is not a bloody garden party," Geoffrey snapped, clutching the end of her bed to prevent him from falling as the ship rose and then suddenly dropped over a huge wave. His sister was less fortunate, sliding across the floor before crashing into the wall. Geoffrey stumbled across the cosmetic upheaval to reach her, uncertain what part of her body to grasp hold of and lift. Grabbing her nightdress he tried his utmost to extricate her from the mess until the material gave way and dumped her back onto the floor.

"LEAVE ME!" she screeched hysterically. "Do not touch me again… I can manage on my own. This is more embarrassing for a woman than you could ever know," she wailed, making a concerted effort to stand.

"In that case, you should appreciate why Mother is asking for you and not me," he retorted.

"I will be there as soon as I can. In the meantime ask Florence. She will help."

"And that is your answer, is it? Even if I knew what cabin she was in, I would not be able to reach the lower deck without breaking my bloody leg. You know Taylor was already ill and she is probably worse than Mother is right now. Rose is no use either, she is as sick as a dog. This is your responsibility, and no one else's!"

Struggling against the roll of the ship, after what seemed like hours they reached their mother's cabin. No sooner was the door opened than another huge wave rocked the ship. Geoffrey managed to grab hold of the doorframe, unlike his unfortunate sister who lurched forward, stumbling across the luxurious carpet into the opposite wall close to where Lady Claudia was now sprawled in a motionless heap.

"Mother…?" she screamed, crawling on bruised and grazed knees to ease her mother into a sitting position by the time Geoffrey was able to reach them, clutching a bed sheet.

"She needs to be covered!" he said, wrapping her as best he could.

"Forget that, Geoffrey. Just help get her onto the bed and locate Dr Beresford. He must attend Mother as soon as he can."

"What if I cannot find him?"

"That is not an option. Why did you not say Mother was this ill?"

"I did try if you care to remember!" Geoffrey retorted before leaving to find the doctor.

After what seemed like hours of searching endless lurching corridors, he eventually found Dr Beresford attending the maid, who looked even more wretched than his mother. At Geoffrey's insistence the doctor agreed to accompany him and by the time they arrived, Lady Claudia had regained consciousness.

Although Geoffrey was desperate to reach his own cabin, convinced he would die if the waves of nausea didn't stop, he forced himself to look in on Rosamund, and when he saw her he was thankful he had. With barely a year's difference in their ages he had no shame in helping her out of her stinking nightdress and washing her naked body and face as well as he could, using what little water he was able to carry over to her bed in one of the few unbroken dishes.

Making her as comfortable as he could in a clean nightdress, he waited until Dr Beresford arrived. Returning to his own cabin he finally gave in to the nausea, oblivious to the significance of the date. It was his eighteenth birthday.

The storm raged for two more days before the skies cleared and the ocean calmed. Apart from two brief visits from Dr Beresford, the only person tending to Geoffrey's needs was the blurred figure of an elderly male steward. After that Marguerite's huge frame was seemingly ever-present when he awoke, making him swallow glasses of fizzing water but failing in any attempt to get him to eat.

A day later, the liner docked in Montreal where many grateful passengers were able to disembark allowing a maintenance crew to come aboard with a gang of carpenters and painters to clean and refurbish the salons, corridors and storm-damaged cabins.

"You will feel better Geoffrey, now the *Lugansa* has docked."

"How long is this stopover in Montreal?" Geoffrey groaned, wishing the port marked the end of their journey and not the halfway point.

"Two nights, I understand."

"They will never fix all the damage in that short time."

"They are not expecting to. Dr Beresford tells me this is only to make it presentable until we dock in Pernambuco."

"And how long will that take?"

"The captain has estimated the overhaul will take between seven and ten days."

"Does this mean we have to remain on board all that time? That could be uncomfortable without that new-fangled air-conditioning unit operating."

"The captain is in the process of arranging suitable hotel accommodation through our shipping agent," she explained.

"And just how are we expected to occupy ourselves after we have seen Father? There will be nothing of interest there." Geoffrey winced as the carpenters began work, hammering in a nearby cabin. "What the devil is that racket?"

"Repair work. It will be essential for the passengers boarding tomorrow."

"For pity's sake, can you ask them to stop banging and work somewhere else until my headache has gone!"

"Why not go out on deck and take the air?"

"Why bother? I might as well stay in here and die instead!" Geoffrey groaned, turning over and plugging his ears with his fingers.

Later that day, desperate to see his mother, Geoffrey staggered to his feet and was only partially dressed when Marguerite entered, carrying a plate of lightly buttered toast but looking just as dreadful as he felt.

"You are so painfully thin, Geoffrey. Please try to eat. You've had nothing in days. It will help until the kitchens are able to serve proper meals again. She was wearing a shapeless gown that he didn't recognise. Her normally shiny, coiled hair hung in a tangled mess, tied away from an ashen face with a scarf, emphasising the dark circles beneath her eyes.

"How is Mother?" he asked, trying but unable to eat any of the toast. "I was about to go and see her. Have you been attending her too through the storm?"

"Most of the time, unless it was Dr Beresford; that allowed time to look in on you or Rosamund," she said wearily. "Now, if you will excuse me, I must retire to my cabin and rest."

Although the carpenters' work in the nearby cabins had ended, the ever-present chatter of frustrated painters and the clattering of their buckets had not. The head-pounding smell of fresh paint prompted Geoffrey to go out on deck but any chance of rest was disrupted by wailing infants and a noisy group of children eagerly racing up and down, their voices shrill and high-pitched in rivalry. Geoffrey decided that when the time came for him to marry, the use of Victorian child restrainers was not such a bad idea after all.

Throughout the remainder of that day the irregular sounds of boarding passengers being shown to their cabins by loud-voiced stewards disturbed any chance of settling down to work on fragments of an elusive composition that had been flitting in and out of his mind. Only the knowledge that the liner would be leaving Montreal later that afternoon kept him sane.

Geoffrey spent most of the following day alone, reading in a deckchair. It had been his intention to spend a few hours practising on the violin but staying below deck any longer than necessary was no longer an option. Instead, he massaged soothing oil into his hands and the joints of his fingers, which still ached from the strain of lifting his sister.

"Might I be permitted to ask what you are doing?" A well-dressed stranger seemed to have appeared from nowhere, and now sprawled uninvited in a deckchair alongside him.

"What does it look like? I massage my hands because they ache like the very devil," Geoffrey grumbled.

"I could do that for you, you know. I massage Mother's feet quite a lot," the man offered.

"That will not be necessary but thank you for the offer, Mr?" Geoffrey said, fumbling with the cork.

"Here, let me, Sir Geoffrey." He took the slippery bottle from Geoffrey's hand and corked it efficiently. "The Hon.

Noel Effingham, at your service," he said, just a fraction too easily for Geoffrey's liking.

"Have we met before?" Geoffrey asked, unsure if he recognised the older man or not. Either way, he wanted to get away from his intrusive manner. At a guess, he was somewhere in his early thirties, although on first impression he had appeared younger. His clothes were expensive, clearly worn for effect rather than for comfort and way too fashionable for Geoffrey's modest taste.

"We were not formally introduced, Sir Geoffrey. We acknowledged each other in the dining salon on our first night on board, when you were accompanying two ladies and a rather overweight maid."

"If you will excuse me, I really must go. I have been out on deck too long." This was not the time to get into a heated discussion with a perfect stranger, so he ignored Noel's rude comment about his sister.

"How disappointing, I was hoping to tempt you into a game of deck tennis," Noel said, indicating a racquet on the decking between them.

"I am sorry… I cannot," Geoffrey said.

"Then maybe tomorrow; my regular partner is a long way from recovery after that wretched storm and I could certainly do with some exercise in this bracing sea air."

"Actually, I do not play much tennis."

"Then what do you play?"

"The violin," Geoffrey said, annoyed at the intense way Noel stared at him.

"You are joking… right?"

"Not in the least. I never joke about such matters."

"A musician, please forgive me, I should have realised." Noel stared at the boy's long, slender fingers. "Even so, Sir Geoffrey, having a friendly knockabout on the court would not cause any damage to your beautiful hands."

"Maybe not but today would be out of the question. I need to practise at least five hours a day and I am way behind," Geoffrey insisted, mistakenly thinking Noel would take the hint and try to ensnare another unfortunate partner.

"Then I shall look out for you tomorrow, Sir Geoffrey. Perhaps you will join me for a game after luncheon?" Noel called after him.

Geoffrey saw nothing of his mother or Rosamund during the remainder of that day, both of them still too ill to leave their cabins. Only Marguerite joined him for dinner, in a private room where they both picked at their food but ate very little.

"You must try to eat more, Geoffrey, otherwise you could blow away in the next gale. You are as thin as a streak of pump-water," she said, pushing her own plate aside.

"Is that what is really troubling you?"

"I am becoming more concerned about Mother. She ought never to have considered making this trip. Seeing her taking so many pills it troubles me there might be something else wrong with her other than the seasickness."

"I agree, she is taking far too many. Mother must have more than one bottle in her possession for this length of journey. Why not take a look in her cabin when she is out?"

"I cannot go sneaking through Mother's belongings. I would be no better than a common thief."

"Strewth, I am not suggesting you take anything... only that you can find out what they are prescribed for."

"Well the answer is no, whatever you say."

It was two more days before Lady Claudia ventured onto the deck on the arm of Marguerite, and was comfortably settled in a shaded area that had been specifically allocated for ladies. Although battered by the storm, most of the potted palms had survived.

By this time, Noel Effingham had convinced a reluctant Geoffrey to partner him on the tennis court. Contrary to Geoffrey's initial thoughts, he was actually beginning to enjoy the pleasures of having a male companion on board after spending so much time in the company of his mother and sisters.

"Your arrival in Pernambuco is timely, Sir Geoffrey. There are many cultural events happening there this month. There is a touring Russian ballet, performing *Swan Lake* at the Apollo. A colonial shooting event and a midweek point-to-point race in the Great Park. There will also be a production of *Samson and Delilah* at the Grand Opera House the day after our arrival."

"Quite the hub of the universe, you might say!" Geoffrey was relieved at the prospect of having a cultural diversion to anticipate after what promised to be a difficult reunion with his father.

"As an alternative, the city offers a Minstrel show, playing at the Vaudeville Theatre, and needless to say the burlesque shows on the other side of town."

"Then our short time there will not be without interest," Geoffrey commented.

"There should also be a spectacular ball one evening, to which I will naturally not be invited!" Noel said archly.

"You seem quite sure about that?" Geoffrey said curiously.

"I am but only because of my father's political associates. The event is being held on the estate of that hatchet-faced old dowager, Lady Harriet Drummond. Such a grandiose function as is rumoured must surely be with the prospect of marrying off that saintly grandson whom she parades about at all of the important events, though in my humble opinion he is little more than an Irish ruffian."

It was clear Noel was not close to his father, a politician who drank heavily throughout the day and could barely articulate anything that made sense in the dining salon. Geoffrey thought that Noel's brief conversations with his overindulgent mother sometimes bordered on the insolent, particularly when she made any comments directed towards Geoffrey. In contrast to Noel's elderly mother, her travelling companion, Agnes Hulme, was a younger woman, neatly dressed in drab, unadorned clothes, who trailed after her mistress with a theatrical subservience that never quite rang true.

"I trust you will not object when I make this observation, Sir Geoffrey, that you have the most beautiful sister imaginable," Noel commented as Rosamund joined her mother in the shade. "Until this moment, I hadn't realised how very alike you are, in both features and colouring."
His sister did look incredibly beautiful that afternoon and Geoffrey was more unnerved by Noel's comparison than he cared to admit. "We do both have fair hair, I grant you but that is where any similarity ends," he said gruffly, though he knew that they had often been mistaken for twins.

"I cannot agree, Sir Geoffrey. In appearance, you are both perfect in every way," Noel said, lighting up a cigarette. "By the way, I meant to ask if your sister has the same musical inclination as you do yourself?"

"None whatsoever. Lady Rosamund does play a little but other than having a keen interest in the latest fashions, she spends most of her time on horseback. My elder sister, Lady Marguerite, is an accomplished watercolourist."

"You have another sister? That is surprising. How unfortunate she could not have accompanied you on this voyage. South America would be a delight for any artist."

"Then it is as well that she is travelling with us. The Lady Marguerite is seated with Mother and Rosamund under the palms," Geoffrey said with grim satisfaction at Noel's discomfiture. He could also see that his mother and sister were preparing to leave, which gave him the ideal excuse to shake him off, along with his overbearing attention. "Now if you would excuse me, Noel, I must return my to violin practice but before I do that, I must speak with my mother."

"Then you must allow me to accompany you, Sir Geoffrey. Our time together on board is limited and I take great pleasure in your company," Noel said and there was nothing Geoffrey could think of to put him off.
When they reached the palmed area, they hung back momentarily. Lady Claudia and Rosamund had already left,

leaving Marguerite distracted from her novel by Agnes Hulme, the companion of Noel's mother. It was clear the woman was in a highly agitated state and with no regard for propriety she was displaying a shocking flash of scarlet stocking on a shapely leg as she sat down beside his sister.

"Why the devil is Hulme out on deck, gossiping? If it would not embarrass your sister, I've a mind to drag the baggage down there to do what she's paid for," Noel said, lighting up another cigarette and inhaling deeply. "Thank God her position will be terminated soon after we dock."

"But how will she get back to England?"

"She is not going back. Some unfortunate man she has never laid eyes on is about to marry the creature, sight unseen."

"You are saying she has never met her future husband? It's like the Middle Ages."

"Where have you been hiding, Sir Geoffrey? That sort of thing goes on all the time. The lower decks are no doubt strewn with lonely spinsters on their own fishing expeditions. There are always unattached men on some plantation or other in need of a wife." As Noel said this he caught her eye, which quickly had her disappearing below deck.

Later that afternoon, once Geoffrey had completed his violin practice, he caught up with his sister, who was making notes in her journal.

"You seemed very engrossed in conversation with that Hulme woman earlier."

"Why do you ask?"

"Only because Noel hinted that she is prone to expanding the truth and is not to be trusted."

"Oddly enough, Miss Hulme was implying you should perhaps not be spending so much time in Noel's company either."

"Really? Did she explain why?"

"Well, since you ask… Noel was expelled from Cambridge with three other students after his first year and that could not be a lie."

70

"Expelled for what? She must have come up with some story."

"It appears that a senior lecturer was involved in the scandal and he was forcibly removed from the building by the local constabulary. What is even more shocking is that all of the students were drunk and in a state of undress, Noel included. Fortunately for him, his father is an influential politician and blocked publication of the news."

"And you believe that trumped-up story?" Geoffrey protested weakly, unsure if a servant would have the audacity to invent such a lie.

Later that afternoon, he discovered from his mother that Florence Taylor's condition had worsened and, according to Dr Beresford, she would be unable to make another ocean crossing for some months to come. His elder sister had already begun making enquiries to find a suitable replacement.

Every day that the liner surged ahead through the now bluer, cresting waves, so the impending continent of South America became more of a reality. The air had become noticeably warmer and Noel Effingham's companionship was proving unshakeable.

Although life for the first-class passengers had resumed its efficiency the only cause for complaint, apart from the lingering smell of fresh paint, was the stifling atmosphere below deck whenever the state-of-the-art air-conditioning unit broke down, which it did frequently.

Accustomed to the freedom of life on the estate in Ashbourne, Geoffrey could only escape the monotony of their confined existence on the liner through his music. Religiously, after each lengthy practice session, he would scan the cloudless sky in search of any sea birds and the prospect of land.

"Did you make contact with Lady Dun-a-bunk, or whatever her name is? Beresford mentioned her to Mother when we were boarding," Geoffrey asked, settling beside Marguerite while she was sketching.

"Lady Drummond. I will, once we are introduced. She must know someone who could help, having a large estate on the outskirts of Pernambuco."

"Have you not even met the woman yet? I thought Mother knew her."

"Only indirectly. Her late daughter married a childhood friend of Mother's from an estate neighbouring Grandfather's in Ireland."

"I suspect that would have been Rufus, the Earl of . Glendower. That Irish ruffian Grandpa made us avoid as children."

"I gather he and Mother were inseparable growing up."

"And that is probably why Grandpa brought Mother back with him to Ashbourne. If you recall, I must have been about six when we eventually went over to visit."

"You were. Mother arranged that trip for my fifteenth birthday. None of us was allowed any further than the gatehouse but I do remember a terrible argument on our last day between Mother and Grandfather after she was prevented from riding over to the Glendower estate."

"What happened?"

"Nothing, but they barely acknowledged each other for months after."

On the following day, the family was at last introduced to Lady Harriet Drummond. It was not an easy introduction for Lady Claudia, who was in a great deal of pain that afternoon and was barely able to conceal it.

"My dear, are you unwell?" the dowager asked, as Geoffrey assisted his mother into a reclining seat.

"Foolishly I seem to have come on deck without my headache pills. Geoffrey, be a darling and collect the small brown bottle from my bedside table."

Before he returned with the bottle, Geoffrey paused to scribble down the name on the label on a sheet of paper from his mother's writing table.

On his return, Lady Drummond was talking at length about the many virtues of her only grandson, one Archie Westbrook. The name was repeated often and in such glowing terms that it began to grate. He made the excuse of needing to continue his violin practice, only to be confronted by Noel sauntering along the deck a short distance away.

"I cannot join you for tennis this afternoon, Noel; I am already late with my practice. I have been held up all morning while the chandeliers were hoisted back into position in the ballroom and now I am running late."

"No matter, Sir Geoffrey. I could not have concentrated properly anyway, having drunk far too much last night to hit anything straight. However, I would like to extend an invitation to you to accompany me and a group of friends to the opera, once we dock in Pernambuco, . After the earthquake four years ago, the acoustics in the opera house are now perfect since the architect who rebuilt it had the foresight to travel to London and visit the Royal Albert Hall."

"An evening at the opera sounds interesting," Geoffrey said, somewhat reluctantly.

"This new production of *Samson and Delilah* promises to be way above average, and would make a splendid evening all round," Noel enthused.

"Then I accept your kind offer. I am sure Mother would be delighted to accompany us," Geoffrey said.

"Unfortunately, this would be a gentlemen-only outing, Sir Geoffrey. Doubtless, Her Ladyship would not object to your joining our party. I am perfectly at home in the city and I would never allow any harm to befall you."

"I am well able to take care of myself, Noel. Of course I will come," Geoffrey said, yet immediately he wished he hadn't, feeling somehow that he'd been entrapped, as was conveyed by Noel's victorious smile.

In the dining salon later that evening, Geoffrey was relieved to find his mother in good spirits and looking radiant, her sapphire earrings sparkling with every movement of her lovely head. Again she wore no other jewellery except for a pair of silver and tortoiseshell hair slides to hold the lustrous dark hair away from her slender neck.

"What do you think of Mama's hair, Jeffy?" Rosamund asked. "I did it for her."

"Then I am impressed to see you *are* actually good at something," Geoffrey said with a laugh.

"If you bothered to find out more about your family instead of fiddling all day long, you might think otherwise," Rosamund retorted, deliberately prodding at her food as if it was her brother.

"Like what exactly?"

"Do not be unkind, Geoffrey dear; Rosamund has spent hours making me look this presentable," Lady Claudia said.

"Rubbish; you always look nice, Mother but even so, why use those worn hair slides on this trip? They must be even older than I am. You wear them all the time at home, so why bother bringing them with you?"

"They are as precious to me as your grandmother's sapphires. I would be devastated if I had the misfortune to lose either," she said, flushing.

"How come you are not wearing the necklace tonight?"

"I have that locked away in the captain's safe with my other jewellery. I would feel overdressed, wearing the necklace at dinner. If it will make you feel any better, Geoffrey, I promise to wear them on the night of the opera."

"Opera...?" he asked nervously.

"Lady Harriet has invited us to share her box for the premiere of *Samson and Delilah* soon after we dock in Pernambuco. There will be no other seats available for weeks."

"Have you accepted the offer?" Geoffrey asked, grinding his teeth with vexation.

"Of course I have, darling. It was a most thoughtful invitation."

"I am afraid you must count me out. I have already agreed to accompany Noel and his party to the same opera that evening."

"Surely you are not considering going anywhere with Noel Effingham once the liner has docked in Pernambuco?" Marguerite commented. "You are far too young to mix with any of that man's group. Who knows what they get up to?"

"It is an invitation to the opera, Maggs. I have not signed up for an expedition into the heart of the rainforest," Geoffrey said, doing his best to laugh it off, but wishing all the same that he hadn't agreed to be in Noel's party after all.

"It matters not who Geoffrey is seated with for the performance," said Lady Claudia. "For a musician such as him it has the promise of a spectacular event. Harriet is on the board of directors and assures me this is a show that should not be missed."

"But it would be so much better if Geoffrey sat with us," Marguerite said.

"Why would any young gentleman prefer spending the evening in the company of chattering ladies? Your brother is no longer a child and having male company will be good preparation for his introduction to London society, when he is accepted into the Royal Academy of Music."

"Why do you talk as if I am not here? I do have an opinion," Geoffrey complained.

"Oh do be quiet, Jeffy," Rosamund said, flushing with embarrassment and purposely turning her back on two men who were ogling her from a nearby table.

"I will inform Lady Drummond tomorrow that you are unable to attend," his mother said, her voice rising in alarm as Geoffrey got up and strode over to the men.

"If either of you gentlemen had an ounce of decency between you, then you would be concentrating on your food and NOT on my sister. She, like other ladies of refinement in this room, is here to dine and not be an object to be stared at by a pair of bloody halfwits! If you persist with this, I will demand the captain bars you from being seated anywhere near our table in future," Geoffrey snapped, glaring at the men. Embarrassed at the unwanted scrutiny they were now receiving from the other guests, they rose and left the salon with muted words of apology.

On the following afternoon, although the air conditioning appeared to be working well in other first-class areas of the liner, there was a problem with the units operating in the ballroom and Geoffrey was again granted permission to use it for his daily practice. Even so, the sweltering conditions made the session seem ten times harder, mainly because of the intricate finger changes required for each movement.

After playing for over three hours without a break, Geoffrey was both mentally and physically exhausted. His fingers ached unbearably and he'd forgotten to bring any oil to massage them, an omission that he fully intended to rectify on his return to the cabin.

After taking a short rest and returning the instrument to its case, Geoffrey unlocked the doors, only to be confronted by Noel Effingham, clapping his hands and beaming like the Cheshire cat.

"Well done… Bravo!" Noel gushed.

"What the hell are you doing here, Noel? I do not like anyone being around when I practise," Geoffrey grumbled.

"You should never keep such musical artistry from others. Practice or not, you should have an audience. Your playing was sublime."

"It was nothing of the kind. There were too many mistakes, way too many!" Geoffrey was embarrassed by this exuberant display from a man he barely knew and by comments which, in his own opinion, were completely unjustified.

"If there were any mistakes, no one else would have noticed."

"They were there nevertheless and you should not have been here. No one should," Geoffrey said, wanting to get clear of Noel's theatrical hand gestures.

"I have not been here long, Sir Geoffrey. I had to wait for your sister to leave before I could get close enough to listen properly."

"Lady Marguerite was listening?" Geoffrey asked with surprise. "She is normally on deck, dabbling in her watercolours."

"Lady Rosamund. I have been back five or six times in the past three hours to get close enough but never could. She has been outside for most of that time."

For a moment Geoffrey was speechless, finding it difficult to take in the information. "That does not make sense at all. Rose loathes hearing me play. She always has."

"Then you are mistaken, Sir Geoffrey. I doubt if she even saw me here, not until she was leaving. She seemed to be hypnotised by those intricate melodies. I swear to you, there were tears in her eyes when we passed in the corridor."

"Then if you will excuse me, Noel, I really must dash." Geoffrey increased his pace as he strode purposefully away with the hope of shaking Noel off.

"You have a remarkable gift, Sir Geoffrey," Noel persisted, trying to keep up with the long legs of the younger man. "You must tell me the name of that piece you were playing. I am familiar with most classical works but cannot for the life of me place that work. It was truly exquisite."

"The composition was my own in preparation for my entrance exam to the Royal Academy of Music on our return," Geoffrey admitted reluctantly as they reached his cabin door. "Now if you will excuse me, Noel, I really must get inside to oil my hands."

"Then will you join me later on deck, after you have rested? I would like to learn more about your musical compositions."

"Not this evening, Noel; I have promised to read to Mother. The electric lighting in her cabin is too harsh and it reflects off the page and is affecting her vision."

In need of a bath and a lie down after the sweltering heat of the ballroom, Geoffrey came back on deck in the late afternoon to a mild and pleasant breeze, in mind to join his mother until he saw her in conversation with Lady Harriet Drummond. To avoid being noticed, he wandered to another section of the deck where Marguerite was leaning against the handrail, cautiously peering down on to a sheltered section of the lower deck.

"What's so fascinating down there, Maggs?" Geoffrey whispered, making her jump.

"How you startled me, Geoffrey. I do wish you would not creep up on me like that. You could have given me a heart attack," Marguerite retorted.

"If you were not so intent on being so bloody nosy, you might have seen me coming." He moved closer to the rail. "What were you watching anyway?"

"Do keep your voice down, otherwise they might hear you."

"Who might that be?"

"Agnes Hulme, the Effingham's maid. It is disgusting behaviour," she whispered, prompting him to look over the rail to catch the flash of red stockings, the woman still in the arms of a brutish sailor with a bull neck and tattooed arms like hairy tree trunks.

"They are only kissing. What is wrong with that?"

"Everything, if she is about to marry someone else," Marguerite said, urging him away from the rail. "Come away, Geoffrey, they might see you."

"Would it matter if they did?" Geoffrey complained.

Folding up her portable easel, she packed away her paints and brushes into the capacious bag she carried everywhere, allowing time for Geoffrey to examine her latest watercolour in the journal.

"I say, Maggs; this is a jolly good impression of the area with the palms and Mother lounging in that blue dress. I will never understand how you are able to breathe such life into these paintings with just a few strokes. Whenever I try, the damned things never resemble anything at all, except a nasty splodge of colour, yet yours look so real. How do you do it?"

"Practice I suppose, like you with the violin."

"When you come to think of it, we are a bit of an obsessive pair." Geoffrey smiled, massaging his fingers,

78

before picking up the folding easel and paint box, leaving his sister to carry the artwork and the omni-present bag.

With every passing day it was becoming noticeably warmer but the cooling ocean breeze gave many unsuspecting passengers a false illusion of the oppressive humidity that would await them on arrival. Recently there had been sightings of other vessels on the horizon, sea birds circling in their wake. The dark shape of a cargo steamer, a dying breed of vessel with tall, spindly masts that, with sails furled, gave the impression of three crucifixes. It belched out black, acrid smoke from its twin chimney stacks as it ploughed its way through the water.

Later that afternoon, two graceful ships in full sail were seen on the horizon, the billowing canvas propelling the vessels across the ocean with the effortless elegance of swans. To Geoffrey, this was a sight as inspirational as a piece of music and he gazed after the second one long after it had disappeared from sight. He came away from the rail saddened by the realisation that, all too soon, sailing under canvas across the Atlantic would become a thing the past. In need of some diversion, he found Marguerite on deck, reading.

"What are you reading? I have never seen you this absorbed, except when you are drawing or painting."

"Take a look," she said, handing over her battered copy of *Lost Tribes of the Rainforest*. "You should read this page. You might find it of interest."

Taking the book, Geoffrey skimmed over the page before finding the paragraph she had indicated. "'Therefore, based on all the relevant information, it is logical that an unidentified tribe of pale-skinned mystics, known as the River People, could actually exist,'" he read back to her. "Surely you do not believe this hokum?"

"There must be some foundation of truth in this mysterious sect. Otherwise, why bother writing about it?"

"Maybe sensationalism would be a start, otherwise why would anyone give the chapter such a bizarre heading?" he snorted. "'The White Rain Gods of the Cloud Forest'" He flicked through the volume. "Or what about this: 'The Mysterious Temple of Light'?" He chortled. "I swear, I have never read anything so outrageous. It reads like a Jules Verne novel."

"Unless you have read it, do not mock. Look through the information yourself and then offer your caustic opinion when I return."

"Where are you off to now?"

"To see if Mother is finished with Dr Beresford."

"Why… is she unwell again?"

"They are discussing the months of convalescence Florence will need before she can return to England and there is not much time to arrange it. The *Lugansa* docks in the port of Pernambuco for only ten days before it continues up the coast to Apalla. I would not imagine it will remain there for more than a few days before we set sail for England."

Once he was alone, Geoffrey was soon absorbed in the book reading of a lost geological site where in the year AD 420, a Peruvian mystic was said to have constructed the Temple of Light, a magnificent structure visible only by moonlight. The temple was reputed to provide a gateway into the afterlife protected by the spirit of the Moon, using a route identifiable solely by starlight when a pathway into the astral plain became clearly visible to the naked eye.

It was on the day the coastline of South America finally appeared on the horizon that Dr Beresford came up to Geoffrey on deck and handed him a bottle of pills.

"Please forgive me for this hasty exchange, Sir Geoffrey but unfortunately there has been an incident below deck which needs my urgent attention. Since I am unable to deliver these in person, I entrust Lady Claudia's medication into your capable hands. Please make sure Her Ladyship takes only one pill, four times a day as prescribed; taking any more than that could prove fatal."

"Fatal? What the hell are they and why does Mother need them?"

"These are the strongest painkillers we have on board for her condition, Sir Geoffrey. More than that, I am not at liberty to say."

"What condition? You cannot just say that and walk away, Beresford."

"Unfortunately I must. Forgive me, Sir, but there is an engineer being untangled from some equipment and he is in danger of losing his life if I do not amputate a leg to release him." He strode away, leaving Geoffrey to contemplate a bottle containing more red pills but much smaller than those he had previously seen.

Any thoughts of questioning his mother about her need for the pills went out of his head as he entered her cabin only to discover Agnes Hulme folding and packing gowns into one of the opened suitcases.

"What is that woman doing here, Mother?" Geoffrey asked suspiciously.

"Noel Effingham has very kindly offered Miss Hulme's services to assist with my packing since Florence cannot," Lady Claudia said, looking distinctly unwell herself. "Be a darling, Geoffrey and see if you can find Dr Beresford. He should have been here an hour ago."

"Are these what you wanted, Mother?" Geoffrey was frustrated that he could not question her further with Agnes busying herself about the room. "Beresford asked me to hand these to you. We met purely by chance on the deck. He apologised for not calling in person but he was on his way to deal with an emergency."

"Thank goodness you have them, darling, my head is splitting." She immediately swallowed two of the red pills with a tumbler of water.

"Beresford said they could be lethal if you take more than the prescribed dose. You should take one, four times a day. It is written here on the label."

"Do not fuss, darling. These are only to prevent the migraines from getting worse," she said lightly, although he wasn't convinced. "Has the steward provided someone to assist with your own packing, Geoffrey?"

"There is no need, Mother. I can manage it myself."

"Are you sure? You were never the tidiest boy. You must have your linen folded properly, or they will be dreadfully creased on arrival."

"If they are, then I will have someone at the hotel iron them."

"Then you must have them press every single item and have what you do not need for two days repacked."

"Repacked, why? The *Lugansa* will be in dock for more than a week."

"Please accept my apologies, darling. I have already informed your sisters about the change of plan."

"What plan? Is Father meeting us somewhere else instead?"

"This is not about your father, Geoffrey. It is important that we stay somewhere more socially acceptable than the hotel. That is why I have accepted Lady Harriet's kind offer of some private accommodation at her plantation."

"What next? First a box at the opera and now we are invited to stay for a week with that old dragon? What about the meeting with Father? After all, he is the reason we have travelled out here and, as we have not laid eyes on him over the last four years, would a hotel not be a more appropriate place for us to become reacquainted?"

"Everything is arranged, Geoffrey. We will be staying at the Maximilian Hotel for the first two nights, by which time the business with your father at the solicitor's office will have been concluded."

"I see, and then we are expected to uproot and relocate somewhere else until the *Lugansa* sets sail, just because that old dragon snaps her fingers?"

"Mind your manners, Geoffrey. That is no way to speak about an offer of kindness. This is what comes of having an absentee father for the past four years. What Lady Harriet has so kindly offered is a separate wing of the main house and the reason I agreed to her generous offer is because, unlike hotel accommodation, there would be an uninterrupted space for your violin practice."

"I am truly sorry, Mother. I had no idea. The last thing I want is to upset you." Geoffrey turned and left abruptly before she could see the tears in his eyes.

Chapter Five
Pernambuco

The heat on deck became almost unbearable once the *Lugansa*'s engines were shut down and the comforting breeze abruptly ceased as the liner was towed into the harbour by the tugs. Even before the ship had docked, the unwelcome reality became apparent. The intense humidity was combined with the putrid stench from a build-up of rotting garbage that caught unseasoned travellers off guard, leaving them appalled by the squalor of everyday life, which could be observed from the vantage point of the first-class deck and which clearly intensified beyond the perimeter of the imposing port buildings.

As the liner inched closer to the dock, Geoffrey could make out the uniformed port officials hastily setting up barriers to keep a throng of human activity from entering a roped-off area where the passengers would eventually disembark.

"I cannot see Papa anywhere!" Rosamund wailed, her voice muffled through a handkerchief pressed up against her nose and mouth.

"Perhaps he was delayed. He had some distance to travel," Lady Claudia said.

"He is not the only one, is he, Mother?" Geoffrey muttered, staring into the crowd, where people were milling around like ants.

"What do we do if he is not amongst them?" Rosamund asked, scouring the sea of upturned faces beneath them.

"We will get more information about where he is once we make contact with the shipping agent," Lady Claudia said through her own folded handkerchief which she pressed to her nose.

"What none of us has taken into account is that Father's appearance may have altered drastically after four years in this dreadful climate," Geoffrey said moodily. "And, like Mother said, he might have got held up along the coast."

"But he promised. He always keeps his word," Rosamund pouted.

"Well apparently not this time. If Father planned on travelling overland rather than by boat, he may not arrive until tomorrow, or even the day after," Marguerite said.

"I just hope he knows the *Lugansa* is only docked in Pernambuco for ten days," Geoffrey added.

"The shipping agent will have made sure of that, darling," Lady Claudia reassured him.

"Even so, why not meet us in Apalla instead of down here?" Geoffrey said, waiting impatiently to disembark.

"It is complicated, Geoffrey. Our solicitors in Lichfield have a connection with a firm in Pernambuco. The paperwork your father must sign has been drawn up there." Lady Claudia turned aside, hoping to prevent him seeing her swallow another of the red pills.

"How many is that, Mother? You do know four is the maximum?" Geoffrey said.

"This is only my second one. The sunlight is affecting my eyes badly today and my head is throbbing unmercifully. A migraine is the last thing I need when we are about to disembark."

Beyond the more regular shapes of the bonded warehouses there was a jumble of architectural influences, the older buildings emphasising the dominance of the earlier Portuguese occupation. In the distance, it was just possible to pick out the stately tree-lined avenues. What piqued Geoffrey's interest more was what the civilised heart of the city might offer and, in particular, the recently rebuilt Grand Opera House.

Having descended a covered gangway on to the dock, they were directed by port officials towards the Customs House. Once passports had been checked, each group of passengers was allowed to make their way to the Arrivals Hall but, because of renovation work being carried out on a collapsed section of the covered way, they were diverted outside beside a ramshackle temporary fence made from corrugated iron. Through gaps in the metal a swarm of beggars pleaded for money.

In the oppressive humidity, the air itself seemed alive, buzzing with flies and mosquitoes. The stench from the dead animals and human waste that had collected at the edge of the quay was almost unbearable. At the moment they entered the sanctuary of the arrival hall, their rescuer appeared in the shape of a florid man wearing a soiled linen suit.

"Henry Strickland at your service, Lady Saint Hubes, your appointed shipping agent," he announced, removing a grubby panama hat with deference.

"I am delighted to make your acquaintance, Sir. I had expected my husband would have been here to receive us. Do you have any information on when he is expected to arrive?"

Thrusting a hand into the inner pocket of his jacket, Strickland produced a crumpled envelope. "Perhaps this communication will have the information you require, Milady. Might I suggest that you and your family accompany me to my air-cooled offices? You will find the temperature more agreeable and the atmosphere less noisy than here. It is from there I have arranged for two carriages that will convey your family to the hotel."

"Are your offices far?" Geoffrey asked, concerned by the way his mother lowered the veil on her hat, obscuring her features.

"If you do not mind the inconvenience of using the rear entrance, we can avoid the more crowded streets."

As well as the oppressive heat, the air was filled with dust and grit from the rumbling wheels of passing ox carts and horse-drawn traffic. Geoffrey longed for the peace and tranquillity of the Derbyshire life they had left so far behind. By the time they reached a tall, dismal building with large patches missing from the eroded stucco of the walls, his mother was tiring noticeably and Geoffrey supported her up the creaking wooden staircase with a reassuring arm around her waist.

Although they had walked only a short distance, it was a shocking introduction into an alien environment, so different from the pictures Geoffrey had seen in books from his grandfather's library.

"Are you sure you are up to this climb, Mother?" he asked, pausing on the half landing. "You look very pale."

"Geoffrey, have you seen my Gladstone bag?" she asked with some alarm.

"I assume Strickland must have it. If so it will be quite safe."

"I have the bag here, Milady," the agent called up from below.

"What has become of Rosamund?" she asked. Her younger daughter was partially hidden by the bulk of Marguerite's frame as she encouraged her sister to let go of the handrail and climb the rickety staircase.

"She and Maggs are on their way up, Mother. As soon as we have reached the office, I will go back for them."

Eventually everyone was safely inside the gloomy interior. It was cooler than he expected as there was an overhead electric fan, cranking erratically on a bent shaft. The feather plumage adorning his mother's brimmed hat fluttered in the down-draught as she carefully read through the contents of her husband's letter.

"Your father sends his profound apologies. It appears that he has been unavoidably delayed. However, he is confident he will arrive here within the week, before the liner is due to set sail up the coast." Lady Claudia opened the Gladstone bag, taking out another red pill that she gratefully swallowed with a glass of water.

"Does Father give any reason for the delay?" Marguerite asked.

"There are no details but it appears there has been an important development from one of the more recent experiments."

"Does he mention what these experiments are?" Geoffrey asked.

"Not in this letter but no doubt he will, if you ask."

"But what if he is delayed again? Has he mentioned what we should do then?" Geoffrey grumbled.

"Your father is confident he will arrive here by the end of the week but, if not, he will be waiting on the quayside when the liner docks in Apalla," Lady Claudia said, glancing at Henry Strickland for confirmation.

"This proposition would be perfectly understandable, milady, since that port is at the mouth of the Amazon and, if so, it would mean only a slight inconvenience to you and your family. Fortunately, the *Lugansa* will be docked there for three days, taking on more passengers. There will be enough time to conclude any business before the liner sets sail."

"Assuming he is there. But what if he is not?" Geoffrey asked.

"I am certain your father will make every effort to be there when we arrive, Geoffrey dear. Apart from signing the documents, I know he will be longing to see his children again," Lady Claudia said.

"There was one other matter I must speak to you about, milady. Doctor Beresford has informed my office that you will be in need of a maid to assist you between here and Apalla, is that correct?"

"Indeed. Did you have anyone in mind?"

"I can assure you, the young woman I have appointed is of good character and local to the port of Apalla. Should the unlikely situation of a further delay arise, Juanita Perez has numerous contacts there, which would enable her to assist you."

"How well do you know this young woman?" Marguerite asked.

"The girl is a niece of my wife's family and, because her mother is recently widowed, Juanita is in need of a passage home."

"That is all very well but is she up to the task, Strickland? Has she had any previous experience in a gentlewoman's service?" Geoffrey asked, impatient to get away from the claustrophobic atmosphere of the dusty room.

"Juanita is from a Catholic family and has been here these three months, nursing my wife through a most difficult confinement."

"I am sure this young woman will suit the position well, Mr Strickland," Lady Claudia declared.

"I need to ask if there is another exit to this building, Strickland," Geoffrey enquired. "That staircase is awfully steep for the ladies to descend in their heeled shoes." He looked around at the mountainous piles of dust-laden paperwork that had been crammed into any convenient space, wondering how anyone could remember what each document contained.

"I suggested the rear entrance to avoid the street beggars. The carriages are at the main entrance, awaiting your departure, Sir Geoffrey," the agent said, wedging a box of paperwork against the door to keep it open. "The drivers have been instructed to transport your family to the Grand Colonial."

"Surely that is incorrect. We are staying at the Maximilian."

"Forgive me, Sir Geoffrey, I should have explained. The Maximilian is recommended only for sightseers, not for visiting dignitaries, therefore I deemed the accommodation unsuitable. The Grand Colonial is far superior to any other hotel in this city and I trust you will be most comfortable there."

"Might I ask if you will be accompanying us as far as Apalla?" Geoffrey asked, as they were guided through the building to the main reception area.

"Unfortunately not, Sir Geoffrey; my instructions are only to represent your family throughout your stay in Pernambuco. An alternative shipping agent has been notified with regard to your pending arrival and will be at your disposal during the short stay. Unfortunately, I know nothing of the gentleman's connections within that port. However, Señorita Perez should prove invaluable in making contact with him."

"My main concern is Father. What if he does not turn up before we re-board the *Lugansa*? What if he's travelling down overland and our paths cross, what then?"

"In this modern age of telecommunications," his mother reassured him, "I will arrange for Mr Strickland to make contact with the agent in Apalla, if only to make doubly sure that cannot happen."

"This is becoming such a mess, Mother. I say that if he does not make an appearance here or in Apalla, then we should continue home on the *Lugansa* and let him trail after us to England instead!"

"We cannot go back, Geoffrey, not until an agreement has been reached and the relevant documents have been signed. It is imperative that he does so for your futures."

"This is such an unnecessary precaution, Mother. You're forty-five, not a hundred. Apart from that, this climate is not good for you. I say to hell with these infernal documents. Show Father we are not to be trifled with and let him have the inconvenience of arranging and paying for a passage back to England. If so, I pray it will be a stormy crossing." Geoffrey ground his teeth with annoyance.

"You will feel different in the morning, Geoffrey. Much as I would like to return home, your father must be persuaded to sign these documents now and not later."

"Mother is perfectly right, Geoffrey," Marguerite said. "It is an inconvenience I agree but, since Apalla has always been the last port of call on our route home, I do not see what difference it will make whether we meet Father here or travel up the coast to meet him before continuing to England as planned; we will at least be sailing with the luxury of air conditioning." She was wafting a fan at the beading sweat over her heaving breasts as their carriages appeared under the portico. Each of the two broughams was harnessed to a matching pair of chestnut mares.

Once clear of the docks, they were conveyed to the Grand Colonial Hotel through a broad, elegant thoroughfare laid out between rows of established jacarandas on either side of the carriageway.

"Just look at those blooms!" Marguerite exclaimed, indicating the clusters of rich, purple flowers, drooping like wisteria.

"What are they, Judas trees?" Geoffrey asked, raising his voice to be heard above the carriage wheels rumbling over the cobbles.

"Jacaranda as far as I know; I am not sure what they are called over here."

"After that awful area around the docks, I would never have imagined any part of this city could be so amazing," Geoffrey said, wondering where to look next. Unlike in England there was a noticeable lack of motorised traffic and the roads were instead full of gleaming carriages, drawn by evenly matched pairs of horses, transporting their elegant passengers at a slow trot, enabling them to exchange smiles and even swift greetings with the occupants of other vehicles.

Soon after this all too brief glimpse of elegant Pernambuco society, their own carriages rattled off the grand drive and drove steadily through a more densely populated area. Here most of the once-grand architecture was crumbling through neglect, and trees were less evident. Open carriages were parked close to the many street stalls which were piled with fine linens and silks where well-dressed women bartered for lengths of the fine material, most seemingly well versed in the art of purchasing from the convenience of their own carriages.

Further on, they were held up behind lumbering carts piled high with timber or stacked with mountainous bales of cotton, pulled by undernourished horses, mules and oxen straining under the cracking of whips in the sweltering heat.

As they were driven further through the poorer quarter, the swarms of flies became an intrusive nuisance. Geoffrey hastily slid up the carriage windows to keep out the stink of open sewers, feeling close to suffocation. "How can anyone breathe here?" he protested. Further on, in an area that clearly had once been a fashionable square, a fire-eater was entertaining a gathering crowd while a group of apparently double-jointed children balanced monkeys on bamboo poles or performed somersaults.

In this poorer quarter there were countless potholes in the road, the endless jolting providing an unforgiving ride. By this time Geoffrey's face was the colour of a lobster, not only from the heat but also from the restriction of the high starched collar, creating deep ridges in his neck.

Once clear of the hustle of traders and street performers, the carriages at last rumbled into an area containing more trees in a welcoming stretch of parkland. As they travelled further, a series of grand homes began to appear beyond the dappled light of the trees. Here life moved at a more leisurely pace, and the tracks through the park were occupied by elegant couples on horseback, shaded from the intense heat of the sun beneath the wooded canopy.

"Have you noticed how none of the European women expose any flesh out here?" Geoffrey commented, indicating two figures sauntering through the park, their features barely visible through a veil of finely woven net suspended from their decorative hats, their parasols held by maidservants. "Surely it cannot just be out of modesty, can it?"

"Those veils are more likely worn against mosquito bites," Marguerite said. "I meant to bring some repellent with me from home, so we must visit an apothecary before we leave for Lady Harriet's plantation. There is a recipe to protect against mosquito bites in Grifka's book. I must buy the necessary items to make it."

"How do you know something out of that old book will work?" Geoffrey asked. "Why not use one of your own herbal remedies, like you do back home?"

"I know nothing about mosquito bites on this continent. There are so many species. It makes sense to follow the author's instructions since he lived in the rainforest for years."

"Or he could have died out here from one of his own concoctions for all we know," Geoffrey laughed.

"I must try something. Mother cannot afford to get bitten if she is unwell."

"But what if her skin reacts badly to it? Have you thought about that?"

"Of course I have, Geoffrey. I thought I would try it out on you first," she said, which immediately put an end to her brother's amusement.

"Why not test it on yourself? Your skin type is much closer to Mother's than either mine or Rose's." She had clearly lost interest so he didn't bother discussing it any longer.

As the carriages entered the refined suburb of Mambuco, the affluence of the town became immediately apparent. The architecture of the grand establishments could be only glimpsed through carefully staged groups of trees within large ornamental grounds, caged behind decorative iron railings.

Inside one of these properties Geoffrey caught a glimpse of a statuesque Negro wearing a broad gold amulet which glinted in the sunlight as he restrained a sleek black panther on a taut leash, its collar studded with diamonds.

The Grand Colonial Hotel was a sprawling, colonnaded building that had been constructed in the late Georgian period but extended more recently to provide the best accommodation in the area. Each of the family's apartments had magnificent views overlooking the elaborate gardens, laid out in the formal French tradition.

Once their luggage had been offloaded from the carriages and taken up to their respective rooms, Geoffrey made the unwelcome discovery. His carefully packed violin had been damaged in transit.

"Whoever was responsible for this should be hanged, drawn and quartered and, if I could find the culprit, I would gladly do it myself with my bare hands!" Geoffrey raged to his mother. "This was no accident. It looks like someone has deliberately kicked it and more than once, to cause this amount of damage. It will take months to get it restored."

"Then I shall buy you another the moment we get home," Lady Claudia assured him.

"It would not be the same, Mother. You bought me this violin when I was twelve. The tone was perfect."

"Any instrument being played with your talent would sound wonderful, Geoffrey."

"You do not understand, Mother. I had a connection with this instrument."

"And you will again. In the meantime we must find you a replacement as soon as possible. You cannot afford to miss your daily practice."

"I know, Mother. It is the shock of finding it like this." Geoffrey knew how well the instrument had been packed before they docked and, for that reason alone, he was certain someone had deliberately unpacked it to cause the damage before wrapping it up again.

As he examined the full extent of the vandalism he realised it would be almost impossible to repair the three vicious holes that had shattered the instrument. As he put it aside, he heard something rattle inside the body and, after shaking it hard, the steel heel cap from a lady's shoe fell out. After carefully examining what remained of the fragmented bridge he found a few silken threads from a red stocking, snagged in the splintered wood, and he knew exactly who the culprit was.

On the following day, Geoffrey and Marguerite set off to purchase the herbal supplies she needed for the mosquito remedy. This also gave them an opportunity to see the local sights in a rented brougham but only on the understanding that they would return to the hotel by noon. After an uncomfortable journey into the poorer quarter of the city they located an apothecary, who unfortunately stocked only a few of the items Marguerite required.

"Where else would you suggest we try?" Geoffrey asked, speaking slowly as he was unsure if the shifty-eyed owner could understand English at all. He was convinced they had been vastly overcharged but decided it would be safer not to question the amount of change the man had handed over.

"Mercado... para brujeria," the storekeeper suggested.

"I am sorry... I did not understand that at all, can you tell me again in English?" Geoffrey asked. Meanwhile his sister was thumbing through an English/Spanish dictionary.

"I think *brujeria* means witch and *mercado* could well be a market," Marguerite said, which got a nodding confirmation from the owner.

"Is there anything in the dictionary for an instrument shop?" Geoffrey asked.

"I doubt we will have any luck finding one in this part of the city. It is too run-down."

"Maybe, but it has to be worth a try," Geoffrey said, vexed that he would never be able to confront Agnes Hulme and find out why she had caused such appalling damage to his violin.

"Have you any idea how that damage was caused, Geoffrey?"

"Possibly but I would rather not say for the time being."

"Perhaps Lady Harriet could suggest where to purchase a new one."

"Can you not understand? I do not want a new bloody instrument. If I did, I would stop off at Harrods on my way home and get one off the rack."

"I do wish you would control your language, Geoffrey. Mother would be horrified to hear you."

"Well fortunately Mother is not here and, since no one in this dump can understand a word of English anyway, what is your problem?"

Ignoring her brother, Marguerite flicked through a few pages of the illustrated dictionary and found some examples of musical instruments, which she showed to the apothecary.

"José, him show," he said, calling to the rear of the store.

A beam of sunlight penetrated the dirty windows, illuminating the murky contents of three huge glass bottles of amber and green liquids on a shelf, each shrouded with a thick coat of dust. The jars were straddled by a mass of thick, matted webs which made Geoffrey shudder at the thought of what creatures might be crawling about on the rough shelving further back, undetectable by the human eye in the gloom.

"You need pay," the owner said.

"But we have already paid and quite possibly too much!" Geoffrey exclaimed.

"It no para me, it para José. You have peseta?"

"We only have English money, you know that," Marguerite said.

"Then give me crown?" he said, eyeing her modest diamond earrings.

"I will be damned if you get another penny," Geoffrey snapped, attempting to lead his sister away by the arm.

"You can have one shilling and no more," Marguerite said, placing the coin firmly on the counter. "That is more than enough for being guided to a market."

"Estar es no bueno lady. It no enough," the shopkeeper exclaimed.

"Then so be it," she said, taking up the coin. "Good day, sir. Thank you for your time."

With some alarm, the proprietor followed her to the door. "Missy, you no go, no without my José. It no safe."

"Then I will offer you the one shilling and three pence more. That is my final offer," she said with grim determination, just as the human hulk named José appeared from the shadows. Handing him a scribbled note, the owner pushed the man towards her and took the offered coins. "You make me a poor man, lady."

"If that bloody halfwit could speak English all along, why allow us to struggle on until now before letting on?" Geoffrey said, following José and his sister outside where the sun was blinding.

"Bartering must be an everyday occurrence for these people, I suppose," she said, allowing Geoffrey to help her into the carriage.

It was almost half an hour before they arrived at the witches' market through a warren of narrow streets where no other pale faces could be detected among the jostling crowds.

Once inside, their senses were invaded with the smells of strong herbs and exotic spices. Here some of the stalls were piled with raw meat of unidentifiable origin. Dried tobacco leaves hung in clusters above others. Every nook and cranny was stacked with sacks of maize or other produce. There were dogs scavenging for food among the thronging hordes pushing and shoving to reach the appropriate stall. Regardless of the produce, everywhere was buzzing with swarms of flies, wasps and hornets.

"I think we should move on," Geoffrey whispered, firmly taking Marguerite's arm to lead her away from a particularly gloomy area.

"Why? I have not found anything I need."

"Can you not see them?" Geoffrey asked, trembling noticeably.

"I can barely see anything in this light, except for those strange wooden carvings on this stall."

"That is exactly why we need to get away, Maggs. They are not carvings. Those things are shrunken heads."

"Do not be so childish, Geoffrey. We are not in the Dark Ages," Marguerite said, peering more closely at one of the items on the stall. "I have to agree they do appear very lifelike but they are carved wood. The sale of such dreadful artefacts would not be allowed." Her eyes widened with horror as she examined the shape closest to her. "Dear God in Heaven… this one has hair!"

"We must get away from this loathsome place while we can," Geoffrey urged.

"We are not going anywhere until I find what we came for," she said adamantly. "Mother will need this and I refuse to leave without all the ingredients."

"Very well then, get on with it."

Gripping her arm once more, Geoffrey manoeuvred them swiftly into a brighter area where José handed them two portions of some unidentifiable food, wrapped in leaves and bamboo containers containing drinks.

"You cannot in all seriousness consider eating anything that has been prepared in this dump, Maggs? What the hell are they anyway?"

"Them much good, señor," José said, biting into one of the wraps and encouraging Marguerite to do the same, who began eating before her brother could prevent her.

"Whatever you do, do not swallow that, Maggs. Spit it out for God's sake."

"Unlike you, Geoffrey, I am hungry. I missed breakfast." She took another bite. "You should try one. They are very tasty."

"I can manage until we get back to the hotel."

"Where is your sense of adventure, Geoffrey?"

"Adventure… you are displaying more of a suicidal tendency than any adventurous spirit, Maggs. Those things could be poisonous." He peeled back the edge of his wrap to see what was inside.

"I would never have considered trying one if José wasn't eating too. They are rather nice. If you do not want yours then I will have it," she said, taking it from him.

"Why are you behaving like this? You are supposed to be the sensible one, not me!"

"Sensible yes but hungry," she said, taking a drink from the bamboo beaker. "If you will not eat anything, then at least drink some of this juice, otherwise you will become dehydrated in this oppressive heat."

"I do not want any of the damned stuff!"

"Stop being an idiot for once, Geoffrey. Try it. I have been using herbs long enough to know there is nothing harmful in this potion. Whatever juices went into making this drink, it is the perfect combination." Still unconvinced, Geoffrey took a cautious sip, and before long had drained the entire contents. They followed José to a stall, which to his relief, had all the items Marguerite needed. After the transaction was concluded, she suddenly asked, "Where has everyone gone, Geoffrey?"

"What, José? I am not sure. He was standing next to me a moment ago." He looked around, searching for the burly figure of their guide.

Because Geoffrey and his sister had been concentrating on the purchase, he had no idea what had become of the previously thronging crowd. Nearly all the shoppers were gone, leaving the market virtually empty except for a few stragglers who were still bartering with the traders.

"Do you think he has cleared off and left us?" Geoffrey said, checking his wallet was still in his pocket.

"José wouldn't abandon us here, not until he has been paid," she replied as they emerged from the market building.

"Can you hear that strange music?" Geoffrey asked, stopping to listen. "It's like no instrument I have ever heard. Where the devil is it coming from?" He shielded his eyes from the glare of the sun as he tried to locate the source of the unearthly sound, while his sister stared at the ground beneath her feet.

"I could swear the sound is coming from beneath us, rising out of the earth." She stopped at the sound of a collective gasp from around the other side of the building.

Rounding the corner into a shadowy street, they saw that a silent crowd had assembled. Curiously they eased a passage through the gathering, where they found that a young woman was pressed up against the market wall, naked, her outstretched arms held securely in what looked like a sacrificial position by two heavily pregnant women while an old hag painted strange symbols onto the girl's stomach and breasts. Barely moving, the captive's eyelids fluttered open to show the whites of her unseeing eyes.

Staged strategically between this strange ritual and the crowd was a low hedge of dried wood and bracken. Close by the old woman's feet was an earthenware bowl from which pale blue smoke drifted. With extreme care she unwrapped a piece of filthy sacking to remove the shrivelled carcass of a huge lizard, a good five feet in length. This she placed in the centre of a chalk circle in which the girl, now alone, had remained in the position of a crucifixion, both of the pregnant women having now moved their feet outside the circle.

Around the dead reptile the old woman systematically laid out five triangular shapes made from human bones. In the centre of each she placed a dead bat, sprinkling them with a blue powder. Finally, she coated the remains of the giant lizard with a fine dusting of powdered gold.

Settling back on her haunches, the crone began making a low, ritualistic chant while mixing together an assortment of herbs and insects in the earthenware bowl. Into this potion she finally added five strips of dried animal flesh and a pouch of powdered bone. Finally, she sprinkled a handful of red earth into the ancient vessel and stepped aside immediately.

A second later there was a huge gasp from the crowd, who all stepped back in unison as the contents of the vessel began to flash and spark violently. The wisp of blue smoke turned green, then orange and red, crackling with an intense light, the smoke spiralling higher. As the old mystic's chant became more intense, she began wafting the coloured vapour into the face of the naked girl.

Moments later there was another collective gasp and the crowd surged forward, carrying Geoffrey and his sister in their midst and rendering them powerless to back away. The mystic had turned the dried-up carcass of the lizard until it was facing the young woman and now began marking identical symbols into the earth around the creature to those she had painted on the girl's stomach.

With a theatrical gesture, the old woman hurled a handful of orange dust onto the low barricade, setting it alight, before linking the drawn images together on the ground, transforming them into the shape of a dragon.

"What the hell is this?" Geoffrey whispered, uncertain whether they should make a break for it or stay to see this fascinating performance right through to its conclusion.

When the mystic's chant had dropped by a full octave, the crowd dramatically surged closer to the circle, open-mouthed and all eyes fixed on the crone, who was now daubing a steaming, viscous liquid from the steaming vessel onto each of the bats, before proceeding to baste every inch of the dead lizard while making a series of finger gestures over the carcass. As she stepped away, the creature spontaneously ignited, accompanied by enthusiastic applause from the expectant crowd. The next moment the mystic's body began to shake uncontrollably and she fell to her knees before the flaming lizard. Frantic to get a better view, neither Geoffrey nor his sister were able to see anything more until some members of the tight-knit crowd began to sink to their knees in reverence.

"What the devil is going on, Maggs?" Geoffrey asked, straining to see above the heads of those standing in front of him. When they also began kneeling, the movement was swiftly copied by others until the moment a child began to scream hysterically as the first of the dead bats began to move. Stretching the membrane of its flimsy wings, the quivering shape began squirming within the framework of bones before becoming motionless once more. The same thing was happening with the second bat and then the third, fourth and finally the fifth.

Although terrified by the nightmarish images, Geoffrey was unable to look away. It was as though he was witnessing nature in reverse, unlocking the mechanism of death via the mystic's ritual. It was then he noticed a slight movement in the desiccated carcass of the lizard, entombed within a membrane of flame, where the shape of the reptile appeared to grow in size until the glowing creature was more than six feet long. Angling its head in the direction of the crowd, it hissed violently through the blanket of flames before the magnificent shape of a golden salamander reared up beyond the wall of flame, swishing its tail and sparking clouds of glittering dust in its wake.

"Geoffrey... we must do something. That young woman is about to be sacrificed!" Marguerite exclaimed, grabbing hold of Geoffrey's arm.

"Strewth, Maggs, this has got to be trickery, an illusion," Geoffrey responded with more conviction than he actually felt. His breath was coming in short gasps, his legs feeling ready to buckle as the salamander's strangely intelligent head slowly pivoted towards the petrified young woman.

Now wide awake and screaming with terror, she slid down the wall and back into unconsciousness. Unceremoniously she was dragged away by the two pregnant women, both clearly wary of any movement from the salamander. Though hemmed in by the barrier of flames and trapped by the surrounding buildings, time the creature's eyes constantly scanned in all directions as if for a possible escape route, the flared nostrils betraying its distress.

As the claws of its feet dug deep into the earth and it turned around, the crowd fell silent with fear. All the time its golden eyes remained alert and searching, as if the creature was scanning the expectant crowd for something – or someone. Its head pivoted towards Marguerite and her brother, focusing on them with such intensity that neither could move a muscle until a shower of sparks exploded around the mystic, enveloping her in a cloak of red mist and momentarily concealing the old woman from sight.

"We must get away from here right now, Maggs," Geoffrey hissed, grabbing her by the arm and pulling her with him through an opening in the crowd, who appeared to be deliberately making way to allow them through.

Looking back, Geoffrey saw with astonishment the drastically altered shape of the mystic, who emerged through the smoke having been transformed into a light-skinned teenage girl with burnished auburn hair, her ringing voice calling after them as they ran.

"Inglesa… estar es muy, muy importante, señorita!" she cried, gesturing clearly towards Marguerite. "Ustedes la madre…" She repeated the same words over and over until they were out of earshot.

Pausing only long enough to allow his sister to catch her breath, Geoffrey glanced back to where the auburn-haired girl had been standing. Her shape had now resumed that of the aged mystic. Behind her, the intimidating mass of the salamander was becoming distorted and, like the fluttering bats, was evaporating into the billowing smoke until it completely disappeared.

"Whatever she was shouting must be a curse," Geoffrey muttered, urging Marguerite to move faster until he saw José ahead of them, waiting by the carriage.

"Where you go?" José asked when they reached him.

"I might ask you the same question," Geoffrey snapped, helping his sister into the carriage. "Just get us away from here and back to the hotel… the Grand Colonial."

"What happened back there, Geoffrey?" Marguerite asked as the carriage rattled away from the scene.

"I am not sure, only that it could not have been real. Perhaps there was something in that concoction we drank in the market."

"Whatever it was, that was the scariest moment I have experienced in my entire life."

"What was that old hag shouting after us? What did she want?"

"Money presumably, since we were leaving before her fantasy exhibition came to an end. If we had watched that performance on stage at the local Hippodrome, we would have paid for the experience beforehand. Admittedly it was an outdoor arena, but they would not put on a show like that for free." She grabbed Geoffrey's arm as the carriage lurched badly when the horses were startled by a pack of barking street dogs.

"I hope this guide knows where we are heading," Geoffrey scowled into the small of José's back as he directed the carriage driver through a warren of streets. "I just wish I had brought my compass along. At least I would know if we were heading in the right direction."

"Surely you did not bring that rusty old thing all the way out here?"

"I never go anywhere without it. Well, except until today, when I probably need it most," he said as the carriage rumbled to a halt at a congested street market.

"Señor, here for música," José called, indicating they should get out and accompany him.

"Where is that maniac off to now?" Geoffrey said, uncertain if it was safe to follow. "Did he say something about music?"

"That is what I thought."

"If so then I'm going too."

"Not on your own Geoffrey. It might not be safe," she said, making as if to follow.

"If there is any trouble, I can always sprint back. I will not take any risks out here."

"Do you have your wallet with you?"

"Yes. I have a one pound and two ten-shilling notes," Geoffrey said, examining the contents.

"That should be enough." She rooted through her capacious bag for her purse. "Take this change in case you need more," she said, handing over some coins. "Remember, you are not shopping at Fortnum & Mason's. Sheet music or strings for an instrument in this run-down quarter cannot possibly cost more than a few shillings."

Although Geoffrey was tall for his age he felt dwarfed alongside José, but took comfort from his companionship, passing shifty-eyed hawkers as they made their way to a stall a short distance away. Once there, his excitement mounted as he immediately spotted an old violin that hung from the rotting canopy, partially obscured by a collection of cowbells and a filthy tambourine.

Contrary to his original opinion of José's reliability, their guide bartered well on his behalf and Geoffrey was soon in position of the instrument at a cost of one pound, four shillings and sixpence. On his return to the carriage, he proudly displayed the careworn violin for his sister's inspection.

"Are you sure about this, Geoffrey? It looks ready to disintegrate at any moment."

"Nobody has bothered with it for years. It just needs to be oiled and then you will see a difference."

"But why buy such a neglected instrument when you are unable to hear the tone with all these missing strings?"

"I just know it will produce a wonderful sound."

"And what about replacement strings? You are going to need those."

"The stallholder had none, only this treasure," Geoffrey said, eager to get back to the hotel and start work on the restoration. "I will use the ones from my old violin. The body is perfectly intact. I checked it over thoroughly."

By the time they arrived back at the hotel, Geoffrey had barely an hour before he was required to escort his mother and sisters into the dining room and return immediately to change for the opera. It had been arranged that he would first join Noel Effingham and his companions for cocktails in an exclusive gentlemen's club that was conveniently attached to the rear of the opera house.

Chapter Six
The Opera

Geoffrey wished he looked older than his youthful reflection in the revolving doors of the hotel but it was, nevertheless, liberating to be out at night, unaccompanied by any member of his family and travelling through an unfamiliar city on his own. His only regret was that it wasn't to meet someone of his own age, someone who, unlike Noel, wouldn't find any excuse to touch him on the hand or arm in that creepy way he had.

When the carriage drew up at the rear of the opera house, Geoffrey was already impressed by the gleaming marble columns of the magnificent entrance and could hardly wait to see the interior, anticipating a wonder of the modern world.

He was barely out of the carriage when Noel emerged from the shadows and gripped his arm, swaying rather unsteadily, his clothes reeking of cigar smoke.

"What a vision of youthful innocence you present, Sir Geoffrey," Noel gushed, waving an empty champagne glass theatrically as he stumbled, tightening his grip to steady himself. His wing collar was badly crumpled and his stained cravat was coming undone. There was a noticeable sprinkling of cigar ash on the lapel of his frock coat.

"Please do come and meet the others, Sir Geoffrey. They will be delighted that such a handsome gentleman will be gracing our box. We had almost given up on you."

"But surely I was here on time, Noel?"

"For the opera yes but not the entertainment; that got under way more than two hours ago. You would have loved the stripper. It was quite a performance. But the night is young and who knows?" Noel shrieked with laughter. "As soon as the opera is over, I have arranged for a visit to a very different venue that will be an education for any young

Englishman." He led the way through a side door and up two flights of carpeted stairs.

None of the London theatres Geoffrey had visited in his young life could have compared to the grandeur of the rooms housing the gentlemen's club, where it seemed no expense had been spared on the refurbishment. This evening, however, the elegance was somewhat marred by a recently shattered chair and six empty champagne bottles scattered about the landing, two of them broken, the contents seeping into the carpet. Cigar and cigarette stubs had been ground into the pile and others left burning on the French-polished surfaces of two elegant Georgian hall tables by the doorway.

Once inside the smoke-filled interior, he was confronted by a noisy, jostling crowd of drunken and in some cases partially clothed young men, apparently liberated by the absence of any female companions. On a makeshift stage there was an unmade, four-poster bed, a garish four-fold screen, an upturned table with a broken leg and a pair of torn silk pyjamas. For reasons unknown the footlights had been left on, which in the dense, smoky haze added to the eerie, debauched arrangement on stage.

"What is this place?" Geoffrey asked, doing his best not to display his alarm as Noel closed the door behind them.

"This club, Sir Geoffrey, is where gentlemen such as you and I can shed the trappings of rank and respectability, allowing us to enjoy each other's company," Noel explained with an oily smile, hailing a half-naked waiter carrying a tray of champagne-filled glasses. "Drink one of these, Sir Geoffrey. It will help you relax."

"I have no desire to relax, thank you and refuse to take any part in this debauchery."

"What debauchery?" Noel laughed. "This is not a house of ill repute, Sir Geoffrey. This is simply a gentlemen's club. There is nothing sinful here. If you had arrived two hours earlier with everyone else, then what confronts you now would seem perfectly acceptable."

"To you perhaps," Geoffrey said, realising there was no polite way to get out until the call was made for the audience to take their allotted seats half an hour before the opera. But that was almost an hour away, so he would have to make the best of it.

"When you have downed that first glass of champagne, Sir Geoffrey, I will introduce my other guests this evening," Noel said, leading him further into the room, as Geoffrey surreptitiously emptied the champagne into a gilded pot containing a large kentia palm.

An individual with strange, hypnotic eyes now accosted them, whose unblinking stare made Geoffrey's skin crawl. The man spoke no English, or at least he chose not to; instead he conversed with Noel in Spanish, the content of which Geoffrey suspected concerned him.

"What is he saying about me?" Geoffrey demanded.

"Nothing for you to get grumpy about, it is all very complimentary."

"I doubt that very much. I do not appreciate being stared at in such a manner."

"Gabriel means no offence, I can assure you. The man is an artist, and is appreciative of the beautiful skin you have. Most young men would be flattered by his attention."

"Well I am not."

By this time, a group of other men were jostling around them, most speaking in Spanish or Portuguese. Geoffrey could understand none of it but, as they eyed him up and down, he knew instinctively he was the prime object of their conversation. The man called Gabriel rattled off a tirade of questions in an unintelligible language, which Noel translated.

"Gabriel has expressed his desire that you might sit for him."

"Then tell him thank you but no. If I wanted anyone to paint me, my sister would do that admirably. She is an excellent artist."

Hearing this, Noel laughed. "You do surprise me. You are saying that you would allow your own sister to paint you in the nude?"

"No, I damned well would not! I would never allow anyone to paint me like that."

"You are overreacting, Sir Geoffrey. You have no idea of Gabriel's talents. Think it over, I beg you. Otherwise you will deprive the art world of what might be a masterpiece."

"You have my answer, Noel. Just tell your artist friend he can go to hell!" Geoffrey snapped.

Although it was no great distance, it took an age to reach Noel's guests, seated at his table. There were seven men in the party that evening. Four were in their early thirties, three of them partially drunk; the other seemed pleasant enough and was perfectly sober. Two of the remaining men, seen in profile, were probably older than Geoffrey's mother. Seated between them was a seventh he couldn't see clearly, who was supported by one of the men and suggestively handled by the other, so close to the stage they could have been an integral part of the earlier show. Geoffrey had never felt so uncomfortable in his life, except perhaps when his mother enrolled him as a Wolf Cub in the local Scout group when he was aged six, where he was made to change in a locker room full of older boys. After a second visit he refused to go back again although he pointedly refused to return his compass, the very instrument which ironically he now carried in his tailcoat pocket.

"What the devil is going on here, Noel?" Geoffrey demanded alarm as the seventh man, barely covered with a bed sheet, stood up from between the two older men and stepped onto the stage to resounding applause.

"There is no need to be shocked, Sir Geoffrey. I told you about the stripper when you came in," Noel said, resting his hand on Geoffrey's thigh.

"Take your bloody hand off my leg before I take a horse whip to you!" Geoffrey shouted, jumping to his feet and knocking over the table between them.

But Noel was too drunk to care, or he couldn't hear above the noise of the shouting and fists beating on tables for the man on stage to continue with the show. Instead, Noel stood up groggily and, moving closer to Geoffrey, made a grab for his crotch.

Outraged by the groping hands, Geoffrey brought his knee sharply up into Noel's groin and with a clenched fist had the satisfaction of punching him squarely in his leering face to the crunching sound of breaking cartilage in his nose.

"You broke my nose you… you toffee-nosed bastard!" Noel shrieked, clamping a handkerchief tightly against the bleeding mess.

"Think yourself lucky I did not have my penknife with me, you bloody pervert, or I swear it could have been a hell of a lot worse!" Geoffrey retorted, with more bravado than he was actually feeling.

With the sound of Noel's screams ringing in his ears, Geoffrey only just caught the half-hour call being announced, requesting the audience to take their seats and determinedly headed for the box office with the idea of buying a ticket in order to blend in with the audience, unaware of the blood that was now splattered across his torn dress shirt.

When he was refused a ticket – whether because they were sold out or because of his dishevelled clothing he couldn't guess – he despaired at his own stupidity for not having paid more attention to his mother when she had told him where Lady Drummond's party would be. Making his way into the foyer he was immediately accosted by two burly ushers. Neither spoke English and, in view of Geoffrey's appearance and lack of a ticket, they seemed more keen on throwing him out than helping to locate his family.

As Geoffrey was being hauled towards the street by the bouncers, their arms hooked under each armpit, he caught sight of his elder sister, deep in conversation with another woman in the foyer and cried out for help as he struggled to get free of their iron grip.

"Maggs...! Marguerite... It's Geoffrey. I'm over here! I need you to stop these idiots from kicking me out!" he screamed as they dragged him backwards across the polished marble floor.

"What on earth are you doing?" Marguerite shouted at the men. "Take your hands off the young gentleman this instant!"

"No comprendo, señora?" the first usher replied but, intimidated by the authority of her voice, the two men waited until she reached them, the other woman close behind.

"Miss Hulme, would you be kind enough to ask these gentlemen to unhand my brother this instant. Unfortunately I do not have my dictionary with me."

"I am not fluent milady but I will try," Agnes Hulme responded, pausing to adjust a large and rather inappropriate hat.

"Anything you can come up with to defuse the situation would help immensely. I would be most grateful, Miss Hulme, if you would try," Marguerite huffed.

Despite what she'd said, to Geoffrey's ear there was very little hesitation or stumbling over her words – or the many obvious expletives – as she demanded that he be released. As he watched this performance, Geoffrey became increasingly aware of how soiled her clothing was under the unforgiving artificial light. There was a tear in her dress and patches of dried mud at the knee as if she had fallen down. Beneath the frayed hem of her skirt, her shoes were badly scuffed and looked as if they hadn't been cleaned in a week.

"Thank you, Miss Hulme, you have been most kind," Marguerite said as the two men released their grip on Geoffrey and left with a curt bow of apology.

"And regarding my request? I would be most grateful to be considered for the position. My situation here is unbearable. I will have no money for food or lodgings by the end of the week. I am destitute, Milady."

"I cannot promise you anything, you understand. The position is already taken but I will speak to her ladyship about your situation as soon as I can."

"But how will I know?"

"I will inform Mr Strickland, our shipping agent, the moment I have any information. Now if you will excuse me, I must bid you good day, Miss Hulme. Thank you once again for securing my brother's release."

As Geoffrey took her arm and they set off up the grand staircase, he could tell that his sister already regretted having agreed to whatever Agnes Hulme had requested.

"What exactly has that woman asked you to do for her, Maggs?"

"It would appear that Miss Hulme's fiancé has broken off their engagement and she finds herself abandoned here without any moral or financial support."

"So he ditched her," Geoffrey chortled.

"This is not amusing, Geoffrey. The woman is clearly distressed, otherwise why would she break with etiquette to approach me at an event like this?"

It was an observation that made a lot of sense, considering the contrast her grubby outfit had made with the glittering array of women in elegant gowns of the latest Parisian fashions, many now staring curiously at Geoffrey as he waited on the half landing where the grand staircase split, for his sister to pause and catch her breath before making the final assault.

"Maybe but, even so, I am pleased for that unfortunate man she was engaged to, who dumped her before it was too late. You cannot deny what we saw on board the *Lugansa*?" Geoffrey said.

"I do wonder where you pick up this dreadful slang."

"*Dumped* isn't slang. It is a valid form of expression and a jolly good one too if you ask me. And, since you are asking, it was something I picked up from Father's American novellas. So what was the Hulme woman after? Money?"

"Not exactly. She was seeking passage to Apalla as mother's maid. She has contacts in that port who will assist her from there."

"But Mother has already engaged the services of someone for the trip and you cannot be suggesting we take a dreadful woman like Hulme along with us too. You could have offered her money instead."

"It did cross my mind but she was so insistent I could not refuse, especially with the help that she gave us."

By the time they had reached the landing, a growing pain in Geoffrey's hand was making it difficult to concentrate on anything else, including the prospect of spending the next few hours crammed into a box with his mother and sisters, the self-opinionated Lady Drummond and her companions the Misses Fleck, two spinster sisters.

"Have you got anything for easing pain, Maggs?" Geoffrey asked.

"If you have developed a headache from carousing with Noel Effingham this evening, then no… I do not have any aspirin with me."

"This is not for my head. The pain in my hand is killing me," Geoffrey winced as his sister examined his knuckles.

"What on earth have you been doing, Geoffrey? Your hand is swollen."

"Never mind that; is there anything in that chemist's shop you call a bag or not?" He gave a sigh of relief when she took out a bottle of oil and massaged some into his throbbing hand.

"How did you do this? And do not lie. I know this was no accident."

"Firstly, you must promise not to repeat any of this to Mother."

"You have my word but, knowing how she fusses over your hands, Mother will most certainly ask you the same question and you must tell her the truth."

"I will come up with something but not that. It would be so bloody degrading!"

"So tell me, what happened? I will not be so easily fobbed off with anything but the truth."

Geoffrey briefly related the events of the evening.

"You actually broke Noel Effingham's nose?" she said with a gasp.

"Yes, and I would do it again." He was aware that the musicians were tuning up in the orchestra pit and they were now the only two people on the landing. "We need to make our way to the box before the performance gets under way," he said. He wondered how Lady Drummond could have managed that sweeping staircase on her sticks, as there was no evidence of any lifts.

Lady Drummond's box was much larger than Geoffrey had envisaged and darker at the rear, where he could avoid his mother's questioning gaze.

"Why have you chosen to sit so far back, young man?" Lady Drummond demanded. "There is a spare seat next to your sister. I insist that you sit closer, Sir Geoffrey, before the performance begins. No aspect of this wonderful show should be missed. The voices of the leading tenor and soprano will unquestionably be the talk of the season." She settled into her seat with anticipation as Geoffrey moved closer to the edge of the box.

Before the lights dimmed, it was apparent how many pairs of opera glasses were trained not on the stage, as he would have expected, but on his sister Rosamund. She did look particularly beautiful this evening and he found himself feeling more protective towards her than he could have imagined.

"Lady Harriet, have you any idea who that young man is, seated in the third row of the stalls?" Lady Claudia asked, rather uncomfortably, a question which made Geoffrey isolate the man in question with his own glasses. Unlike those around him, this man had his gaze focused not on Rosamund but on her mother.

"He did arrive on time! That handsome young man you speak of, Lady Claudia, is my grandson, Archie

Westbrook." She beamed, fluttering her fan towards the young man in question just as the orchestra struck up the overture and the house lights dimmed.

When the luxurious tabs were slowly drawn apart, there was thunderous applause as the stage setting for Act One of *Samson and Delilah*, the public square of Gaza, was revealed. It was clear that no expense had been spared on this elaborately staged production, although perhaps the leading tenor was a little overweight to be perfectly cast in the role of Samson. What was unquestionable, however, was the range he could project with that amazing voice.

As the first act reached its halfway point Geoffrey was feeling decidedly uncomfortable and finding it difficult to breathe, which he assumed was a delayed reaction to the evening's traumatic events but when he looked across at his mother she appeared to be even more unsettled than before, holding tightly onto the edge of her seat as the final sequence of Samson's passionate aria was concluding.

"At last the hour has come, the hour of the avenging God," he sang, building up the emotion as he raised his eyes towards heaven. *"I hear his fury explode in the clouds."*

The tenor was positioned between two of the temple columns, positioned to create a dramatic image as the sound effects were set in shuddering motion accompanied by thunderous orchestration with the added drama of the highly realistic lighting. The realism of the staging bordered on the miraculous as the colonnade shook amid further powerful and dramatic flashes of light and a dense cloud of smoke belched out from the wings, accompanied by even more of the unearthly tremors that seemed to be resonating from far beyond the stage.

Peering over the balcony, Geoffrey looked down into the orchestra pit as an ear-shattering thunderclap sounded, pre-empting the bemused percussionist who was poised in readiness to deliver a grand crescendo on a huge kettledrum which, although shaking as moved by a ghostly hand, remained untouched.

In the centre of the beautiful domed ceiling, high above the stalls, the magnificent chandelier began to sway erratically, rattling a thousand crystal droplets which twisted and jangled before crashing violently together.

On stage, Samson's voice noticeably faltered as he uncharacteristically glanced towards the prompter, as though in need of reassurance. *"Yea before his wrath, all flee in terror,"* he sang, now jarringly off-key, just as one end of the backdrop broke loose from its coupling, crashing on to the stage a few feet behind him. The tenor staggered off the stage as if he were drunk, colliding with one of the wing flats as the newly rebuilt opera house was again shaken to its foundations.

"What the devil's happening?" Geoffrey cried in alarm, jumping to his feet ready to help his mother.

"Dear God, it is an earthquake, Geoffrey!" Marguerite exclaimed, grabbing hold of her bag as the angular backcloth crashed to the stage floor to reveal the staging for Act Two. The chaotic shambles of trembling fake walls lurched downstage amid the sound of tearing canvas and splintering wood as stage braces snapped from their weights and the unsupported set collapsed in a shuddering heap.

Geoffrey's first thought was how to get his mother and sisters out of the building to safety and after that to assist the aged Lady Drummond down that seemingly endless staircase into the foyer.

Below them women were screaming as the audience scrambled over seats, pushing and shoving to get clear of the broken scenery that was tumbling from the stage. Electrical spotlights rocked violently with each tremor, sending unnatural beams of light across the unfolding chaos before their stands toppled over and crashed noisily onto the stage. By this time the orchestra pit had emptied as the musicians abandoned their instruments amid a snowstorm of broken plaster, the scattered sheet music swirling around in a powerful updraught. Moments later the decorative centrepiece of the proscenium arch broke free and crashed into the pit. A huge section of plasterwork collided with the edge of the stage and shattered, a jagged section of masonry crushing the kettledrum into a pulp as the flying fragments of plaster peppered out a sinister death rattle on the twisted cymbals. As the orchestra pit was enveloped in a swathe of asphyxiating dust another section of plaster fell, crushing the grand piano and sending out an eerie discord to accompany the frantic pandemonium in the stalls as the audience fled.

"Quickly, Mother, follow me," Geoffrey said as he reached her. "You must allow me to get you all out of here."

"I can manage perfectly well, Geoffrey and so can your sisters. You must attend to Lady Harriet first. She has difficulty walking and will be in need your assistance."

"I can come back for her later, now the earthquake is over."

"This might be only the beginning, Geoffrey. I fear there could be worse to come." Moments later a further tremor rocked the building and the floor began trembling beneath his feet as if the box had been constructed from jelly.

"I need to get you out of here, Mother."

"Do as I say, Geoffrey and help Lady Harriet."

"But Mother… the building may collapse before I get her clear. You must allow me to help you first. Then I promise to come back for her," he insisted. He had hoped that by now the Fleck sisters would be assisting the old lady into the corridor. But instead they were flapping around like headless chickens before dashing out of the box as one.

"I am perfectly able to walk unaided and I have your sisters with me. You must assist Harriet to safety. She will direct you to the moving staircase at the rear of the building. Once she is clear, then do help whoever you can to safety but do not take any unnecessary risks!" She raised her voice to be heard above the screams from the adjoining boxes and more crashing of crumbling masonry. He knew it would be pointless to argue.

"Are you sure there is a moving staircase, Mother?" he asked, helping her as far as the door.

"One had to be installed for those who are unable to manage the stairs. Lady Harriet knows how to reach it. But hurry, as the power may go off."

Once Rosamund had reached their mother in the corridor, he helped Marguerite out to join them. After that, he made his way to Lady Drummond, who was sitting as calmly as she might have done at any garden party until he reached her. She was barely out of her seat when the next tremor hit and a huge section of plasterwork at the front of their box broke away. Grabbing hold of her arm, Geoffrey pulled her back to prevent her from pitching forward and falling headfirst into the stalls.

Peering through the haze of dust swirling along the corridor, Geoffrey supported his elderly companion as they moved towards the escalator. Unlike the grand staircase, it had been installed in a plain, functional style, with no decorative plasterwork in sight. Two bath chairs were littered with broken masonry and a red fire bucket had been ripped off the wall and crushed flat beneath a toppled storage cabinet. The floor was littered with shattered bulbs from the state-of-the-art light fittings and scattered tins leaking brass and furniture polish that made it even more difficult to remain standing.

It took some time to position Lady Harriet on the moving staircase to prevent her badly torn dress or shoes from becoming entangled in the mechanism, which thankfully was still working, although the rumbles from beneath the building suggested that the worst wasn't over.

They were a few feet away from the ground floor when a terrifying quake rocked everything about them with such a biblical ferocity that Geoffrey feared for his own life. The escalator lurched to a grinding halt amid the stench of burning rubber and showers of sparks erupting between gaps in the wooden treads.

"We should not remain here any longer, my dear boy. Just take hold of my corset and keep me steady," Lady Drummond said, remaining impressively calm as she lifted the hem on either side of her shredded gown and tucked it firmly into her knee-length bloomers as more chunks of plaster crashed into the foyer ahead of them.

"But Lady Harriet… what if someone sees you?" Geoffrey faltered.

"Then so be it. Getting out of this building is our priority, Geoffrey, so to hell with public opinion I say!" she announced grandly, making him laugh and find more courage despite the horror of the situation.

Helping the dowager down the remaining steps and over the rubble and crushed palms, he soon had her seated on a bench in the square, a safe distance from the opera house and any other buildings that might collapse.

"I do not see your mother or sisters, Geoffrey. Perhaps you could see if they are safe?"

"If you wait for me here, I will find them." Geoffrey sprinted off among the crowds of dishevelled and distressed people, coughing and wailing and covered in dust. Just as he was about to go back inside he found his mother, seated on what remained of a decorative fountain, nursing an injured knee.

"Did you get Harriet out safely?" she asked as he helped her to her feet. Her dress was badly torn, and she had lost the heel off one of her shoes, which hampered their progress until she removed them.

"Yes, Mother, I did."

"I cannot see any sign of either of your sisters in the crowds, Geoffrey, and that troubles me. I have been looking for them from the moment we were separated."

"I had assumed all three of you would be clear of the building by this time, my dear," Lady Drummond said as they reached her. "Archie was here a few moments ago, checking if I was safe. He went off to find the two Miss Flecks. Had I known, I would have asked him to find your daughters too. I am sure they will be safe."

"There is no guarantee of that. I must get back in there and find them," said Geoffrey.

"You must leave that to the emergency services, Geoffrey, my dear. Now they have arrived, no one else will be allowed inside," Lady Drummond pointed out.

"Not everyone, it would seem. I just saw a man dash into the building." Geoffrey said, determined not to waste any more time in talking.

"That would have been one of the Irish fire-fighters. They will work tirelessly until every last soul is accounted for."

"No one is going to prevent me from getting in there, fire-fighter or not!" Geoffrey said, turning away before anyone could prevent him.

Scanning the dust-covered stragglers on his way towards the crumbling facade, he saw no sign of either sister, nor as he made his way cautiously up the shuddering staircase. He breathed a sigh of relief when he finally made out Marguerite's shape on the opposite landing through the haze of dust, clutching her ever-present bag as she gripped the wrought-iron landing rail, surrounded by piles of debris and fluttering programmes.

"Maggs!" he called, waving frantically.

"Get away from here, Geoffrey, this building might collapse at any moment!"

"Where is Rose?" he cried, clambering higher up the groaning staircase.

"A young gentleman is assisting her." She coughed hoarsely as swirls of billowing dust belched out from a corridor behind her.

"Is she injured?"

"Not badly, I think. She has a sprained ankle and is unable to walk."

"Stay where you are, Maggs, until I can reach you," Geoffrey called. At that very moment a dishevelled young man clambered into view over a pile of rubble, carrying Rosamund like a sack of potatoes. Just as they got clear a violent aftershock shook the entire building with such tremendous force that Geoffrey was sent sprawling over a pile of rubble.

"Geoffrey... Geoffrey!" Marguerite screamed across the stairwell, still clinging to the twisted balcony rail. Behind her, Rosamund was barely visible, supported around the waist by the young man.

From immediately above Geoffrey's head came a fearful rumbling noise, as if the opera house was about to collapse around them, and within moments a huge section of the landing floor caved in with a violent crash. Through this gap Geoffrey could hear the unnerving screams of the buried and injured, pleading for help, while ghostly, dust-covered shapes staggered aimlessly through the rubble, calling out the names of the missing.

Trapped on the opposite staircase, Geoffrey watched with relief as Rosamund leapfrogged onto the stranger's back with the confidence of a twelve-year-old, her coiffure now tangled and wild, the beads of her torn Parisian gown covered with plaster dust. Making his way to Marguerite, the man assisted her down the fractured staircase. Even now she refused to let go of her bag.

By the time Geoffrey emerged from the building, emergency rescuers had cordoned off a large area and formed a human chain to pass buckets of water from two horse-drawn fire engines in a futile attempt to control the flames that now roared through the windows of the upper floor. Survivors from the wreckage were being helped to reach an open space where the injured could be stretchered to a motorised ambulance and a row of emergency vehicles.

Dodging an official who urged him to get clear of the crumbling facade, Geoffrey saw no sign of his sisters as he searched through the faces among the crowd, and was about to dash back inside the building when he heard an Irish voice calling his name.

"Geoffrey! The ladies are over here, they are all safe," the man called, ducking under the cordon to reach him and take him firmly by the arm.

"It is *Sir* Geoffrey, you Irish imbecile and you can take your damned hands off me," Geoffrey snapped, assuming this was one of the rescue team Lady Harriet had mentioned. Unlike the gentlemen who were standing around in top hats and tails, he wore only a shirt, covered in so much plaster and masonry dust that he looked positively ghostly.

"For God's sake come with me before you get yourself killed, you arrogant little prick," the Irishman said, yanking Geoffrey out of the way as a huge section of masonry crashed down from a building barely ten feet away from them.

"Have either of my sisters been injured?" Geoffrey demanded, attempting to wrench his arm free as the man shoved him under the barrier.

"Neither of them but we will be, to be sure, if we don't get crushed under the façade. It looks about ready to come down." He called urgently to one of the firemen and pointed towards an upper window where a group of people were trying to attract attention.

"Where are my sisters now?"

"They are waiting for you to join them in carriages on the far side of the square. Your mother and Lady Drummond are with them. You should join them before there's another aftershock," he said, loosening his grip on Geoffrey's arm to listen to what one of the Irish fire fighters was shouting. "I will be with you in a moment, Doyle!" he called.

"Are you not coming with me?"

"I need to join the others and see if I can help," the Irishman said and, before Geoffrey could say another word, he had gone.

Geoffrey found the ladies were not yet in the carriages but clustered together awaiting his return.

"You were gone for so long, Geoffrey!" Lady Claudia said, brushing back the hair from his face.

"It was awful, Mother… I could see both the girls inside but it was impossible for me to reach them. It was such a relief when a fireman told me they were safe. There are still people trapped inside. Maybe I could be doing more to help. That fireman dashed back without a second's thought."

"You cannot risk going back, my darling. These men are trained for the job and you are not. That is when accidents can occur." The two Miss Flecks hobbled past, one with a broken toe and the other with a twisted knee and hair like a hayrick after a storm.

As if by an act of providence a carriage bearing a splendid coat of arms now appeared and it was apparent from the deference the coachman showed to Lady Drummond that it came from her estate. Because their hotel could have been affected by the quake, it was quickly arranged that Lady Claudia and her family would accompany the dowager to her plantation home on the outskirts of the city, where they would be safe and comfortable.

Geoffrey was about to help his mother into the carriage when he realised that the dishevelled young Irishman had returned and was already assisting her. "You came back," he said.

"I did, but only because I seemed to be more of a hindrance than of any use. I had forgotten how organised the emergency crews are here, so I came to see if I could be of any further assistance to the ladies."

"Since you are already familiar with my two sisters, then allow me to introduce my mother, Lady Saint Hubes," Geoffrey said. "Mother, this is the fire-fighter I told you about."

"I am greatly indebted to you, sir, for assisting my daughters out of that building. That was very brave," Lady Claudia said cautiously, scanning what little of his features were visible beneath the layers of dust on the man's face.

"Anyone would have done the same in those circumstances, Lady Claudia," he said, his dark violet eyes seeming to deepen in colour under her gaze.

"How do you know my mother's name?" Geoffrey asked, bristling at the man's familiarity.

"Lady Claudia and I have met once before, although I doubt if her ladyship would remember me as a child," the young man said in his pronounced Irish brogue.

"How could that be possible? She has barely returned to Ireland since childhood." Geoffrey guessed the man was related to one of his grandfather's tenant farmers.

"Irishman or not, that is no reason to assume that your mother and I could never have met," the man said dismissively, before addressing her again. "Milady, Archie Westbrook, from Elgore, at your service."

Geoffrey noticed his mother adjusting the tortoiseshell combs in her hair.

"Westbrook, you say... from Elgore?"

"Rufus Westbrook is my father."

"Oh, my dear… do forgive me, I ought to have known your parentage immediately from the unusual colour of your eyes, so like your father's. Even so, it is hard to imagine that you recall our meeting when you were just a child."

"I remember it quite vividly, Lady Claudia. We met in Knightsbridge with my father. You were making purchases from the woollen department in Harrods. In fact, I wore the Fairisle sweater you bought me every day until I outgrew it. Even then, I was loath to part with it."

"You are too kind, Archie dear."

"My father will be livid that he was not here to meet you himself. He speaks of you often."

"Rufus should have been here too?"

"That was the plan until he went down with a fever, so I came on alone."

"A fever?" she asked with alarm. "Nothing serious I hope?"

"I was assured not, otherwise I would never have sailed without him. However, I fear I have delayed you long enough, Lady Claudia and I would advise you to depart this area before the next aftershock, or before another building collapses." As if on cue, the corner section of a building on the far side of the square crumbled in an upsurge of dust, spooking the horses, which the coachman had some difficulty bringing under control.

Once Geoffrey knew his family were all safe, his anxiety transferred to his recently acquired violin and he decided he would not go directly to the plantation but return to the hotel to collect it, even though he had no firm idea of the location of either.

"You must go on ahead without me, Mother. I will join you at the plantation later. There are things I must do first," Geoffrey said, closing the carriage door firmly.

"Geoffrey, please get into the carriage," Marguerite scolded. "There is nothing else you can do here."

"I have no intention of remaining here. I must get to the hotel. You of all people should know why."

"You cannot be serious, Geoffrey! It isn't safe to return there after the earthquake. Mr Westbrook has already said there might be another aftershock."

"Earthquake or not, I have already lost one violin and I am not going anywhere without this one," Geoffrey said, scanning the now vacant stands where rows of hansom cabs had been lined up when they arrived. "Besides, there's no room in your carriage for me."

"Please, Geoffrey," his mother pleaded. "We will all be safer in the country." She was about to get out of the carriage again when Archie returned.

"You must set off without further delay, Lady Claudia. I have instructed your driver on the safest route to reach Lady Drummond's estate."

"I cannot leave here without my son, Archie; he might get killed. Please make him see reason."

"You must leave now, Lady Claudia. I will take your son in my own conveyance. No harm will befall him, I can assure you."

As far as the eye could see the square was a scene of ruin and devastation, made even more sinister by the eerie light of a full moon. On the far side of the square, flames were roaring through the open windows of a municipal building, below which a group of firemen were backing away from the intense heat as a modern pumping engine spluttered into view. Within moments the men had unreeled the hose, previously making more impact than the buckets of water.

"What have you done to your hand?" Archie asked. "Let me see."

"It's nothing," Geoffrey said, wrenching his hand away.

"It doesn't look that way to me. You need some antiseptic on that."

"Just leave me alone, it will be all right."

"Only an idiot would say that. This is not England. Infection is rife here and who knows what you might have picked up in that rubble. Something needs to be done about this, or you could lose an arm from gangrene in a week," Archie insisted, striding ahead.

"It was not done in the rubble. If you must know, I broke someone's nose before the show started!" Geoffrey shouted after him, trying to ignore the throbbing that was spreading up his arm.

"You broke someone's nose?" Archie stopped, waiting for Geoffrey to catch up. "Brawling with another young ruffian, were you?"

"This was no youngster, I can assure you. He was probably older than you."

"Then you must remind me never to get you enraged. Are you sure you are not an Irishman too?" Archie laughed easily.

"That is not funny. Unlike you, Mr Westbrook, I can trace my family tree back to William the Conqueror."

"How reassuring that must be, Sir Geoffrey." Archie walked on ahead without saying another word until they arrived at an archway. "And here we are and it's high time we got under way before the moon clouds over."

"What makes you think I am prepared to go anywhere in that?" Geoffrey asked, grinding his teeth as he surveyed the sturdy open cart, harnessed up to a pair of workhorses.

"Unless someone else is willing to take you, then if you do not ride with me how do you expect to find the hotel on your own?"

"I can find my own way. I would rather be dead than be caught riding in that farm cart."

"You talk like an idiot, Geoffrey."

"Geoffrey! Who gave you leave to address me like that, you bloody halfwit. Unlike you, Archie Westbrook, I have a title. Even if you drive around in a farm cart, you might show me some courtesy," Geoffrey shouted.

"Actually I will call you what the hell I like, you pompous ass. And, just for the record, my father Rufus is the Earl of Glendower. Therefore I outrank you in both age and position." Archie released the harness from the horses as Geoffrey was about to climb into the carriage. "Now mount up on one of these and keep a watchful eye out for falling masonry. I have no intention of having either of my horses injured just because you can't sleep without cuddling up to some blasted violin."

"You have no idea what you are talking about. This violin is unique."

"Quite frankly I don't give a damn. I am only doing this because I made a foolish promise to your mother to keep you safe. Now get astride one of the horses before I throw you on her back myself."

"Your father might be an earl but he obviously spawned an idiot, if you expect me to ride through the streets at night on horseback… without a saddle!"

"You can ride, can't you?" Archie challenged, leaping easily astride the larger mare.

"Where I was brought up, a gentleman is taught to ride with a saddle."

"And where I come from, gentlemen prefer to be less formal and have no need for them," Archie retorted, roaring with laughter after Geoffrey's third and finally successful attempt to mount the horse. "Now that you are seated at last, just make sure that you don't fall off."

"Bloody Irish gypsy," Geoffrey muttered through clenched teeth, holding onto the horse's mane for grim death as Archie set off at a brisk trot.

"Make sure that you follow close behind me and keep an eye out for any crumbling buildings," Archie called back to him.

As he followed him through a maze of streets littered with debris, Geoffrey had to admit that it would have been impossible for anyone to drive through them in a horse and cart. They hadn't gone far before there was a deafening rumble as one of the taller buildings ahead collapsed into a pile of rubble with the cracking of joists and a clatter of skidding roofing tiles. The moon was barely visible through the cloak of brick dust, so Archie guided his horse into another, even narrower street. Here men were scurrying about, levering up sections of a crumbled dwelling where pathetic cries could be heard from beneath.

"Geoff. Stay where you are and take hold of the reins of my horse and do not let go whatever you do," Archie said, leaping down from the animal.

"Where are you going?"

"Someone is trapped under that rubble and needs help." He rolled up his sleeves as he strode purposefully towards the rescuers, merging into the lingering haze of dust from the building.

Remembering his earlier outburst, Geoffrey felt suitably ashamed and immature. What he wanted to be was strong, sensible and in control, in just the way Archie Westbrook was at that precise moment. Gritting his teeth, he got down from his mount and tethered the two horses securely to the wheel of an overturned carriage.

"What can I do to help?" Geoffrey asked, clambering after Archie over the mound of rubble. "The horses are tied up away from danger."

"Have you done it securely?"

"I do know how to tie a knot, for Pete's sake."

"Then help me to lever this door open a bit more. If I can just squeeze through the gap, I might be able to reach whoever is trapped inside."

Straining together, they managed to wrench the shattered wood partially open, allowing just enough room for Archie to squeeze through.

"I think whoever is down there must be under a staircase. If this door leads into the main passage, I can probably get to them before the rest of the building collapses."

"If you are going in there, I am coming with you."

"You can stay outside. It is not safe. I promised your mother I would look after you. If you want to make yourself useful, get searching and tear up any strips of material you can find, and bind them tightly around this." He handed a broken chair leg through the gap.

"Why?"

"I need light. It is as dark as pitch. The idea is to make a torch, so if you can find some oil to douse it in, even better."

Geoffrey tried to find a piece of curtain but having failed to find anything suitable decided to tear up his own shirt. Scrambling back to where the horses were tethered to the abandoned carriage he saturated the bound material with oil from one of the carriage lamps.

"This is the best I can do... but how are you going to light it?" Geoffrey called into the darkness to the barely discernible figure as he reached through the gap.

"Clearly you are not a smoker," Archie replied, lighting the flaming torch with a match. "Thank you... you have made a good job of this. This should last for quite a while."

"I am coming too whether you like it or not; you might need my help," Geoffrey said, determined not to be left behind.

"Very well, but only if you do exactly as I say and stay close behind me. Hold on to my shirt tails."

A short time later, Geoffrey clambered back through the shattered doorway alone, clambering over the rubble to enlist the aid of three rescuers who quickly went underground to lend a hand. Not long after Archie came out carrying a small child, followed by two distressed women and an old man.

"Dear God, Geoffrey, you look like crap. What the hell happened to your shirt?" Archie laughed.

"There was nothing else so I wrapped it round that chair leg and you burnt it."

"What is your mother going to say when you turn up looking like this?" Archie laughed again.

"No doubt it will be similar to your aunt's comments. For the son of an earl, Archie Westbrook, you do not look that great yourself."

"What are you staring at?" Archie asked, feeling at a damp patch on his own temple.

"Your head; you are bleeding."

"It probably looks worse than it is." Archie examined his hands before wiping the blood on his trousers. "It will heal."

"That is quite a gash. Does it hurt much?"

"Not yet but it might in a bit. Hey… what are you doing?" Archie shouted, unable to prevent Geoffrey reaching over and tearing a panel from the back of his shirt.

"I would have used mine but, if you remember, you burnt it," Geoffrey said, tearing up a broad strip. "If you hold this pad on your forehead I can bandage it up."

"We must get back to the horses," Archie said, once Geoffrey had fixed the makeshift dressing in place.

Although the alarmed horses were tugging frantically at their reins, Geoffrey's knots had held but it took Archie a little while to calm the animals and, as his shirt caught on the broken hood of the shattered carriage it tore further, exposing the top of his spine and shoulder blades.

"I think it would be unwise for us to continue to the hotel until daylight," Archie said.

"Then I will get our coachman to bring me out tomorrow. That way I can collect my family's luggage from the hotel, as well as the violin."

"There is no need; I will take you," Archie said.

"I say, Archie… you have a tattoo!" Geoffrey announced with some surprise as the moonlight caught his companion's torso. "Why would you want to have a flying dragon printed on your skin?"

"That is not a tattoo. The mark is hereditary. It occurs only in the male line of our family. My father has the same birthmark; my grandfather had one too."

"What… all in the same place?"

"They are; unlike you and I, who should not remain in this place any longer. The horses are spooked already and we need to get off. Follow me at a steady trot. I know a short cut out of the city."

The following morning, Geoffrey emerged from the house having had barely any sleep and wearing a shirt that was two sizes too large, which he suspected had been supplied by Archie via Lady Harriet. Even worse, because his sisters were still sleeping he had no access to the aspirin, oils and arnica in Marguerite's bag. His swollen hand had kept him awake through most of the night and was causing him a considerable amount of pain. His fingers in particular would scarcely bend.

Geoffrey found Archie impatiently waiting for him in the driving seat of an open cart that had been harnessed to a pair of mules. Considering the situation the Irishman had been in the previous night and that he had probably had even less sleep, it irritated Geoffrey how anyone could appear so roguishly charismatic, despite a blackened and bloodshot eye.

"Mules…? Is that the best you can come up with?" Geoffrey commented moodily, clambering up beside him.

"What did you expect, a pair of thoroughbred mares? This is hardly Derbyshire," Archie retorted crankily, ready to set off.

"No, and it's not a backwater in Ireland either. What I meant was that they look a bit temperamental."

"I can handle them well enough. So… are you coming or not?" Archie asked tersely.

Once Geoffrey was settled at his side it became clear that Archie was still suffering from the crack on the head, given the amount of blood that was seeping through the fresh bandage but he was too annoyed to care.

"If I didn't, you would never know where to look for my violin."

"It is a musical instrument, for God's sake. It wouldn't be that hard to find," Archie grumbled, flicking the reins to get the mules moving.

"That is where you are wrong. I keep it hidden. Apart from that, it would not be seemly for you to rummage through my mother's closet for her clothes, or my sisters' for that matter."

"I have no intention of repacking any of your family's clothing. I will arrange for a maid to do that. I know this hotel and some of the staff. If the place is still standing after the quake then we will return to collect everything you and your family need."

"You cannot know that, not for certain."

"Can you PLEASE shut up just for ten minutes? I have a raging headache and listening to you squawking in my ear is not helping one bit." Archie reined up briefly to swallow two aspirins with a swig from a hip flask before they set off again, and Geoffrey made up his mind to say nothing at all until they reached their destination.

Although a whip was attached to the handler's seat, Geoffrey doubted it had ever been used. All Archie needed to do was give a click of his tongue and a light flick of the reins to encourage the mules, which set off at a brisk trot down the long drive to the gatehouse where the avenue was bordered by sweeping lawns and immaculate flower beds filled with exotic plants.

Although he refrained from making any comment, Geoffrey couldn't help but be impressed by his first glimpse of the Drummond estate in daylight. He also grudgingly had to admire the way his companion handled the mules through the quake-damaged areas to reach the hotel.

Although the Grand Colonial Hotel had suffered some damage to the main frontage, it was minor in comparison to three others in the area that had been reduced to rubble. Fortunately the family apartments had hardly been affected and it didn't take long for Geoffrey to emerge from his room, clutching the violin case and his recent compositions in a briefcase.

"You must forgive me for asking but is that what you intend wearing for the remainder of your stay here?" Archie asked with a wry smile.

"What the devil are you on about?"

"Clothes, Geoffrey, clothes. You need to go back inside and pack them. We won't be able to get through here again, not once the clear-up gets under way."

"I do not pack clothes... a valet from the hotel can do that."

"Not today. I have it on good authority that any staff who turn up today will be fully occupied attending to the guests. My advice would be to throw everything you need into a suitcase. Lady Harriet will arrange to have the jumble sorted out after we get back."

"And what about the ladies' clothes; have you applied any thought to that?" Geoffrey asked, noticing the door to his mother's room was open.

"That has all been taken care of. The two señoritas who were available have been at work from the moment we arrived and have packed everything carefully into the ladies' trunks." Archie disappeared into Lady Claudia's apartment and returned moments later, dragging the first of three cabin trunks which he loaded onto a sack barrow. "And before you ask, there are no porters available either."

"Then how do you propose getting that lot down the stairs?"

"The staff lift is still working. We can use that."

A task that Geoffrey had thought would take no time at all required a good two hours of manhandling the trunks and suitcases before the mule cart was loaded up with every item of luggage.

"Surely this cannot all belong to my family. There must be some mistake?" Geoffrey said.

"Not at all. I supervised the packing myself. Presumably the ladies have brought along a suitable garment for every occasion they might encounter. That is nothing out of the ordinary. Lady Harriet travels in exactly the same manner."

"I had forgotten how many gowns my mother and sisters brought with them," Geoffrey said, examining the name tags on each item of luggage.

"You look puzzled, Geoff?" Archie said, as his companion moved the luggage about.

"I don't think everything is here."

"You must be mistaken. Every wardrobe, closet and drawer has been emptied. I double checked through the rooms myself once the packing was done."

"Probably not well enough. Lady Marguerite's trunk of art materials is not here. She will never forgive me if her sketch pad and that bloody journal she is forever scribbling in have been left behind."

"Are you sure her trunk isn't buried under this other stuff?"

"Of course I am. I would know that box anywhere. I am not leaving without it. It's more than my life's worth to turn up without that."

"What is it with your family? Firstly you are obsessing about a violin and now it's your sister and a missing box of paints? Holy Mary… Are we ever going to get away from here?" Archie put a couple more aspirin into his mouth, swallowing them with a cupped handful of water from a wall fountain.

"Then I will tell you what it is, you bog-Irish halfwit," Geoffrey blurted out. "We are not being obsessive for the sake of it. My sister and I are both artists. Not muscle-bound freaks who would not know one end of a bloody paintbrush from another!" His tone was as much a reaction to the pain in his fingers, having missed his footing on a cracked step on the way down and banged his already bruised hand against the wall.

"Feel any better now, after getting that out of your system?"

"Yes, since you ask. And have you got any more of those aspirin on you? I could do with a couple myself."

"Sorry, sport, they were the last two. I can probably rustle some up from reception if you are desperate."

"No need. What I must do is get the manager to allow me access to the hotel safe."

"Not thinking of looting the place, are you?" Archie said in a half-hearted attempt to lighten the situation.

"Hardly. Mother asked me to collect some jewellery that was deposited there."

"Then you should have mentioned it before we set off. Do you have any identification on you?"

"Why would I need any? They know me here."

"Not all of the staff. Leave it with me. I will try to round up the relief manager, who fortunately I know. Lady Harriet employs his brothers on the estate. Did you want to come along with me? I can vouch for your identity."

"No thanks. If you can handle it on your own, there is a more pressing matter in need of my attention."

After fifteen minutes Geoffrey returned carrying a small pine chest splattered with paint, a box that would not have looked out of place in any garden shed, and was surprised to find Archie already waiting.

"Good lord, is that what you went back for?" Archie laughed.

"Of course it is. What beats me is how anyone could have missed it. This box was on the floor near the window seat, in full view."

"I didn't miss it at all. In fact I almost broke my neck on the blasted thing. I thought the maid must have got it ready to be thrown out. I did not expect anything like that would belong to Lady Marguerite."

"We are a family of compulsive collectors. If it feels right, we keep it, whatever it is," Geoffrey said defensively.

"Like your violin?"

"Exactly… what were you expecting, something grand and inlaid with marquetry?"

"Maybe, maybe not; you are something of a riddle, Geoffrey Saint Hubes. You never can tell what people are really like until you look deeper and I confess I am rather pleasantly surprised."

"And how did you get on, breaking into the office safe for Mother's jewellery?" Geoffrey said in a feeble attempt to cover up his embarrassment at the compliment.

"All I needed was to sign some paperwork, once he remembered Lady Claudia was wearing those sapphires when she left for the opera." Archie handed over the casket, which he'd wrapped in a piece of old cloth. "Put this under your seat, Geoff, just in case we get jumped on our way out of the city. There will be a lot of lawlessness about at a time like this."

They returned to the plantation by the coastal route, a twisting road with wide vistas of an aquamarine ocean and cresting waves that took Geoffrey's breath away. Once the road branched inland, however, the lane became narrower, more uneven and badly pot-holed in places. Still, Archie easily coaxed the mules along until it eventually petered out into nothing more than a cart track, with a surface that jolted Geoffrey's spine and did nothing to relieve the pain in his hand.

"What are we stopping for now?" Geoffrey blurted out as Archie unexpectedly halted the mules, causing the mountain of luggage in the back to slide forward and ram up hard against the seat. He stood up in horror as a huge snake slithered across the road ahead of them.

"Sit down, for God's sake, Geoff before you fall off and break your bloody neck."

"You cannot stop here; what if that thing sees us?"

"It is not interested in us, only in getting to the other side and away from the wheels of the cart. Now sit down and save your breath, or you might attract something else."

"You expect us to sit here and wait for that damned reptile to slither across? Can you not do something?"

"How can I, you idiot? What do you expect me to do, run the thing over? I am not an Englishman, wantonly killing any creature for no reason. It's only a snake and it's not doing any harm to either of us."

"But it's huge and probably deadly poisonous," Geoffrey said, settling awkwardly back onto the seat.

"What do those private tutors of yours teach you? That snake is a boa constrictor. They don't use poison. They just crush you to death instead."

"They crush you?" Geoffrey began, until Archie grabbed his arm and yanked him along the driver's seat towards him.

"Get your bloody hands off me!" Geoffrey raged, before grabbing onto Archie's own arm petrified as a green snake with yellow markings dropped out of a tree immediately above him, missing his shoulders by inches and landed, stunned, on the luggage piled up behind Geoffrey's head.

"Let go of me, you idiot. I need to pitch that blasted snake away from here before it gets its wind back or we are both dead!" Archie snapped. Unclamping Geoffrey's hand from its vicelike grip on his arm, he hooked the end of the whip underneath the reptile's body and flung it into the dense undergrowth.

"I swear I loathe you and everything else in this godforsaken continent!" Geoffrey shouted in a tone bordering on hysteria, ready to jump out of the cart and race back to the hotel on foot had his legs not felt as if they were made from jelly.

"You will thank me later when you realise what a narrow escape you just had. A foot closer and that blasted snake would have landed squarely on your shoulders and killed you in seconds."

"What the hell made you take this route away from the town and bring us through a bloody jungle you… you bog-Irish halfwit?" Geoffrey shouted in his face. "What was wrong with the way we came out?"

Until that moment Geoffrey hadn't noticed how much fresh blood was seeping through the bandage on Archie's head and he might even have offered to rebind it had he not been so wound up by his own narrow escape.

"This way is shorter and the mules get more shelter from the sun."

"You chose this way to prevent these bloody mules from getting sunstroke? What about the promise to my mother to keep me safe? I loathe snakes. I cannot even look at them in a book because they scare me so much. Did the danger to anyone else except for your bloody mules ever cross your mind?" Geoffrey raged.

"As a matter of fact, yes it did and this is the route I chose," Archie responded, ashen-faced and tight-lipped. "And I would seriously advise you to curb your language. I am not one of your hired lackeys to be spoken to in that manner. Any more abusive talk about my Irish heritage from you and you can damned well walk back."

"You would not dare!"

"Try me… I have met twelve-year-olds with more common sense than you seem to have. Wake up, Geoffrey. You are in South America, for Christ's sake, not rural England!"

"Bollocks!" Geoffrey retorted angrily.

"If and when you eventually develop a pair, then perhaps you will behave more like a gentleman and less like an arrogant prick."

"I was born a gentleman, you… you arse!"

"Then why not try and act like one!" Archie fumed, flicking the reins to speed up the pace and making no effort to reduce the jolting of the cart all the way back. They continued to the plantation in complete silence, where Geoffrey's mother was there to greet them.

"I feared the manager would not allow you to collect my possessions from the safe without my written authority," his mother said, when Geoffrey handed over her jewellery casket.

"Actually, I did not get them. Saint Archie arranged everything with the manager. He seems to know what buttons to press with anyone worth knowing," Geoffrey said peevishly.

"Saint Archie…! You are so funny, darling. I am delighted the two of you are getting along so well together." Lady Claudia smiled, planting a loving kiss on his cheek.

Chapter Seven
An Unexpected Departure

It was inevitable that Archie Westbrook would also be staying at the plantation for the short time Geoffrey and his family were house guests, so he tried to avoid the Irishman as much as possible. He did notice, however, that Archie was spending a lot more time in his mother's company than he did with either of his sisters. It was also clear from the moment they arrived that Rosamund was infatuated with him, even though he did little to encourage such admiration. While he did his best to engage Marguerite in conversation, she spoke very little, seeming more engrossed in her work than ever before.

"Why do you spend so much time in Westbrook's company, Mother?" Geoffrey asked petulantly, since there never seemed enough time to enjoy her company alone.

"Surely, now you have got to know Archie more, you must value what an engaging conversationalist he is."

"I would not expect anything else from an Irishman."

"He is a remarkable young man, Geoffrey, so easy to get along with. There is nothing that could please me more than if you would make more of an effort with him. He is so like his father."

"Hopefully he was not a liar too!" he said, regretting it immediately on seeing his mother's shocked reaction.

"Geoffrey! Why would you say such a dreadful thing?"

"He lied to me about not having had a tattoo, when it was blatantly obvious that he has."

"Are you certain about this?"

"I am positive, Mother. Westbrook has a dragon-shaped tattoo between his shoulder blades. I saw it clearly through a tear in his shirt on the night of the earthquake."

"Then what Rufus once told me must be true, if Archie has this mark also." Her smile seemed to illuminate her face.

"You do not seem that surprised, Mother."

"Archie's father and I grew up on neighbouring estates in Ireland. We often went swimming on those hot summer days. It would appear he has the same birthmark as his son, which I trust will alter your misconceived opinion of him. Please make friends, darling; it would mean a great deal to me if you can."

"I would, Mother, if only to please you but I cannot since he has no respect for my title and treats me like a spoilt child," Geoffrey complained.

The conversation was broken when Lady Harriet beckoned them over to the terrace to tell them that a team of workmen would be arriving later that day to complete work on the archery targets and the rifle range and to erect staging for the coming entertainment.

This five-day event was to honour the tenth anniversary of the death of her late husband. Some events were of Scottish origin, in respect of the laird's ancestry, while others were for the enjoyment and sporting entertainment of the gathering. In respect of this important occasion, every silver cup and trophy had been meticulously engraved with an image of Netherdunn Castle, the Drummond clan's estate on the west coast of the Scottish Highlands.

Geoffrey was rather more pleased when the dowager offered him the use of a neglected ballroom in the west wing for his violin practice while the one in the east wing was dressed in preparation for the Grand Ball that would be the culmination of the memorial events.

Later that day, after an extensive search, Geoffrey located his younger sister in a strangely pensive mood, alone and wandering aimlessly through the rose gardens.

"What are you doing out here on your own, Rose? I looked everywhere for you."

"Mother is resting, and you... you were hidden away somewhere, practising."

"Admittedly it is rather hidden but it is perfect as it's out of everyone's way. Why did you not find Maggs? She would have accompanied you."

"Not today; she is too engrossed in more drawing for her journal."

"Did you know anything about this tournament?" Geoffrey asked.

"Naturally… did Archie not tell you?"

"Not a word."

"Well… that is probably your own fault because you never stay long enough to make any conversation with him," she commented but his interest was already focused elsewhere. On one of the many formal lawns that could be seen through a row of topiary shapes was another spectacular terraced garden, beyond which it was just possible to make out a large marquee being erected.

"There are archery and shooting contests as far as I know," Rosamund said.

"I trust you are not considering taking part in any of those events; not unless you want to suffer the indignity of coming in last?" Geoffrey laughed.

"Actually, I was not… but now I most definitely shall!" she said, brightening.

"And which one would that be, for Pete's sake?"

"Neither of them. There is also a steeplechase. I think I will enter that."

"Rubbish. They would never hold one here, not with this sodden ground and so many fallen trees after the earthquake."

"They might and, God willing, if they do, then I definitely intend to compete," she said gaily, prompting him to walk away in the direction of the marquee to investigate. He was taken unawares by the arrival of a pony and trap.

"Geoffrey, my dear, how perfect to find you out here," Lady Harriet called, hailing him over. "Yet again, I am in need of your assistance, my dear boy." She refused his offered hand as she clambered down from the trap.

"How is that, Lady Drummond?"

"Quite simply, I need you to stay close to dear Archie throughout the events," she said, tying the pony's reins to a fallen tree.

"Would you mind if I ask why? I have not laid eyes on him today. Apart from that, Lady Drummond, Archie Westbrook and I are not really the most suitable companions."

"Then I insist that you try; if not for me, then for a very dear friend of your mother." She allowed him to help her over the uneven ground until they reached a park bench, where he sat beside her.

"And who might that be, Lady Drummond?"

"Why, dear Rufus of course… Archie's father." She drummed her fingers on the arm of the bench. "If you do not oblige me in this, Geoffrey, then I fear my grandson's future could be in considerable danger."

"But if Archie is in danger, Lady Drummond, would a manservant not be a more suitable choice? I am a musician and almost a stranger to him."

"Your mother and I have already discussed this, Geoffrey. She agrees you would be the perfect choice. Indeed it was her express request that I seek your assistance immediately."

"If you would care to explain in more detail, then naturally I will do whatever I can to help, Lady Drummond."

"This danger is of a more destructive kind and one that I, as a devoted grandmother, cannot challenge. Archie has the kindest nature but some day he will also inherit his father's estate and title. This combination has made him the matrimonial target of every eligible female in Pernambuco society."

"If you will forgive this observation, Lady Drummond, surely at his age Archie would see through any such schemes?"

"With the less devious ones perhaps but you will understand my concern once you are confronted by the Viceroy's niece, Isabella Moreno."

"Where is Archie now?"

"Out of harm's way for the moment, helping clear the racecourse for the final event. So can I assume that you will help?"

"I will, of course, if it will please both yourself and my mother," Geoffrey said. Yet the thought of trailing around after the fiercely independent Archie Westbrook as a male chaperone was almost laughable and he was determined to take up the issue with Lady Claudia at the first opportunity.

To his relief, there was no sign of Archie at dinner that evening but even so, Geoffrey had no opportunity to speak with his mother about his situation. She was happily laughing and reminiscing about her teenage years in Ireland with Lady Harriet, her drop sapphire earrings sparkling magically in the candlelight with each turn of her lovely head.

The following morning, Geoffrey awoke late with a throbbing headache having sneaked a glass of an unidentifiable drink in the Games Room when no one else was about. By the time he was bathed, dressed and ready to set off it was almost noon.

Carriages had been arriving at the main house long before Geoffrey tumbled out of the comfortable bed. The valet had already been sent away twice, until he could no longer block out the shrill sound of bagpipes heralding the commencement of the first day's events. By the time he arrived at the arena the opening tug-of-war was over and the hammer-throwing was well under way.

The third and final event of Day One was an archery competition. The ladies' event was dominated by the stately figure of Isabella Moreno, who positioned her magnificent body to great effect before releasing each arrow. Although she never missed the target she never quite managed to hit the bullseye but her command of archery far exceeded that of her eight gentrified rivals and, as the clear winner she received a splendid silver trophy.

As the cup was being presented by a seemingly gracious Lady Drummond, Geoffrey observed a clear alteration in her attitude when a tousle-haired and mud-spattered Archie made an unexpected appearance to receive an engraved silver tray on behalf of the tug-of-war team. Wearing a pair of torn and grimy trousers and an equally stained shirt with rolled-up sleeves, he would have looked the picture of rugged health had it not been for the bandage on his forehead.

"Dear God, you look dreadful. What ails you?" Archie asked when Geoffrey managed to reach him, moments before the immaculately attired Isabella Moreno swished across the ornamental bridge, waving in their direction.

"Nothing, I overslept and had to dash to get here. The tug-of-war was over by the time I arrived but congratulations anyway," Geoffrey managed to say before Isabella arrived and pushed herself between them.

"Archie Westbrook, I do declare you are the most elusive scoundrel. My aunt and I have been here for hours without laying eyes on you once and yet here you are, conversing with this angelic schoolboy."

"Isabella… might I present Sir Geoffrey Saint Hubes, a family acquaintance of my grandmother's from England."

"Sir Geoffrey, how very nice this is," she responded, manoeuvring her body for Archie's better appreciation and barely acknowledging Geoffrey's existence after the brief introduction. "Congratulations, my dear Archie, on such a magnificent win." She removed the tray from his hand for a critical examination. "You must be devastated to receive such an insignificant trophy after such strenuous effort."

"It was done for the sport, Isabella. Might I enquire what you have done with your own trophy?" he asked, taking the tray back.

"It is in safe keeping with Aunt Agustin."

"Then presumably Xavier Juarez has arrived also?"

"He has indeed. The Viceroy will be handing out the trophies tomorrow. It was he who taught me to shoot so it will be a great privilege to receive my trophy from his hand."

"Do you presume this competition to be a foregone conclusion, señorita?" Geoffrey asked, speaking directly into her back and making her turn around.

"My skill with a firearm is indisputable, Sir... Geoffrey. The Viceroy is predicting a display case of Drummond trophies at the Embassy by the end of these memorial events." She laughed, seductively linking arms with Archie. "If you will excuse us, my uncle, the Viceroy, is most eager to renew his earlier acquaintance with dear Archie."

"Perhaps later, Isabella but first I need to get scrubbed up before this evening's entertainment ," Archie said, firmly disengaging her arm and striding off towards the house, leaving Geoffrey perched on a wall and the statuesque Isabella to make her own way back across the ornamental bridge.

That evening's entertainment was not a performance in the grand marquee as Geoffrey had expected but a collection of thrilling circus acts inside a big top erected in one of the paddocks. The evening began with a nail-biting high-wire performance, followed by a group of midget jugglers and a chilling knife-throwing act as well as a troupe of awesome trapeze artists before the interval. The second half was opened by twelve kabuki-style dancers from the Orient, followed by plate spinners performing on stilts and concluding with a party of shoulder-balancing Cossacks on trampolines. Finally, to a collective gasp of appreciation from the audience, the end of the big top was lowered to the ground to reveal a magnificent firework display, staged on an island in the centre of the ornamental lake.

On the second day, although Geoffrey tried to locate Archie there was no sighting of him until the polo match got under way in the afternoon. Here Archie proved his skill as both a horseman and a team player. After a tense and thrilling match, the opposing team scored in the final moments of the game and were presented with the silver trophy by Xavier

Juarez, the small, impeccably dressed Viceroy, overshadowed by his domineering, broad-shouldered wife.

"Who is that awful creature cornering Archie?" Rosamund pouted, as the now all-too-familiar figure of Isabella shadowed Archie from the polo ground.

"Isabella Moreno... a woman who believes she will dominate the ladies' events and claim most of the trophies."

"Well, that remains to be seen. Are you aware that Mama has been entered for the rifle competition?"

"Why would Mother do such an impulsive thing? She has never even held a gun," Geoffrey protested.

"Where are you going now, Jeffy?" Rosamund called after him, hitching up her skirts and racing to keep up.

"Off to find Mother and put an end to this hogwash!"

Lady Claudia, however, had taken to her bed with a migraine and did not reappear until the following morning for breakfast. When he broached the subject of the rifle competition it was clear that she had no intention of getting into any exchange on the subject, instead insisting that he must not allow the events of the week to interfere with his violin practice.

The first competition on the third day was the gentlemen's clay pigeon shoot, scheduled to begin at noon. As a result of the earthquake and subsequent storm many of the clay discs had been destroyed and, with insufficient numbers remaining, these were allocated for the gentlemen's competition only.

For the ladies' tournament, twelve replicas of animals had been created from planks of wood and erected a considerable distance away across open ground. At the other end of the field there was a seated viewing platform for the gentry, sandwiched on either side by four banks of terraces for the local spectators.

Staged inside an arena of hay bales, the event was preceded by an exciting exhibition of horsemanship by four circus performers. Two were balancing on the shoulders of the others as they entered the arena, transferring from one horse to another at great speed then somersaulting on to the ground, leaving the other two men straddling both horses. One then positioned himself at the edge of a seesaw as the other clambered up a scaffold and jumped down on to the end of the plank, catapulting the first man through the air to land squarely on the shoulders of one of the riders.

Once the staging crew had reassembled the bales into a stepped wall and sectioned off numbered shooting positions, the twelve marksmen took up their positions. As the propelled clay discs hurtled over in rapid succession, each of the men fired off six shots before the steward rang a bell, thereby ending the first shoot. At the end of the each round one of the marksmen was eliminated and by the end of the second, it was easy to speculate as to who would be the next man to drop out. One of the four who remained was Archie.

"How Archie resembles his father in the way he shoots," Lady Claudia observed, watching the event closely through field glasses.

"What is Rufus Westbrook like, Mother? Is he much older than you?" Geoffrey asked.

"Our birthdays were a year and a day apart. He was a shade taller than Archie is now; but their features are very much alike and they both have the same violet eyes."

"What else do you remember about him?"

"He is the kindest person I have ever known," she said, caressing one of her worn hair combs. "Rufus was a wonderful artist and could draw anything in perfect detail. He did a sketch of me once which your grandfather had framed, even though he disliked him so much."

"That sketch next to the desk in his study?"

"Yes."

"But I thought that was a portrait of Maggs as a girl," Geoffrey said, shocked by the revelation. He had never imagined that extraordinary portrait was of his mother and not his sister; they could have been identical twins. "We are talking about the same portrait?"

"I was young once, darling. All parents were," she laughed.

"That portrait is incredible."

"If Rue had not been born into the aristocracy, he could have achieved international recognition as an artist, or as a sculptor in any material at all, had his father allowed it."

"What is the story behind these hair combs mother? There must be one, seeing the fondness you have for them," Geoffrey asked, examining one close up.

"Rue fashioned these for my fifteenth birthday from the shell of his dead tortoise."

"They are very beautiful but what about the silver inlay? Surely he didn't create such an intricate design as this?" Geoffrey remarked. To his astonishment, as he examined the exquisite workmanship he realised with a jolt that it was a perfect replica of Archie's birthmark.

"He had an inherent talent to create anything with those skilful hands. These combs took weeks to complete… in secret," she smiled. "And yet he mentioned nothing about them until he gave them to me on my birthday." She replaced them in her glossy dark hair.

"What else do you remember about him?"

"Mostly that he was always in trouble and more often than not when I was with him." She laughed gaily, amused by some distant memory and appeared happier at that moment than Geoffrey could ever remember.

"If you liked him that much, why did you never mention him until now?"

"I suppose because spending time with his son has brought those dear memories flooding back. Besides, this all happened so long ago."

"You might have been a lot happier if you had married your childhood sweetheart, instead of Father."

"If I had, my darling, then I might never have had you," she said lovingly, bringing an end to their conversation.

By the end of the gentlemen's shooting tournament Archie was the clear winner and duly went up to receive the trophy from the sweating hands of the flustered Viceroy, who almost dropped the engraved silver tankard as it was being presented. There had only been rare sightings of his daughter as she was preparing herself for the ladies' event. With two hours before it was due to begin, Geoffrey found his mother in the Morning Room, deep in conversation with Lady Harriet Drummond.

"There is no need for this modesty, my dear. It is well known that either you or my dear Rufus won every shooting tournament in the county of Dublin in your teens."

"Yes we did, Harriet but I am not as young as I was and it would be foolish of me to even consider that I can still shoot accurately."

"But if you do not try my dear, that Isabella is going to walk off with this trophy too. Strong competition is what we need today and you are the ideal candidate, especially as she is also sure to scoop up the Gold Cup for the fourth consecutive year."

"Then might I suggest you allow my daughter to take my place?"

"But surely Rosamund is not suited to such an event?"

"I was referring to my eldest daughter, Lady Marguerite."

"Are you implying the artist can also shoot?"

"Personally I have never seen her handle a rifle but I am told by my gamekeeper that she is more than capable and, as I have not handled a weapon in years, it is quite feasible my daughter will prove a more accurate markswoman than I. If I can persuade Marguerite to take part, I am convinced that she will not disappoint."

It was clear the information Rosamund had given him was no exaggeration but, although he had many unanswered questions for his mother, he decided to wait until later.

Whereas the gentlemen had used shotguns in the clay pigeon shoot, the ladies' event was allocated .22 rifles, which had less kickback when fired and lessened the chance of damage to their shoulders. There were twelve ladies

150

competing and a broad walkway of planks had now been laid behind the hay bales to cover the waterlogged ground.

When the imperious figure of Isabella Moreno entered the arena, followed closely at heel by four deferential competitors, Geoffrey thought that the only thing missing was a fanfare of trumpets. He nervously waited for his mother to appear.

Having failed to persuade Marguerite to take her place, Lady Claudia was competing in ninth position. From a distance she might easily have been in her mid-twenties. He was shocked to see that, unlike the other competitors, she chose to load the rifle herself rather than allow the handler to do this for her. Although he could barely come to terms with his gentle mother taking part in such an event, it was soon clear from the way she handled the rifle that she was no stranger to firearms.

Soon after the competition got under way, one of the more elderly competitors stepped back too far, fell off the planking and took a nasty tumble in the mud. Lady Claudia looked nervous and, although she never missed the target ,she was falling some way behind Isabella. The leader flashed a radiant smile in Archie's direction after every shot, until her overconfidence led her to glance his way while firing and she missed the target completely.

Her error was the cue for Lady Claudia to rediscover the skill of her youth, scoring a bullseye with every shot thereafter, resulting in a tiebreak with Isabella. By this time, Lady Harriet was fanning herself furiously with one hand while gripping Archie's arm with the other. After a tense play-off Lady Claudia was declared the outright winner and received the coveted silver trophy from a clearly unhappy Viceroy.

"I had forgotten the stories I was told about what a fine shot the Lady Claudia was," Archie said, catching up with Geoffrey on his way to the house.

"Then you have the advantage of me. Until today, I had no idea Mother could even hold a rifle, let alone shoot straight."

"She never told you? My father often spoke of it when he taught me to shoot."

"No, she never did."

"It must have been quite a shock for Isabella not to have won the competition but at least all is not lost; no doubt she will get the Gold Cup tomorrow. Her seat is magnificent on a horse. Unfortunately for the other competitors, there is no woman in South America who can match her in the saddle," Archie said.

"Well, that remains to be seen; no one else could have outshot her until today."

"Surely you are not suggesting Lady Claudia could outride her too?"

"Not in the least; I just hope there is someone here that can," Geoffrey said, breaking away towards his own apartment.

That evening there was entertainment in the marquee with *Les Fausses Confidences*, a three-act comedy by the French playwright Marivaux. Although the play was in French, with only a narrator to translate, it was beautifully acted, staged and costumed and the talented performers had the audience – or most of them – in gales of laughter.

"Did you not find it amusing, Jeffy?" Rosamund asked as they were leaving.

"How could I? It was all in French."

"Then you should have paid more attention to your lessons back home!"

"You were the one with a French governess, Rose, not me!" Geoffrey grumbled, storming off before his mother and Archie could catch up with them.

"Well if Archie could understand everything, why not you?" she called after him.

"Go to hell, Rose," Geoffrey growled.

Having slept badly that night, Geoffrey woke early, determined to make amends with his sister at breakfast but finding that she had already eaten and left, he set off in search of the stables. On the way he met the very last person he wanted to see.

"Where are you off to, Geoff?" Archie asked, leading a temperamental mare across the cobbled yard.

"I am looking for Rose since you ask. Have you seen her?"

"Yes, I have. I trust you are going to apologise after that idiotic outburst last night," Archie said, gripping the reins tightly when the startled mare reared unexpectedly at the clatter of a bucket.

"It would be none of your bloody business if I was!" Geoffrey snapped.

"One of these days you will decide to grow up. I just hope I live long enough to see it!" Archie shouted after him, wrestling with the mare as it clattered across the cobbles.

Geoffrey found Rosamund in the stables deep in conversation with a bow-legged, grizzly old man who was dressed like a tramp.

"What are you doing here, Rose?"

"If you are here for an argument, Jeffy, then I am not, so please go away."

"I am sorry I was so churlish last night."

"Childish would be more appropriate! What is it you want?"

"I just came here to say I am sorry."

"Are you now? Then now that you have said so, perhaps you could give your opinion of this horse."

"Naturally… that is, if it is not French!" Geoffrey smirked, receiving a pinched arm for the comment. "Why are you looking at horses?"

"Simply because I do not approve of the way that dreadful Isabella Moreno behaved towards Mama when she received the trophy. Because of that, I have decided to enter the ladies' challenge race this afternoon and beat her," Rosamund smiled, smoothing the horse's thick and ungroomed coat.

"Surely you will need a better mount than this, Rose," he said. The horse looked as though it had been working on the estate.

"There are no other mounts suitable for the race," the old man said knowingly, patting the mare with affection. "Charmer is the master's pride and joy. She may not have the sleek looks of the others but she would never let the young lady down."

"But you can't expect my sister to ride that creature. She could easily get thrown and trampled underfoot!"

"I will be perfectly fine, Jeffy. You of all people should not question my ability to ride."

"And I do not, only that this animal seems better suited to a rodeo or a medieval jousting arena than as a mount for the ladies' competition."

"I will get her measure soon enough and she mine, if you leave me alone with her. This horse needs to know who will be riding her and that she can trust me."

"But that won't make her move any faster and it is speed you will need."

"Charmer will outrun the others, just mark my words," Rosamund said, running her hand lightly down the animal's legs. "These muscular legs will do well over boggy ground. A ride like this is in her make-up."

"Is this an actual breed?" he asked with some disbelief. "If so, what the hell is it?"

"It would be obvious if you took any interest in horses, Jeffy. This is a Chilean mare. They were bred for herding cattle on the pampas." She stroked the horse's flat forehead.

"Well I would have put it down for pulling a rag and bone cart, rather than anything so exotic," Geoffrey commented but his sister's knowledge of horses was undeniable and what she said made sense. "But can you ride side-saddle on this animal?"

"I have already informed the young lady there are no ladies' saddles available," said the groom.

"No matter, I shall make do with this one." Rosamund dusted down a worn gaucho saddle from the rack.

"I do beg you to reconsider, milady. This is a working saddle. Your competitors will regard your selection as an outrage. This is not what a respectable young lady would use," the old man protested.

"Nevertheless, since you have no alternative I shall make do with this and the ladies can think what the heck they like," Rosamund said, bringing an end to the conversation.

Usually the ladies race would be a regal affair, with all the young women riding side-saddle on their perfectly groomed horses, eager to display a shapely ankle as they trotted along the grand drive towards the starting point of the track.

Following the earthquake and subsequent storm, the arena marked out in the Great Park was no longer firm underfoot but sodden and in some parts waterlogged. Although the estate workers had done their best to remove whatever debris they could, some fallen trees had proved impossible to lift in the limited time available. As a result, the course had been altered from the expected point-to-point into more of a cross-country event. Had it not been for the importance of the occasion – and the lure of the gold trophy – the race would surely have been cancelled.

Even so, the course was more treacherous than any of the young ladies were prepared for that afternoon, mounted on a variety of light saddle horses all groomed to show off their riders' feminine charms. The only breeds Geoffrey could recognise were two Arabian mares, one Andalusian stallion and a Friesian. Apart from those, he had no idea other than they all looked decidedly superior to Rosamund's mount as she cantered up to the starting position. She had dispensed with the usual veiled riding hat, instead plaiting her shining hair and coiling it into the nape of her long neck. Since she had come unprepared for such a formal event, Rosamund wore a pleated charcoal skirt with a fetching cream blouse made from a fine Honiton lace, both items on loan from her mother; on top of these was an embroidered gentleman's waistcoat that Geoffrey instantly recognised as his own. Unlike the other ladies, especially Isabella, mounted regally on a black stallion, Rosamund wore no items of jewellery and looked all the more beautiful for the lack of it.

When the flag went down it came as no surprise that the black stallion carried Isabella out in front of the pack like a warrior princess riding into battle. It seemed inevitable she would be the clear winner but as she galloped into the boggy ground, the stallion began to slip and flounder, splashing mud everywhere, its rider needing all her skill just to keep her seat. Close behind, two other contestants were not so fortunate, both plunging head first into the mud.

It was at this point that it became clear that Rosamund was a strong contender. Although she was just as mud-spattered as the others, there was a radiance about her that caused Geoffrey to smile, remembering that same determined look from their competitive childhood before her beauty began to emerge and she became more interested in the latest modes of fashion.

As she came up from the rear, the superior intelligence of Rosamund's horse came into play. Other competitors skidded about on the boggy ground, bucking more of the genteel riders off but this horse held its ground as it gradually overtook one after another of the competitors. Soon there were only two riders between his sister and a clearly nervous Isabella.

From the corner of his eye Geoffrey briefly noticed Archie, shouting through cupped hands as Rosamund and her mount were jostled away from the drier ground by the two trailing contenders. Any hope of catching up with Isabella seemed doomed as a fallen tree now lay across their path until, as Archie shouted out again, instead of stopping, the courageous horse charged full tilt at the obstacle and sailed clean over it.

Had Rosamund not been the rider she was, she could surely not have stayed in the saddle, yet determinedly she hung on, now urging the horse to gallop hard after the black stallion who was being guided into still boggier ground by the grimly determined Isabella. The spectators held their breath as the stallion again lost its footing, slipped and pitched its rider into the mud, allowing Rosamund to gallop past to the winning post.

So it was Isabella Moreno who received the runner-up silver plaque but only after a dishevelled but beaming Rosamund was handed the coveted golden trophy by a reluctant Viceroy to resounding applause, not least from Lady Drummond herself.

"What will you do with it, Rose?" her brother asked as they walked back from the stables, arm in arm.

"Mama suggested that I leave it here with Florence Taylor, just in case Father is not waiting in Apalla when we arrive."

Neither of them had noticed Archie, waiting to congratulate Rosamund on her win.

"You should not congratulate me. I did none of the work. It was that lovely mount you allowed me to ride that deserves this trophy," Rosamund said, brushing mud from her face.

"I disagree. Having you ride her was the perfect combination for my Charmer. She is an incredible horse. I am only surprised that she did not try to buck you off but allowed you to ride her around that obstacle course as if you were welded together. None of the other ladies would have dared ride her the way you did."

"I think we would all agree on that," Geoffrey said, breaking away and allowing Archie to escort Rosamund the rest of the way back.

The Grand Ball to mark the culmination of the celebrations was held three days before they continued up the coast on the *Lugansa*. It was nearing the end of their stay and Florence

Taylor's health had not improved, so a decision had to be made. The dowager had arranged for their maid to have rooms in the servants' quarters until she was well enough to travel. All this was dependent on the advice of Doctor Beresford who dutifully called in every day to check on her. Their hostess had also arranged that Archie would accompany them to Apalla on the understanding that he would remain with them until they were finally reunited with Lord Oliver. This was a decision that was well received by all of the family except Geoffrey, even though he admitted, though only to himself, that whenever Archie was with him, arguing or not, he had never felt safer in his entire life.

"Jeffy, do come and join us in the Morning Room!" Rosamund called from the far side of the lawn in the late afternoon before the ball. "We are having fortunes read in the tea leaves. It is going to be great fun. We can find out if you will pass your entrance exam!"

"Thank you but no, I really must catch up with my exercises; if not I will never get accepted anywhere, regardless of what any fortune teller has to say," Geoffrey called back. He wanted no more diversions to prevent him from putting the violin through its paces, having spent the past hour nervously restringing the instrument, wondering if it would live up to his expectations.

Having set up a music stand on the stage of the old ballroom, Geoffrey applied oil to his hands and fingers before taking up the instrument. After playing only a few short pieces he knew instinctively that he had indeed found the perfect violin and vowed that he would never allow the instrument out of his sight again. He had been practising one of his own compositions for less than fifteen minutes when he became aware of someone close by, concealed in the wings of the stage.

"Whoever you are, please go away. I need to concentrate. I cannot play with anyone watching," Geoffrey grumbled, pressing the violin tightly against his chin.

"No need to worry, sport, it is only an Irishman and according to some, they do not count anyway." Archie smiled good-naturedly as he reached the music stand and turned over a page of sheet music precisely when it was needed. "Just pretend I'm not here and continue."

Geoffrey was soon immersed once more in the perfect pitch from the instrument and grateful to have the pages turned, allowing him more control over the many challenging and intricate sections of the score. Even so, he was never able to completely ignore Archie being in such close proximity.

"That was magnificent, Geoff," Archie said with unconcealed admiration as Geoffrey finally lowered the instrument.

"Rose likes this composition too."

"I cannot imagine anyone who would not."

"Why are you here, Archie?" Geoffrey asked. He had been deliberately secretive about where he practised. Even his mother had no idea where he would be that day and, as far as he was concerned, no one other than Lady Harriet knew of his whereabouts at all.

"Lady Claudia asked me to let you know that dinner will be served in half an hour but that was over an hour ago, so you had better come up with a good excuse, Geoff, otherwise my grandmother will be serving you up as the main course!" Archie chortled.

"How did you know where I would be?"

"I saw you sneaking past the veranda earlier, clutching that old violin case. It made sense to follow the sound of the music, so here I am."

"A servant could have found me easily enough, so why you?" Geoffrey grumbled, packing away the instrument.

"I came because of the animosity that has formed between us. I genuinely would like us to be friends, Geoff. We were getting along so well to begin with, until that unfortunate incident with the snake," Archie said, collecting the sheet music from the stand.

"There is absolutely no way, Archie Westbrook. For God's sake, you are old enough to be my father!" Geoffrey blustered to cover his embarrassment, hoping that would get rid of him. But instead of leaving, Archie burst into peals of laughter.

"Now I have heard everything. How old do you think I am?"

"I have absolutely no idea."

"Then take a wild guess."

"Ancient... is that good enough!" Geoffrey retorted, realising as he did that he was again making a complete ass of himself.

"I am twenty-five and that makes me two years younger than your eldest sister. Not even an Irishman can procreate at the age of seven! So how about we bury the hatchet and spend some time together? I have no male friends in these parts and, it appears, neither do you."

"I cannot afford any further distraction from my studies. Besides, we are leaving for England as soon as we have made contact with Father," Geoffrey retorted. "However, what I did want to say is that I am sorry if I offended you with that snake business. I should have behaved better but they do make my blood run cold."

"I ought to have realised from your reaction it was something like that and that was my fault," Archie said as he left the room. Watching him go, Geoffrey felt more at ease and wished he had handled the offer of friendship better. He was determined to make peace with Archie properly that evening before the ball.

Crossing the lawn on his return to the house, he found Archie waiting outside.

"Were you waiting for me?"

"There is something I want you to have before we go in for dinner. It would have been inappropriate to hand it over inside." Archie reached into his pocket and handed over a hunting knife with a silver and horn handle. "Make sure that you keep this with you at all times after we dock in Apalla

160

and be careful how you handle this weapon. The blade is sharp and deadly, so be sure to keep it safely in this sheath."

"I cannot take that thing!" he exclaimed, eyes wide as he looked at the fearsome blade. "It is horrible."

"This is not a gift, Geoff. This is just on loan in case we ever get separated on our way to, or in Apalla."

"Well that is not going to happen is it? Rose and Mother never let you out of their sight," Geoffrey scowled.

"Now you are being ridiculous."

"Like hell I am," Geoffrey retorted angrily.

"What I am offering is important, you idiot. Having this knife with you might just save your life one day. You need this as a precaution. If you saw sense for once in your life, you might understand I am trying to be bloody helpful." Archie gave him a withering look.

"I am not a child. I do have a penknife, you know. I can manage well enough without this disgusting weapon," Geoffrey snapped.

"I am sure that you can," Archie said, doing his best not to smile. "What you will not be aware of is that Apalla is renowned for being lawless. If the search for your father separates us in one of its more unpleasant quarters then you will need to be armed. This knife will help fend off any threat."

"You are just being overdramatic. I have already said I do not want it!" Geoffrey insisted, pushing the sheathed knife away.

"For Christ's sake, TAKE IT, Geoffrey! Why do you have to be so bloody stubborn all the time?"

"Who the hell do you think you are, talking to me like that you... you bloody moron? You are not my elder brother!"

"Listen to me, you little prick, you would be a damned sight more respectful to other people than you have been in the past if we were related. Now take the bloody knife before I am tempted to use it on you!" Archie snapped, thrusting it into Geoffrey's hand before he could object further and storming away without another word.

"Go on… piss off, Bog Boy. BOG BOY!" Geoffrey yelled after the rapidly departing figure, whose only response was an expressive gesture with his middle finger.

Seen from the darkening gardens, the interior of the ballroom was already a blaze of light, reflected in the elongated Georgian mirrors along every wall. Inside there was a sense of frenzied activity as immaculately liveried servants scurried about with flower arrangements and extra seating as the musicians tuned up their instruments for what promised to be a perfect finale to the memorial celebration.

On his way back to his rooms to change into his evening wear, Geoffrey had decided to leave the knife on the bedside table with a note asking for it to be returned to its owner but, having second thoughts about the practical benefits of Archie's loan, he tore up the note and packed the knife into his bag.

After apologising for his late arrival, Geoffrey had barely cleared his plate of the first course when everything was thrown into confusion by the delivery of a cablegram.

"Please forgive me, Lady Claudia but I must speak with my grandmother on an urgent matter," Archie said, folding the paper as he escorted Lady Drummond from the room. "Please continue eating, as this could take some time."

There was clearly an emotional exchange going on between them as their voices faded away in the corridor and, with the exception of Marguerite, they ate little and were toying with their dessert by the time Lady Harriet reappeared.

"My grandson has asked me to pass on his apologies for leaving so abruptly but there is an urgent matter in need of his attention."

"Is there any way I can be of help, Harriet?" Lady Claudia asked, seeing how distressed their host seemed.

"Thank you, my dear, but there is nothing anyone can do now, except pray for a safe journey and manage the best we can without him. Archie must sail for Ireland tonight and my fear is that he will board any tramp steamer on which he can find passage at this hour, anything to get him back home."

"Might I enquire why Archie is so desperate to get to Ireland?" Lady Claudia asked.

"Archie's father's condition has worsened and the physician has advised a swift return. I just pray he may be the tonic Rufus will need to improve."

While Archie's departure put a dampener on the evening's events for everyone Geoffrey observed the strong effect on his mother, who seemed as if she might faint on hearing the news. She stayed in the ballroom for less than half an hour after dinner before retiring to her bedchamber complaining of a migraine.

There was the sound of hysteria echoing along the hall where Isabella, the Viceroy and his wife were nearing the end of a tearful exchange. It was a shock to see the normally self-possessed Isabella oblivious to anyone else and devoid of the independent aura she presented in public. He realised how much older than he had originally thought she now appeared, certainly a good deal older than Archie himself. Finding her so unaccountably distressed, like some deflated balloon, Geoffrey felt genuinely sorry for her, sensing that her feelings for Archie ran deeper than his grandmother had anticipated

"But he cannot go!" the distressed Isabella continued wailing, her features bleached white, her eyes red and puffy from weeping. "You must go after him and prevent him from leaving. He has a moral duty to return here and ask for my hand in marriage, otherwise my reputation will be forever ruined!" she cried.

For most of the evening Geoffrey partnered his younger sister, not so much through any desire to be on the dance floor amid the blurred rustle of swirling dresses and twirling frock coats but more to prevent any of the eager young men from whisking her away from his protection. As he expected, Marguerite showed no interest in taking to the floor but spent most of the evening in the company of Lady

Drummond, sketching characters, immersed in the gaiety of the event.

"Will Archie be coming back, do you think?" Rosamund asked after they had found a cool seat on the dark terrace beneath a palm as far away from the dance floor as Geoffrey could get, as a South American adaptation of the Highland fling sprang into noisy life.

"I doubt it, Rose. By now he is probably on a creaking tea clipper, bobbing up and down like a cork in another wretched storm. If he had not left here in such a hurry, he could have travelled back to England on the *Lugansa*. As it is, we will probably arrive in Liverpool before he does anyway," Geoffrey said.

"What would you think, Geoffrey, if we broke from tradition and visited Mother's estate in Ireland now that Grandpapa is no longer able to dictate what we do?"

"Why would you want to do that? You never bothered about going over there before?" Geoffrey asked, suspecting that he already knew the answer.

"It would be nice for us all to go over and visit as Archie lives in Ireland most of the time and, after all, his father's estate is next to ours. Surely you are interested in seeing the place where Mother spent most of her childhood?"

"If Mother agrees, then yes, I suppose we could."

"But we must. Archie cannot just be erased from our lives as if he never existed."

"Why would you care if he was? You could have any chap you wanted. Why is he so special? We have only been acquainted with him for less than a week. That Irishman could be an axe murderer for all we know!" Geoffrey blurted out, which sent Rosamund into peals of laughter.

There was no sign of Lady Claudia throughout the following day, which was fortunate for her since the noise was almost deafening as the entire estate appeared to be overrun with workmen dismantling the marquee and the big top. In other areas, horse-drawn carts and wheelbarrows were being piled high with seating, while others were loaded with bales of hay and archery targets as order was restored to the Drummond plantation.

The only disruption inside the main building came from the dismantling of the decorations in the ballroom, none of which affected the west wing where Lady Claudia had remained in bed with curtains drawn. Here the silence was only disturbed by one of the servants packing for their departure the following morning.

"Thank goodness you remembered to collect my chest from the hotel, Geoffrey. I could never have managed without it," Marguerite commented, packing away a folding easel and her precious tin of paints into the battered pine box.

"If I had forgotten, you would never have let me forget," he laughed. "Where did you acquire this ratty old box from anyway; Violet Dobson's junk shop?"

"There is no need to be offensive, Geoffrey. Mother gave me this box before you were born."

"Mother would never give you a battered old trunk like this, caked in paint and God knows what else." He picked at some of the peeling paint on the lid. "Grandpa would never have allowed this in the house. You know what a tyrant he was about everything needing to be perfect."

"Well Grandpapa is not here. Besides, someone else used this box long before I ever did." She snapped down the catches.

"What about your precious journal? Is that inside here too?" he asked, buckling down the straps securely.

"Certainly not, I have that in my bag."

"If Mother gave you this trunk, do you think it might have belonged to Archie's father? Mother said he was a fine artist. She was right too; his work is brilliant."

"How could you possibly know that? You have never set foot on that estate."

"I didn't need to. Archie's father carved the hair combs Mother wears all the time. He also drew that fabulous sketch of mother, hanging by Grandfather's desk in the study."

"He drew that? I imagined that sketch was by an important artist but when I asked Grandpapa, he would never say who it was. Mother was very beautiful, even at fifteen."

Geoffrey was about to add that he had originally thought the portrait had been of Marguerite but decided not to say anything. If her eating habits hadn't run so out of control over the years, she might easily have matured into a younger version of their elegant mother.

Chapter Eight
Apalla

On the morning of their departure from Pernambuco, Lady Claudia and Rosamund made their way up the gangway with inadequate lace handkerchiefs pressed tightly against their nostrils. Geoffrey was left to assist his elder sister as Marguerite's fear of water and her laborious ascent slowed their progress.

Unlike their departure from Liverpool, the lower decks were crowded with noisy coastal passengers, bound for the port of Apalla. Once the *Lugansa* was tugged clear of the harbour and had got up steam, they moved away from the intense humidity into the cooling sea breeze.

There were no familiar faces among the passengers on the first-class deck, which for Geoffrey, came as a relief. However, the unwanted attention his younger sister was attracting from the male passengers meant he worried unless she was in the company of either his mother or Marguerite.

Soon after Geoffrey was settled into his own cabin, he was introduced to Juanita Perez, his mother's replacement maid, who he guessed was no more than twenty. She was an attractive young woman with an engaging smile, her dark hair plaited and coiled neatly at her neck.

"I quite like the look of this Perez woman," Geoffrey admitted to his elder sister.

"Me too. I only wish I had not been obliged to engage Agnes Hulme as well. Fortunately, her services will no longer be required once we dock in Apalla," Marguerite replied.

"And that could be the longest three and a half days in history," Geoffrey grumbled, pulling down the brim on his panama hat against the reflected glare of the sun. "How on earth do the locals manage to keep working when the sun is so strong?" He paused at the sight of Agnes Hulme approaching.

At a distance the maid seemed much more presentable than she'd appeared at the opera but only until her serviceable skirt caught on a deckchair, briefly exposing her red stockings and pair of scuffed boots.

"Where are you going?" his sister asked, as Geoffrey took his leave.

"I need to practise a new composition. I am not comfortable with it." He checked the time on his pocket watch. "If I go now, I can meet up with you all in the dining room by seven."

Although Juanita Perez attended his mother in a caring and respectful manner, the drawback was her lack of understanding of the English language. This was a defect that Agnes Hulme took advantage of by stepping in to interpret whenever possible.

On the second day, as Geoffrey was about to join Marguerite on deck, he overheard Agnes in conversation with his elder sister, saying that the local girl was sly and ought not to be allowed access to Lady Claudia's valuables.

"I am sure you are mistaken, Miss Hulme. Juanita appears to be most trustworthy. Mother is very happy with her services, as too is my younger sister."

"Please forgive me, milady, if I disagree. I caught Perez going through Lady Claudia's Gladstone bag, where her jewellery is kept, when I came into the cabin to collect a fan for her ladyship."

"That is an odd request, Miss Hulme. Mother never uses a fan until the evening but there is no need for any concern regarding Miss Perez. I was with Mother when she asked her to collect her pills."

"Pills, milady?"

"The ones prescribed by Dr Beresford. They are kept in the bag you mentioned," Marguerite said. Just then, Agnes noticed Geoffrey and retreated quickly along the deck.

"I say, Maggs, what is this?" he asked as she tried to close her journal.

"It is nothing… just a rough sketch."

"Rubbish. This is Archie Westbrook. I would recognise that enquiring smile anywhere." Geoffrey examined the image in more detail. "How on earth did you capture that look so perfectly without getting him to do a sitting?"

"It just happens sometimes," she said modestly.

"But a relative stranger… I guess you must have studied him quite a bit to reproduce such a lifelike image. So… can I assume then that you rather like him?"

"I do, but not in the way you are implying. This drawing was never intended for me, but for Lady Harriet in appreciation of our stay on the plantation."

"Then why did you not give it to her?"

"You have seen the marvellous artwork she has on display. I changed my mind in case she might be offended by the gift of a simple drawing after all her kindness."

"What planet are you on? This is far better than anything I saw at the plantation," he said with exasperation, wondering how anyone could imagine that a doting grandmother like Harriet Drummond would not have treasured such a perfect likeness of her only grandson.

"Sadly the problem I have now is that I cannot leave this in the journal with my other drawings; it would not be appropriate when I hand these sketches over to Violet Dobson," she said, carefully detaching the page.

"You can't throw that away!" Geoffrey protested, half hoping that she might offer it to him as a keepsake. "What are you going to do with it now?" he asked, watching the paper flutter in the breeze.

"Put it into a portfolio when I go down to my cabin."

"Better still… why not give it to me? I can keep it safe with all my sheet music." He snatched the page from her hand before she had chance to object. "It will be much safer there than anywhere else until we get back to England."

"Well do not forget where you put it. I know how disorganised you are."

"Never with my compositions. Archie will be perfectly safe with them," Geoffrey said, setting off for his cabin before she could change her mind.

Although on departure his mother had appeared to be in good spirits, her mood had rapidly deteriorated and she had taken to her cabin by the late afternoon with a severe migraine, requesting that only Juanita attend her. However, to Geoffrey's relief she made a brief appearance at dinner in the Grand Salon on their second day at sea, although this did little to reassure her anxious family that she was feeling better.

"Mother looked very pale this evening," Geoffrey observed, toying with his food.

"You know how these attacks affect her. She was pale, admittedly, but then Mother often is. She was perfectly dressed and there was not a single person in this room that did not see Mother join us," Rosamund said.

"And that is it, is it? Mother must be feeling better because everyone in the room noticed her? Every man's eyes were on you too, if you bothered to look," Geoffrey scoffed.

"Actually I did but I chose not to notice any of them. They only focus their attention on me because I am young. I do not have the elegance Mother has."

"Then why assume she is feeling better?"

"Because if you had any sense in that music-fuddled head of yours, you would have noticed Grandmama's sapphire earrings; Mother was wearing them tonight."

"Oh those old things. Of course I saw them, who could miss those dangling from her ears!" Geoffrey complained, secretly relieved that his sister thought their mother had recovered.

As the *Lugansa* surged along the coastal route on the third day, the cooling breeze and light ocean spray offered welcome relief for the travellers. Geoffrey made his way to the shop on the second-class deck to enquire after a waxed bag, telling himself it was to protect his portfolio of sheet music when in fact it was more a case of preserving the recently acquired image.

Once the bag was in his possession, he made his way down to the cabin but, as he passed his mother's door, he noticed it had been left ajar and he went inside to discover a tearful Juanita repairing a nasty tear in one of Lady Claudia's evening gowns.

"What on earth is the matter?" Geoffrey asked.

"My lady, she… she think it me. I no do this bad thing," she said, clearly distressed.

"How did this happen?" he asked, examining the tear. "There must be a perfectly reasonable explanation."

"Aganesse, it she make bad, no me," the maid said, miming the opening of drawers before continuing with her neat sewing.

"Agnes Hulme, is she responsible for this?"

"Si, señor. Please, you no say I speaking you?" She crossed herself nervously.

"Well, if that is what you want but if anything else happens, you must promise to tell me immediately."

"Si señor, gracias."

On the morning of the fourth day, the humidity on deck had become almost intolerable. The *Lugansa* had slowed its speed to navigate a safe passage along the rocky coastline, narrowly avoiding a collision with a barque sailing under full rigging dangerously close to the liner.

"There is something magnificent about the old way of sailing, don't you think?" Geoffrey mused.

"They are very beautiful under full sail but I for one, am relieved that we did not sail here on a ship like that," Marguerite said.

"It would not have been much fun in that storm we came through, that is for sure." He was wondering again what type of vessel Archie might have sailed on. It would be some time yet before he reached Liverpool and sailed for Ireland.

"Any information on how long the *Lugansa* will be docked in Apalla before it sails for home?"

"Approximately three days."

"Three days? What are we supposed to do if Father is not there either?"

"He will be there to meet us, if only to see Rose again. You know how he dotes on her. Besides, if we miss that departure there will be others sailing for England."

"Then let us hope for one that is also equipped with this new-fangled air conditioning," Geoffrey said, peering over the rail on to the lower deck with interest. "I thought Hulme was asked to pack Mother's things this afternoon, in preparation for tomorrow?"

"That is what I understood. Why?" Marguerite asked, joining him at the rail.

On the lower deck, Agnes Hulme was deep in furtive conversation with the first mate and a swarthy gentleman wearing a white linen suit, who was examining the glittering contents of a handkerchief the maid held out.

"What the devil is that woman up to?" Geoffrey whispered, as she took the items back from the man and slid them away in her skirt pocket.

"It is none of our concern who Agnes gets involved with."

"It is until tomorrow. She is being paid to assist Mother with packing and not for hanging around like some common tart with that brute of a first mate and his companion."

"This conversation is making me very uncomfortable, Geoffrey. We should go and see if Juanita is attending to Mother."

"It will not need two of us. Anyway, I need to round up that Beresford chap again. Mother is suffering with too many of these beastly migraines and I need some answers."

"Dr Beresford would not be allowed to tell you anything, Geoffrey; only Mother can do that."

"I will take my chances and try anyway. Mother has not been herself in months, and that was before deciding on this crackpot scheme." Geoffrey removed his collar stud and opened the top button of his shirt. "Before you say anything, I am fully aware this is inappropriate but if I keep this blasted collar on any longer, I swear I will pass out from the heat!"

"This awful climate cannot be helping Mother either. Maybe that is what is affecting her."

"Whatever it is, as soon as we get home she must be persuaded to consult a specialist in London about these migraines. It may be her eyesight; she could need spectacles," he said.

"Maybe. If you do speak with Dr Beresford today, could you ask if Mother has enough painkillers to last for the voyage home?"

By evening, the dense forestation on the coastline had misted over in a heavy downpour, which cleared the deck of all but the more seasoned travellers. By mid-morning the next day, although the rain had stopped, a dank heavy mist almost obliterated the busy port of Apalla as a fleet of rusting tugs manoeuvred the gigantic liner into the dock. From Geoffrey's vantage point on the upper deck as the *Lugansa* was towed towards its berth, he could see teeming activity as men and boys swarmed like ants around the docked vessels.

Moored at one of the many cargo docks was a steamer loaded with caged animals and exotic birds crated for export. Other ships were stacked with recently felled hardwoods. A smaller vessel was bristling with unrecognisable plants that were in the process of being lowered into the hold. There were sacks of coffee and cacao beans stacked up on the dock waiting to be hoisted aboard, while barrels of rubber and bales of cotton swung in mid-air from cranes.

With hats swathed in veils of muslin against the hordes of mosquitoes, Lady Claudia and Rosamund disembarked down the gangway with Geoffrey following behind, supporting his hesitant elder sister by the arm. There was no sign of the half-forgotten features of his absentee father, or even anyone that resembled him.

When Geoffrey had last laid eyes on his father in England, it had been five days after his fourteenth birthday, "as gawky as a streak of pump-water," as his mother had laughingly called him. Now he was determined to look his father in the eye as a presentable young gentleman of eighteen, a choice he was already coming to regret as the starched, restrictive wing collar and bow tie he had selected made breathing almost impossible and chafed his sweating neck whenever he turned his head. He was convinced that if they didn't get a move on he would vomit from the nauseating stench emanating from a nearby steamer that was being loaded with huge bundles of animal hides and pelts. From the piles of caiman hides, the hollow eye sockets in the flattened heads seemed to be focused on the passing liner. Geoffrey longed to return to the tranquil, cooling dales of his beloved Derbyshire.

Even inside the once-grand waiting hall there was little relief from the oppressive heat. Two overhead fans creaked and juddered menacingly above them and, as his mother's veil lifted in the downward draught, he became suddenly aware of just how ill she was, her features showing increasing distress as fruitlessly she scrutinised the throng for any sign of her husband.

"Father is not here again, is he?" Geoffrey declared vehemently, taking his mother firmly by the arm. "Since we cannot stay on the liner until it sails for England, we must get you into a decent hotel, Mother. You cannot wait here in this insufferable heat if Father can't even be bothered to turn up."

"Papa would not be so cruel as to keep us waiting for him again, Jeffy," Rosamund said, looking around with growing desperation.

"I am sure your father would be here to meet us if he could," Lady Claudia said in a weak voice.

"And why is that? Because of how he might benefit from the divorce settlement, or because his darling Rose came all this distance to see him?" Geoffrey fumed, pulling off his bow tie with a firm tug and releasing the stud on his collar.

"Geoffrey, apologise to your sister. Your father would have wanted to greet all of his children today," Lady Claudia said, taking hold of Marguerite's arm for support. "And please re-button your shirt, Geoffrey. I cannot have you arrive at the hotel half dressed."

"If you insist, Mother... and I am sorry, Rose. There... I have apologised and I will fasten up my collar but not until we set off for the hotel, otherwise I will surely be dead from asphyxiation. If Father does arrive, then he will have to see me in a state of undress."

"Very well, Geoffrey, if you insist but now I must locate our shipping agent. Once our luggage has been accounted for, the gentleman can arrange transport to an appropriate hotel," Lady Claudia said firmly.

"Father might not have arrived in Apalla yet," Marguerite observed.

"Well he damned well should be here. It was his decision to meet in this frightful dump, not ours!" Geoffrey exclaimed, ready to confront his father eye to eye on a number of issues. "We cannot stay cooped up here on the off-chance Father or some shipping agent will show up. At this rate, we could be waiting until midnight." He was convinced that he would take great pleasure in breaking a second nose on this eventful trip.

"We should not stay here a moment longer than necessary, Mother. The heat is unbearable," Marguerite agreed.

When the shipping agent finally appeared, standing a head taller than most of the crowd and holding up a board with the family name written on it, Lady Claudia was preoccupied with searching among the baggage piled up on a cart beside them.

"I cannot see your Gladstone bag, Mother. Are you sure it was not sent on ahead with the other luggage?" Geoffrey asked, having gone through the pile systematically.

"It was most definitely not. I purposely asked Miss Hulme to make sure the bag travelled with me." She checked her hat and straightened her gown as the young man came towards her, removing his own hat in deference before offering her an official document of identification.

"Emile de Costa, milady, your authorised shipping agent. I have been engaged by the express instruction of a Mr Henry Strickland of Pernambuco. He has been most precise with his instructions for your stay here. Might I also be allowed to enquire if you are unwell, milady?" he asked with some concern.

"It is nothing more than a mild headache, Señor de Costa, due to this oppressive heat."

"Then I should arrange transportation to the hotel immediately."

"Before we go, do you have news of my husband's whereabouts?"

"In the communication I received two days ago, his lordship reassured me that he would arrive here no later than yesterday. Unfortunately, as you can see, he has not arrived yet and there has been no further communication."

"Then what the devil are we supposed to do now?" Geoffrey grumbled. "Wait here indefinitely and hope he will suddenly appear? What we need to know is where he is now." He assisted his mother to a bench.

"That is a question I cannot answer, Sir Geoffrey. When the note was delivered to my office, the writing was barely legible."

"Surely you questioned whoever delivered it."

"The note was deposited in the mailbox overnight and I was unable to interview anyone. Communication from remote regions can be very unpredictable. As I am sure you will appreciate, there can be many unforeseen difficulties which might delay a traveller unused to the treacherous currents of the rivers and the many dangers concealed within the banks." His assertive response silenced Geoffrey, and he was preparing to take his leave when Lady Claudia intervened.

"It is imperative that I locate a missing Gladstone bag before we leave here, Señor de Costa." She rested a gloved hand on his arm. "There are some important documents inside for my husband to sign. Without them, our journey to South America will have been wasted."

"Then allow me to put your mind at ease, milady. Because of this intemperate climate and the importance of these papers, Mr Strickland has taken the precaution of sending duplicates. They arrived here by steam packet two days ago." He removed a set of papers from a worn leather satchel for her to examine.

"We cannot know for certain that it is lost, Mother. All we know is that it is not here with the other baggage," Geoffrey said.

"Then allow me to make enquiries immediately, Sir Geoffrey," said the agent, hailing a porter.

"Before you do that, de Costa, maybe this woman can help," Geoffrey said, as Agnes Hulme appeared through the crowd, empty-handed. "She may have some knowledge of the missing Gladstone."

The maid insisted the bag had been dispatched from the *Lugansa* with the other luggage but when Juanita Perez was sent to search their cabins, Agnes Hulme needed no persuasion to follow her immediately.

During the long wait that followed, Emile de Costa arranged for two porters to load their luggage onto a cart in preparation for departure. He also ordered a pitcher of cool lemonade to be brought to them, just as Juanita reappeared, clasping the Gladstone bag tightly against her.

"Should I get your pills, Mother?" Marguerite asked, reaching for the bag.

"Not until we reach the hotel," Lady Claudia replied, clearly distracted by the maid's attempts to cover up marks on her arms. "What on earth have you done, child?" she asked but, instead of answering, the maid simply handed Marguerite the bag.

"Where did you find it, Juanita, in the cabin?"

"No, señorita. Estar es con mal hombre."

"The señorita is saying that some man had it," Emile de Costa intervened.

"What was this man doing with it?" Marguerite insisted.

"Estar es no claro, he... el amor – con la inmodesto mujer... Aganesse," she said tearfully, which made no sense to any of them until the shipping agent interpreted that she had seen this man many times during the voyage in the company of Agnes Hulme.

"Was this Mr O'Brian, the first mate?" Marguerite asked and, although she had addressed her question to the shipping agent, the maid responded.

"Si, señorita," she answered hesitantly, nursing her bruised wrist.

"Whatever have you done? Did you fall?" Marguerite asked, examining the injuries. It was clear the maid was unhappy at being unable to give a full explanation, so she asked Emile de Costa to interpret.

"It appears that when Señorita Perez saw the bag, this maid – Agnes Hulme – and her male companion refused to hand it over."

"But she has it now? How did Juanita get it?" Marguerite asked.

"She pretended to leave but crept back inside when she heard them arguing and tried to get away without being seen. The bruises came from struggling with Agnes Hulme, who saw her."

"How dare that woman behave in such a manner?" Marguerite scrutinised the crowd for any sign of the absent maid. "She will definitely come back, since she has not been paid for her recent employment."

"You can forget unpaid wages," Geoffrey said "That baggage approached me earlier about what she was owed, so I paid her then. At least Mother has the bag again and I, for one, am glad to see the back of the woman." Picking up the bag, he noticed that it was more scuffed than he remembered and heavier than he had expected.

The Empress Hotel had the faded elegance of a bygone era. A spacious suite of rooms had been reserved for Lady Claudia overlooking the gardens at the rear, while Geoffrey and his sisters had rooms that, although smaller, were comfortable and airy.

Another welcome surprise was the private sitting room the agent had arranged for the family's use. This was a glazed, L-shaped veranda with a series of French windows. One section had a spectacular view over the gardens and the mountainous region beyond, a space that was well furnished with a comfortable seating area and several bookcases.

The second area, which angled around the corner, had an uninterrupted view over the ocean providing a more restful space, if required, that could be sectioned off with folding tapestry screens. Here the furnishings were of cane and bamboo, some of the latter inlaid with mother of pearl.

After Geoffrey had thanked de Costa for arranging their accommodation in such a fine hotel, he returned to his own room where he had already unpacked the violin. He was just about to scribble down a few bars of a new passage of music when his elder sister barged in.

"Do you ever knock?" Geoffrey snapped, waving a blank sheet of music paper in her face. "I had the perfect intro in my head before you came barging in!"

"I apologise but this is more important. You need to accompany me to Mother's apartment immediately."

His mother's apartment was furnished in pale, painted wood. There was a slight breeze billowing through the light folds of pale-silk drapery, partially drawn to cover the open French windows. Although it was impossible to distinguish his mother's features clearly in the subdued light, it was apparent that she was in considerable distress.

"This Gladstone bag is not mine, Geoffrey, it belongs to someone else," Lady Claudia said.

"That cannot be… it never left my side from the moment we left the dock," Geoffrey said, examining the label where his mother's name had been clearly written.

"There has been a mix-up. Just look at the contents. None of my red pills are there, not one."

"I wrote all the labels out myself and this is most definitely my writing," Marguerite said, examining the label again before unclipping the bag. "Oh my giddy aunt…?" she said with disgust, emptying out a pile of soiled male underwear, grimy vests and unwashed socks.

"Do you need to do that?" Geoffrey complained. "We can all see the contents are not Mother's."

"I am not doing this for pleasure, I can assure you. I am simply trying to establish who owned this. There may be something in here with a name on it and, once I have that, this bag can be returned to its rightful owner in exchange for Mother's."

Also crammed amongst the clothing was a brass telescope, a pair of red stockings clearly in need of darning, a pair of women's shoes, one missing a heel, a worn paperback romance, three empty ring boxes and Lady Claudia's jewellery case.

"Mother… do you have Grandmama's sapphires with you?" Marguerite asked.

"I have the earrings," she said with a slight movement of her head, the dangling pendants glinting reassurance in the half-light. "The necklace was in its case, inside the Gladstone."

"This one?" Marguerite asked, opening the case for her inspection.

"What I fail to understand is why anything of mine would be in someone else's bag," Lady Claudia said, examining it more closely. "This is not the case for Mother's sapphires. My pearl choker with the diamond clasp belonged in here. I packed it myself yesterday."

"And these empty ring boxes, do you recognise these?" Geoffrey asked.

"Yes I do, but how could this have happened? Only Juanita had access to where my jewellery was kept."

"You seem to be forgetting Agnes Hulme," Geoffrey said, taking a pencil from his pocket to prod through the clothing for any clues.

"Possibly, but I cannot be certain. Only Juanita was allowed access."

"I think this evidence is enough to incriminate that Hulme woman," Geoffrey said, lifting the red stocking from the pile as he might have done with a deadly snake. He examined the shoe with the missing heel, which he was convinced had ended up inside his shattered violin. "She needs to be horsewhipped."

When the apparent mix-up with the luggage was explained to the agent, Emile de Costa's immediate suggestion of involving the police was rejected by Lady Claudia.

"It is imperative, milady, that we establish exactly what items are missing, and present a detailed report of this to the policía," de Costa insisted.

"The police must not become involved, Señor de Costa. It might be harmful to Juanita's reputation by association and I cannot allow that."

"Please, Mother, you must allow Señor de Costa to help retrieve the bag and the missing jewellery. Those heirlooms have been in our family for generations," Marguerite urged.

"If the policía are not to be involved, milady, there is very little I can do to trace them. Without help from the authorities, my hands are tied."

"There must be another way, señor... there has to be. There are possessions in my own Gladstone bag that I could not bear to lose, more so than any jewellery," Lady Claudia said.

"What could be more precious than Grandmama's sapphires, Mother?" Marguerite asked.

"Treasured memories that I keep in a tin box; I must have every one of those items returned at all costs."

"And those red pills, Mother, you cannot be without those," Geoffrey said.

"I do have an alternative that Dr Beresford entrusted to me prior to our departure, in case of an emergency," Marguerite said, rummaging through her own capacious bag and handing two white pills to her mother with a glass of water.

"All crew members are required to leave their contact details with the company office," da Costa suggested. "I can access that information within my official capacity. If this woman is no longer with her companion, he may know where to contact her."

The shipping agent did not return until late the following morning.

"Although I have the information you require, Sir Geoffrey, the address I have is in a run-down neighbourhood into which I would not advise a young gentleman such as yourself to venture unaccompanied," he warned.

"My brother will not be alone, Señor de Costa. I fully intend to accompany him," Marguerite said firmly.

"You misunderstand, milady. This is an area frequented by rogues and villains of the worst kind. If you both go that will double the need for protection."

"I am sure that a firearm will protect us from any attack, señor," Marguerite reassured him.

"I do not own a gun, let alone know how to use one!" Geoffrey exclaimed, thinking the intense heat must have addled his sister's brain.

"Just because I am a woman does not mean I have not anticipated arriving on this vast continent without adequate protection," Marguerite said, removing a service revolver from her bag.

"Oh my God… you can actually shoot that thing?" cried Geoffrey.

182

"You are full of surprises, milady," de Costa smiled. "However, I would be most obliged if you would allow me to engage a reliable escort who is familiar with this area, a man well versed in the art of finding routes that will avoid any possible confrontations. I will continue looking into your father's whereabouts. I have many people assisting me with this."

"Then let us hope they can be quick about it. The *Lugansa* is due to sail for England in two days and we would like to be safely on board by then," Geoffrey said as the agent took his leave. He had barely closed the door behind him when Geoffrey's interrogation of his sister began.

"I overheard Mother saying at the plantation that you were able to shoot but now you own up to carrying a revolver around? What if someone had accidently barged into you at dinner and the damned thing went off? You could have shot Mother!"

"Not with the safety catch on. I am not an idiot, Geoffrey."

"And you would really fire that thing if you had to?"

"I can hit any target I choose."

"I do not believe that for a second. To become as proficient as you claim would take years of practice. No one is that good, not even that self-opinionated Isabella Moreno."

"Very well, if you want the whole truth then I will tell you," she said firmly, and he could see by the way her eyes narrowed that she was going to do just that.

"Go on. I am listening."

"I had my first lesson four years ago. Since then I have been practising three times a week."

"Four years ago? How could you have kept it secret for so long without the estate manager finding out? No one could get away with that, no one. He knows everything that goes on."

"I did not have to 'get away' with anything," she said. It was the manager's son Giles who had taught her through an agreement that, if his father did not mention anything to their mother, then she would keep quiet about finding Giles poaching out of season.

"You actually blackmailed him?" Geoffrey asked, barely able to contain his growing admiration for his sister's swashbuckling attitude. "But why take up a firearm in the first place? It is so unlike you."

"I did it for protection."

"Why would you need protection, in Ashbourne of all places? Was it because Father left for South America?"

"Quite the opposite. I vowed if he ever laid a hand on Mother again, I would kill him where he stood."

"What...? You were planning to shoot Father?"

"Do you remember when Mother fractured her skull and broke her arm after she supposedly tripped and fell down the stairs?"

"How could I forget, when she was rushed to hospital in the ambulance."

"And do you have any idea how that accident happened?"

"Well yes, she missed her footing on the stairs. Even Rose remembers that. Mother was in a coma for three whole days. How could either of us forget that night?"

"Well I can assure you that was no accident. I was there, Geoffrey. I saw him beating Mother on the landing. I was too far away to stop him from pushing her backwards down the stairs. That is why she sustained such dreadful injuries and that is why I intend to kill the swine if ever he tries anything like that again."

To begin with, what his sister was saying seemed so outrageous that it could not be true. But lying was something she never did and now everything began to make sense. The way his father had simply taken off four years earlier, only two days after his wife came out of the coma, saying his research project was of immense importance. On the following day he had caught the train to Liverpool, leaving his wife in a life-threatening condition at the Derby Royal Infirmary.

184

Until that moment, Geoffrey had never suspected how much his elder sister must have loathed their father. It was shocking to hear her swear for the first time in his life, if understandable but, the fact that his normally placid and artistic sister could shoot someone still had him reeling. Marguerite had always lived by a strict moral code and was surely much too sensible and God-fearing for that to ever change.

"I could never work out until now how Father could be so uncaring as to leave Mother in that semi-comatose state," Geoffrey said.

"It was probably to avoid being hanged had she died from her injuries."

"What baffles me is how he managed to get posted to South America, of all places, so soon after Mother recovered. I know he was supposedly well regarded in his department but, even so, it was all too convenient if you ask me, having this so-called research work to escape to."

"Not if you consider he worked for Mr King at the Hospital for Tropical Diseases. All he had to do was to contact his scheming wife and everything would have been arranged. Her husband must have been an old fool, not knowing that she had been Father's mistress for years?"

"WHAT! Surely that cannot be true?"

"You saw how the woman behaved before we set off, acting as if she owned the estate."

"But how could Father get away with it for so long? Mother is not stupid. She must have guessed." Geoffrey had long suspected his father of being unfaithful and, if he had been carrying on with this former Gaiety Girl, then it made sense why he chose to work in London. It also explained the arguments that followed long into the night after he returned home, short of money.

"I am sure Mother knew. That is probably what started the row the night he attacked her."

Considering the physical abuse his sister had witnessed, he was surprised she had been able to keep the secret from him until now. On reflection, however, his father had never been kind to Marguerite, not in the way he way he had been with Rosamund, barely acknowledging her remarkable artistic talent. It was as if Lord Oliver had been trapped into a loveless marriage and it was his sister's fault since she had been born in the first year of their union.

An hour later, Geoffrey and Marguerite set off in a Victoria carriage under the protection of Omar, a colossus of a man who sat up front with the coachman. They soon entered a squalid area of the town, rattling along ever-narrowing cobbled streets strung across with washing lines. While some of these were hung with laundry, others were drying bunches of tobacco leaves, hanging in stark contrast against the white sheets.

Turning into a street barely wide enough for the carriage to pass through, the wheels rumbled over what few cobbles hadn't been buried beneath years of compressed horse dung. Here a gang of urchins appeared like swarming ants from dingy alleys between the buildings, yelling and gesturing obscenities at the passengers, pelting the carriage with rotten fruit and even the decomposing body of a cat as the driver whipped the horses into a canter. The maze of narrow streets now widened out into a square where the carriage rumbled to a stop before what had once been an impressive dwelling, now converted into a boarding establishment.

Once inside, Omar began questioning the brute of a concierge in a language that was unrecognisable to either Geoffrey or his sister. The hulking figure emerged from behind his desk jangling a bunch of keys and indicated that they should follow him up the creaking stairs to the second-floor landing.

Surrounded by the acrid stench of dried urine and stale beer in the unaccustomed gloom, Geoffrey and his sister waited for the man to fumble with the keys and push open a door with a splintered panel. Inside, the room was not much lighter than the corridor, since little sunlight could penetrate the yellow, grimy window panes. Had they been cleaned, the light would have revealed a well-proportioned space with an imposing fireplace but it would also have highlighted the awful mess left by the tenants.

Against the main wall was an unmade bed and lying on this was the missing Gladstone bag with its lock and clasp shattered.

"What have they taken?" Marguerite asked as Geoffrey opened the bag fully for inspection.

"I have no idea what Mother kept inside here. If you have, then maybe you ought to take a look yourself." He began to empty the contents out on to the crumpled sheets.

"No Geoffrey, you cannot do that!" she cried. "If Mother's pills are inside, we cannot allow them to be contaminated by any of this filth!"

"You are too late," Geoffrey said, looking at the contents he had already emptied out on the soiled bedding.

"Anyone with an ounce of common sense would have known not to do that," Marguerite complained, pressing a handkerchief against her nose and using her free hand to open a jewellery case. "This is the one that contained Grandmama's sapphire necklace. There is nothing inside."

"They must have sold it," Geoffrey said, trying to push up one of the sash windows. "I swear if I do not get one of these open soon we will both choke to death." He jolted it open and returned to the bed. "I cannot see any of Mother's red pills here."

"We must keep looking, Geoffrey and get away from here before they come back."

"Mother's documents are not here either. What the hell has she done with them?" Geoffrey got down on all fours to look under the bed. Beside a brimming chamber pot he found what remained of the paperwork, torn, stained and soggy. "Ugh! I swear if I ever see the Hulme woman again I will swing for her gladly. Either she or that bloody first mate have been using Mother's documents to wipe their backsides!"

"Forget them, Geoffrey. Thankfully the shipping agent brought duplicates. Her pills are our priority."

"The only medical stuff I could find is this," Geoffrey said, offering her an empty pillbox with no lid.

"Then the red pills must be here somewhere. We cannot leave without them." She replaced the items they had found into the Gladstone bag, before starting on an unproductive search through every drawer and surface in the room.

"What the hell have they done with them?" Geoffrey said, getting down on his knees to make another search under the bed. Just as he was about to crawl back out again, he spotted the pillbox lid, and close by a scattering of red dots near the skirting board.

"There are maybe a dozen or so under here," he said, carefully gathering them up. "If there is anything I should know about Mother's illness, then please tell me," he continued, handing over the pills.

"I cannot... Mother made me promise not to repeat the conversation I overheard between her and Dr Beresford. She does not want you or Rosamund to worry."

"Well I can assure you it is too late for that and I swear Rose will not hear anything from me."

"Mother has a brain tumour. It was diagnosed by a specialist in Harley Street four months ago. That is why she was so insistent on making this trip to get her affairs in order." Marguerite held on to the headboard for support.

"Mother cannot die!" Geoffrey shouted. "What are these red pills? You must know if anyone does."

"Morphine, to help ease the pain and it is imperative that we find as many of them as we can."

"Then we carry on looking," Geoffrey said, back on his hands and knees to search every inch of the floor where he found three more of the pills buried in piles of fluff.

After half an hour of searching the quantity of pills still only half filled the box but they decided it would be fruitless to carry on.

While repacking his mother's items in the bag, Geoffrey unwrapped a fine linen cloth from around a battered biscuit tin. Opening it, he found a bundle of letters. Lady Claudia's name was written clearly on the envelopes in a bold, boyish hand, and the numerous ink smudges only made them more endearing.

Beneath the letters were the treasured tortoiseshell hair combs and rattling loose at the bottom of the tin he found a plain silver locket threaded onto a fine gold chain. In one side of the locket there were locks of hair of two different shades, lovingly plaited together. On the opposite side was an inscription, etched into the metal by a meticulous hand: *For ever one love.*

As he was returning the pack of letters to the box, a single photograph became dislodged and fell onto the bed. It showed two young people who had clearly just been swimming. The girl, aged between twelve and thirteen and undoubtedly his mother, was laughing at a wild-looking boy, perhaps a year or so older. He was kneeling beside her and had not had time to turn and face the camera before the self-timer went off. Clearly displayed on the upper section of the boy's naked spine was a birthmark resembling a flying spirit, positioned centrally between his shoulder blades and identical to the mark Geoffrey had seen on Archie Westbrook's back on the night of the earthquake.

Absorbed by the images in the photograph, neither of them heard a man stealthily entering the room.

"Tu estar Inglesa?" he challenged them aggressively.

"If you are enquiring if we are English, sir, then yes we are," Marguerite replied, stepping firmly between the man and her brother.

"Then might I ask, madam, who you are and what purpose you and your son have in breaking into this private apartment?"

"Firstly, the gentleman you are referring to is my brother and we are well within our rights to be here," she retorted.

"Not in this apartment, madam," he said. His tight shirt, besmirched with food stains, barely stayed buttoned over his bulging stomach and his crumpled linen suit was equally dirty.

"Then I might well ask you the same question. Who are you?"

"I am Enrique Sabatini, the proprietor of this establishment and I insist you tell me why you are here before I call in the policía." He glared at them with bullfrog eyes.

"Actually that would suit us both admirably," said Geoffrey. We are perfectly entitled to be here to retrieve our stolen property." Marguerite offered up the empty jewellery case. "We need no permission to search for what is rightfully ours, Sabatini," he continued, now remembering exactly where he had seen the man in the linen suit before.

"I must insist that you remove nothing from the premises without my tenant's approval, otherwise I will summon my security guards," Sabatini responded, sweat spreading noticeably across the taut fabric of his shirt from his armpits.

"Then the police might be interested to learn that you were on board the *Lugansa*, negotiating with Agnes Hulme on the valuation of our mother's jewellery," Geoffrey challenged and knew he'd hit a nerve when Sabatini retreated to the doorway, yelling for assistance.

Geoffrey thrust his head through the open window and called down to Omar. Soon after there was a sound of breaking furniture and a man screaming before their bodyguard entered with blood spattered over his arms and shirt and they left the building with no sign of Sabatini or his men.

The moment they entered his mother's darkened apartment, Geoffrey knew something was wrong. Lady Claudia was groaning with pain, lying fully dressed on the bed, her dark hair loose and her ashen features beaded with sweat.

"Geoffrey and I have retrieved the Gladstone and what we could of the red pills, Mother," Marguerite said, easing her into a more comfortable position before giving her one of the pills with a glass of water.

"Were all the contents still inside?" she asked urgently.

"Sadly Grandmama's sapphire necklace and all of your other jewellery was missing."

"Then I am fortunate I still have the earrings with me."

"The tortoiseshell hair combs you treasure were in there and a tin box with a bundle of letters," Geoffrey said, sitting beside her and taking her hand.

"Do you have the locket?"

"I have it here with the letters."

"Please secure the locket around my neck, Geoffrey," she said, pressing it against her throat once it had been secured. "When my end comes – as it will to us all," she added hastily, "what I ask of you both is for this locket to be around my neck and for the hair combs to hold back my hair. They are more precious to me than anything else I own."

Throughout the next day there was still no communication from their father and, with the *Lugansa* due to sail for England the following morning, Geoffrey was adamant his mother should return to England for the best medical attention.

"Surely there must be some means of communicating with my father, de Costa. I am not prepared to wait here forever on the off chance he will show up. It is imperative we get her ladyship aboard that liner before it sails tomorrow." He and Marguerite had received the shipping agent in the private sitting room where there was less chance of being disturbed or overheard. Marguerite sat in one of the cane chairs to give her a clear view of anyone approaching along the corridor, should their mother decide to join them earlier than arranged.

"You do realise there is no way Mother will be talked into leaving here until those papers have been signed, Geoffrey," Marguerite said.

"But she must go back to England immediately."

"I fully appreciate the distress caused by this delay, Sir Geoffrey," said the agent, "and would assist you in any possible way but, as there has been no communication from your father, nor any information from when the previous contact was made, my hands are tied."

"So what are the options if we cannot make the crossing tomorrow? When is the next liner due to sail for England?" Geoffrey asked.

"I have been informed there will not be another crossing from this port for six weeks. The only alternative would be to return to Pernambuco and wait out the time there."

"Surely other liners will be making the crossing sooner than that?" Marguerite said.

"Unfortunately not. Three passenger vessels are reported missing during the storm that your family experienced. Only ocean liners such as the *Lugansa* will be sailing that route until this unusually severe hurricane season is over."

"This is the devil of a predicament, de Costa, unless I can persuade Mother to agree to what I have in mind," Geoffrey said.

"What idea is that?" Marguerite asked.

"That I go up the river on my own and force that... that wicked bastard to sign the papers myself!" Geoffrey snapped.

"If Señor de Costa has no clue where Father is, how could anyone as inexperienced as you expect to find him on your own?"

"I could damned well try. Mother cannot miss the crossing tomorrow. All I need is a map and a reliable guide," he said through gritted teeth.

"Geoffrey, you are barely eighteen. If you were older and had more experience then perhaps you might have a chance. Most of the tributaries of the Amazon are unmarked on the charts and the forest goes on for ever, with no roads to speak of, only rivers."

"I would take a map," Geoffrey said, with rather more bravado than he was actually feeling. He caught himself wishing he could be more like Archie Westbrook.

"Be practical, Geoffrey. The only time you went exploring on your own, you got lost in the Dales. You had a map then."

"So what, I was only ten. If you lend me that book Violet Dobson gave you, then I should be all right," Geoffrey persisted.

"It is an admirable gesture but Mother would never agree."

"You cannot know that; not for sure," Geoffrey said, turning abruptly as Rosamund folded back the screen. She and their mother had clearly been seated there for some time.

"Having inadvertently overheard your conversation, I wholeheartedly agree with your sister, Geoffrey," Lady Claudia announced. "If anyone is to venture upriver to locate him it should be me and no one else. Only I can make him fully understand that he will never get control of all of my father's estates in the event of my death. Your father will only get one of my choosing, not his."

"If only Archie were here with us, he would know exactly what to do and where to look," Rosamund said.

"But he is not here, is he?" Geoffrey retorted.

Although he would only have admitted under torture that she was right, he knew all too well that Archie was a natural leader and, in truth, he would have readily followed the Irishman deep into any part of the rainforest if he'd been asked. As it was, it was now down to him.

"I love you dearly for your proposal, Geoffrey, except I must insist that all three of you return to England. It is my intention to ask Mr de Costa to make the appropriate reservation on the *Lugansa*," Lady Claudia said.

"The girls can go back if they like but without me. I am staying with you, Mother, whether you like it or not."

"Geoffrey, see reason. Your sisters cannot travel back unchaperoned. It is your responsibility to accompany them."

"Not in the least. De Costa can arrange for a suitable chaperone, because I have no intention of leaving your side for one second if you propose sailing off up the Amazon unaccompanied. Lord knows what dangers are lurking out there."

"Milady, please reconsider this decision. I have no idea where your husband might be located," the agent pleaded.

"My husband is a creature of habit. Whatever route he took four years ago he would be travelling back the same way. All that I ask is that you discover exactly what that was. There must be a record of his movements somewhere."

"That is something I have been attempting to achieve from the moment you arrived, milady."

"I may be able to help, señor," Rosamund broke in, speaking for the first time. "I keep all of Papa's letters. He told me everything about what he saw on the journey to his compound."

"You have letters?" Geoffrey asked, barely able to contain his surprise.

"Shall I get them, Mother? They are in my room," Rosamund said, deliberately ignoring her brother.

"Please, darling."

Although he was shocked to discover that his father had been secretly communicating with Rosamund when he hadn't bothered writing to him or to Marguerite, Geoffrey also realised that his sister had been smart enough to bring them with her. All at once, it made the prospect of journeying up the Amazon a little less daunting.

In under half an hour Lord Oliver's first port of call had been established, and both sisters had declared they had no intention of allowing anyone to venture further alone. On reflection, Geoffrey was relieved there would be two people in the group who could handle a loaded weapon, although the prospect of having Rosamund tagging along was less appealing.

"I do not think you should allow Rose to be included, Mother. It is not safe."

"I refuse to be left behind like a piece of unwanted baggage, Jeffy, whatever you say. I have as much right to go as either you or Maggie, probably more since you would never have found where Papa is without my help!" she pouted.

Chapter Nine
Anger and Disappointment

The safety of his family was his primary concern. Geoffrey spent the night formulating a plan in a way he thought Archie might have done. Marguerite would be able to take care of herself and their mother as she was armed and able to handle a gun and, with Archie's hunting knife clearly visible in his belt, only an idiot would have the nerve to challenge him. His only problem was Rosamund, as he couldn't protect both her and his mother if they became separated. Since the last attempt to dissuade her hadn't worked, he decided to try another approach on the following morning before they set off for the docks.

After a short conversation, the shipping agent agreed to arrange for Rosamund to stay in a private villa in Apalla, chaperoned by Juanita Perez until the family returned to the port. What Geoffrey had not taken into consideration was his sister's determination not to come down for breakfast that morning and to ride in her mother's carriage with Juanita, leaving Geoffrey no opportunity to offer up this suggestion since he had to travel with his elder sister to the docks.

On their arrival, Emilio de Costa introduced them to their new guide and his uncle, Don Julio Salamerez, impeccably attired, with the exception of a single black leather glove on the left hand. Not only did this look bizarre but it must have been extremely uncomfortable in the sweltering humidity.

It was clear from the agent's distracted attitude and the dark circles under his eyes that there was a problem weighing on his mind and Geoffrey wondered if it might explain his apparent hesitancy about leaving Apalla with them that morning.

Reassuringly, Don Julio had the document satchel slung across his shoulders, enabling Geoffrey to fully appreciate the fine detail of the workmanship. He was particularly fascinated by the zippered compartment inside the satchel, having only seen an illustration of this extraordinary invention in his grandfather's catalogue from the Chicago World's Fair of 1893. He now noticed that the bag had the logo of the World's Columbian Exposition embossed into its leather flap, confirming the satchel was an authentic souvenir of that very event.

It was soon established that Don Salamerez was a well-educated man who spoke and understood the English language well and had manners that were unquestionably correct in every respect towards Geoffrey's mother and sisters. This was a relief as it became clear that Emile de Costa would be accompanying them only as far as the first port of call before he was obliged to return to Apalla and fulfil his responsibilities as an agent of the Trident Fleet.

However, just as the family were about to board the paddle steamer that would carry them upriver, Geoffrey caught sight of a man handing a note to the agent before disappearing into the throng. Once de Costa had scanned the contents, the note was handed to his uncle and they went into an intensely whispered discussion.

It was already late morning and the heat seemed more intense than ever as Geoffrey was finally able to approach his younger sister.

"If you have something to say, then you can get it off your chest as we walk. There will not be any shade until we get on board that frightful-looking boat," Rosamund demanded from beneath an inadequate parasol.

"That is just it, Rose. I do not want you setting foot on this dreadful old tub. I appreciate what you said yesterday, but I hope that now you have had time to think it over you may have changed your mind and, before you reject this proposal out of hand, please hear me out."

"Why should I? I just knew you would try to find another way to leave me behind! Why else do you think I have been avoiding you all morning?" Rosamund snapped.

"You can protest all you like, Rose but I have made arrangements for you to wait here in a private villa with Juanita."

"How dare you do that?" Rosamund retorted, looking at him in amazement.

"How dare I...? Can you not get it into that empty head of yours this is for your own safety and for no other reason?"

"How could you arrange such a thing behind my back when you know I have every intention of going with you?"

"It is for your own good, you idiot. Why the hell will you not listen to me for once?"

"Because you never listen to me... ever. If you did, you would know the reason I will not change my mind is because Mama has been so unwell since we first arrived in this beastly place and she must go back home as soon as possible. If, as you and Maggie both seem to think, Papa will do anything I ask, then I will get him to agree to whatever Mama wants, then we can all go home... together."

"There is no need to be so bloody dramatic, Rose. I cannot protect both you and Mother if we get into any kind of trouble. You would never be able to defend yourself without my help."

"Have you the remotest idea how ridiculous you sound? How could *you* possibly defend my honour, or anyone else's come to that? You are barely a year older than I am. Besides... we will be floating on the water most of the time, so what possible harm can befall us there?"

"Why do you have to be so bloody-minded when I ask you to do something?" Geoffrey asked irritably.

"I do not recall you *asking* me to do anything. Would you change your own plans if I tried to tell you what to do; well, would you?" she demanded in a way she knew would always rile him. "If you think I would agree to being held captive in this dreadful town until you get back, then you can think again."

"Sometimes you can be quite impossible, Rose. Anyone in their right mind would be relieved to avoid this trip and not be so bloody stubborn. The reality is you have never really cared about anyone but yourself and that shallow father of ours. If I were you, I would take those blinkers off for once and see that monster for what he really is."

"That is a beastly thing to say, even for you. I adore Mama, and would never dream of allowing her to travel anywhere without me by her side and certainly not into whatever vile places you imagine might lie ahead. It is true enough that I want to see Papa but not for the idiotic reasons you imagine."

"I am only doing this to protect you, Rose," Geoffrey insisted, gripping her by the wrist before she had any chance to prod him with her parasol.

"Get out of my way, Jeffy, and allow me to board before I bite you. You know I will do it and it will hurt... I promise!"

"You would never dare, not here, where people would see."

"I am not playing games. If you do not let go of my wrist ..." Her nostrils flared and her eyes narrowed and he let go immediately, knowing all too well the rage that would follow had he not.

"Very well, have it your own way but if anything happens, it will be your stupid fault and not mine!" he called after her slight figure as she made her way on to the vessel.

The *La Verde Angel*, a once-grand paddle steamer, was dwarfed by the majesty of the passing *Lugansa* as the liner was towed away from the dock by a fleet of tugs. Geoffrey could only watch it glide effortlessly into the clear water of the vast ocean, cursing his absentee father that he and his family were not now safely on board, bound for England and the tranquil countryside of the Derbyshire Dales.

Emile de Costa had supplied him with a map of the area, which although sketchy in detail had a few names marked and gave Geoffrey some idea of where they were heading, which was along a wide tributary of the main river towards the final destination of Coyacuche, little more than a smudge on the chart. From there the steamer would return to Apalla.

After the luxury of a sleek, air-conditioned ocean liner, the voyage up river on the ageing paddle steamer was far less enjoyable. From its shabby appearance to the general lack of maintenance, the crowded little vessel was a far cry from the immaculate *Lugansa*. What made it worse was that, because of the slower speed, there was very little breeze, which made the heat even more unbearable.

The unidentified grey meat that was served up in the dining salon made the prospect of eating anything on the plate questionable and, once Geoffrey had retired to his cabin he could barely sleep on the unforgiving flock mattress. In the morning he made sure that Don Salamerez was aware of how insufferable the conditions were for his mother and sisters, and their guide quickly arranged for their meals to be served in a private salon provided by the captain. On the second day the riverboat docked for half a day at a port that was not even marked on Geoffrey's map. Here the majority of the passengers disembarked on to a wide, purely functional dockside where two rusting cranes were loading a mountainous collection of barrels on to a cargo steamer.

"What is this place?" Geoffrey asked Juanita, after fruitlessly consulting his map.

"This is Karaka," she said, assisting Lady Claudia into a shady area of the deck as de Costa and his uncle re-embarked. Moments later Don Salamerez began a lengthy, hushed conversation with Lady Claudia.

"What are they loading in those barrels, de Costa?" Geoffrey asked as the shipping agent approached.

"That would be rubber, Sir Geoffrey."

"And what news do you have of my father? Have there been any sightings of him in this place?"

"It appears that his lordship did dock here once, a year ago, on his way upriver, but nothing has been seen or heard of the gentleman since."

"Was there any mention of what he was doing here?"

"From what I understand, he was here to collect a shipment of medical equipment that had been sent out from England and also an amount of essential tinned produce before the start of the rainy season."

"Did they say where he was based? Surely my father would have mentioned something to the dock officials."

"One man I asked gave the impression that Lord Oliver had diverted his return by way of Coyacuche, a place with a very bad reputation, where I would strongly advise against any lady in your party disembarking. If your father is to be found there, Sir Geoffrey, my uncle will most certainly locate the gentleman and return with him."

"And what would we find so shocking in this port, de Costa?"

"Coyacuche is a port frequented by travellers in need of female companionship, which the women of the town are more than willing to supply... for a price," he answered, lowering his voice as Juanita stared questioningly in his direction.

"Then how am I supposed to explain this to Mother? Both she and my sisters are unused to the restrictions on this steamer and will be eager to disembark."

"Unfortunately, Sir Geoffrey, the port of Karaka is where the captain must terminate the journey upriver."

"But what are we supposed to do now? We cannot go back to Apalla, yet this rotting hulk is about to leave us here, high and dry!"

"There are other vessels available, Sir Geoffrey and my uncle is already seeking out the most suitable craft. At this late time in the season, the waters are much too shallow for our paddle steamer to continue. Don Julio will be taking over my duties as your shipping agent and will escort your family beyond this point. I offer my sincere apologies that I am unable to offer my services beyond Karaka. I shall be returning to Apalla on the *La Verde Angel* this afternoon. It will take a minimum of four days to reach Coyacuche and I cannot delay my return a moment longer."

In response to Geoffrey's protestations the shipping agent explained that his sister was in considerable distress and in need of support having received a ransom demand following the disappearance of their youngest brother, a boy of fourteen. On hearing of his departure, Lady Claudia requested that he should allow Juanita to accompany him since, from what she head overheard, her reputation might be in danger if she accompanied them to Coyacuche.

"But Mother," Geoffrey complained, "would it not be more prudent if you allow me to go on ahead with the documents that need signing? It would be much safer for everyone if you and the girls travel back with de Costa here because, if what he says is correct, Don Julio will be capable of getting the information I need to trace Father."

"You do not know your father the way I do Geoffrey… not where wealth or property are involved and I have every intention of making him see reason." It was clear there was nothing Geoffrey could say that would change her mind.

As their belongings were removed from the paddle steamer, Emile de Costa assured them that his uncle fully understood the importance of finding Lord Oliver and knew exactly who to approach in Coyacuche. They had a relative there named Armand, he explained, who had many contacts throughout the area.

The shipping agent pointed out a small cargo boat, only half the size of the steamer, with thick rust encrusted around the rivets above the water line.

"You cannot expect us to go anywhere on that blasted thing!" Geoffrey exclaimed. "What about that other boat over there?" he asked, indicating a much larger and more well-appointed vessel further along the dock.

"This is the only vessel with a shallow enough draught to be capable of reaching Coyacuche until after the rainy season. You must understand, Sir Geoffrey, the depth of this tributary will now be very low in parts, and no responsible captain would risk grounding their vessel."

"But there must be another alternative, de Costa. No one could expect Lady Claudia and my sisters to travel anywhere on that wreck."

"The only alternative I can offer is that you return with me to Apalla. That would be my advice under the circumstances. My uncle will discover the whereabouts of your father and report back to Lady Claudia and your good self to avoid any unnecessary hardship."

"My mother will not change her mind on this issue, de Costa. Not now."

"Then unfortunately, Sir Geoffrey, you have no alternative."

"So if we do agree to travel upriver on this rust-bucket, how long will it take to reach that wretched town?" Geoffrey asked.

"My best estimate would be a five-day journey… as a minimum."

"Five days! Surely to God there must be another alternative," Geoffrey said, barely able to contain his frustration.

"As I have already explained, Sir Geoffrey, there is not."

"One day would be bad enough to consider travelling in this pile of junk, but for my mother and sisters to spend that long, cramped together on that floating disaster would be a nightmare. Therefore please assure me there are suitable cabins available for them?"

"My uncle is already in the process of arranging that with the captain. However, we must bear in mind this vessel is not equipped to cater for passengers of your family's status."

"But what if my father is not there either? How much further up the river does this crate go after Coyacuche?"

"No further than that, Sir Geoffrey. Once there, it will collect a cargo of caiman hides and then return here. That is why I consider it essential that you persuade the Lady Claudia and your sisters to return with me to Apalla."

"However much I would wish that, Mother will not change her mind and both my sisters are determined to accompany her." Geoffrey was beginning to feel more vulnerable than he would have cared to admit.

Juanita bade them a tearful farewell, with the reassurance her services would be required immediately the family returned to Apalla. The maid was escorted by de Costa back on board the paddle steamer, which pulled away from the dock almost immediately.

The antiquated cargo vessel wasn't due to leave for another two days and, as the only decent hotel had a gambling casino on the ground floor, alternative accommodation was hastily arranged for them in an assortment of rooms above a local restaurant.

To begin with the owner offered some resistance to the amount of space they would require, but it soon became clear that Don Salamerez was not a man to be trifled with. Once the negotiations were concluded the alteration in the courtesy shown to Lady Claudia and Geoffrey's sisters was remarkable and the amount of space that was allocated to each of them was nothing short of miraculous, except that the three ladies had to share one bathroom.

Geoffrey was not so fortunate, as his narrow room was situated above the kitchen and furnished with a single bed and a mattress that felt like it had been supplied by the Spanish Inquisition, despite the clean sheets. There was also a faded mahogany chest with one drawer missing a handle and another that stuck badly but the most embarrassing concession was sharing a lime-washed lavatory at the end of a long corridor with the owner and his three sons. Next to this was a small bathroom with no lock or bolt on the door.

On the following morning, although Geoffrey complained loudly, Don Salamerez was clearly concerned only with the comfort of his mother and sisters and Geoffrey realised he must suffer in silence for the next two days.

Because there was no convenient place for him to practise on the violin, Geoffrey used the time to work through a new composition about the spirits of the rainforest and barely had time to put the sheet music away when Rosamund appeared in the doorway.

"For goodness' sake, Jeffy, have you taken root? Mother is waiting in the carriage. If you do not get a move on, you will just have to wait here on your own until we return!"

"What have you done with all your bags, Rose?"

"Don Salamerez has taken care of everything. Our luggage is already on board."

By the time Geoffrey had manoeuvred his own heavy suitcase to the bottom of the stairs with one hand, refusing to let go of the violin with the other, his arms and back were aching unbearably. By the time he arrived at the entrance, his shirt was sodden with sweat and he was ready to fly off the handle at the least provocation.

"I thought you said Mother was waiting?"

"She was but it was too hot so she went on ahead with Maggie," Rosamund said, opening out her parasol. "Don Salamerez arranged for another carriage to collect us."

Geoffrey assisted his sister into the waiting Victoria as the coachman strapped his case on to the luggage rack.

"Once we dock in Coyacuche, do not set foot off the boat whatever you do," Geoffrey said, releasing the stud on his wing collar before he choked to death.

"For heaven's sake, Jeffy, do stop being coy and tell me what everyone is so afraid of; and you can save your breath about preventing me from going with you."

"Object all you want but you are not coming with us. I will arrange something with Salamerez," Geoffrey snapped.

"Do not dare to try and stop me, Geoffrey Saint Hubes, or you will live to regret it." Her flaming eyes dared him to interrupt. "Apart from Mama, the other reason I have for going up this river is to confront Papa."

"What, you… confront Father? You would never dare."

"You have no idea what I am capable of, not after what he has done!" she retorted.

"Maggs told you about Mother?" Geoffrey asked in a daze.

"Mama... no, what have I not been told?"

"It is too complicated to explain now. But why would you want to provoke him?" Geoffrey asked as they arrived at the dock.

"For reasons you could never understand," she said icily, gripping on to his arm as she stepped down from the carriage.

"Why not try me?" he fumed.

"Very well then... I simply want him to justify having ruined the only true friendship I had before he left. Liam Hardy treated me like a real person and not like an empty-headed ornament. He taught me a lot of useful things and he made me laugh."

"Who the devil is Liam Hardy?"

"The young porter you were so objectionable about on Ashbourne station. He had a limp, in case you have conveniently forgotten. He was the only real friend I ever had."

"Rubbish. You had me and Maggs."

"All you ever bothered about was your music. You never gave a fig about me or anything else after we grew up. As for Maggie, she was too busy painting to bother with what I had to say."

"Even so, what would someone like you have in common with a fellow like Hardy? It doesn't make sense."

"Not to you, because you do not live in the real world most of the time." Her eyes narrowed. "Now if you would please move, I need to get onto the boat. Get out of my way, you idiot." She poked him with the parasol.

"No I will not, not until you tell me what Father did to make you so angry."

"He was jealous, seeing what fun we were having, fishing with nets that Liam made. The boat was perfectly safe, and yet Papa got rid of him the very next day."

"Father must have been concerned for your safety."

"Think whatever you like but I am convinced he sent him away because we were too close and, what is more, he deliberately crushed any opportunities Liam might have had to get work locally."

"You cannot be certain."

"But I can. I overheard Violet Dobson tell Maggie how Papa had threatened her not to employ Liam at the bookshop. Now please step aside," Rosamund demanded, jabbing the end of her parasol hard into the soft leather of his boot.

As he watched his sister walk up the gangway and the pain from his throbbing toe faded, Geoffrey's thoughts turned to the letters in his mother's tin box and the photograph of the tattooed boy and he began to wonder whether his father had been worried that history was repeating itself.

Later that afternoon the rusting, shallow-draught steamer chugged off up the Amazon. In the early hours of the following morning Geoffrey was awoken as the boat altered course, veering sharply away from the main river and into tributary heading in a south-westerly direction. Not long after breakfast there was more manoeuvring to negotiate a large projection of rock that seemed to rear up out of the water. Geoffrey began to revise his opinion on the need to change boats as he changed out of his trousers, soaked from his overturned cup of tea.

Throughout the day, even in the shadiest corners, there was no escape from the sweltering heat as the steam packet chugged laboriously along the murky waters. On either side of the river, the banks were overshadowed by an unbroken swathe of the most enormous trees he had ever seen. In some sections only a minimal amount of light filtered through the dense, overhanging foliage and, the further they went, the thicker the vegetation became, offering no indication of human habitation, native or otherwise.

"Have you got that reference book handy, Maggs? That one that creepy Dobson woman gave you about unknown tributaries and other stuff?" Geoffrey asked, placing his compass on the worn linen map.

"If you made more of an effort to get to know the locals in Ashbourne, you would realise there is nothing creepy about Violet Dobson." Marguerite lowered the net veil from her wide-brimmed hat to rummage through her bag until she handed him the battered volume.

"Have you had a chance to look at this yet?" he asked, thumbing through the pages with renewed interest while checking his map against an entry in the book.

"Not all of it, no, but I will," she said, rolling down her sleeves against an invading swarm of midges before attempting another sketch in her journal.

"Compared to that modern map de Costa gave me, this book is crammed with all kinds of information." Geoffrey eagerly unfolded a detailed chart attached to the centre of the book. "According to this, the river we are on now is known as Zu-nia."

"Surely one blue line looks much like any other."

"Going by this mark here, we should be seeing some weird outcrops of rock along the far bank," Geoffrey said, shielding his eyes from the bright reflection off the river and searching fruitlessly for any break in the impenetrable forestation.

The following morning, Geoffrey ventured on deck to find visibility reduced to a minimum, a dense mist on the river meant he could scarcely make out on either bank. To his surprise Marguerite was already on deck, sketching an impressionistic image of their surroundings.

"How can you see to draw anything in this?" Geoffrey asked, flattening a blood-sucking insect on his arm.

"I could not allow this opportunity to pass." Marguerite was still sketching furiously when Rosamund joined them.

With visibility no more than a few feet ahead, the steamer had manoeuvred closer to the left bank, slowing down to almost crawling speed to negotiate a wide passage through an intimidating, irregular outcrop of rock. As the boat got nearer, a cave gradually became visible in the rock face through the mist. Projecting from this was a tongue-like shelf, reaching out over the river. On either side of the cave were the twisted outlines of two colossal trees.

"Oh, what a beautiful shape your dragon has," Rosamund said, peering inquisitively over her sister's shoulder.

"What dragon? It is just a pile of rocks," Geoffrey scoffed.

"You can be such a bore sometimes. Can you not see the beauty in anything except music?" Rosamund scolded, as her brother shaded his eyes to stare at the cave.

"I say… look over there! If we were back in Pernambuco, I would have sworn that was the old woman from the witches' market," Geoffrey exclaimed as a shadowy figure emerged from the entrance before the mist grew thicker once more.

"I do not see any old woman, only a girl," Rosamund said.

"What girl?" Geoffrey asked, squinting hard to focus on the pale, indistinct shape of a young girl, emerging from the entrance to the cave exactly where the old woman had just been.

Seemingly unaware of the passing steamer, the girl came down to the water's edge where they could see her more clearly. Her pale, ivory skin had a strange, ethereal quality, framed by a cascade of auburn hair, shimmering in the sunlight like strands of burnished copper. She cupped her hands against her mouth as if she was about to call out to them but no sound was heard. Moments later the lone figure merged into a cloud of billowing mist and she was lost from sight.

"Who could she be, Maggie? A white girl stranded all the way out here? We must ask the captain to turn the boat around and go back. We cannot leave her here," Rosamund said, shielding her eyes as the sun broke through once more.

"That would not be possible, Rose. You saw how difficult it must have been for the captain to navigate past those submerged rocks. Turning around here would be almost impossible." Marguerite looked back as the mist began to clear away from the rock formation. "This mist must be distorting our vision, because I am not sure any of us saw the same thing at all."

"Why, what did you see, Maggs?" Geoffrey asked curiously.

"To begin with I thought the figure might have been a woman but in that blinding glare, it looked more like a giant lizard than anything human."

"Well I cannot be sure what I saw," he said. "It might have been a girl, except she was standing in exactly the same place, wearing the same clothes as the old hag I saw, as if she'd transformed into the girl! To be perfectly honest, whatever it was back there it seemed happy enough. I side with Maggs and say we should not try to go back."

As the mist had rolled back in Geoffrey realised that he had not been staring at a young girl, or even an old hag but at the glistening wet scales of a golden salamander. Even in the wretched heat he felt goose-pimples prickling his arms as he relived the memory of those intense, smouldering green eyes, focused not on him but on his elder sister by his side.

"It was a girl. I know it was!" Rosamund insisted.

"Very well, Rose, have it your way if you must," Geoffrey said, focusing not on her but on Marguerite. Her features had become chalk white as she gripped tightly on to the handrail, her pencil slipping unnoticed from nerveless fingers, allowing her precious journal to drop dangerously close to the open rail. Geoffrey grabbed hold of it just before it slipped through and into the water below, before helping her to sit down on a crate.

"For a moment I thought I was going to pass out." She fanned her throat.

"You should go below deck and keep out of this heat." He held her steady so that she didn't topple off the crate.

"I cannot go inside, Geoffrey. It is difficult to breathe even out here on deck. If you would help me into the shade, I will feel better soon."

The further the boat progressed during the following two days, the more rocky outcrops appeared among the trees on the far bank, but nothing was comparable with the dramatic dragon formation. Around midday Don Julio announced the steamer would arrive at their destination by evening but there were still no signs of any habitation for several more hours. The first indication of any human activity on the bank was a small dugout canoe but one unlike any Geoffrey had seen before. This one displayed intricate workmanship in the beaten metal designs that had been hammered into the wood.

The craft had been hauled up from the river and left on the bank but, in the dense, sprawling forestation, there was no sign of a footpath leading away from that place` and no obvious reason why anyone would leave such a remarkable craft unattended.

"Just look at this, Maggs. Imagine the strength it would take to haul that tree trunk away from the water."

"You would never get me into one of those things, not for all the tea in China." She hurried to sketching it into her journal before the steamer had passed.

It was an extraordinary craft, hewn from a trunk of ebony. Three shooting stars had been carved into the prow, each one perfectly outlined by a strip of beaten silver. At the stern there was a series of ancient symbols intricately worked into the timber, again from beaten silver, a design that would have had wowed any art critic in London.

After a few more hours of chugging along the river there was evidence of one or two isolated clearings along the left bank, where a cluster of flimsy shelters had been erected on stilts. The roofs were thatched with palm fronds but there was no sign of life.

Beyond this, stranded high on a projecting ledge above a bank of jagged rocks, was the astonishing spectacle of a

Spanish galleon. According to Don Julio, the vessel had been carried along on a raging torrent of floodwater caused by a freak delay in the rainy season in 1568, the force of which had smashed a corridor through the forest and carried the galleon all the way from Karaka.

"Surely that would be impossible," Geoffrey said.

"Look across there, Sir Geoffrey and tell me what you see." Don Julio indicated a section of the dense rainforest on the opposite bank.

"Only trees, the same as everywhere else," Geoffrey said, uncertain what his point was.

"Correct, but if you check the height of the trees beyond that rock over to the left, and then compare those against the enormous height of the trees way over to the right, you will notice a considerable difference in growth. Although those on the left are quite substantial after more than three hundred years of growth, they cannot be compared to the ancients on the right, thus confirming the devastating force of the floodwater that year."

"That must have been a corker of a spectacle"

"Not for the few villagers who survived, Sir Geoffrey. I have witnessed two disastrous floods in my lifetime but nothing on that scale and, hopefully, I never shall."

"Then we should pray there will never be another delayed rainy season," Geoffrey said.

"I pray you are right, Sir Geoffrey," said the agent but Geoffrey was more interested in seeing the old galleon in closer detail than listening. It struck him that Don Julio too had barely shifted his gaze from the shipwreck as the steamer chugged closer.

The fact that most of the vessel, including a single mast, had survived virtually unscathed might have been remarkable enough, had it not been for the astonishing garden that had been created on what had once served as the main deck, transforming it into an oasis of vibrant colour. Immediately beneath the prow, a vine had secured a root-base in a crevice of rock and was now flourishing among the mass of sprawling ferns and orchids.

"Who would have imagined such a garden could exist in this godforsaken wilderness?" Geoffrey said.

"It seems to me that God's hand is very much in evidence," Marguerite said as they moved slowly past.

"Estar es muy bella hacienda," Don Julio commented enigmatically.

As the steamer chugged beyond the stern of the wreck, they were able to see not only that most of the original leaded windows had remained intact but also that extra living accommodation had been incorporated on the landward side of the vessel. The spacious dwelling prompted Geoffrey to ask their guide if there would be any decent hotels for his family to stay in once they had docked in Coyacuche.

"I cannot allow my mother and sisters to remain on board this dreadful boat for a moment longer than is necessary," he added.

"There would be nothing suitable, Sir Geoffrey. However, you and your family will be most welcome to stay here," Don Julio said, proudly indicating the galleon.

"You cannot expect my mother and sisters to stay there, Don Julio!" Geoffrey said, staring back at the old ship's lofty position on the rock.

"Oh Jeffy, where is your sense of adventure? It would be so romantic!" Rosamund exclaimed.

"You cannot be serious? What we need is a hotel with running water, not a rotting hulk with river sanitation. Snakes or God alone knows what might be crawling about inside." Geoffrey was unable to repress an involuntary shudder.

"I must agree with my brother, Don Julio, since it is wedged in a most precarious position above the river," Marguerite added, while sketching as much detail of the galleon into her journal as she could before they rounded a bend in the river.

"But you do admire it, milady?" Don Julio said.

"I cannot imagine anyone who would not. However, while I have no wish to offend you or to spurn your generous offer, Don Julio, for our family an hotel in the town would be preferable."

"Well I disagree. The prospect of staying on that galleon is a wonderful idea. If Archie had been with us, he would most certainly have agreed," Rosamund said defiantly.

"Then it is fortunate Archie Westbrook is not here and you are outvoted," Geoffrey grumbled, annoyed that his sister needed to mention the Irishman at all.

Not far ahead of them, where a section of the river branched off towards an area of rapids, two natives were paddling furiously against the current in a flimsy canoe. Wedged tightly between them was an unidentifiable figure protected from the sun by a sheet that even from this distance was clearly stained with blood.

The younger of the two natives wore the bleached skull and upper jaw of a young caiman, suspended from a beaded belt that barely covered his genitals. His older companion was equally naked, but wearing the extraordinary trappings of an Amazonian witch doctor. An array of small animal and reptile skulls hung from his belt while two amulets of snakeskin were plaited around his biceps. What denoted his status were the two scarlet macaw feathers suspended from a bleached rod pierced through the septum of his nose.

"Wai-Wai!" Don Julio called anxiously through cupped hands but he failed to attract the attention of either canoeist over the roar of the rapids. Within moments of the canoe reaching calmer water they were out of sight, still paddling at tremendous speed.

Chapter Ten
No End in Sight

Rounding a bend in the river about a mile further on, the boat pulled into a mooring near a shanty town of irregular dwellings, which, by contrast also offered two well-constructed docks. Moored in the smaller of these were three shallow-draught vessels. In the other dock there was a collection of barges and two more steamboats of a similar size to their own.

On higher ground close to the forest edge were two sprawling bungalows, in the colonial style. Further on there was a scattering of run-down shacks near an open-framed warehouse, its roof thatched with layers of palm leaves and clearly a depository for all trading goods.

The steamer had barely docked before Don Julio vaulted over the side and within seconds was lost amongst a crowd of dockers and the inevitable cluster of beggars. A short time later he returned with news that arrangements had been made for transport to be brought to the quayside to collect them.

"What the devil are these?" Geoffrey asked, when two shabby carriages arrived, harnessed to a pair of carthorses.

"I can only apologise for the poor condition of these conveyances, Sir Geoffrey but, unfortunately, they are the best available at short notice."

"Even so, the hostelry can surely do better than send us this pair of old nags?"

"Unlike England, Sir Geoffrey, there are no surfaced roads through the rainforest. Tree roots are frequently exposed above the compacted earth and, during the rainy season, the roads can become mud-baths overnight. In such conditions this breed of horse is preferable," Don Julio said, clearly impatient to be off.

With apologies to Lady Claudia for the hasty departure, their guide mounted a waiting mule and escorted the carriages away from the town with an urgency uncharacteristic of his normal placid character. He brandished his riding crop like a cutlass, pointing into the crowd and barking threats at anyone who dared hinder their progress.

"What the devil has got into Don Julio today?" Geoffrey complained to his mother, supporting her as best he could in the jolting carriage. "I cannot make the man out… he was perfectly collected earlier and, without warning, he has transformed into Napoleon."

"Do not judge him too harshly, my darling. There has been a life-threatening incident involving his nephew and Don Julio is desperate to be at his side, which is perfectly understandable."

"But what has that to do with us, Mother? Why do we have to go with him? Shouldn't we be going to a hotel?"

"The only hotel Don Julio had in mind is undergoing reconstruction and there has been no time to make alternative arrangements. To leave us unprotected was not something a gentleman of his character was prepared to do."

"So where are we going in this old crate without any suspension?" Geoffrey complained, as the carriage lurched over a hole that felt like a bomb crater.

"That was unclear, Geoffrey but he assures me the accommodation will be most agreeable, and we shall want for nothing."

"But should we not have made enquiries about Father before setting off?"

"There was no alternative. Don Julio has agreed that we can accompany him into the town tomorrow to make further enquiries at the shipping office."

After travelling a couple of miles, although it seemed much further, the vehicles veered off the road into a long, rutted track through a pair of elaborate wrought-iron gates. Beyond these stretched a magnificent, well-maintained drive between cultivated trees, interspersed with unidentifiable flowering shrubs. It was an awesome approach that eventually, to their surprise, ended at the rear of the shipwrecked galleon, the landward size of which had a sizeable extension with an elegant Georgian facade.

Just as the carriages reached it, a breathless servant ran out of the house, waving his arms and jabbering incoherently at Don Julio, then pointing to a small track through the forest from where a flat-backed cart, harnessed to a mule, was now rumbling across the manicured lawn.

Driving the cart was the young canoeist Geoffrey had seen earlier. Riding on the back was Wai-Wai, the shaman, busily tending a badly injured man by sprinkling handfuls of red seeds into his many open wounds before dusting them with an acid green coloured powder.

The cart had barely come to a halt before Don Julio leapt aboard and was kneeling beside the injured man, questioning the shaman urgently in his native tongue, none of which Geoffrey could understand, although the name Armand was repeatedly used.

It was clear that Don Julio had grave concern for the injured young man as he lifted him cautiously down from the cart, his features partially obscured by the bloodied sheet as he was carried towards the entrance of the property, followed by Wai-Wai in his red feathers.

"Can I be of any assistance, Don Julio?" Geoffrey asked, convinced the bleeding man was either dead or very close to it as he and his family cautiously followed them inside.

"Gracias, señor but that will not be necessary. I do apologise for the inconvenience, but if you would be kind enough to escort the ladies further inside, the staff will do everything possible to make you and your family comfortable."

"You must think no more about our comfort, Don Salamerez," Lady Claudia reassured him. "Your nephew should be your only priority now. We will be perfectly fine here."

"Then if you would excuse me, milady, I must go. Wai-Wai has important medicine to prepare for Armand's injuries." He called two female servants to show the guests into a nearby room, still cradling the injured man against him as he backed open a sturdy, medieval door.

Stepping forward to help, Geoffrey was too late to prevent the door from closing on Don Julio as he struggled to carry the injured man clear of the doorway, which jolted him and caused Armand to moan with pain. Just for a moment Geoffrey saw his eyelids flutter open, revealing bloodshot eyes that stared directly into the distressed face of Don Julio.

"Papa..." Armand gasped weakly, before he fell unconscious.

There was a bright rivulet of blood running down his bare arm, which swung lifelessly as Don Julio passed through the doorway into the ballroom beyond, ordering the young canoeist to close the door firmly behind them. The very last glimpse Geoffrey had of the room was of a makeshift table on which Wai-Wai was setting out some crude surgical instruments.

A long wait followed, relieved only by the interest of their unexpected surroundings. They were shown into a long gallery that would have been the envy of any country house in England and its contents and furnishings were of considerable interest to Geoffrey's mother and sisters. For Geoffrey himself, what fascinated him more than any of the fine porcelain objects, sculptures or artwork was the scene beyond the leaded windows of an original section of the wrecked galleon that had once been the captain's quarters.

As well as a spectacular view over the river and the white foam of the rapids beyond, the light that was reflected off the river, filtering into the long interior, making the opulent space even more appealing. Had Geoffrey been alone, it was a place where he would have been overjoyed to continue work on his latest composition.

"How lovely this place is, Mother," Rosamund said, unaware of how captivating she was herself in that unguarded moment as she paced the length of the gallery.

"It is remarkable how anyone could have achieved such magnificence inside the wreck we saw from the river," Lady Claudia agreed.

"How sad it is that Archie could not be here to witness this."

"Why would you think that Irishman would be in the least interested?" Geoffrey protested.

"If you need to ask that, then you would not understand!" Rosamund pouted.

"Perhaps I might, if it was a bad-tempered mule or a lame duck but certainly not the interior of a converted wreck," Geoffrey sneered.

"Why do you have to be so horrid about Archie? It is not surprising that you cannot make any friends at home if you refuse to see the good in anyone!" Rosamund challenged him, striding away.

"If you like Archie Westbrook that much, I am surprised that you have not already agreed to marry him!" Geoffrey called after her.

"I might well have done, had he asked me," Rosamund parried before seating herself next to her mother.

"Will you please stop… both of you. We are guests here," Lady Claudia said.

"This climate is affecting us all, Mother."

"Quite possibly but these argumentative exchanges cannot be excused, especially when our host is having to deal with those frightful injuries."

"I am truly sorry, Mother," Geoffrey said, collecting himself.

"Would it be appropriate if I offered them my assistance?" Marguerite asked.

"It is a kind thought, darling but I suspect their customs regarding women might be very different to ours and your offer might cause offence. I just pray that Don Julio and that strange character with the red feathers pinned through his nostrils will have everything under control." Lady Claudia broke off with a shudder upon hearing a terrifying scream from beyond the closed door, followed by a deathly silence.

An hour passed and, with nothing else to occupy him, Geoffrey explored the sumptuous furnishings that surrounded them, examining the impressive artworks, marble and bronze sculptures and other antiquities, eventually running his fingers lightly across the keyboard of a grand piano.

"I do wonder how anyone could come by such an amazing collection of valuables in this backwater," Geoffrey commented to his mother as she admired the fine texture and gold thread-work of the lavish Venetian drapery around the gallery.

"They are indeed wonderful. This fabric alone must have cost a king's ransom. They must have been inherited," she said, examining a collection of miniatures.

"Or it is more likely these have been acquired through piracy? That could certainly explain how he came by those awful wounds."

"Why do you always think the worst of everyone, Geoffrey?" Rosamund complained.

"From what little I saw of him in passing, he appeared to have been mauled by some wild creature. Those horrific gouges in his chest looked as if they had been clawed out," Marguerite said but, by now her brother wasn't listening as he peered through a corner window where he could observe the witch doctor at work.

Outside, Wai-Wai crouched on a projection of rock, adding wood to a blazing fire. Suspended over it was a shallow, blackened pot. Taking four fleshy succulents from an overhanging vine, he then sat cross-legged within reach of the fire where he cut and twisted each fruit until only strands of green fibre remained after every drop of the yellow juice had been squeezed into the pot.

"You should see this, Maggs," Geoffrey said, beckoning his sister to join him at the window. "What do you think he is up to?"

"I have absolutely no idea, unless this is a ritual of some kind." At that moment the young canoeist appeared, apparently having climbed up the rock face from the river.

"Why would they be doing that?" Geoffrey asked, keeping his voice low so that neither his mother nor Rosamund would hear at the far end of the gallery.

Cautiously the young native handed over a handful of damp earth he had collected from the riverbank, which Wai-Wai began dropping in bits into the bubbling pot. He then grated a section of lime-green tree bark into the mix, chanting in a low, unintelligible voice, all the time stirring perfectly in rhythm. Very carefully, he then crushed a cluster of brilliant blue shells against the rock, adding them to the mixture at regular intervals and, with each deposit, he spat in the liquid with the same, ritual intensity.

"Ugh… how disgusting!" Geoffrey said but, even so, he was unable to look away as Wai-Wai removed two snake eggs from a leather pouch on his belt. Cracking open the first against the rock, he tipped the writhing green contents into the concoction. Repeating the same action with the second egg, he added the wriggling red embryo.

"This is too macabre! Come away, Geoffrey; you will have nightmares if you watch any more of this," Marguerite said, taking her brother firmly by the arm.

"Not yet," Geoffrey said as he saw Don Julio appear outside, urgently summoning Wai-Wai and his young companion through an open door. Before leaving, the shaman ladled out some of the paste and layered a thick amount of the steaming substance onto a torn strip of linen, before also disappearing inside the building.

When Don Julio reappeared in the doorway of the long gallery after an absence of three hours, the alteration was shocking. Gone was the immaculate, gentlemanly demeanour.

The grey frock coat and silk cravat had been discarded, revealing a raw masculinity; his sweat-stained shirt was streaked with a thick grey slime with the sleeves rolled back to expose a series of scars, cut and tattooed along his right forearm. This depicted the outline of a salamander that descended down the limb. The electrifying shape appeared alive with each movement of the sinews beneath the taut skin.

"Please forgive me for having neglected you, Lady Claudia but my Armand has been badly injured and might not recover and I cannot remain with you for long," he said wearily, perching on the edge of a chair.

"We are perfectly comfortable here, Don Julio. You must remain with the invalid for as long as necessary," Lady Claudia said calmly.

"If you will forgive the liberty, I have arranged suitable accommodation for you and your family, milady, which I hope will be to your satisfaction. The servants will inform you as soon as the rooms are ready."

"Thank you for your kindness during what must be a very trying ordeal."

To Geoffrey, able to observe their host at close quarters, it seemed from the scale-like texture of his skin that Don Julio's left forearm had been badly scalded but seeing his gloveless hand without a forefinger or thumb made him shudder with horror. Stretched between his three elongated fingers was a fine webbing of skin. The steel-grey hair, which earlier had been so fastidiously slicked back and tied neatly at the base of his neck, now hung matted about his ashen features, emphasising the dark patches under red-rimmed eyes, fathomless pools haunted by a fear of the unknown.

"Excusar," Don Julio said, stumbling as he tried to replace the glove over his hand but unable to prevent it from falling against the chair.

Instinctively Geoffrey retrieved it from the floor, only then noticing the shape of a wooden thumb and finger concealed inside the leather as he helped button it securely about Don Julio's wrist.

It was only after Don Julio had returned to the sick room and his mother and Rosamund had gone to freshen up that Geoffrey brought up the subject that had been bothering him for some time.

"Do you think Rose was serious earlier, Maggs? Saying she would have married Archie Westbrook if he had asked?"

"You know Rose will say anything to rile you if she's angry enough," Marguerite replied with a smile.

"Well, it sounded convincing enough to me."

"Then if it was in her mind to accept, it would be a perfect match."

"And you would not mind?" he asked with surprise.

"Not at all; why do you ask?"

"I just thought you might be rather keen on him yourself," Geoffrey said cautiously.

"Why on earth would you assume that? Surely it cannot be just because I made that sketch of him?" Marguerite laughed. "Admittedly Archie is a remarkable young man but I am not interested in him, or in anyone come to that. I am a confirmed spinster and I intend to remain so. Archie Westbrook, on the other hand, would make the perfect husband for Rose."

"But that drawing you made of him from memory. It was so lifelike. Why do that if you have no feelings for him?"

"If you need a reason, it was simply because I needed to record that handsome face of his for posterity."

"You think Archie Westbrook is that handsome?" Geoffrey asked reluctantly. Marguerite only smiled and made no reply.

The sleeping facilities they were allocated were four cubicle rooms in the lower section of the galleon, with restrictively low ceilings and a pair of glazed doors that opened out onto a long balcony running the length of the ship.

Barely able to draw breath in the sweltering heat inside his room and with his mind a jumble of conflicting thoughts, Geoffrey pulled aside the mosquito netting from across the open doors and stepped on to the balcony. Positioned immediately outside his room was a solitary, well-serviced cannon that was doubtless an original fixture. Others had originally been fitted inside what were now the converted bedrooms of the ship. However, this particular weapon appeared to have been deliberately bolted down in its position, aimed at an indistinguishable point on the opposite bank. Geoffrey found it difficult to focus on, even in the moonlight because of a low mist that obliterated any trace of the rapids.

"Could you not sleep in this dreadful heat, Geoffrey?" Marguerite called from her doorway, unwilling to step on to the balcony.

"For Pete's sake, I almost jumped out of my skin," Geoffrey said sharply, massaging the joints of his hands. "Have you any of that lavender oil handy? This damp air is an absolute killer, every joint in my fingers aches."

"I did wonder why you have not been practising this week," she said. "You are a talented musician, Geoffrey but you cannot afford to make any errors in your entrance exam."

"I can assure you that I do practise whenever I can, but there has not been much opportunity recently. All I want is somewhere quiet but even you must agree that was impossible, since there was not an inch of space on that bloody awful steamer."

"You could have practised on the deck," Marguerite persisted.

"There is nothing on earth that would convince me to do that, not with that crew of cut-throats looking on. I doubt if anyone in that gang of thugs knows one end of a violin from another."

"So what are you going to do about it? There is no knowing when this business with Father will be resolved. You cannot just abandon your talent."

"You think because I cannot practise each day that I will do nothing. If you must know, I am in the middle of a new composition for the entrance exam, so my time will not have been wasted."

After a short silence when Geoffrey imagined his sister had fallen asleep and a few bars of a melody were beginning to form in his head, she reappeared in the doorway and the notes disappeared.

"Do you not find the situation here strange, Geoffrey?"

"Absolutely and do you not find the relationship between Don Julio and the pirate a bit weird also?"

"These are not fictional characters from one of your adventure books. If Armand is anything like his uncle, then he is most likely a perfect gentleman. You only have to assess the furnishing in this property to realise what Don Julio's nephew is like. You do talk rubbish at times."

"Well, for your information, this Armand is not his nephew. He is his son. I know that for a fact, because I heard him call Don Julio 'Papa' as he carried him into the room."

"That is impossible. I distinctly recall Don Julio referring to Armand as his nephew. You must have misheard."

"Extramarital affairs happen all the time, Maggs, so it is not out of the question. Take Father as a prime example."

"I would rather not continue with this conversation, Geoffrey. I am going to bed, and if I were you I would do the same," Marguerite said, returning to her room.

After a sleepless night, Geoffrey did his best to use the washstand in his room and found himself longing for the convenience of running water, however beautiful the jug and bowl might have been. Staying clean had been a torturous experience in the meagre facilities available on the steamer but facing similar restrictions in this luxurious home was positively annoying. He found his sister sketching on the balcony.

"This is not a hotel where you would expect running water on tap. We all have to adapt. For future reference, the next time you find me out here drawing, please do not interrupt me with any more of these childish complaints."

"Does it not bother you that Mother will have to wash in this primitive manner?"

"Perhaps it would, if that were the case."

"What do you mean?"

"I am saying that Don Julio has arranged for Mother to stay in Armand's private apartment."

"Even so, it cannot be much better than what we have."

"If you look in on Mother later this morning, you may be pleasantly surprised." She slipped an elastic band around the journal before putting it into her bag.

"You should take more care of that book if Violet Dobson is ever going to get it published," Geoffrey said. "The air is always damp and it can tip down with rain at any moment. Why not use that oilskin bag to keep it dry? What you really need is a satchel with one of those zippers, like the one Mother's papers are in."

"Why are you obsessing about my journal, Geoffrey? I have no intention of allowing anything to happen to it. It will be perfectly safe."

"Here on land, maybe, but not on the river. You almost lost it once and what if the rainy season starts earlier than expected and we get soaked? Have you even thought about that? There are too many drawings that might get damaged."

"There is nothing I could not draw again, except perhaps that sketch of Archie. Have you got it safe?"

"Yes, for now, along with my latest composition," Geoffrey said, debating whether his music might be safer in Don Julio's satchel too.

"If it bothers you that much, Geoffrey, then do go ahead and ask Don Julio but only on the clear understanding that you will keep that satchel with you at all times."

"Then you think it a good idea?"

"Yes, if the journal is safe. Lightening the weight in my bag will be somewhat of a blessing too."

On the following morning, Geoffrey was met by a haggard Don Julio, deep in conversation with Lady Claudia in the apartment belonging to Armand. The luxurious suite of rooms was a revelation after the cramped conditions he and his sisters had endured. The dressing room was light and airy, with embroidered silk hangings depicting exotic birds of paradise and other flora and fauna. There was also a fully functioning shower and even a flushing toilet.

Although Armand's injuries were no longer life-threatening there had been a further complication from the trauma which had left him in a comatose state. Understandably Don Julio had no intention of leaving his side until the young man regained consciousness. Whatever information had been obtained on the whereabouts of Geoffrey's father, he would therefore be unable to accompany them beyond Coyacuche.

"What do you suggest, Don Julio?" Lady Claudia asked.

"Since I must remain here, the only person I would trust, apart from Wai-Wai, would be Churuma, the young man who delivered Armand here safely," Don Julio replied.

"Then on those assurances I would be happy to continue in the search for my husband with that young man as our guide. Could I meet him?" she asked.

"That would not be possible today, milady. Churuma set off at daybreak to collect any information he can find on Lord Oliver's whereabouts. Armand's apartment is at your disposal for as long as you require. I think it would be advisable if you rest here until you get more positive information."

"Don Julio is right, Mother," Geoffrey agreed. "We just need information on where to find Father. I shall go on my own with Churuma. If Father is in town, then I shall return with him. If not, then we can plan our next move when I get back."

"I cannot allow you to go there alone, Geoffrey. I would fear for your safety."

"But I will have Churuma with me."

"Geoffrey will be perfectly safe if I go along too," Marguerite chipped in.

"There is no need. I am perfectly able to take care of myself," Geoffrey retorted, scowling at his sister.

"Well I am coming, Geoffrey, so get used to it. There is nothing for me to do here, and Mother needs to rest."

"There's no reason for you to tag along. If you are bored, why not draw something," he said spitefully but he could tell by the glint in her eyes that she was not going to change her mind.

"Well then I am coming as well," Rosamund said determinedly. "And before you ask, no, I will not change my mind either."

Although Geoffrey was unsure whether their safety should be entrusted to someone who couldn't have been much older than him and had scant knowledge of the English language, he was at least local to the area and was clearly trusted by Don Julio. Geoffrey made sure that it was he who was entrusted with the leather satchel which now contained not only the documents for his father to sign but also his sister's journal and his own composition, along with Archie's picture, tucked safely between the pages.

On the outskirts of the town they came to a large warehouse, Churuma went inside to make enquiries and, after a good fifteen minutes there was still no sign of him returning.

"If Churuma stays inside any longer, then I shall go and see for myself what he is up to," Geoffrey said impatiently.

"You must not get out of the carriage, Geoffrey," Marguerite warned. "Don Julio was most specific that we should avoid attracting any unnecessary attention. It could prove to be dangerous."

"Very well. I shall wait but not for much longer," he warned, just as their guide finally reappeared.

"Come!" Churuma said abruptly, urging Geoffrey and his sisters to follow him into the warehouse where a clerk led them into a large storage area. Here there were two rough crates scheduled for transportation to the trading post at Yanoa and clearly labelled for collection by his father. There was nothing else and nothing to inform them whether he was still in the vicinity.

"Can we find out when these crates are due for collection?" Marguerite said. "That way we will know when Father will return. I am certain Don Julio would accommodate us for a while longer if asked."

"Quite possibly but if Father has gone to ground, then it is down to me to uproot him. The sooner we can get away from this frightful dump and return home, the better," Geoffrey said. Taking hold of Churuma by the arm, he indicated his father's address on the crates and then pointed to a mound of ledgers behind the clerk's desk. "Tu comprende... do you understand?"

"Si... Si, señor," Churuma said, asking the clerk to find the appropriate ledgers and bring them out into the light.

"Well done, Geoffrey," Marguerite whispered with a smile. "I am sure even Archie could not have done better."

"Hmm," Geoffrey grumbled but he couldn't prevent a satisfied grin from lighting up his face as he went carefully through the final entries. "I think I have it. What I do not understand is why these crates are still here if they were due for collection last month. That would be the same time Father should have been setting off to meet us in Pernambuco, which makes no sense."

"It would... if he never had any intention of being at the port to meet us," Marguerite said.

"But then these crates would have been collected and not left here gathering dust," Geoffrey said, swatting an insect on his arm and scratching irritably where he'd been bitten.

"What is in these boxes anyway?" Rosamund asked the clerk, who had been unable to takes his eyes off her from the moment she stepped inside the building. In his befuddled state he had clearly misunderstood the question and before anyone could prevent him, he began prizing off the first lid with a hefty crowbar.

"It will only be chemicals or medical equipment for his research," Geoffrey said. "What might be of use is if there is something in there to help against any infection we might come in contact with in this disgusting environment."

"You could not be further from the truth," Rosamund said.

"Why, what is it?"

"It can only be a surprise; for me... I think," she said hesitantly, removing the tissue paper from an ornate gown, festooned with clusters of silk flowers in brilliant colours.

"Dear God in heaven, that is awful!" Geoffrey exclaimed. "Not even you would look presentable wearing a costume like that, Rose."

"Why would he buy something like this? It cannot be for me, surely?" Rosamund lifted it into the light where it looked even worse.

"He would never have dared buy anything like that for Mother. She would not have allowed it in the house," Geoffrey commented.

"Well it cannot have been ordered for me either," Marguerite grimaced, inspecting the tiny waist. "I cannot imagine what would have possessed him to purchase such a bizarre garment. It is absolutely frightful."

"I agree and surely he could have ordered a more appropriate gift for every one of us, not just for me," Rosamund said, reluctantly opening out another vividly coloured garment against her.

"If they were intended for you. How many are there in that crate?" Geoffrey asked.

"There must be at least twelve," Rosamund said. She handed Geoffrey an envelope addressed to her father. "You should open this, it might be important."

"This is an invoice from a French dressmaker in Apalla, asking a king's ransom for the contents."

"So what do we do with them now? Take them back with us?" Rosamund asked.

"They can stay here. Father can collect them when he's ready," Geoffrey grumbled. "And when we get back, Rose, do not breathe a word about this to Mother."

"You must think I am the biggest dimwit ever, if you imagine I would mention any of this to her but, before we go, don't forget Papa has another package waiting to be collected," she said.

After a short wait the clerk prized open the second crate, which contained a quantity of jars of pharmaceutical goods, powders, crystals and bottles of liquid.

"This ought to have been collected weeks ago. These pharmaceutical materials from North America must have been vital for his research, especially at this price," Marguerite said, examining the receipt. "I think we should take this crate along with us."

"Is there any information on Papa's laboratory?" Rosamund asked.

"Not exactly, only that this is for his attention c/o the trading post in Yanoa, wherever that is."

"Maybe Churuma can find someone who can pinpoint it on the map in Violet Dobson's book," Geoffrey said, following his sisters towards the open door, where a warm, but welcome gust of wind billowed out Marguerite's shapeless gown as she moved ahead, like a galleon under full sail gliding towards the daylight.

On their return it was clear that Armand's condition had worsened but Don Julio welcomed them back warmly, serving them a plain but appetising meal.

"Her ladyship has asked to be excused from dining with you this evening since she has already eaten and is taking this opportunity to rest," he told them.

"I should look in on her to ask if she needs anything," Geoffrey said.

"I understand from the maid who is assigned to her that Lady Claudia has requested not to be disturbed, Sir Geoffrey."

"That is most kind of you, to have provided our mother with a maid."

"It seemed appropriate. Nia is Churuma's sister and, though she has only a scant knowledge of the English language, she is ideally suited to serve her ladyship on the next section of your search. It has been arranged that both she and Churuma will remain with you until you return here safely."

"We appreciate your assistance and allowing mother to occupy Armand's private apartments," Marguerite said.

"There is no need, milady. The boy needs as much fresh air as possible. A bed has been set up on the eastern section of the veranda, shaded by the forest. It will be much cooler for him there."

"Has there been any improvement in his condition?" Marguerite asked.

"Unfortunately there has been no sign of him waking," Don Julio said, turning away swiftly but not before Geoffrey caught the glint of tears his eyes. "If you will please excuse me, I have been away too long." He stood up and left abruptly.

After dinner they retired to the long gallery, where Geoffrey had barely settled into looking through an old *Country Life* magazine when Rosamund opened the French windows and looked along the expanse of the veranda.

"Did either of you hear that?" she asked.

"Hear what?" Geoffrey grumbled.

"I cannot be sure but it sounded like a scream."

"What direction did it come from?" Marguerite asked, stepping out to join her sister.

"I am sure it came from down there, where the invalid is recovering," Rosamund said, indicating the far corner of the veranda.

At that moment Don Julio appeared from around the corner, distraught, haggard and spattered with fresh blood.

"Please go back inside. There is nothing to be alarmed about," he said, although his dishevelled appearance did little to reassure them.

"Is there anything we can do to help, Don Julio?" Marguerite asked.

"Unfortunately not. Wai-Wai is trying every conceivable way of returning my boy from the inevitable," he said, clearly struggling to keep control of his emotions.

"We heard screaming?" Geoffrey said.

"Then I apologise sincerely if my own despair has caused you any alarm, since I fear that my son is slipping away." He turned on his heels and disappeared around the corner.

"There must be something we can do to help," Geoffrey said.

"You should play for him," Rosamund mused. "Everyone knows that music can be a wonderful healer."

"Now you are being ridiculous!" Geoffrey retorted.

"Wilting plants respond to music, so why not a person? I read about the healing properties of music in a book."

"A romantic novel, no doubt," Geoffrey scoffed.

"It was a gardening book actually, one that belonged to Liam's father. Mother once said Mr Hardy was the most natural gardener she had ever met; 'a gifted man', she called him."

"Most people are good at something. Gardening obviously applied to him."

"You might have altered your opinion had you read the same article. I clearly remember it stating that certain rhythms in music can help ailing plants to recover."

"This is not a giant hogweed we are talking about but a young man; what he needs to recover is peace and quiet, not me scraping out a tune in the next room!"

"You could at least give it a try," Rosamund snapped, curling up against her sister on a day lounger.

"Rosamund could be right, Geoffrey," Marguerite agreed. "You have the violin with you, so why not play something light and soothing that we could all enjoy?"

"I suppose I could give it a go if what Rose says is correct but I do question the notion of playing anything light or soothing in a situation like this. Surely it requires something more uplifting and dramatic."

"Then you will do it?" Rosamund asked eagerly.

"I suppose I could."

"Will you play one of your own pieces?"

"Definitely not. If any music is going to reach out to him, then it would need to be a recognisable piece. Let me think about that while I collect the violin."

"At last, logic penetrates! Will it be one of the Russians?" Rosamund called after him, but got no response.

After a lot of thought and abandoning many pieces that did not quite fit the requirements, Geoffrey settled on a dramatic variation of 'Winter', from Vivaldi's *Four Seasons*. Although it had been almost a week since Geoffrey had taken up the violin, he was eager to play something that wasn't geared towards the entrance exam or more of those endless scales.

Striding purposefully through the gallery with his mind set on the music, he chose to say nothing to either sister when they asked, or indeed to his mother who had joined them in his absence. Making his way to the far end of the veranda, Geoffrey made sure he was out of sight of the expectant faces of his family and, more importantly, out of the light. Although he had played this particular piece a few times at home, that was over a year ago and without any sheet music to follow he needed no distractions.

The night air was still and seemingly expectant, his only visual audience the ancient trees that surrounded them and whatever creatures were concealed in the blanket of darkness. Positioning the violin against his chin, he smiled confidently as he placed the bow across the taut strings and, drawing it across with slow deliberation, the passionate recital began.

The isolated position he had selected was perfect for setting the mood and he never faltered throughout the sometimes manic and volatile piece in the all-encompassing darkness, as if it were the easiest piece he could have selected to play. Nothing in his life until then had seemed so important as he unconsciously incorporated his own frustrations and unconscious desires into the performance.

His fingers skimmed over the strings as lightly as a breath of air, not only performing for the injured man but reshaping the piece for the dark, intense beauty of the surrounding forest, where the trees themselves seemed attuned to every alteration of pitch and tone of Vivaldi's masterpiece. However inappropriate 'Winter' may have seemed in the humid depths of the Amazonian rainforest, when the final section came to an end, the clusters of leaves all around him seemed to rustle in appreciation for the extraordinary gift they had been given.

Once the final note had faded into the darkness, Geoffrey's only thought was to give thanks to whatever ancestral gene had enabled him to play in such a way. Close to tears, he did his best to wipe his cheeks with the back of his hand, until someone passed him a handkerchief out of the darkness.

"Thank you, Maggs," Geoffrey said, blowing his nose while keeping his head turned away from his sister; or so he thought until Don Julio spoke, close to his ear.

"You have my heartfelt gratitude for that recital, Sir Geoffrey. Less than an hour ago I was preparing for my beautiful son to depart this earth but your wonderful music has penetrated the dark recesses of his mind, returning him to this realm."

"It worked?" Geoffrey said with astonishment.

"His eyes are fully open and he called me by name," Don Julio said, taking Geoffrey by the arm. "I would be obliged if you would accompany me to his bed, where you can see for yourself the miracle your music has worked."

"Would that be wise, Don Julio?"

"Armand adores music above anything else. It would be an honour if you would allow him to meet you in person, Sir Geoffrey."

The young man's features were nothing like Geoffrey remembered from the fleeting glimpse he'd had of the shrouded, blood-stained figure the previous day. Although hollow-eyed and sallow-cheeked, the charisma of the face staring at him from the makeshift bed was unmistakable. In age, Armand was perhaps a few years older than Archie Westbrook, if not as ruggedly handsome but Geoffrey's assessment of him as a rogue pirate could have been a perfect fit.

"Maestro… Thank you," Armand mumbled, peering through half-closed eyelids. "Before your music penetrated the walls of darkness, there were devilish creatures waiting for me to topple into a bottomless pit."

"I cannot take all the credit. It was my sister Lady Rosamund's suggestion that I should play for you. To be perfectly honest, I never imagined it would work," Geoffrey said, taking Armand's offered hand.

"Then please offer my grateful thanks to your sister also."

In the fading light it was difficult for Geoffrey to examine the unnaturally cold, clammy hand as Armand withdrew it but, compared to the softness of his own skin, the texture felt almost scaly.

The onward journey to locate Lord Oliver would inevitably involve yet another downgrade in the quality of transport, with even more restricted accommodation. Geoffrey tried once again to dissuade his mother and sisters from accompanying him any further but none of them would agree with his reasoning. It was eventually agreed that any clothing in need of washing would be left behind to be freshly laundered and ironed for their return.

With the exception of Marguerite's cumbersome bag and Geoffrey's violin, only 'essential' clothing and toiletries were packed. This still involved four tightly packed shipping trunks, three large suitcases, two trunks, two hat boxes, a Gladstone bag and a portable music stand.

"Well I must say we did jolly well reducing the luggage," Geoffrey said, praying that everything would fit aboard the boat.

"I must say, Geoffrey, this trip has been very good for you," Marguerite said as their carriage rumbled along the dock.

"What do you mean by that? More grown-up?"

"Not exactly; more focused on practical issues."

"Well maybe you will be too when you lay eyes on the rusted hulk we are expected to sail on."

"Oh my goodness... is it safe?" Marguerite asked.

"Well it is floating, so that would be a plus," Geoffrey said, unzipping the leather satchel. "I thought we agreed you would keep that journal of yours with my composition and Mother's papers?"

"What worries me is if you leave it behind."

"What do you take me for? I have no intention of leaving it anywhere. If I lose this satchel, then this bloody awful journey will have been for absolutely nothing."

"Well, if you are sure," she said, tentatively handing over the journal.

"I can promise you this satchel will stay slung across my shoulders even when I am sleeping."

Chapter Eleven
A Glimpse of Destiny

Whatever name the vessel had been given many years before was barely distinguishable on the rusting prow. More worrying than the flaking paintwork or the overpowering stench of rotting flesh was that there was no prospect of them returning to Coyacuche on the same vessel. This was because on the outward journey it was travelling empty, enabling the crew to return fully loaded with caged birds, animals and reptiles as well as uncured caiman hides for export.

"I must ask you again, Mother, to reconsider taking this voyage and just wait for me here," Geoffrey pleaded.

"Darling, I cannot allow you to venture any deeper into the rainforest on your own. What sort of a parent would I be in allowing that?"

"A sensible one," Geoffrey muttered. "You do know this boat can only take us one way. The captain has already warned Churuma there is no guarantee that another boat will be available, or that it would be willing to transport us back. If only one person needs to get back, then I'm sure the captain of this tin can could squeeze me on board for the return journey, even if it is jam-packed with animal crates. I would not take up much space."

"It is imperative that I should be the one negotiating with your father to protect your rightful inheritance. He can be a monster when money and property are involved and, if that frightful Mrs King has had her say, he will be twice as mercenary. Without my involvement the three of you would be fortunate to inherit the dower house between you. That is why I must negotiate this deal and no one else."

"But then how do we get back? Churuma says the river is already low, and there will be no other boats of this size until after the rainy season, which could be months away."

"If we offer to reimburse the captain for any loss of income from leaving some of his trading goods behind he would surely allow us to return with him?" Marguerite suggested.

"I seriously doubt that. Churuma did say that a smaller boat was already en route for the trading post with provisions and will be returning empty. That seems to be our only practical option for getting back."

"But even if you confront Father in person, he would never concede to anything he did not agree with?" Marguerite asked.

"I have leverage in some damning letters written to him by Mrs King, proving beyond doubt that the affair with your father began while she was still married. Your father would never allow his reputation to be tarnished in fashionable society and, if he is unwilling to see reason, those letters will appear in next month's edition of *The Lady's Realm*. It is imperative I secure his signature to every condition and clause, otherwise this terrible journey will have been for nothing."

"But even so, Mother, we all know he never backs down from anything once his mind is made up," Geoffrey said.

"Perhaps not, until I confront him with my intention of blackening his character by also detailing his infidelities to Lord Harbury at *The Times* and in Lady Drayton's society column in the *Illustrated London News*. I am determined to protect your grandfather's estates from falling into the wrong hands, at any cost. Once that is achieved, I shall demand that he returns with us to Pernambuco where I shall file for an immediate divorce."

"He would never agree to that, Mother. How would he exist without your financial support?" Marguerite asked.

"I have arranged to sign over your grandfather's estate in Ireland. That would include all of the breeding stock and the stables. Even your father would be hard pressed to offer any resistance to that."

Two hours later, together with Churuma and his teenage sister Nia, the family boarded the *La Constantia*, on which they were allocated only two of the eight cabins available. The larger had the convenience of a manual water closet, a washbasin and just enough space for Lady Claudia and Rosamund to hang up a change of clothes.

Crammed against the wall in the second cabin there was a double bunk with only one mattress, which Geoffrey insisted his elder sister should occupy.

"But what about you, Geoffrey? Where will you sleep?" Marguerite asked.

"Churuma will come up with something. He seems pretty resourceful."

Soon after the steamer left the dock, Churuma erected a shelter of palm fronds on the deck. Beneath this he placed three worn cane loungers for the family's convenience and then rigged up a separate shelter as Geoffrey's sleeping quarters under the stairs leading up to the wheelhouse, affording him a three-sided area of privacy. On the open end he attached a length of mosquito netting.

To begin with Geoffrey had been uncertain about the intended route and was surprised when at first the boat steamed back down the river for a short distance, until it branched off the main waterway. Here the skipper immediately reduced speed, piloting the craft into another shadowy tributary beneath the imposing Dragon Rock.

From this different angle, it was easy for Geoffrey to understand what had captured his sister's imagination, since the strangely shaped rocks gave the distinct appearance of a huge dragon rearing up from the river. This time, however, there was no mist, nor any evidence of a pale-skinned girl, only the mouth of the cave sprawling with vegetation.

"Do you think we did actually see anyone?" he asked curiously, staring hard into the depths of the cavern.

"I think that was the culprit," Marguerite said, pointing out a thick trailing vine, dangling curtain-like across the partially obscured entrance and moving in the breeze.

240

"That would not explain the red-haired girl."

"Whatever it was, there is nothing there now," she said, but Geoffrey was already examining the map in Violet Dobson's book on the uncharted tributaries of the Amazon to pinpointing their exact position.

"Rio Zu-nia is the name of the river we are on and that mound of rock is marked as Lizard Head but, for my money, Dragon Rock suits it better," he grinned.

"You should thank Miss Dobson for her kind gift of those books on our return, after the countless times you have referred to them."

"If it will make you happy," Geoffrey mused. "This river is so small it is barely marked on here."

"It might be of more interest if you can work out how much further we must travel before we arrive at this wretched trading post," Marguerite said irritably, swatting another mosquito and lowering the netting attached to the brim of her hat. "You should get something to cover your head too, Geoffrey. We could all get bitten to death before we reach our destination."

"If you think I would be caught dead wearing anything like that, you can think again," Geoffrey said, squinting hard at the map.

"Take a look through this." Marguerite handed him a folding magnifying glass from the depths of her bag.

Soon after, Geoffrey found the elusive tributary, a narrow stretch of water branching off the main river barely two hundred yards before the Paputa Falls. At the end of this slim but lengthy waterway, there was a web of spidery tributaries, fanning out from an area marked Yanoa.

"I have found a place called Yanoa but there is nothing about any trading post."

"This is a very old book. The trading post might not have been in existence when the author documented this area."

"What could have possessed Father to travel so far away from civilisation just to conduct his research? Why would anyone in their right mind do that? This is virtually uncharted territory," Geoffrey said.

"I have absolutely no idea… unless his research might be less than legitimate," Marguerite said.

"Surely the hospital would never allow him to dabble in anything unorthodox?"

"Maybe not, but who can tell what he and Mr King were experimenting with? After all, none of this was funded by the hospital as far as I am aware. This was a private venture."

Over the next three days, Geoffrey and his family rarely got off the boat, preferring instead to stay on board and take it in turns to use the functioning lavatory and washbasin in Lady Claudia's room, rather than share the disgusting toilet facilities with the crew.

At mealtimes the food they ate with the captain in his private quarters was edible enough, although Geoffrey chose not to enquire about what meat the cook had used.

Because of the cramped conditions his violin lay idle. Geoffrey attempted to concentrate on composing but that didn't work either, with the constant clanking of the engine sending up clouds of billowing black smoke as the boat chugged slowly along the murky water. Their progress was shaded by the overhanging canopy of trees from either bank, forming a dank and sinister tunnel. Remembering with a shiver, the reptile that had fallen into Archie's cart, Geoffrey had good reason to bless Churuma's ingenuity in constructing a palm awning that offered ample protection from any creatures that might otherwise have dropped into the boat as it passed slowly beneath.

At night Geoffrey slept fitfully on his lounger under the stairs, now inadequately hung with a torn piece of stained canvas, which Churuma had found, a covering that Geoffrey found preferable to the see-through mosquito netting. His makeshift bed was constructed from a bamboo framework, made private by a barricade of empty crates that he and their helpful guide had piled up to obscure him from prying eyes.

"I swear I would have been eaten alive if I had stayed outside any longer," Geoffrey grumbled as his mother bathed the insect bites covering his face, neck and hands.

"It must be your pale skin that is attracting so many insects."

"I doubt these bites are to do with my skin, Mother. The stench from that canvas awning where I sleep is frightful. I am convinced those brown stains must be dried blood, and I dread the prospect of spending even one more night under that wretched thing."

"Then you must put aside any thoughts of propriety and sleep in the cabin with your sister and me," she said, dabbing the reddening areas with one of Marguerite's concoctions. "I am sure we can make room."

"I will ask Churuma to rig up an alternative cover. There must be something on board this rusting hulk."

"How can you remain so calm Geoffrey, this is so unlike you?" Rosamund said, wincing visibly at a violent shriek of agony from an unidentifiable creature that was clearly being dragged off by its predator through the dense undergrowth.

"I am as worried as you but I try not to show it," Geoffrey admitted.

"I wish I could be more like that."

"Quite the contrary; no one knows you better than I do, Rose, not even Mother."

"How grown up you seem. Archie would certainly approve of this alteration in you. You are so dependable now."

"I doubt Archie Westbrook would notice anyone else if you were in the same room."

"Do you think he only liked me because I am pretty?"

"Well you look like rubbish first thing in a morning but he will not have to endure the shock of that, unless he pops the question!"

"Do you think he might?"

"It is unlikely that anyone in their right mind would knowingly burden himself with a wilful creature like you Rose, but then he can be unpredictable too."

"Do you think Maggie would draw him for me?"

"Would that be a good idea, if she is hoping to get her drawings from this trip published on our return?" Geoffrey said guiltily, praying she wouldn't say the same to Marguerite and then demand the portrait of Archie for herself.

"Why does Maggie never confide in me like that? Why does it always have to be you? I think publishing her work is a splendid idea and I would have told her so had I known. Does Mama know?"

"I believe so."

"Then that makes it ten times worse. I am not just a pretty face, you know. I do have an opinion, if any of you bothered to ask!"

"And so you do, which proves what I said earlier. Once what you present to the world fades, as it eventually will, then behold… the Rose with thorns will emerge!" Geoffrey laughed which ended with a well-aimed kick on his shin.

The further inland the steamer chugged, the more the ancient majesty of the monumental trees took hold of his imagination, compelling him to scribble down passages of music before they evaporated and were lost forever.

Often, Geoffrey had the uneasy sensation they were being watched from the bank but, stare as he might, he saw nothing except for a few brilliant flashes of copper glinting among the dense foliage, all within moments of each other, yet in different areas of the undergrowth. He became convinced it wasn't just an overactive imagination when he saw Churuma staring just as intently at the same section of forest.

Shouting something unintelligible to his sister, Churuma waited until the boat came to a narrow section of the river and then leapt from the deck, landing awkwardly on the bank. Limping, their guide disappeared in the direction of the coppery light.

Shortly afterwards the captain dropped anchor close to a rocky outcrop to replenish the tanks from a waterfall. At around the same time, Churuma reappeared from the forest, clearly tired but with a look of elation in his eyes. Still limping, he had some difficulty in clambering back on board, hindered by his refusal to unclench his hand until he was well clear of the crewman helping him over the rail.

"Where the devil have you been?" Geoffrey demanded, intrigued by the expression on the young guide's face, as if he'd been subjected to some holy vision.

Sitting beside him, Churuma opened his left hand to reveal three long strands of what looked like a fine wire of copper or gold. He remained seated in the same position for well over an hour, painstakingly plaiting the strands into a gleaming cord. When this was done, he wrapped the band three times around his wrist, finally knotting the trophy in position with the aid of his strong, white teeth.

From then on, instead of sleeping on the boat, around midnight Churuma would select a clear space on the riverbank where he would sit cross-legged, chanting with his face turned upwards to the moonlight, his hands cupped as if to catch the beams of light, where they illuminated the plaited band around his wrist so that Geoffrey could have sworn it was on fire. Oddly enough, the rhythm of his voice had seemingly quieted every nocturnal animal in the immediate vicinity.

On the second night, when the moonlight was at its most brilliant, Geoffrey became aware that Marguerite had stealthily appeared and was also witnessing this strange ritual.

"What are you doing out here, Maggs?" Geoffrey whispered.

"Watching… the same as you" she said, reaching for the satchel across his shoulder.

"What the hell are you doing?"

"I need my journal right away, Geoffrey."

"You must be bonkers if you think you can draw anything in this light."

"Just hand it over," she hissed, realising from her tone that if he didn't do as she asked she would never allow him to keep it safe again.

Marguerite immediately perched on the edge of his makeshift bed and began sketching the striking image onto the page. She had barely completed the outline when, following Churuma's gaze, she and Geoffrey looked up into the starlit canopy. To their disbelief, the ethereal, silvery shape of a winged spirit was gliding above them.

Barely aware of his sister's furious sketching, Geoffrey could only watch open-mouthed as the spirit passed across the face of the moon, the translucent wings infused with glistening silver as it crossed the night sky, fluttering with a hypnotic grace until the shape was obscured by the treetops.

When Geoffrey awoke the following morning he was unsure whether what he had witnessed had been a dream but only until Marguerite asked him to return the journal to the zipped section of the satchel.

"Did you manage to capture what we saw last night?"

Instead of answering, she opened the journal for him, first displaying a sketch of Churuma which was so incredibly lifelike their guide could have risen from the page and spoken.

"This is amazing work, Maggs."

"Thank you. I could not be happier with the way this has turned out, although this other one I find rather disturbing. Do you think it could have just been a passing cloud?"

"No… it was definitely not that." Geoffrey stared transfixed at the flowing shape of the bird-like spirit.

"Then what was it?"

"I have absolutely no idea. What is important is that you have recorded whatever it was in perfect detail. This sketch is astounding. You must show this to Mother."

"She is not well this morning. I have given her an extra red pill to ease the pain."

"Did you have to?"

"Had you been there, Geoffrey, and seen how much pain she was in, you would have done exactly the same."

"What bothers me is how many of these pills Mother has left for the journey. We did not find very many in that disgusting apartment."

On the final stages of the trip the food consisted of boiled rice and fish, which Geoffrey particularly enjoyed when garnished with an unfamiliar, crushed fruit that had been pounded into a sticky substance, giving it a texture not dissimilar to honey.

"If the captain does not alter course soon, this old tub will get pitched over the falls and us along with it," Geoffrey said, studying his map with growing concern, trying to work out how much further ahead Yanoa could be.

"I just pray Father's compound will be close to this trading post so that we can find him before we all expire from this infernal heat," Marguerite commented.

"Or get bitten to death by swarming mosquitoes," Geoffrey added, swatting at one that was settling on his arm. "What could have possessed Father to base himself in this godforsaken place?"

"Quite possibly because his research could not be conducted anywhere else. Father would never have relinquished the comforts of home without due cause, so I imagine he selected this area because of what might be found growing here. There must be countless unknown plants out here, Geoffrey, varieties of flora and fauna which could have properties that are invaluable for an experimental programme."

"That is possible but only if he foregoes any need for creature comforts, and that is not very likely."

"Maybe not… but there are other possibilities," she said thoughtfully.

"I suppose debauchery would be one contender," Geoffrey retorted cynically.

"Considering his blatant disregard for his patients' welfare at the hospital in London, there is another possibility: being so far removed from society would be ideal in the event of something going wrong during his trials."

"That is a dreadful thought!"

"Indeed but, wherever he is based, its remoteness might serve to prevent the spread of any unforeseen infection," Marguerite said, before staring towards a distant patch of open ground on the far bank.

"What have you spotted, Maggs?" Geoffrey asked, blinking furiously to dislodge an insect in his eye. Through his blurred vision he could just make out what appeared to be an elderly man in a priest's cassock, urging a hefty mule towards a steep rise.

"Dear God in heaven!" Marguerite gasped as a youthful, wild-looking figure with a mane of auburn hair now broke cover and went haring after the priest, brandishing a spear. Bounding alongside him was a ferocious-looking wolfhound.

"Oh my hat… he is naked… and white!" Geoffrey cried, unable to see properly before his view was obliterated by the dense foliage bordering the clearing. Anxiously, they listened for the priest's screams from the attack that had seemed inevitable but heard nothing above the usual sounds of the rainforest.

"Geoffrey, hand over the journal," Marguerite urged him.

"Not now… I have something in my eye. I can barely see."

"Just hand it over," she snapped. Once it was in her possession, she began sketching furiously and didn't look up again until the dramatic images of the old priest, the wild youth and the wolfhound were etched on the page.

248

"If you have captured any of what we just saw, I am convinced this will be an extraordinary book, whatever that Dobson woman says."

"Do you honestly think so?"

"Of course I do. I mean, who would have expected to see anything like what you have just drawn, here, in this godforsaken country?" Geoffrey said, unable to get the images out his head.

Chapter Twelve
Yanoa

Around lunchtime on the following day, a Jesuit mission came into view, built high on a cliff at the junction of two rivers. At the base of the cliff was a modest landing stage shaded by a large tree.

"Who in their right mind would build something so inaccessible? It seems more like a fortification against marauding raiders than a religious establishment," Geoffrey observed.

"I think I can see a road leading up from the forest," Marguerite pointed out, shading her eyes.

The captain approached. "Señor… you need speak me?" he asked.

"It is imperative that we stop off here, captain. I must question this priest about the whereabouts of my father, unless of course he was the man I saw being pursued by an armed savage, in which case I fear for his safety."

"El Americano es no 'ere."

"You misunderstand me, captain. I am asking to see the priest, the priest from the mission up there," Geoffrey said, pointing to the building.

"Si señor, him Gringo… boat gone mean him no 'ere. Mañana we at Yanoa, señor; ask there."

Although the map showed that they were now nearing Yanoa, it was clear this part of the river would be more difficult to navigate and the steamer chugged on slowly for three more days. Two of these nights Geoffrey spent cramped inside the cabin with his elder sister to avoid being eaten alive by the swarms of mosquitoes that descended on the boat like an avenging cloud.

When the trading post of Yanoa at last came into view at the intersection of five rivers, it was clear the channel they had used was by far the largest of them. Like the mission, the building had been constructed on high, rocky ground but, because of its reliance on trade from the river, it was easily accessible via three levels of staging, connected by steps leading down to the dock.

Above this was a barnlike structure, irregular in shape and somewhat lopsided. The supporting frame was formed of four twisted tree trunks, each with a number of branches which supported the palm-leafed roofing. Although the building had been positioned for access from the river, from the well-trodden tracks leading out of the forest, it was apparent that this was a well-used place.

Just beyond the landing stage there were two independent tributaries, running parallel. Tied up against the dock were three dugout canoes, while moored close by was another shallow-draught boat, its grimy boiler belching out plumes of black smoke over its filthy, shredded awning. Hard at work underneath, was a figure that appeared to be a local tribesman, though dressed in grimy European clothing, who was stoking up the fire in preparation for departure once the boat had been unloaded.

"What is the delay?" Geoffrey asked when the captain ordered the engines to be cut, and the anchor dropped, a short distance away from the dock.

"It better wait, them mal hombres, señor. Bandidos." The captain indicated three unsavoury white males who were struggling up a section of the rickety staging, all loaded down with packs of untreated caiman hides. From where they were anchored, Geoffrey had a clear view of the group. One of them, who seemed to be the leader, was negotiating with a large and bizarrely dressed woman, who was shouting down from the clifftop and could be clearly heard from the boat as she bellowed out that the men should not come any further up the steps.

After a brisk negotiation with the brute, whom she addressed as Valdez, she called to someone inside to bring out two sacks of produce, three clinking cases of bottled spirits, a rifle, some boxes of cartridges and two gleaming machetes.

These were then lowered down on a hoist by two burly tribesmen, leaving Valdez to order his accomplices to transport them to the boat. The only items that Valdez handled himself were the rifle and a pack of shells.

"Dear lord… what is that horrific smell?" Marguerite asked, clamping a handkerchief tightly against her nostrils against the stench of rotting flesh as the wind shifted in their direction just as the caiman hunters began loading their provisions onto the filthy steamer. When the first man stumbled against his colleague, the jolt caused him to drop some of the cargo, struggling with his one hand to grab the sack of provisions before it fell into the river. The wasted section of his left upper arm, severed beneath the elbow, waved grotesquely as he attempted to regain his balance.

However, as macabre as his disfigurement was at a distance, the sight that his companion presented to the onlookers was infinitely more terrifying when he turned his maimed features towards them. Most of his nose was missing and what remained was covered in scar tissue, as too was a section of his crooked lower jaw. Above this, a blinded right eye seemed to stare menacingly at them with its milky-white gaze, as if he could hear Marguerite whimpering like a child, pressing the screwed-up handkerchief against her mouth to prevent her from screaming aloud.

"God in heaven… this place must be verging on Hell!" Geoffrey said in horror, unable to tear his gaze away from the nightmarish ensemble as the brutish Valdez now clambered aboard the steamer, clicking the firing bolt of his rifle off and on with military precision as if in anticipation of the next killing session.

Unlike the other two hunters, Valdez appeared to have acquired no physical defects from the savagery of their trade other than the stained and rotting teeth exposed inside his vicious gash of a mouth as he snarled at one of the tribesmen from the trading post, who nervously dumped a sack of produce some distance away from the boat and scurried back towards the steps.

Valdez now withdrew a vicious knife from his waistband, clearly ready to embed it into the retreating back of the tribesman and was only persuaded against doing so when the owner bellowed down from the clifftop, indicating two more tribesmen positioned strategically to the left and right of her, each with a blowpipe against his mouth.

To Geoffrey's immense relief, within a few moments the paddles of the hunters' steamer began to rotate, threshing the water into foam as they veered off the main course of the river and chugged up one of the nearby tributaries, leaving the stench of their cargo and unwashed bodies hovering like an invisible cloud across the dock as *La Constantia* pulled up alongside.

With Churuma leading the way, Geoffrey urged his mother and younger sister to go ahead up the rickety staircase with the captain, while he assisted Marguerite. More troubling was that, now Valdez had left, there was no sign of any other vessel moored in the dock, contrary to what he thought Churuma had told him.

Once they had reached the top, he discovered his mother and the captain engrossed in conversation with the proprietor. Her overweight body was slouched in a throne-like chair beneath the conical thatch of the store roof, a covering that precariously straddled the rotting timbers. Adjacent to this were two other buildings, one of which had been built on wooden posts. This construction had a veranda running the entire length, unlike the smaller one that was accessed by two steps and was of a more basic design.

The proprietor, one Misqualla, was broad-featured and of mixed race, her skin chalky and patched with dark blotches. She was of medium height but gave an illusion of increased stature with the aid of a turquoise silk turban pinned together with a glittering green brooch, presumably as a symbol of her authority. Her broad, intimidating body was swathed in an elaborately embroidered material fashioned in the manner of a sarong, an unflattering choice in view of the evident stubble on her chin and the hairy, muscular arms.

"Massa Olibo? Him no 'ere," Misqualla responded to Lady Claudia's inquiry.

"Then where is my father?" Geoffrey asked, barely able to contain his exasperation and unsettled by the glint in those bullfrog eyes that had not looked away from him from the first moment he had appeared.

"Him no say where go," Misqualla replied, gesturing theatrically with open palms amid the jangle of multiple bangles sliding down her muscular arms as members of the crew began bringing up the family's luggage and piling it beside him.

"We cannot have our luggage up here, captain," Geoffrey protested. "We must continue our journey with you as my father is not here."

"I not take back, señor. My boat… it soon full." Below them his crew was already loading up a collection of caged hyacinth macaws, hoatzin birds, jaguar cubs, golden lion tamarins, sloths and other smaller creatures that Geoffrey was unable to identify.

"But Captain, you cannot simply abandon my family out here in the middle of nowhere. It is inhuman!" Geoffrey protested.

"Have you seen Mother?" Rosamund asked unexpectedly.

"Not recently, why? I had assumed she was with you." It was clear the captain had no intention of changing his mind. "They cannot be far away," he said with as much reassurance as he could muster. "Mother will be perfectly safe with Maggs. Just stay close to me and we will look for them once I have been able to sort out our return passage, otherwise we could be stranded in this godforsaken dump until we rot!" Geoffrey strode after the departing man and grabbed him by the arm. "Please reconsider our situation, captain, I beg you."

"It no possible, señor," the captain said, shaking his arm free and moving away to supervise the loading of the cages and crates of livestock onto the boat.

"I understand your situation, captain but, if you cannot transport us back, then I need your assurance that either you or another boat will return here to collect us as soon as possible."

After a lengthy discussion the captain agreed to deliver a note to Don Julio, asking him to arrange for a vessel to collect them from Yanoa at his earliest convenience. Even so, it could take two weeks before any steamer could reach them so, until then, they would have to make the best of the situation at the trading post.

To Geoffrey's immense relief, his mother returned during this exchange, appearing as if from nowhere carrying a worn, leather bag across her shoulders.

"Where did you get to, Mother?"

"There were a few essential items I needed to purchase," she said with a glimmer of satisfaction.

"You should not have gone into that place on your own. I could have obtained whatever you needed," Geoffrey said with alarm.

"You would not have known what to choose, my darling, and it did not take long. Marguerite will be out in a moment."

"What on earth would possess her to stay inside that building on her own? God alone knows what could be lurking in there."

"We were offered use of the facilities in the smaller bungalow. You and Rosamund should also take advantage of the water closet, darling. It is all rather primitive but at least it is clean."

Four muscular natives carrying packing crates of medical equipment now approached them from the main building and dumped them alongside their already considerable pile of baggage. These were followed soon after by three chests of tinned foods from North America.

"What are we supposed to do with this lot?" Geoffrey said moodily.

"We will find a solution," Lady Claudia said, in her reassuring way when faced by a difficult situation.

"Mother, sit in the shade; the sun is scorching out here in the open."

"Then you must sit with us too, Geoffrey."

"I will, but only after I have checked these crates for any other information."

"Then I shall help," Rosamund cut in, "otherwise you will be more impossible than ever if I just sit in the shade and watch." She clicked open her grossly inadequate parasol as she began examining some chalk scrawls on one of the chests.

"You will only get in the way."

"Or maybe not… how about the name Scaggoa, marked here on the end of this case?"

"That sounds more like an Italian dish," Geoffrey said with annoyance, as yet another crate of medical supplies was deposited with their luggage.

"Then maybe you should have paid more attention to his letters."

"Perhaps I would have done, if he ever wrote a letter to me," he said, desperate to find some other clue before his sister got the upper hand.

"That is rubbish, Jeffy. He must have done."

"Why would I lie? He never writes to any of us… except you and, after what I found out about his carryings on, I am rather glad he did not."

"Then pretend for a few moments I am not as stupid as you and Maggie seem to think and credit me with having some common sense for once. Scaggoa is a village he mentioned once as being a possible place to begin his research. And look, the same name is written in Papa's handwriting on this tag." Rosamund showed him a water-stained luggage label.

"You are probably right. The problem is, my Spanish is absolutely hopeless and so is yours come to that."

"I can speak French," Rosamund said defensively.

"Are you barmy? What use is that? We need someone who can find out where this Scaggoa place is exactly. That creepy Medusa who owns this dump must have some idea."

"Why not ask Churuma?"

"I would, if he could understand more than two words of English."

"I can ask the captain; I am sure he would not be averse to helping," Rosamund said, smiling prettily as she reopened the parasol.

"He is too busy loading."

"Then ask the owner. She seemed to understand some of what Mother was asking. All you need is to get her over here and show her this mark."

"Ugh… there is no chance. She looks me up and down like a joint of meat in a butcher's shop. That woman scares the hell out of me."

"Oh for goodness' sake stop putting obstacles in the way. If you are going to be so melodramatic, then I will do it," she said, trying to remove the tag. "Damnation… I cannot undo this leather strap. It must have got wet and swollen up."

"Let me have a go," Geoffrey said, fully expecting to undo it in seconds and gain the upper hand but he couldn't shift it either.

"So what do we do now?" Rosamund asked.

After a moment's thought, Geoffrey pulled Archie's hunting knife from the leather satchel and sliced through the leather strap in a single cut.

"Where on earth did you get that?" she demanded.

"I got it from Archie, why?"

"I know who it belongs to, you fool. What I want to know is why you have it in your bag. Archie would never have given it to you willingly."

"It was not stolen, if that is what you are implying. It wouldn't be in this bag if he hadn't given it to me, would it?"

"That knife is a family heirloom; it belonged to Archie's father. He would never have given it to anyone and least of all to you."

"Well, contrary to your idiotic assumptions, he gave me this on the night before he sailed for Ireland. There was absolutely no point saying anything about it before, either to you or to anyone else, because I never thought I would use it, not until just now. Satisfied?"

"Not in the least. Why would he give his knife to you? You cannot tolerate violence; even Archie must have been aware of that."

"It was for our protection on this journey."

"That does not explain why he would give that knife to you, of all people. You never spent much time together and whenever you did, you were usually arguing."

"He made me take the blasted knife on loan. I am to give it back when we return and, having seen some of the shifty characters here, I am glad that he did as we might need it later." He attached the now sheathed knife to the belt around his waist, which immediately made him feel more secure than he had in weeks.

"Do not allow Mother to see you wearing that, Jeffy. Can you not cover it with a handkerchief? You look like a bandit." Rosamund smiled and linked his arm as they made their way after the retreating Misqualla.

"This search for Father is becoming more insane with every place we stop," Geoffrey complained. "How are we supposed to continue without a boat?"

"Maybe there is a way overland. There are plenty of tracks leading away from here," Rosamund suggested.

"That is worth a try, but not together. I need to get the three of you to the mission until I return. It will be safer there with the priest, assuming he is still alive. Rather that than wait here. Father cannot be that far away now, and I swear I will bring him back to sign the paperwork, even if I have to drag him by the ear; and trust me, if I have to do that, I will."

"That will never work, Jeffy. Mama will never budge from her decision."

Once inside, they were barely able to breathe for the nauseating stench of rotting animal hides hanging from drying frames like ragged red carpets. The base of each post stood in a bowl of paraffin to keep ants and other flesh-eating insects away.

After a difficult and halting conversation with Misqualla, she confirmed it would be impossible to reach their Father's research encampment on foot. The only safe means of transport was by river and, because there were no shallow-draught boats available, their only option was to travel by dugout canoe. Adding to this already nightmarish proposal, there were only three craft available and, because each dugout would need to be accompanied not only by the owner but by one other tribesman acting as paddle-man, it was clear that the lack of space would make for a most unpleasant journey over the coming days.

When this singular travel option was revealed to Lady Claudia and Marguerite, it was immediately clear that his mother was no less determined in her resolve, unlike his elder sister, who he was convinced was about to pass out when she learnt the family would be paddling upriver crammed into hollowed-out logs.

"There must be a way to dissuade Mother," Geoffrey said in a final bid to avoid any more discomfort for her. "Waiting at the mission has to be the only option... for all of you."

"Mama will never change her mind about this, or wait while you go off on your own," Rosamund reasoned.

"But she must. You and I might survive travelling by canoe but Mother cannot, not in her condition. Maggs is terrified of water and, from what I have seen, they are so narrow she would never even get that backside of hers into one without using a crowbar!" Geoffrey said, unable to resist a smirk despite the gravity of the situation, which was rewarded with a pinch on the arm from his sister.

"Sometimes I swear you have no sense of anyone's feelings except for your own," Rosamund said.

"Actually, I do not give a damn what you think, because I am trying to be practical. I am not being insulting and, if you cannot see that, you can go to hell!"

"I would say we are already there." Rosamund's beautiful eyes welled up. "I am sorry if I sounded beastly."

"My days would not be the same if you were not," he said gently, resting his arm across her shoulders. "I suppose that crowbar comment was a bit much?" he added, relieved to see her laugh.

As he waited for his mother and Churuma to complete negotiations for the use of the dugouts and an overnight stay in the smaller bungalow, Geoffrey examined Archie's family crest, chased into the silver handle of the knife, unaware of Lady Claudia approaching until she was almost upon him.

"Please be careful, darling, you might cut your fingers with that knife. It looks terribly sharp. Where did you get it?"

"This is on loan, from… a friend." Geoffrey said, returning the knife into its scabbard.

"You should not wear it on your belt either, Geoffrey. What if you fall over and cut yourself? This is not Ashbourne. There are no hospitals here."

"I will be careful, Mother, I promise. I know I am not like Grandfather, obsessed with stag hunting and winning trophies for being a crack shot."

"Actually, darling, most of the trophies in Grandpa's cabinet were mine, not his. Archie's father and I were very competitive in our youth. We entered every competition we could. I was an excellent markswoman in my day and, if he did not win first prize, then I did," she said, smiling at the memory.

"When you won that trophy at Lady Harriet's it did come as a shock but if you were that good, why did you stop?" Geoffrey asked, barely able to take in the new information.

"Only because your grandfather insisted I went hunting with him. Naturally I refused to take part in any blood sports, so he banned me from ever returning to Ireland.

After I married your father and had Marguerite, I lost interest."

"Even so, you did rather well with those targets at Lady Harriet's."

"Once you learn to ride a horse, you never forget. The same applies to a firearm. That is why I decided to purchase a revolver before we ventured any further."

"You bought a gun!" Geoffrey exclaimed.

"Indeed I have. You said it yourself, Geoffrey. We need some means of protection and I have no intention of having any of my children harmed. Who knows what creatures might be lurking out there."

"Or people," Geoffrey muttered, eyeing Misqualla's band of muscular bodyguards.

While Geoffrey checked through the luggage his mother sat in a shaded area with Marguerite who had brought her a drink in a cup adapted from a cow-horn, allowing her to swallow two of the red painkillers.

"We must find a way to get you more of these, Mother, or something comparable."

"Your father will be able to help. He must have something in his laboratory, since there appear to be regular deliveries of medical supplies. We shall be there in three days, and I have enough to last until then."

The reality of being propelled along the river in a hollowed-out log only hit home as they examined the primitive craft beside the dock.

"I suggest we should try out the canoes first and see if we can all fit. Two of them seem extraordinarily narrow," Marguerite said nervously as Geoffrey and Churuma arrived with the violin case and some folding chairs.

"Bear in mind, Maggs, the biggest of these will need to accommodate our luggage," Geoffrey said.

"There is no reason for us to take everything, surely, if we are returning in less than a week?"

"Do you honestly imagine that anything would be here when we got back? That Misqualla creature would have sold off the lot by that time," Geoffrey retorted.

"They seem very low above the surface of the water already and we must all have some form of seating if we are travelling in these for three days," Lady Claudia commented.

"I have asked Churuma to borrow some folding chairs from the trading post," Geoffrey said, opening them out before assisting Rosamund and his mother into the narrowest of the canoes.

Once they were in position, padding was inserted to wedge the seats tightly against the sides of the hollowed-out trunk and, although this didn't afford much space, it did at least allow them more comfortable seating.

"If you must insist on taking every piece of luggage, Geoffrey, then your father will need to arrange to collect these crates of food later."

"But if we leave it behind, what about us, Mother, we could starve?" Marguerite complained.

"There will be enough to eat when we arrive. Your father was never one to go without," Lady Claudia said decisively.

It was arranged that Churuma and his sister Nia would travel with the luggage in the widest of the canoes, leaving more space for Geoffrey and Marguerite in the other.

Marguerite was clearly mortified at the prospect of being afloat on the murky river in a hewn-out log and it was impossible to calm her down until Churuma came over and, with an air of reverence, knelt before her to offer her the narrow plaited band from his wrist.

"What are you doing, you silly man? Please get up now before anyone sees you. Geoffrey, make him take away whatever it is he is offering," Marguerite said, backing away.

"He does not mean you any harm. He is offering you a charm for the journey to keep you safe. Please take it, otherwise he might be offended," Geoffrey said, watching with relief as his sister allowed the young man to put the bracelet on her wrist.

"This workmanship is very beautiful," she said more calmly, as the intense sunlight glinted on the burnished copper threads, causing them to glow like a band of red-hot metal. What she had failed to notice, which Geoffrey did not, was that where the bracelet had been removed from Churuma's wrist it had left marks on his flesh, as if each detail of the band had been branded into his skin.

"Master, him he come," Churuma muttered, speaking in semi-coherent English, his voice oddly mesmeric.

"Who will come?" Geoffrey asked, but their guide remained on his knees as if kneeling before a Madonna.

"Tu estar la madre" he whispered. To Geoffrey's amazement, Marguerite offered no resistance when Churuma pressed his lips against each of her fingertips with a slow deliberation, chanting rhythmically after each contact.

Throughout this strange ritual Marguerite seemed transfixed, unable to pull away until it was over. Afterwards, turning his unseeing eyes directly into the heavens, the young guide stared unblinking into the brilliance of the sun before he passed out cold.

"What the devil is wrong with him?" Geoffrey said, emptying a pitcher of water onto his upturned face before dragging him into the shade in the care of his sister Nia.

It soon became apparent, however, that the dugout Geoffrey was to share with Marguerite would not accommodate her. A long session of bartering with the owner of the canoe, involving a steel mirror, one gold sovereign and a silver pocket watch, finally persuaded him to hack out more space in the log until finally there was room for her. This unexpected delay and the imminent nightfall, meant that more negotiations were necessary with Misqualla. Only then was the family able to spend the night in the smaller of the two bungalows, which to their relief was well furnished and comfortable.

Although his mother tried to persuade him otherwise, Geoffrey chose to spend the night out on the veranda, finding a spot with some privacy behind a pile of empty crates where he set up a place to sleep. It was a sweltering night and it wasn't long before he discarded his damp nightshirt and fell fast asleep, shrouded beneath a length of shabby mosquito netting on a rickety cane lounger.

Never an early riser, Geoffrey was painfully woken by the blunt end of a spear prodding his exposed groin, thrusts that kept him pinioned as another was shoved under his chin, making it impossible to move.

"Let me go, you bastards!" Geoffrey hissed, as much alarmed that his mother and sisters might come out on to the veranda and see him naked as he was intimidated by the two men, wishing he'd had the presence of mind to have kept Archie's knife close by.

In the dawn light he recognised his antagonists as two of the paddle-men, seemingly intent on inflicting as much pain as possible and prodding at his groin with mounting amusement. The ordeal came to an abrupt end when Churuma, who had crept up on them unawares, held a knife against the throat of the main antagonist, calling out to the other man to back off.

"There must be other men with canoes instead of these idiots, Churuma? I will not allow my family to travel with those perverts," Geoffrey grumbled in an effort to cover his embarrassment. His anger had not lessened by the time he had buttoned up his shirt and yanked on his trousers.

"I speak Misqualla, señor," Churuma said, which surprised Geoffrey since their guide had barely spoken or even acknowledged the English language before. After an offer of five more gold sovereigns, Misqualla produced an elderly paddle-man and a boy of no more than thirteen. Geoffrey had no option other than to accept the replacements.

Once the old man and boy had loaded the larger canoe with luggage, the violin was wrapped with a double layer of oilskin Churuma had collected from the trading post, along with the mosquito net Geoffrey had used on the previous night and a groundsheet with which he covered the mound of baggage.

"We are almost ready to set off, Mother," Geoffrey said as she came towards them with a bulky raffia bag.

"I had to make a practical purchase for the journey since there will be no lavatories available and, before any of you make any comments, I will not be subjected to using torn-up newspapers or banana leaves as an option." She handed Geoffrey and his sisters a roll of toilet paper each.

Once his mother and Rosamund were comfortably seated and shaded by their parasols they might well have been studies for a Renoir painting, had their canoe not been a hollowed-out log.

Apart from the old man and the boy, there were four grey-haired paddle-men, each wearing body paint to ward off evil spirits. All the men had a spear close by and carried a sheathed hunting knife on a plaited belt, from which also hung a barely adequate loincloth.

After the baggage canoe was already on the river, Lady Claudia and Rosamund's vessel was launched. Negotiating Marguerite around a large mound of freshly chipped wood, Geoffrey was finally able to persuade his reluctant sister to squeeze her hips into the recently enlarged hollow of the dugout, where she sat on a wooden box. Geoffrey climbed gingerly on board and, moments later, the paddle-men launched the primitive craft into the river.

Late that afternoon Geoffrey noticed that the paddle-men in each of the canoes had stopped calling out to each other and were carefully guiding the dugouts away from the centre of the river and closer to the right bank. The reason became clear when Geoffrey's canoe rounded a bend and was paddled even closer to the bank where trailing, willow-like fronds snagged at their hair and lashed against their unprotected faces as the caiman hunters' encampment came into view on the opposite bank.

Two of the hunters were gutting a caiman strung up on rack. Neither the one-armed man nor his scar-faced companion was aware of the passing canoes until their brutish commander called out as Geoffrey's dugout rounded the bend where he had been urinating into the river.

The older paddle-man and teenager were having difficulty keeping the canoe away from the centre of the river as they fought against the strong undertow that was bringing it steadily closer to the encampment. There Rodrigo now stopped hacking at the carcass and, grabbing a handful of bloody entrails piled at his feet, hurled them at the dugouts with surprising accuracy. Although the gory projectiles fell short by a few feet, both Geoffrey and his sister's faces were splashed from the bleeding flesh before it sank. Barely had his sister wet her handkerchief in the river to rub her face clean, heedless of the rocking this created, than the waters erupted around the resurfacing entrails, frothing against the canoe as they were torn apart in a savage feeding frenzy by a swarm of red-bellied piranha.

That evening, Geoffrey and his family were hardly able to relax and sat huddled together beneath a sloping canvas sheet tied to the lower branches of a tree overhanging a clearing on the bank.

A fretful night was interspersed with the jarring death-cries of unidentifiable creatures and the following morning it was clear from the way Marguerite was walking that she was in a considerable amount of pain. Finally she had to admit that her hips were both sore and swollen from being so tightly wedged in the dugout but when Geoffrey had Churuma ask for more wood to be hacked out of the trunk, the old paddle-man refused.

The second day would have seemed endless had it not been for the sense of relief that, the further they travelled into that remote region, the more they distanced themselves from the menacing caiman hunters. At midday they were able to take a break, eating a lunch of grilled fish with a tasty red vegetable that Nia prepared before they clambered back into their individual dugouts.

In the evening, Geoffrey helped Churuma erect a section of a canvas tent, which they roped on to an overhanging bough. Although it started raining heavily before dark, the paddle-men managed to keep the fire from going out until it began to come down in torrents, at which point they huddled together until dawn, sheltering beneath an upturned dugout supported on logs. It was still raining when the boats were eventually re-launched, and, although Geoffrey had intended wearing his panama hat, he couldn't find it anywhere and he was soon soaked to the skin.

Although it was a tight squeeze, his mother and Rosamund were at least able to share the only umbrella they had with them, while Marguerite sat hooded beneath a section of the tent. Because of the intense downpour and the possibility of the documents getting wet, Geoffrey persuaded his mother to keep hold of the satchel and shelter it beneath her umbrella.

That night they made camp in a convenient clearing on the bank, where Churuma rigged up the makeshift tent one more. By then the rain had stopped, leaving a dense mist that had barely cleared by ten o'clock on the following morning.

In mid-afternoon they passed a number of unoccupied dwellings on raised poles that clearly hadn't been lived in for months. Geoffrey hoped they were at last nearing the Scaggoa compound and the long-delayed confrontation with his father.

Immediately ahead of them, the paddle-men in his mother's canoe began jabbering agitatedly as a modest docking area became evident, projecting out into the river. On the bank close by, two giant condors were tearing apart some unfortunate creature.

On a section of higher ground, closer to their canoes, another huge condor was dragging its victim to the very edge of a promontory, from where it now launched out across the river directly towards them, its prey dangling awkwardly from the vicious talons. The bird's dramatic eight-foot wingspan was a nightmarish sight as it swooped down towards Geoffrey's canoe and he was able to identify the swinging carcass of a half-eaten tribesman, grasped tightly by the head so that he dangled like a grotesque rag doll.

The bird had barely passed beyond his mother's canoe when the weight of the swinging carcass pulled it away from the head with a resounding crack as the torso crashed on to the dugout below, striking one of the pole-men across the shoulders, the crushing weight of the flailing legs shattering the other man's arm and pitching them both into the river.

Moments later the condor released the detached head, which plummeted like a cannonball into Geoffrey's dugout, landing just a few feet away from his sister's legs. Screaming with terror, she struggled wildly in an attempt to free herself from her wedged position, wailing hysterically as the severed head rolled over her feet. Both paddle-men, screaming with fear, scrambled clear of the canoe just as Geoffrey tried to reach her, their combined weight capsizing the hollowed-out trunk, rolling the dugout over and pitching Geoffrey overboard.

Grabbing hold of his violin case, Geoffrey briefly saw the tribesman with the fractured arm resurface, frantically trying to stay afloat with his one good arm and swimming slowly after Lady Claudia's canoe that was now drifting towards the projecting dock until the water surrounding him suddenly erupted with a frenzied shoal of piranha. The horrific intensity of his tortured screams gave Geoffrey all the impetus he needed to dive under the canoe to release his trapped sister.

Underneath the water Marguerite was straining desperately to get free, her arms flailing in the murky green water. A long coil of unloosened hair thrashed about her face like seaweed as Geoffrey grabbed her head and pushed her nose into a pocket of trapped air inside the canoe, all the time struggling to release her voluminous dress which was snagged on an improvised paddle holder, her hips still

268

wedged tightly in the dugout. Sucking in a lungful of air, he twisted his body upside-down, ignoring the water that was forced up his nose as he struggled to cut the material free with Archie's hunting knife. He was amazed to see a bright amber glow from the woven band around his sister's wrist, helping him to find exactly where to cut as he straddled his legs either side of her for leverage. On the third attempt at locking his elbows under her armpits, he wrenched her clear of the makeshift seat, tearing another gaping hole in her tattered garment.

As they reached the bank, Geoffrey stretched every sinew to drag Marguerite well clear of the river, supporting her shuddering body as she began retching up a mixture of river water and bile. With relief, he saw that his mother and Rosamund had reached the landing stage in the drifting dugout and were safe. Seeing Marguerite in her distressed state, they made their way towards her, forgetting to secure their canoe, which began drifting away on the current. On the opposite bank Nia was knee deep in shallow water, surrounded by floating luggage, slowly submerging as it drifted into the centre of the river.

What neither his mother nor sister noticed was Churuma re-boarding the remaining dugout canoe, now empty of their belongings, in an effort to stop the remaining paddle-men from abandoning them too. At first he seemed to be gaining some control over the men, until four tribal hunters appeared through the bushes carrying a gruesome array of decapitated human heads dangling from a pole carried between two of them.

Without hesitation one of the head-hunters leapt into the shallows, caught hold of Nia by the hair and dragged her screaming onto the bank, while another loaded up his blowpipe as the girl was yanked out of sight beyond the bushes.

Powerless to help on the other side of the river, Geoffrey could only watch as Churuma leapt into the shallows from the dugout, bellowing unintelligible threats at the hunters above the sounds of Nia's screams, wading through the water until he was able to clamber on to the far bank, his gleaming hunting knife held in readiness to strike. Then, without any warning, he fell backwards into the river, thrashing about like a wild creature, clawing at the poisoned dart lodged deep in his neck. From the other side of the bushes came the sound of an axe, Nia's screams ceasing abruptly as Churuma's lifeless body sank below the surface.

Chapter Thirteen
A Change of Direction

Their frantic questions about Marguerite's condition made it clear that neither Rosamund nor his mother had been aware of the dramatic events on the opposite bank and Geoffrey had no idea how he could tell them what he had seen. It was obvious that something needed to be done to get his sister away from the river and together they got her to her feet and supported her along the bank until she was seated on the edge of the dock.

Geoffrey had never felt more frightened and alone in his entire life than in that moment. What he desperately needed was someone like Archie, someone who could instil in him the confidence he so desperately needed as he watched the remaining dugout being paddled furiously back up the river, where it rounded the bend and disappeared from sight.

"What should we do, Jeffy?" Rosamund asked, jolting him back to reality.

"Did you see what happened?" he asked cautiously, grateful that his mother was occupied in tying a shawl around Marguerite's waist.

"What was it?" she asked. It was clear she had not seen the horrific events, so he quickly diverted the conversation.

"The dugout that you were in was not secured to the landing stage and has drifted away," Geoffrey said, relieved he had come up with something practical to say. If you stay here with Mother, I will try to save what I can before it all sinks in this damnable river!" He grabbed a dead branch as he hobbled towards the landing stage in his bare feet.

"That will never work," Rosamund called after him, hitching up her damp skirts and overtaking him at a run. "I saw some fishing nets at the end of this staging when we got out of the canoe."

"What use are they?" Geoffrey shouted, trying to keep up, but finding it impossible without shoes. When he caught up with her, Rosamund was already swirling a weighted net around her head like a bolas before releasing it towards the nearest pieces of luggage. It dropped squarely over Geoffrey's padded violin case and their mother's Gladstone bag.

"Take hold of this rope, Jeffy and pull hard, while I snare what I can of the others," Rosamund called, yanking on the rope. Geoffrey hauled the bundle on to the staging while his sister repeated the operation three more times before the remainder of their belongings either sank below the surface or were carried out of reach on the current.

"Where did you learn to do that, Rose?" Geoffrey asked, with undisguised admiration.

"Liam Hardy taught me down at the lake. Where on earth are your shoes, Jeffy?" she asked, staring at his feet, one in only a sock and the other entirely bare.

"Somewhere at the bottom of the river by now; it was impossible to swim with them on."

"But you cannot swim, Jeffy, everyone knows that!"

"Well fortunately I can. Father forced me to learn and today has proved that he did me a favour."

"Well I think you are immensely brave."

"Where are Churuma and Nia?" Marguerite asked, joining them with their mother. "We cannot get separated, not now the paddle-men have gone."

"Maybe they went back downriver to get help," Geoffrey lied, praying that his father would find a solution to get them back to the nearest port.

"We cannot rely on seeing them again in this wilderness," his mother said, in the matter-of-fact way she used whenever she was protecting them from anything unsettling. The sidelong glance she gave Geoffrey made him realise that she had in fact seen everything that had happened. "Darling, where are your shoes?" she asked.

"Probably at the bottom of the river," Geoffrey said, removing his only sock and debating how to make some temporary footwear. From a bush on the bank he cut off some of the thick, banana-like leaves, which he shaped into pads with Archie's knife and, after cutting up one of the fishing nets he placed his feet squarely on the pads and wrapped them securely with the net, tying them firmly with a length of cord.

"How ingenious you are, darling," his mother commented, opening the sopping wet Gladstone bag to examine the tin box containing her pills. "And bless you, Rose, for saving this bag with my painkillers."

Among the other items rescued, along with Geoffrey's violin, were a portmanteau and two suitcases belonging to Lady Claudia, two others from Rosamund's luggage, and one of Marguerite's. There was also a trunk of sheet music and a box of medical supplies.

Removing the satchel from her shoulder, Lady Claudia took out an object wrapped in a cloth before handing the bag over to him. "You should take care of this, darling, now that we are safely on dry land," she said, calmly unwrapping the revolver and loading it with bullets.

"Mother... you have a gun!" Rosamund exclaimed in horror.

"Please allow me to take care of that, Mother. I know how to handle a firearm," Marguerite said.

"I am well aware of that, darling... practising with such regularity at eleven o'clock every Tuesday, Wednesday and Thursday."

"You know about that?" Marguerite asked, shocked.

"What mother would not?" Lady Claudia said, firmly retaining control of the weapon.

"I think we have stood here long enough, Mother," Geoffrey urged. Without the sound guidance of Churuma he had to get the family to safety before nightfall. "The baggage should be safe enough here. It is time we confronted Father." Geoffrey was about to lead the way until his mother caught hold of his arm.

"No, Geoffrey, we cannot take chances; there may well be hostile tribesmen ahead." She released the safety catch on the revolver. "The girls must follow close behind me, with you at the rear, but keep your knife unsheathed in readiness to defend yourself."

His mother led them cautiously along a narrow track to a point where the roofs on a cluster of low buildings could be seen through the dense forestation.

Marguerite recoiled at the sight of something beside the path. "Something awful must have happened here recently," she murmured.

The partially eaten body of a man lay slumped against a tree. The skeletal corpse of a woman had been dragged into the undergrowth a few feet away. Further along the track they came upon the decomposing remains of six more bodies among the stumps of fallen trees, coming to an abrupt halt when Rosamund screamed as a huge spider crawled out of the gaping mouth of a one of the corpses, the added weight of the giant creature jolting the skull to face them like a grotesque apparition from Hell.

"I do so hate this place," Rosamund said hoarsely, clinging on to her mother's arm.

"Why not let me take the lead, Mother?" Geoffrey asked, gripping Archie's knife firmly. "It is too quiet. Someone must be aware of us by now."

"A knife would count for nothing if we were attacked by more than one tribesman. This revolver is loaded with six rounds and I will make every one of them count if need be. All I ask is that you follow at a distance with your sisters. You will need to protect them if I cannot." She walked on ahead as calmly as if she were attending a public function.

The pendulous drops of her sapphire earrings shimmered like drops of frozen ice as she unconsciously rearranged the loose strands of wet hair, as if in preparation for the inevitable meeting with her husband, or with her maker. Vapours of steam lifted from the sodden hem of her gown, the incongruous train trailing behind as she walked, dusting up a cloud of dried earth in her wake.

At the end of the pathway was a clearing and in it a compound that appeared to be be abandoned. At the centre was a raised, colonial-style bungalow with a wrap-around veranda, accessible by a broad flight of steps. It was an imposing dwelling, ambitiously conceived and painstakingly executed by native labour. Connected to it by a wide and open breezeway was a long building at the far end of the compound. Hanging between the columns were tattered lengths of stained muslin, blanking off any view of what was inside.

There were three other structures in this area, modest by comparison and angular in shape. A fourth, much sturdier cabin was set apart from the others on a high ridge accessed by a set of rough wooden steps. Nowhere was there any sign of life.

"Stay here, all of you," Lady Claudia said firmly, making her way cautiously up the steps of the main bungalow.

"You cannot go in there alone, Mother," Geoffrey called as he bounded up the steps, closely followed by his sisters. He froze as he caught sight of a distorted shape, silhouetted by the sun, moving slowly behind one of the sheets on the breezeway. When he looked again there was no sign of any figure but there was also barely a trace of his mother, apart from the faint sound of her trailing gown, swishing over the roughly hewn boards within the darkened interior.

As Geoffrey's eyes became accustomed to the gloom it was soon obvious that no expense had been spared on the furnishing of the interior. The emphasis had clearly been more on his father's creature comforts than on any show of ostentation, yet had their situation not been so dire Geoffrey would have laughed out loud at the elegant shape of a grand piano, which would surely have gone out of tune in a matter of days in this climate. On the closed lid stood an untidy collection of family portraits, amid stacks of notes and half-empty liquor bottles. Littered on the floor were piles of typed papers, open folders and more empty bottles.

Leaning against the arm of a torn leather armchair was a pile of plates with remnants of food encrusted with mould and, perched on top, an ashtray piled high with cigarette stubs. The smell of decaying food was overlaid with the sickly-sweet stench of death, an odour that became ever stronger near a curtained doorway leading into an internal room.

When Lady Claudia pulled back the curtain, it was impossible to see anything in the pitch-black interior. Following his mother inside, Geoffrey threw open the shutters. The bright sunlight revealed a scene that he could interpret only as the debauched inner chamber of his father's private harem. From the moment the shutters were opened, a swarm of winged insects began buzzing angrily about the room.

In the centre of the bedroom was a bed with a decorative iron framed, on which lay the decomposing body of a native woman, clearly well advanced into her pregnancy, her once youthful shape now twisted in the final agony of death. The body was clothed in a dress of European manufacture, the bodice of which she had torn open to expose a horrific mass of weeping sores. Her unseeing eyes were blanked over with the white film of blindness.

Beyond this room they found a sectioned-off area made from panels of woven palm fronds. A four-fold screen served as a makeshift doorway, beyond which were five narrow beds. On four of these were the bodies of more native women, each of them in European dress and, without exception, their skin was covered with identical eruptions and open sores. Two were clutching at their throats while the others lay twisted on the torn, bloodied sheets with gaping mouths, as if their limbs had been paralysed.

Against one wall there was a long rack, hung with more gaudy dresses. Scattered across a narrow table was a collection of cheap, glittering jewellery, theatrical cosmetics and two large bottles of perfume but, before he could investigate further, Geoffrey turned at the unmistakable sound of a child's whimper from an adjacent room.

Inside the nursery were five pale-skinned children, all under the age of three. Four of the infants were dead, laid out like royalty. The fifth child stared at Lady Claudia with white, sightless eyes as she lifted her gently from the cot and carried her into the light. Apart from one of her tiny arms, her limbs were locked rigid. Her once pale, delicate skin was now red and hideously inflamed, a sight that was clearly affecting his mother as she tried to comfort the infant by rocking her gently against her breast.

"Mother... you must put the child down, this disease may be contagious," Marguerite pleaded.

"This child is in the final stage of her life and in need of a mother's love. It is the very least I can do. Your father must be found immediately and made to do something... anything to help ease this child's suffering. Oliver must have a laboratory close by. If you want to help, please find him," she said, cradling the infant. "However lacking your father might have been morally, he would never allow an ailing child to suffer."

Their father's laboratory was connected to the building by the breezeway and would have been easily accessible had it not been for the number of rough wooden beds that were positioned along one side. On each lay a corpse, twisted in the final spasms of death. Even outside the stench was appalling.

"Mother, please stay inside the bungalow," Geoffrey pleaded as she began to follow, still comforting the infant.

"Geoffrey!" Marguerite called from inside the laboratory, her voice high-pitched and wavering. "Father is here."

Although Geoffrey had seen so much death recently, he was unprepared for the sight of his own parent's agonising demise. It was clear that he had died just a few hours earlier. His rigid, contorted body lay on the floor amid a splintered rack of test tubes, their contents pooled against him amid the shards of shattered glass.

There was a column of ants tracking across his face, unseen by his sightless, bulging eyes. His once handsome features had been ravaged by open sores, leaving him barely recognisable behind a shaggy beard, a far cry from the fastidiously groomed gentleman who had left Derbyshire four years earlier. His greying hair was long and tied back with coloured beads, which emphasised the suffering etched on his haggard features. What few patches of skin were free from infection had the texture of dark-brown leather. The exposed flesh on his emaciated body was as taut as a drum where his grimy, vomit-spattered shirt had been torn away as he'd fallen. His collarbone and ribcage were covered by a wafer-thin layer of parchment-like skin.

"Unfeeling monster," Lady Claudia hissed, prodding his lifeless carcass with her foot.

"Mother… you should not be in here," Geoffrey said.

"How could he… how could anyone expose a child to this in the name of science?" she raged, choking as the tears began flowing down her cheeks.

"We cannot know that for certain," Marguerite said.

"Of course we can! That monster was trained in all manner of disease control at the hospital in London. He knew what precautions had to be taken and would have known the risks he was taking by keeping his children close to his experiments. How could anyone in their right mind allow that?"

Fearing that she might collapse, Geoffrey lifted the struggling infant from his mother's arms. Moments later the infant's back arched as her tiny arm reached upwards, the hand grasping at the air for a final intake of breath. Then it was over.

"All I can hope is that your father will rot in Hell where he belongs!"

"How could Papa have been so unfaithful?" Rosamund hissed as Geoffrey placed the infant on the only unoccupied bed outside. Tearing down a panel of muslin, Geoffrey covered the child.

278

"It is fortunate there was only one child here," Rosamund said, breaking the silence that had descended amongst them.

"There are more but only this one was alive." Geoffrey could not find any way to lessen the impact of his revelation.

"There are others?" Rosamund asked in horror. "How many?" she called after him as Geoffrey strode back into the darkened room.

"There are four!" Geoffrey called, checking each child for any sign of life but finding none.

"Are you positive, Geoffrey? You have not had any medical training," Marguerite said, pushing past him in the doorway.

"Check for yourself," he said, but saw clearly that he hadn't made any mistake when she came out, ashen-faced. "I swear if Father was not already dead, I would willingly strangle him here, on this very spot!" Geoffrey hissed.

"Were they all his children, do you think?" Rosamund asked.

"I would imagine so." Geoffrey studied the child's features. "This girl has the same hair colour as ours."

"That does not mean they are Papa's," she responded defensively.

"I think it is inevitable. This child's mother would have been a local tribeswoman."

Marguerite re-emerged, staring at the woven band around her wrist that was casting an amber glow over her skin.

"You should get rid of that thing, Maggs, it might be contaminated," Geoffrey said, leading her away from the breezeway where he got her to sit on a low crate.

"I did wonder but I cannot seem to get it off. Would you try?" Although Geoffrey did his best, even trying to insert the knife under the threads was hopeless. There was a cracking sound and sparks flew from the blade but he made no headway.

"What the hell is this stuff?" he said, confused and baffled but unwilling to risk the blade slipping and cutting her skin.

"Perhaps being underwater has made the fibres swell, or maybe some sort of flint in the material is making it spark," she said, breathing heavily as she got up from the packing case.

"Where is Mother?" he asked with alarm, looking back along the walkway. "The child has gone too."

"Mother has taken her inside to lay her out with the others for burial," Marguerite said.

"We need to get her out of there before she becomes infected herself," Geoffrey said, rushing into the darkened room.

Still cradling the dead infant in her arms, his mother was framed in a strong beam of light from the open shutter, murmuring a soft lullaby that he remembered from childhood while staring at the row of tiny bodies.

"Mother, you should not be in here."

"I cannot leave their tiny bodies so exposed in this way. It is not Christian."

"If you come outside with me, I promise we will return to cover them over with muslin. They are safe in here, it will be dark soon and we need to find somewhere safe to rest overnight."

It was Rosamund who found a length of clean muslin and swiftly cut into appropriate lengths, which they placed over each infant, laying a token flower on each from a vine on the veranda.

Lighting the oil lamps his father had installed, Geoffrey worked feverishly to clear away some of the mess from the living room and, with his sisters' help prepared makeshift beds for the night.

"Why are there are only three beds in here, Geoffrey?" his mother asked.

He did not reply but said "I shall be out on the veranda, keeping watch. I have no intention of being taken by surprise. In the dark, I will have the advantage."

"You would not be safe, my darling. You must sleep inside with us. However deadly you imagine that knife is, it would be no match for a skilled hunter." After a short discussion it was resolved that she would stay outside with him on the veranda with the revolver.

After cleaning their hands and arms with disinfectant they found in the laboratory, a meal of sorts was concocted by their mother from fruit growing nearby and some European biscuits Marguerite found sealed in a tin.

Geoffrey and his mother spent the night on a cane lounger, both wrapped up like mummies in layers of muslin. It had been his intention to talk to her about the fate of Churuma and his sister but the care with which she stripped down the revolver, checking and oiling each of the components like a soldier, confirmed that she had seen everything.

After a breakfast of the same food they had eaten the previous evening, they gathered outside the darkened room at his mother's insistence, allowing her to work alone behind the closed doors, washing down each infant and re-dressing them in clean shirts that had belonged to her husband.

After she had laid out each child in separate cots, Geoffrey and his sisters were finally allowed inside to place around them whatever green fronds and clusters of flowers they had been able to gather.

"If only we knew what names father had given his children," Geoffrey said.

"Your father would definitely have kept records of births and deaths. Probably with the help of the Jesuit missionary, since he would most certainly have had all his children baptised. There must be a record of their names before they are buried. I will go through his papers immediately."

"There are more pressing issues that need to be dealt with before the children are buried, since their mothers have been dead for much longer and are more likely to spread disease," Marguerite said.

"Digging graves is not women's work. I will look around that overgrown vegetable patch at the rear of the bungalow. There should be a shovel somewhere," Geoffrey volunteered.

"Even if you do find a spade, what do you propose we do about the others? There are so many bodies here," Marguerite said.

"I could help bury them," Rosamund offered, somewhat reluctantly.

"There are too many, not to mention those in the other passageway," Geoffrey said. More adult corpses, in a worse state of decomposition, were laid out there on rush mats.

"With so many trees the ground here will be thick with roots and burying so many could take weeks. The longer they are above ground the more we are at risk," Marguerite said, closing the door on to the breezeway.

"What are you suggesting... a mass funeral pyre?" Geoffrey asked.

"I was thinking more practically. The river is swarming with piranha and caiman. Those scavengers could be the answer to getting rid these infected carcasses."

"You know Mama would never allow anything like that, Maggie, it is not Christian," Rosamund retorted.

"Maybe not but Mother is practical and, considering the risk we all face from contracting this virus, we have no other option," Marguerite said firmly.

"Mama would never consider allowing this to happen to Papa and his children," Rosamund persisted.

"There is no need for that. Once I have located a spade and found a decent burial site, then I will do exactly what I proposed earlier and dig those graves myself," Geoffrey said.

"Before that, Geoffrey, we must find the best way to remove the other bodies," Marguerite said.

"And how do you propose we get them there... carry them?" Geoffrey said irritably, swatting a spider off his arm.

"Archie would know exactly what to do."

"Well you only have me Rose." he retorted.

"We could wheel them there in a barrow," Marguerite said calmly.

"If there is one... if not, are you volunteering to drag them down to the river on canvas sheets?"

"You cannot expect me to do that? I am too... too..."

"I think 'fat' is the word you are searching for."

"No, Geoffrey, I was actually going to say that I am too tired, before you were so... so rude! It is exhausting for me to even breathe in this climate," she said, verging on tears. "You know I will help as much as I can."

A short time later, after finding a pair of his father's sandals, Geoffrey located a small handcart at the rear of the bungalow. After wrapping a sheet around the first corpse, he looped a length of rope under the armpits and, with Marguerite's help, hauled him on to the cart.

They worked tirelessly until late afternoon, when the final body was heaved off the dock. As it flopped into the river, like all the others, the remains had barely drifted away from the dock before the water was a seething mass of fish scales as the shoal of piranha tugged at the carcass, the mummified shape jerking horrifically in an eruption of water before the body was dragged beneath the surface.

"Do you think God will punish us for committing this awful sin?" Rosamund asked as they returned to the compound.

"We had no choice," Geoffrey reassured her, putting an arm around her shoulder.

"Are we burying the children tomorrow?" Rosamund asked.

"Mother was adamant that is not going to happen until the day after, which will allow us time to clear and disinfect the buildings," Marguerite said.

"That is not the most important issue. It is essential that we find a reliable source of food," Geoffrey said.

"We could start in that awful kitchen at the rear of the bungalow," Marguerite said, flopping down with exhaustion on the lower steps.

"After we report what we have done to Mother," Geoffrey said, sitting down on a higher step.

"Where shall we bury the children?" Rosamund asked.

"I will find somewhere appropriate close by," Geoffrey promised.

"It should be on higher ground, not here. I would hate to think my last resting place on earth was here," Rosamund said, looking at the dark, overpowering foliage.

"I will do my very best, Rose. You have my word on that," Geoffrey said, as the tears began welling in her eyes.

"We cannot carry Father up the hill," Marguerite said.

"Then I vote we dump him in the river. That is what he deserves," Geoffrey scowled.

"You cannot mean that, Jeffy. Papa and those children must have Christian burials. Mama would not want it any other way and neither would I."

"I agree. They must all have a Christian burial," Marguerite said, bringing an end to the discussion.

When they entered the bungalow, they discovered their mother had already cleaned and disinfected the room where the children were laid out, and, having fashioned a crucifix of vines, she was applying lemon-scented leaves and delicate flowers to it.

"Be a darling, Geoffrey and hang this from that nail. It is too high for me to reach," she asked.

"How lovely this is," Marguerite said.

"This is perfect, Mama," Rosamund agreed, taking hold of her mother's hand.

"So it is but you should have waited for me to help before moving these beds on your own," Geoffrey said. The tranquillity his mother had achieved through a minor

284

rearrangement of the furniture had transformed an unsettling scene of death into a calming chapel of rest.

Checking around the exterior of the main bungalow, Geoffrey discovered a primitive but functional shower set a short distance away from the rear of the building. Although bizarre in appearance, it worked very well. The showerhead was an adapted rose from a watering can, attached to the end of a collection of pipes and guttering. The flow of water was operated by a cantilevered system attached to a lavatory chain which, when tugged, would channel a flow of tepid water from a source beyond an outcrop of rock that backed onto the rear of the shower.

There was also the added bonus of a functioning water closet in the adjacent shed. When he entered the structure, expecting to find a wooden board straddling a stinking pit, he was amazed to discover an imported porcelain lavatory, decorated with blue flowers and flushed by another ingenious system of pipework, with the waste pipe channelled underground. Hanging from a hook on the door was a piece of looped string threaded with squares of torn newspaper, giving him reason to smile for the first time since his arrival and to give grudging credit to his father's unexpected ingenuity.

That evening the family ate frugally from an unopened pack of cream crackers, with the addition of freshly picked bananas and a sliced mango collected from the overgrown garden. In a cupboard Marguerite found a tin of peaches and a rusted tin of evaporated milk, which Geoffrey eventually opened by hammering two holes into the top with the aid of a rock and a nail.

"Will this be poured over the fruit?" Geoffrey asked his mother.

"No, it is to make up a drink," she replied, pouring water into a jug from a pump attached to the sink.

"That water could be contaminated, Mother."

"Your father would not have had this fitted if the water source was unsafe."

"We could make certain if it was boiled first. There is a primus stove on the back porch. I could see if it has any paraffin."

An hour later, having cooled the boiling water in a sink full of more pumped water, his mother served up the pale, unappetising liquid after the family had eaten.

"Ugh… this is horrible!" Geoffrey exclaimed, thrusting the tumbler aside. "I cannot drink this, Mother!"

"But you must, Geoffrey dear. There is goodness in milk, tinned or otherwise. You must drink every drop. Your sister has done remarkably well in finding this tin. It was probably the last one."

"Unfortunately not; there are another six tins of this awful stuff," Geoffrey said, gulping the remainder down in one go.

That evening they slept in the small cabin that was set apart from the others on higher ground. Although it had clearly been used for storage, it proved a much safer place to sleep, well away from the infected area. Attached to the cabin was a modest-sized stable with two empty stalls. At the end of the structure was a metal bin with a hasped-down lid, which explained why it still contained a quantity of animal feed.

The cabin itself comprised two rooms. Stored in the larger of these were a double and a single bed, including mattresses and a box-spring for both. There was a large camphor-wood chest in the corner, containing sheets and blankets which were thankfully lizard, spider and insect-free.

Stored on a high shelf he found an oilcan along with a few tools. On another were four hurricane lamps, three containing paraffin. Lighting one of them, Geoffrey hung it between the rooms as he began assembling the beds. A second lamp he took on to the veranda, leaving the third unlit as a spare.

After a struggle, banging his knuckles hard on the frame every time the spanner slipped on the worn bolts, Geoffrey assembled the larger bed. Once constructed, it was large enough for his mother and Rose to sleep together.

In the smaller room he made a better job of assembling the single bed for Marguerite, which, although inadequate for her size, was at least a place for her to sleep. In the remainder of the space was a range of shelving accommodating some of his father's books, reading material that had clearly been neglected for some time, with mould on the spines. Boxed up in cupboards underneath were stacks of his research papers.

"Where will you sleep, Geoffrey?" Marguerite asked, cautiously testing the bed.

"There are a couple of cane loungers on the veranda. All I need is a mosquito net and one of the oil lamps."

Wrapped in a length of mosquito net and wearing only his underpants and a shirt, Geoffrey had just settled himself down for the night when Marguerite came out and sat beside him in the spare lounger.

"What is it? Did the bed collapse?" Geoffrey asked, struggling to sit up in his mummified state.

"Mother is in a lot of pain tonight and quite restless. Rose is with her. I have given her an extra dose of the painkillers but they will take time to work. What she needs is the bigger bed on her own, so Rose will use mine instead. Besides, you need the company out here and it would take an hour to unwrap yourself if an attacker got on to the veranda," she said dryly.

"I would have heard anyone," Geoffrey retorted, longing for the privacy of his own room where he could bolt the door and take off the remainder of his clothes in the infernal heat. "Besides, I keep Archie's knife handy."

"Not much use against a jaguar on the prowl if you are wrapped up in that cocoon of netting."

"Then what alternative do I have, other than being bitten to death by mosquitoes or eaten alive by some prowling creature?" he asked.

"I will be here. I have borrowed Mother's revolver while she is resting." She calmly stripped down the weapon and oiled it from a can with the eye of a professional.

"Would you actually use that thing?" Geoffrey asked, hastily putting on his clothes.

"If I had to, yes I would."

"On an animal, perhaps but what about a native, how would you react then?" He clambered on to the handrail where he rigged up a makeshift tent from the mosquito netting, draping it over the two of them, wondering why he hadn't thought of that to begin with.

"The threat of looking down the barrel of this revolver would be a good deterrent against an attacker, without even needing to squeeze the trigger," she said, relaxing back on the lounger with the revolver resting on her lap, exactly the way their mother had done on the previous evening. "I do wonder why Mother never acknowledged, until now, that I could shoot?"

"Mother seems to be aware of everything we get up to," Geoffrey said, all the more determined to keep the knife razor sharp and close at hand. After what the head-hunters had done to Churuma and his sister, he knew that if he were ever presented with a life-or-death situation he would have no hesitation in taking the other's life.

Most of the following morning was spent in the main bungalow, removing the empty cots, and piling them away from the building where he intended to burn them at a later date. Once the contaminated items had been cleared, the family began to disinfect every inch of the breezeways and the bungalow's interior, leaving only the nursery untouched. By midday the task was complete and a meal had to be arranged.

"What is there to eat? There must be something other than fruit," Geoffrey asked.

"There are some chickens penned at the rear of the garden. They might have laid some eggs," Marguerite said.

"Roast chicken and some of Mrs Bailey's mashed potato would go down a treat right now," Geoffrey said, thinking back to happier times in the grand kitchen on the Waterlilies Estate.

"Well, since Cook is not here, you will have to make do with boiled eggs... if I can find any," Marguerite said.

"Anything would do, except for more fruit. What a secretive creature you are, Maggs. I never suspected you could cook."

"Boiling an egg cannot be that difficult," she said, taking a wicker bowl from the veranda as she went outside.

"Did you know Father kept chickens?" Geoffrey asked Rosamund as she entered, tying back her hair with a length of ribbon. "Why is Mother not with you?"

"Mama had to lie down. I did say she was doing too much scrubbing on her hands and knees but she would not listen and now she is feeling unwell again."

"Does she need anything?" Geoffrey asked with concern.

"Chicken broth would be good for her, if Maggs knows how to make that."

"Not without a dead chicken and I cannot imagine her killing one."

The kitchen was quite primitive and stood separate from the main building in a wide horseshoe shape. It comprised three walls plastered with mud, each decorated with mysterious symbols cut deep into the surface. It was well protected from the weather by a thatched roof of palm fronds, with sections of corrugated iron clearly visible under the thatch. In the centre there was a long, rough-cut table and nine hand-crafted chairs. Where the fourth wall would have been, there was a primitive stove and, against it, a pile of logs.

After countless attempts to light the fire, Geoffrey tried dousing the wood with paraffin, which resulted only in singed eyebrows as flames roared out of the grate before going out again. Eventually he got it going with screwed-up paper and a few dry sticks.

Equally tragic were Marguerite's attempts to boil the eggs, with batches that were either sloppy and undercooked or rock hard and inedible. Finally, they dined on the remaining biscuits and more fruit.

After a second uncomfortable night, with no easy access to the shower or lavatory, it was decided they would relocate to the main bungalow as soon as the building had been thoroughly disinfected and they could each move into one of the other cabins later.

The next day, before the burials were due to take place, Geoffrey and his mother set off to find an appropriate site on higher ground, well clear of the river. After a climb that exhausted his mother they found an ideal location, well shaded by trees, with grassy banks and a stream meandering through, which would provide the perfect resting place for the children.

"What about Father? Is he going to be buried here or somewhere else?" Geoffrey asked reluctantly.

"We cannot deny him a resting place here, Geoffrey. They are his children and he should be laid to rest with them."

"That is all I needed to know, except we have not decided where the graves will be," Geoffrey said.

"Doubtless the tree roots will dictate were they can be buried, Geoffrey. I will help dig the graves." She gazed at the dramatic vista from their vantage point near the cliff edge.

"You must leave that job to me, Mother. You will need to prepare the children for burial and, to be quite honest, I do not want to be a part of that."

Returning to the compound, Geoffrey found exactly what he had been looking for in a tumbledown barn close to the overgrown vegetable garden. Stored inside were two garden spades together with a fork and few other tools. There was also another, slightly larger handcart that would be perfect for transporting the children, although a return trip would be required to collect his father.

Back in the kitchen, Marguerite had been slicing up the contents from a tin of bully beef that she had found in a cupboard, along with a can opener.

"Are you sure this stuff is edible?" Geoffrey asked, prodding at the rubbery substance. "God alone knows how long it has been in that cupboard. It might have gone off."

"In a tin, it should stay fresh for years," Marguerite said.

"Not banged and rusted."

"Oh do shut up, Jeffy and eat your dinner," Rosamund said, forking up a section of the meat and nibbling it cautiously.

"You see… you are not sure either," Geoffrey said, half expecting her to choke or spit everything out.

"There is nothing wrong with this meat," Marguerite said, having already cleared her own plate. "If you are not going to eat yours, Geoffrey, then pass your plate over, because I will!"

Collecting two scalpels from the laboratory, Geoffrey picked up the garden fork and a spade from the barn before making his way up the narrow track to the burial site, well away from the prying eyes of his sisters.

He was surprised how easy it was to dig out the five shallow graves for the children. In contrast, his father's plot was more difficult, in the only other space clear of roots, closer to the cliff edge and away from the others.

Once all the graves were dug, he hacked down a fence pole with Archie's knife with the intention of creating a weapon but, after lashing the two surgical knives to it, he was uncertain if the home-made spear would be enough to deter any head-hunter who might venture on to their side of the river.

Scarcely had the thought crossed his mind when he was startled by a crashing noise, as if something was heading towards him through the dense vegetation. Geoffrey leapt to his feet just as, to his astonishment, a huge wolfhound staggered clear of the bushes, its hackles raised like an Elizabethan ruff. Baring its ferocious teeth as it struggled, snarling, to regain its balance, the dog seemed about to leap at him in attack.

"Steady, boy… I am not going to hurt you." It was all he could think of to say, wondering how he could get away from the clearly wounded creature without having to spear it, while avoiding being mauled to death in the process. Unable to get Archie's knife unsheathed from his belt, Geoffrey gripped tightly on to the makeshift spear as the throaty growl intensified and the ferocious creature moved stealthily closer.

As the creature got nearer Geoffrey realised that he was no longer staring at the glare in the dog's eyes but at the intricately braided copper-mesh collar that it wore, identical to the band on his sister's wrist. Now he realised that the threatening growls and baleful stare were not directed at him but instead were focused somewhere over his shoulder. As he spun around awkwardly, the spear slipped to the ground.

Staring at him from the edge of the clearing were two fearsome head-hunters, the shrunken trophies of recent victims hanging from their belts. On the pole they carried between them their most recently acquired heads hung by their hair, swinging like a row of pumpkins on bonfire night.

One of the men wielded a wicked-looking machete, while the other now held a blowpipe against his mouth and fired it at the hound as it launched itself towards him. To Geoffrey's astonishment the lethal dart appeared to twist in flight, rebounding from the mesh collar in a shower of sparks. Before the tribesman had time to reload, the snarling hound sent him crashing to the ground, sinking its teeth into his throat.

Screaming with rage, the second hunter raised the machete and was about to strike when Geoffrey leapt between them and with a powerful thrust rammed the garden fork deep into the tribesman's side, sending him crashing headlong into the bushes.

It was clear the first native was already dead but, on closer inspection, Geoffrey realised with horror that one of the heads dangling from the pole was Nia. He instinctively covered her face with handfuls of grass before turning to find the wolfhound caught up in the deadly coils of a bright green boa constrictor that had silently caught him.

He detested snakes, especially since the incident with Archie in the carriage, yet Geoffrey found himself jabbing at the reptile with his home-made spear until the writhing creature released its grip. But rather than slither away into the undergrowth as he had expected, the enraged snake now launched itself directly at him, its gaping mouth open and hissing.

Although terrified, Geoffrey stood his ground, knowing this was a battle he had to win or be crushed to death. Desperately, he tried to get close enough to reach the dead man's machete, all the while stabbing at the enraged reptile with the makeshift spear until the weapon shattered against the creature's trunk-like body and it rose up, poised to strike. As Geoffrey stared into the gaping mouth it suddenly twisted away as the wolfhound now sank its teeth deep into the snake's back.

Caught up in the threshing coils, Geoffrey was yanked off his feet and sent crashing into a nearby tree, his body dragged agonisingly back and forth across the rough bark before he was eventually released and hurled into the bushes.

Scrambling to his feet, Geoffrey grabbed the machete and clambered up a section of rock, bracing himself for what he had to do. Gauging each movement of the snake as he might have done with a rhythmic section of music, he waited for the gaping mouth to twist back towards the dog until its neck was at the perfect angle.

Summoning every ounce of strength, Geoffrey swung the blade at the creature's arched neck and embedded it deep in the reptile's throat, forcing it to release the struggling hound. In the fray, he was dealt a severe blow to the head from the death-throes of the reptile's thrashing tail, which sent him sprawling.

When Geoffrey eventually came to, he was soaked in blood and found it difficult to move. Directly in his line of vision was Nia's decapitated head, staring blindly at him though the grass with her sightless eyes. Staggering to his feet, he was barely able to comprehend the brutality of what had happened, yet he felt no remorse.

It was clear the wolfhound had been badly injured earlier, perhaps a jaguar in view of the slashed skin and the flap of flesh that hung from its side. He could only marvel that the animal had still been able to carry out its ferocious attack first on the hunter and then the boa constrictor. This dog had saved Geoffrey's life and he prayed there was some way he could do the same in return.

Despite the excruciating pain from beneath his torn shirt, Geoffrey found the strength to dig five more holes using Archie's knife. Barely able to look at Nia's lifeless face, he buried her head in the first of the holes, covering it with flowers before he filled it with earth. He repeated this again with the other heads – a woman and the three men who he, realised from the similarity in their features, must have been two young boys and their parents.

Saying a prayer over each, Geoffrey returned to where the huge dog lay in a twisted heap against a boulder. The only sign of life was the flicker of an eye and the tiniest twitch of its tail. He felt powerless. Lifting it bodily, Geoffrey laid the hound gently on a flat section of ground in the shade and removed the poisoned dart carefully from where it had wedged into the mesh of the animal's collar.

Blinded by rage at the atrocities of the head-hunters, Geoffrey caught hold of the first native's feet and dragged him to the edge of the cliff, heaving the corpse over the edge with immense satisfaction. He watched it splash into the river below, attracting a group of basking caiman. He also noticed a small canoe, no doubt belonging to the hunters, pulled up the bank a short distance away.

Returning to the clearing, Geoffrey had every intention of disposing of the other body in the same way but, as he was confronted by the twitching carcass of the huge boa constrictor, the enormity of what he had done hit home. He began to retching and didn't stop until his stomach was empty.

Although he feared the hound would be dead, when he returned it was miraculously still alive, although barely breathing. Oddly, the woven band around the animal's neck now seemed to be glowing, even pulsating, though he couldn't be certain of anything since his eyes were not focusing well after the recent blows to his head. All he could think was that he must get the injured animal back to the compound, away from any predators roaming the area, so he chose to leave the second hunter for the condors or other scavengers to dispose of.

It would have been impossible to carry the hefty dog back to the compound but he remembered an engraving of North American Indians that hung over his bed at home and decided to make a travois. To create the frame he hacked down two straight saplings with the machete for the main carrying poles, then lashed three shorter lengths across them. Between these he wove a lattice of vine, knotting it securely in the way he remembered from his brief time in the Scouts. Removing his torn shirt, Geoffrey draped it across the frame, buttoned up to give more support, knotted the sleeves on to the top section to hold it in position and bound the shirttails on to the wider part at the bottom. Although the result was rudimentary, he felt confident that even Archie Westbrook would have been impressed with his handiwork, although his mother would not be happy that he had used his only decent shirt.

Tying more vines across the upper section, Geoffrey harnessed himself to the travois by hooking them across his chest, leaving his hands free to grip the poles. Once the unconscious animal had been secured in place, he cautiously dragged his burden down the narrow track to the compound.

"My darling, are you injured?" his mother cried with alarm from the veranda. It was clear from her ashen features that she was unwell and suffering herself.

"It probably looks worse than it is. I got badly caught up in a thorn bush," Geoffrey lied.

"You are covered in so much blood, Geoffrey!" she exclaimed.

"Do not be alarmed, Mother, the blood is not mine and I need Maggs' help to treat this wolfhound before it dies from loss of blood," Geoffrey called back. The last thing he wanted was to cause her any more distress by telling the truth about what happened. "This animal saved my life, and now I must save his if I can," he continued, removing the harness to lay the animal flat. "Where is she, Mother?"

"If you are looking for Maggie, she is down by the river," Rosamund said, coming on to the veranda and handing her mother a glass of water, along with two of the red pills and a large fan.

"Do me a favour, Rose and look after the dog until I bring her back," Geoffrey called over his shoulder, running towards the river as fast as he could in his father's sandals that were a size too large.

"How on earth did you find a dog out here?" Rosamund called after him. By then he was out of earshot.

Once Geoffrey had made Marguerite understand the need to get up to the compound quickly, if there was to be any chance that the animal's life could be saved, he raced back to prepare the things she would need from the laboratory.

When his sister finally arrived at the compound she was not only completely out of breath but even more distressed by the state of the unconscious hound than Geoffrey would have expected.

"I cannot do this, Geoffrey. I am truly sorry, but I cannot. These injuries are horrific. You know the sight of blood makes me faint." She looked away abruptly.

"But you must… the animal will die if you do not!" Geoffrey hissed, handing her the needle and thread she had requested. "You said you could do this, so for pity's sake try."

"Very well, if you insist, I will do what I can," she said, taking the needle with a trembling hand, still unable to make a start.

"For God's sake, Maggs, get on with it," he snapped irritably, desperate for her to stitch back the flap of skin that hung over a savage wound, a swarm of flies buzzing around it but she seemed quite incapable of inserting the needle into the torn flesh.

"I am so sorry, Geoffrey. I cannot do this to a living creature."

"Well then I will." Snatching the needle from her hand, he began stitching the sections of torn flesh together, taking some comfort that, unlike him, the unconscious animal would feel no pain as the thread pulled the jagged edges together.

It was a lengthy, worrying process but as he completed the final stitch he realised that he had made a neater job than he could ever have imagined.

"We must do something about those nasty cuts on your chest and arms," Marguerite said, recovering her composure. "How did you come by them?"

"Getting free of a thorn bush," Geoffrey lied again.

"A thorn bush did this?" Marguerite said doubtfully.

"It must have been that. There was nothing else," Geoffrey insisted, not wanting to alarm either her or Rosamund, who had been tending to the unconscious hound throughout the stitching operation, dabbing away the blood from the gradually closing wound.

"Some of these cuts are very deep, Geoffrey," Marguerite said, before looking away again.

"Do any of them need stitches?" he asked, dreading the inevitable answer.

"All of them, I would say. You cannot risk the chance of…," Marguerite said, still barely able to look at the wounds.

"Well I cannot do it myself, can I? If you could not stitch up this animal, then how will you manage to fix me?" Geoffrey said warily.

"I will ask Mother; she has a much steadier hand. She will be able to stitch up these wounds perfectly."

"You cannot ask Mama," Rosamund interrupted. "She has been unwell all morning and has gone inside to rest. You would have known that if you had not gone off to do more of your drawings."

"But Mother must help. It would be impossible for me to do this on my own," Geoffrey said.

"Then I shall do it," Rosamund said confidently. "You have always complimented me on my needlework," she said, trying to bring levity to the situation.

"I am not a bloody pin cushion for you to go prodding needles into, Rose," Geoffrey said with alarm, the throbbing pain from his head and the open wounds becoming more intense each moment.

"Well, who else is going to offer?"

"Are you sure you can do this, Rosamund?" Marguerite asked tentatively.

"Why do none of you think I am capable of doing anything practical? Perhaps you might explain to me one day why my entire family regards me as a dimwit who is unable to do anything except choose a new dress!"

"No one doubts your ability but there is so much blood already and there will be a lot more once you puncture the skin," Marguerite warned.

"In case you have forgotten, the object of your proposed needlework practice is here with you... listening!" Geoffrey complained, wishing one of them would just get on with it.

"Oh do be quiet, Jeffy!"

"Why the hell should I? You are not the one about to undergo surgery, for God's sake!"

"The dog did not whine when you stitched it together and your handiwork would not have even rated a 'C minus'!"

"If you cared to look, the bloody thing was unconscious!" he shouted but he could not help smiling weakly.

"That can be arranged!" Rosamund retorted.

"Are you sure you can do this, Rose, if Maggs cannot?"

"All I need is whatever Maggie can find in Papa's lab to numb the pain and then I will make a start." She tied back her hair with the piece of string that she now always carried in her pocket, before beginning to clean up the areas of torn skin.

"Ugh… I must leave before I am sick!" Marguerite said.

"Well be sick if you have to… but just get me what I need," Rosamund said angrily. "Can you not see Jeffy is in pain and needs our help? I have no idea what to look for in there, otherwise I would find it myself."

"It does look a bit of a mess," Geoffrey groaned as Marguerite hurried off, biting down on his lip to prevent himself from crying out.

"It is but I can do this. Then I want something from you in return," Rosamund said.

"Are you blackmailing me?" Geoffrey protested.

"Why are you always so dramatic?" Rosamund threaded the needle with slow deliberation. "It is quite simple really. All I want from you is the truth."

"About what exactly?"

"I want the truth about what really happened this afternoon."

"I have already explained …"

"All I have heard so far are lies. Do not deny it. Something else happened up there to get you and that poor animal into such a dreadful state, so stop trying to brush it aside by saying you got caught up in a bush and were slashed by a few thorns. Honestly, is that really the best you could come up with? I always know when you're lying, so before Maggie gets back I want the truth or, I promise, this stitching is really going to hurt!"

"Very well then but only if you promise not to mention a word of it to Mother." Geoffrey proceeded to give a watered-down account of the boa constrictor but chose to say nothing about the deaths of the two head-hunters, or what they had been carrying.

"You saved the dog from being crushed by a snake?" Rosamund exclaimed, wide-eyed. "But you can't even look at a picture of one without feeling ill."

"There was no choice. It was either tackle that reptile or allow the poor dog to get crushed to a pulp."

"This is all very commendable but how did you slay such a beast without help? You don't have a gun."

"I found a machete that belonged to Father," Geoffrey lied, hoping the doctored explanation made sense.

"What were you doing with that?"

"I was trying to make a spear, if you really must know. I was in the Scouts once."

"You went twice if I remember correctly and learned about different types of knots," she said, as Marguerite reappeared with a bottle of chloroform and a pad of cotton wool.

"You remember that? It was years ago," Geoffrey said, groaning from the pain.

"That is probably because you tried out most of those knots on me, since you have so conveniently forgotten. If Mother had not come along when she did, I might still be roped up in the dustbin!" Rosamund took his hand comfortingly and that was the last thing he remembered as Marguerite placed the chloroform pad over his nose and mouth.

Chapter Fourteen
Changing Pace

When Geoffrey awoke, although the pain hadn't lessened, the first thing on his mind was whether the wolfhound was still alive. Miraculously, it was.

"Did the stitches hold?" he asked.

"Rosamund has made a very neat job," Marguerite said, helping him into a shirt that had belonged to his father.

"Not me... I was asking about the dog."

"You messed up a couple of sections but there is no need to worry. I was able to re-stitch them while he was unconscious," Rosamund said.

"Thanks, that means a lot." He struggled to get up and stood unsteadily.

"What on earth are you thinking, Geoffrey?" Marguerite said, fussing like a mother hen. "You need to rest. Some of those wounds were very deep and they will need time to heal."

"Maybe so, but there are more important things I must get on with and first I need to check on the dog."

"Maggie and I put him in the shade around the back of the bungalow. It is cooler there," Rosamund told him.

"Thank you." Geoffrey hobbled out of the room in excruciating discomfort in every part of his torso and down his right arm. The shooting pains from his right thigh and knee became almost unbearable with every new step, and it took all his resolve not to cry out as he made his way outside, forcing himself not to stop as he knew he was being followed.

"Do you need help?" Rosamund asked.

"I can manage on my own, thank you," he grumbled.

"It is obvious that you cannot but you will try of course, even if it kills you."

"Then what do you want me to do?" He was desperate to rest, though he felt he might never get up again.

"I just thought the dog might want this. A dish of raw egg. It is full of protein."

"Then hand it over," Geoffrey snapped, keen to get rid of her so that he could suffer alone in silence.

"We might be in the middle of God knows where, Jeffy but there is no need to be so frightfully rude. You are still a gentleman." Rosamund stepped in front of him, blocking his way.

"I honestly did not mean it to sound like that," he said, wretchedly.

"Very well then, I will let you off, just this once." She moved out of the way, still holding the bowl.

"Can I have it then?" he asked, leaning against the veranda. "Now that I have apologised, give it to me."

"You would only drop it, you idiot. You can barely walk, for heaven's sake, so I propose you lean on me until we get there. After that, I promise to leave you alone."

"You promise?"

"Yes, but only after you take these." She helped him to a bench, where he could rest against the wall and swallow the aspirin she gave him. "There must be something stronger in Papa's laboratory but these were all I could find. Maggie has promised to look for something else."

Although the hound was alert when they arrived, it showed little interest in moving, at least not until Geoffrey offered it the bowl of egg, which disappeared in moments.

"He could do with some more of this; he must be starving," Geoffrey said.

"You are far too weak to get anything at the moment. You can barely stand. I could go down to the river and catch a few fish. But I am not killing them. You would have to do that, and cook them too."

"You can't go down there, Rose, not on your own, it isn't safe," Geoffrey panicked. "Anyone could be out there."

"Who exactly would that be? There is no one else here but us. Even Churuma and his sister have abandoned us."

"Maybe they had no choice."

"They did not have to leave us here, surrounded by dead people. They could have been less selfish and stayed behind to help." Her eyes were misting. "I sometimes think that if Archie had not had to go back to Ireland we would never have ended up in this mess."

"He would have stayed here for you and Mother, if there had been any option," Geoffrey agreed.

"What I do not understand is why you disliked him so much and went out of your way to be so unreasonable? Would it have been so hard to let down your guard and make an effort to be friends with him?"

"That is not fair," Geoffrey said, hoping to end the conversation so he could try to find more food for the injured dog without depleting the family's own supplies. He felt horribly sick, his head was pounding whenever he moved and he could only wish that she would shut up and not embarrass him more. His limbs were trembling badly and, despite the heat, his body felt icy cold.

"Then explain this if you will. How come you spent so much time in the company of that pompous Noel Effingham on the way out here, yet you shunned the offers of friendship Archie made during our stay at his grandmother's? If it was not for his bravery, Maggie and I might never have survived the earthquake." She paused, finally aware of the change in him. "Oh my God, you look dreadful!" was the last thing he heard her say as he crumpled into a heap on the floor and passed out cold.

When Geoffrey came to his shirt had been changed again, his face cleaned, and the pain had eased considerably. Rosamund was close by, feeding the wolfhound.

"I see you found him some more food," he said, struggling to sit up.

"Sort of… I went fishing," Rosamund said.

"Even after what I said?"

"I have no wish to argue, so just be happy I did. Mama showed me how to gut them. After that, we grilled them over an open fire."

"At this rate I will be in your debt for ever."

"I will remind you of that when we get back home," Rosamund smiled and, from the look in her eyes, Geoffrey knew she meant every word.

That night seemed the longest in Geoffrey's short life. His head was aching again, and, whichever way he moved in the chair to get more comfortable, it only increased the raging pain from his wounds. He wanted to scream out loud but instead, he could only groan and hope no one would wake. Only the dog, lying near him, seemed aware of his discomfort and perhaps because they were both suffering from similar wounds this somehow made it more bearable.

The following morning, after Rose had redressed and bound up most of his torso, Geoffrey set off to collect the handcart, once more attended closely by his sister. Collecting the first of the children's wrapped bodies from the bungalow proved even more distressing than he had imagined.

"What are you doing, Mother?" Geoffrey asked, meeting her as she was preparing to descend the veranda steps, cradling one of the infants in her arms.

"You need my help, Geoffrey. There are too many children for you to carry down these steps on your own in your condition. Your sisters will bring out the others."

It was clear that his mother was suffering badly that morning and it gave him some relief to see Marguerite administer the medication and persuade her to rest on one on the loungers. Once the infants had been carefully loaded on to the cart and Geoffrey was about to set off, Rosamund appeared at his side once more.

"Before you even speak, Jeffy, I am going to help you, so do not try to stop me," she said, talking hold of one of the handles. "This is a steep slope and it will need two of us to pull the cart up there."

Although he was reluctant to admit it, it was an immense relief to have Rosamund helping him with the handcart up the incline and they arrived without incident. Geoffrey went back on his own to collect his father but, to his distress, the body slipped off the handcart three times on the way up, the makeshift shroud becoming smeared with Geoffrey's own blood as he lifted it back o the cart.

A little later, Lady Claudia and Marguerite joined them at the burial site, where his mother said a few compassionate words and laid a flower on each child. Over their father, she read a passage from a Bible that he kept in the bungalow. Unlike the children's, this was a cold, unfeeling ceremony and she placed no flower on his grave. None of his family noticed the row of small graves Geoffrey had dug nearby for the head-hunters' trophies.

It took more than a week for the agony of his wounds to ease, during which time Rosamund had to re-stitch two sections of torn skin but, thanks to a numbing solution that Marguerite had found in the laboratory, the pain was minimal.

"These injuries will heal in time but they will scar badly," Marguerite said, helping her sister to dress his wounds.

"I do not give a fig, just as long as they hurry up and mend. It is not as if I will be attending any social function without a shirt."

"If you want them to heal quickly, then do not try and lift that awful dog on your own, otherwise these stitches will burst." Marguerite said.

"I am the only one capable and I cannot allow the animal to lie in its own mess. It needs to be cleaned up. I will be more careful next time," Geoffrey said.

For some time after the wounds began to heal, Geoffrey found it difficult to lift or move anything without the pain returning. This was frustrating when all the contaminated beds needed to be cleared and the area disinfected. On top of this, more food had to be sourced and soon, as the nagging threat of head-hunters remained. Until he could devise a more substantial weapon than the prototype spear, he accompanied his sisters and mother whenever they ventured near the river.

A week after the burials, with their diet reduced to grilled fish and fruit, Geoffrey set off in search of another food source. He was convinced that his father would have kept back-up supplies, being so far from the trading post. Armed with a hefty length of wood, he set off with Marguerite to investigate.

"I thought the chicken coop was on the other side of the compound?" Geoffrey said, balancing cautiously across a felled tree that bridged a fast-running brook.

"We are calling there on the way back. The building I saw is over there," she said, pointing beyond a group of trees.

"Are you coming? The log is perfectly safe."

"You go ahead, Geoffrey, I will wait here," she said nervously.

"Very well but do not wander off without me. I will be back as soon as I can." He made a mental note to fit a handrail across the brook when he felt better.

A short distance away he came upon a makeshift corral, where the bleached remains of two mules lay beside an empty food trough. A third mule, barely alive but somehow still standing, leaned against a roughly constructed barn that backed on to a rock face. At the far end of the enclosure there was a patch of rough ground pecked clean by a straggling brood of escaped hens.

"What have you found?" Marguerite called anxiously.

"There is a mule here, and a barn."

"Is it alive?"

"Barely… and there are another two that are not. There must be a food source inside."

"Do be careful, Geoffrey, there could be anything in there."

Entering the barn, Geoffrey discovered an inner door that he opened cautiously, peering inside the dark, cool area. From what little he could see, this was clearly a cave in the rock face, the walls of which had been lined with shelving. On these were stacked orderly batches of tin cans. Grabbing an armful, he went back outside, not wanting to leave his sister alone any longer. He could return with an oil lamp and investigate further.

By the entrance he found a galvanised bucket and three wooden containers of animal feed. Two of these had been gnawed through by rats and what remained of the contents was scattered across the rock floor. Gathering up what he could, Geoffrey put it into a trough near the emaciated mule, which refused to be fed by hand. Filling the bucket from the stream, he at least managed to get the mule to drink.

As he was about to return to the bridge his nerves, already on edge, were shattered by a fearful braying sound. He whirled around just in time to see the mule topple over, fall on to the trough with an ear-shattering crash and, ironically, end its wretched existence in a pile of scattered food.

Turning away, Geoffrey caught a glimpse of a small figure lurking among the bushes, just beyond where Marguerite was standing. Ignoring the pain, he raced towards his sister like a maniac, brandishing the club with all the ferocity he could muster and shouting for her to watch out.

"For heaven's sake, Geoffrey, what is it?" she cried.

"I saw someone a few moments ago… hiding in those trees," he gasped, barely able to draw breath. "I did not imagine it. We were definitely being watched."

"Dear Lord… you are bleeding!" Marguerite said, paying more attention to his shirt than to their surroundings. "We must take a look at this the moment we get back."

"Well before we do I have some good news. There is a pile of canned food Father had stored over there. I brought some samples." He offered up a tin of bully beef and another of chicken broth.

"This is wonderful news, Geoffrey but it must wait until your injuries have been attended to." She took him firmly by the arm, leading him back towards the compound.

"Rosamund went to catch more fish before we set off, so there will be something to eat, even if the contents of these are not palatable."

"Why does she keep doing that, knowing it may not be safe down there?"

"Mother insisted on going too. She took the gun with her as a precaution."

Back at the bungalow, Geoffrey checked that his mother and Rosamund were safe and was relieved to find there had been a slight improvement in the wolfhound's condition too. After checking no one was around, he rolled the animal on to a rug and dragged it along the veranda, where he made up a padded bed on the floor, close to the cane lounger that he slept in.

"Are you sure that animal is safe, Geoffrey?" Marguerite asked, skirting past the dog cautiously.

"If he was not, I would not be alive," Geoffrey retorted, immediately wishing he hadn't after the suspicious look she gave him, quickly adding, "What I mean is, he could be a really good deterrent against any intruders."

"That is ridiculous. The animal could not protect anyone in this state."

"Maybe not now but he will recover, and soon. We both will."

"Then it is to be hoped it will go looking for its owner and not become a permanent fixture. Feeding the four of us will be hard enough without the addition of a hungry dog. The creature must have come from somewhere but if someone does own it, they have clearly neglected to feed it, judging by that ribcage."

"This is a hunting dog, not domesticated. It goes out and feeds itself, except for times like now when it cannot. Anyway, I need to ask Rose if she caught any fish for his supper."

"You might dislodge those fresh bandages if you do. I will find out," Marguerite said.

"Did you mention those cans of bully beef I found?"

"We are having that for dinner tonight. Mother will come up with something tasty, I am sure. She seems much more at ease in the kitchen than I would ever have imagined."

"Probably because she grew up in Ireland; they do things differently out there."

"Yes, I suppose they do."

"Did you find any clues about what Father was working on in his notes?"

"Father's laboratory is such an unholy mess that I can barely make sense of anything at all. So many of the labels have peeled off the bottles with this awful humidity. Either that or the ink has smeared, making it impossible to read."

Later that afternoon, before dinner, Geoffrey went into the kitchen to look for a carving steel to sharpen Archie's knife and found his mother struggling to open the tin of bully beef.

"When you return to the store, Geoffrey, could you bring back samples of the tinned food and list the amounts? That way I can estimate how long we can manage."

"Let me do that, Mother," he said, opening the tin with the opener Marguerite had found, finding the contents fresh and edible.

"Did you say there are more tins of this?" Marguerite asked moodily, eyeing the plate in front of her with its modest portion of sliced beef and fresh tomatoes from a plant on the veranda.

"There was not enough light to see much but I am sure there were," Geoffrey said.

"We must be prepared to limit the amount we eat daily, supplementing the tinned food with fruit and whatever fresh vegetables we can find in the garden," their mother responded.

"But if there is plenty, why bother rationing?" Marguerite asked, clearing her plate before the others.

"Because we have no idea how long it will take before we are rescued, my darling. Rationing is our only option, unless you are prepared to kill an animal?" That brought an end to the discussion.

On the following morning, Geoffrey realised with alarm that they were not alone in the bungalow, He had secretly opened a 'spare' can of bully beef that he had brought from the store to feed the dog before his mother and sisters were awake. Once he had emptied it into an enamel dish he went outside to get rid of the tin before anyone saw the evidence. When he returned an hour later the dish was empty but the hound clearly hadn't moved from its bed.

With his mother and sisters safely chattering in the other room, Geoffrey began a search of the building but found no one. He scoured the compound but there too he found no evidence of an intruder. Nevertheless he kept a watchful eye out for any unexpected movement throughout the day. Rosamund was repairing one of the weighted fishing nets on the veranda, while his mother prepared food for later and rearranged the furnishings in the living area, transforming the space into a comfortable sitting room. Sadly, because of the humid atmosphere it was no surprise the grand piano was badly out of tune. Marguerite spent most of her time scribbling notes into the journal, or adding sketches of exotic plants.

At the end of another exhausting day, having collected more tinned food from the cave, Geoffrey made another attempt to make a substantial weapon before giving up in frustration. Needing to distance himself from his mother and sister to avoid any interruption, he sat cross-legged on the veranda, close to where the wolfhound lay, working fast to write down a wild section of music that had popped into his head before the sound evaporated and was lost forever. Engrossed in the creative process, he was interrupted by what he at first thought was a rumble of thunder in the fading light, until he realised it was a warning growl from the hound.

Instantly, Geoffrey reached for Archie's knife and leapt to his feet. Grabbing one of Rosamund's fishing nets en route, he made his way cautiously towards the kitchen.

"Where are you going, Geoffrey?" Marguerite called after him as he lit an oil lamp.

"Do not follow me; there is someone back there," Geoffrey hissed, inching his way towards the open doorway. As he paused on the threshold, a shadowy, dwarfish shape crept past in the darkness.

Rushing forward, Geoffrey hurled the fishing net after the pygmy-like figure as Rosamund had taught him. By yanking hard on the rope, he toppled the struggling creature off its feet and lashed the end onto a door handle as Marguerite ballooned her way past him with an oil lamp to stoop over the motionless captive, trussed like an animal in the coarse netting.

"For pity's sake Geoffrey, what have you done?" she asked, holding the lamp above the small bundle.

"Keep away from that thing, Maggs, it could be dangerous!" Geoffrey shouted.

"It is a child," she said, winding up the wick on the lamp to increase the flame. "I think you have killed him! Why can you never think before acting so… irresponsibly?" she said accusingly.

"Do you imagine there is any time to think logically in this hellhole? We could all be dead by now if it was left to you," he retorted, relieved to see the child was breathing. "How was I to know it was not someone hostile?"

"Anyone could see this was a child."

"Not in the bloody dark. I thought it was a pygmy."

"This is South America, Geoffrey, not the African Congo. Did you not learn anything in your geography lessons?"

"Well obviously not!" Geoffrey grumbled, helping her untangle the fishing net.

"Then you should think before you do anything like this again. We are the intruders here, Geoffrey. Not this child."

"How old do you think it is?" Geoffrey asked.

"*It*... is a little boy, not some random object, Geoffrey. He cannot be more than six years old."

"Well that comes as some relief since Father has only been out here four years, so at least this is not another of his illegitimate brood," Geoffrey said.

When the boy opened his terror-stricken eyes it was indeed clear that their father was not the parent as, despite the lightness of his skin, it was the eyes staring up at them that told a different story.

"It seems Father was not the only white man in these parts," Geoffrey said, staring into the piercing blue eyes. "But from what I can recall there were only natives among the dead here. Did you see another white face among them?"

"No, I did not," she responded thoughtfully. "But what also occurs to me is how this boy managed to survive the virus, when it appears no one else in this community did."

"We may never know the answer to that. All we can do is pray that whoever sired him will eventually return and we can persuade him to arrange a way to get us back to civilisation."

"Can you get the boy something to eat? I will stay with him in case he decides to run away." She began comforting the boy as Geoffrey's mother might once have done with him, and he felt even worse at having caused the child's ordeal.

During the days that followed the child began to follow Marguerite around, which she readily accepted, while Geoffrey wondered why she had never displayed this maternal side before.

With the boy tagging along, Geoffrey and his sister made a search of the laboratory for any records that might suggest who the father was and if there was any indication that he was likely to return.

"Whoever the man was, I think he had been here recently," Geoffrey said.

"How could you know that?" Marguerite asked.

"When we arrived here there was a half-completed game of chess set out in the living room. Mother must have cleared it away."

"Are you sure?"

"Positive." He began sorting through a pile of worn ledgers and files.

"What have you got there?" Marguerite asked.

"Proof of what happened here. Take a look for yourself and see what you make of this." He handed over one of the files. In it his father described the outbreak and symptoms and listed all the kinds of fungus, swamp-root and plant extract which had been used in the process of seeking an antidote, detailing the precise measure of distilled juice they produced. Since each plant was given an unfamiliar local name and there were no pictures, as far as Geoffrey was concerned they could have applied to anything in the surrounding forest and, with no one left to ask, the documented research meant nothing.

Among the piles of paperwork there were also three well-thumbed notebooks, bound together with string. Written In the first two was a mass of information in his father's neat, distinctive hand, cataloguing every reaction to the controlled experiments with fanatical precision from the first sign of having contracted the virus and listing every stage of its development until death.

In the other notebook he had recorded the early construction of the compound, which gave some insight into his struggle for acceptance within the native community. His design concept for the Scaggoa compound was aesthetically pleasing but it also involved the creation of a community, which gave Geoffrey some understanding of the happiness his father had experienced in being so far removed from the moral standards required by his earlier, provincial life.

"What have you found, Geoffrey?"

"Some interesting stuff; take a look," he said. "This must have been the first record he made after he arrived, although there's a later entry that Father must have jotted down quite recently… Oh my God!" he said.

The inevitable blindness and creeping paralysis have not only proven unstoppable, but are developing at an alarming rate. Death from contracting this virus is happening in less than a month now and is no longer gestating over an eight-week period as it did in the beginning.

Today, my Benedict's beautiful spirit left this earth a sadder place but he is no longer subjected to that unbearable pain. His rapid deterioration has been unbearable to watch, knowing that I could not find a cure, or suffer any of his pain instead. There is no escape or comfort in sleep, now that only my darling Abigail clings to life. Very soon she, like my other beautiful children, will be taken from the pain inflicted in their earthly existence.

It is so hard to bear the agony of this loss, knowing that we will not be reunited in the afterlife, a thought which is tearing my soul apart. Only Lorenzo could begin to understand the pain of losing each of my beautiful children and, in his wisdom, help me find forgiveness for having unknowingly created this devastating infection.

I pray to God he will return soon, since it will be impossible to fight off the next phase of paralysis and the prospect of abandoning my sweet Abigail to pass from this life without having me to comfort her in those final hours horrifies me. It is a terrifying thought that the curse of this virus is down to my experiments and, for that stupidity alone, my soul should be dammed for an eternity. I can only pray that my penance for all of this avoidable suffering will be to burn in Hell.

There is nothing on God's Earth that can prevent the inevitable asphyxiation which will take me before my last child and it makes my heart break. My constant prayer is that the Lord will allow me enough time to nurse Abigail through her final hours and that, in His infinite mercy, he will return Lorenzo here before my death, and allow him to guide the souls of my innocent children along the spiritual way into the afterlife.

"Geoffrey, you look dreadful, you must sit down," Marguerite said, taking hold of his arm, which he wrenched away without saying a word before dashing out onto the breezeway where he was violently sick over the handrail.

"We need to get away from here immediately," Geoffrey said, once he could speak.

"You know that is impossible, until Churuma can arrange for another boat to be sent from the trading post," she said, trying to wipe his mouth with the hem of her apron.

"He is not coming back, Maggs. We can't stay here for even one more day. We are at risk from that hellish virus. If you don't believe me, then read Father's final entry in these notes."

"Please allow me to help, Geoffrey," she called after him as he moved away.

"If you want to help then leave me alone!" he shouted back, stumbling out of the building. Somehow he had to come up with a plan to get his family away from this place.

"Jeffy! Wait!" Rosamund shouted, helping the wolfhound down the veranda steps towards him.

"Can you not keep him with you? I need to clear my head."

"No I can't. I am helping Mother to clean up and, wherever you are going, this dog clearly wants to go with you. Heaven alone knows why." Rosamund steadied the hound until it reached ground level and staggered towards him. She wore a cotton apron over a simple dress and, with her hair tied back, he realised that she had never looked lovelier. If only Archie could have been there to see her.

Geoffrey led the dog slowly up the narrow track to the burial site, regretting his antipathy to his father and wished he had been more sympathetic towards his tortured remains during the funeral.

Leaving the hound resting in the shade, Geoffrey laid a floral tribute on the tiny grave of each child and another on his father's, where he then knelt for a long time.

"I am truly sorry for all of the suffering you went through, and want you to know that Abigail was not alone at the end of her life. Mother comforted her as she would have done with each of us, until her spirit finally departed. She is buried here with her brother and three sisters, just a few feet away from where you are."

Sitting in the shade with the dog, Geoffrey felt all too aware of the dangers threatening his family in that isolated place. Archie's knife alone would not be enough of a deterrent if he was ever attacked again – something that seemed inevitable – so he would need a more substantial spear. The design of such a weapon could surely be found in his father's collection of encyclopaedias.

Chapter Fifteen
The Arrival

When Geoffrey returned to the compound, he found Marguerite alone on the veranda with one of his father's notebooks, clearly unsettled by what she had read.

"You have been gone for hours. You had everyone worried. Mother in particular."

"I needed to be on my own after what I read. Have you gone through it?"

"I have and so has Mother. It gave her some comfort, knowing how much Father cared for those children."

"It is good to know that and I am sorry for what his final days must have been like."

"I am sorry too but I cannot mourn him, not after the way he treated Mother."

"Who do you think this Lorenzo might be?" Geoffrey asked.

"Well, if he has piercing blue eyes, then perhaps he fathered this poor child," Marguerite said. The boy was lurking just out of Geoffrey's sight in the doorway.

"And what did you make of those spiritual references?" he asked, stopping when his mother came on to the veranda and went over to apologise for having caused her any distress.

After another restless night and finding nothing useful in the encyclopaedia, Geoffrey slipped away with the wolfhound and, by a longer but gentler route, they made their way up the incline to the store cabin where more of his father's reference books were kept. Finally he located a volume with the information he needed and sprawled on the veranda to examine the illustrations, where Marguerite found him some hours later.

"What on earth are you doing up here, Geoffrey? I have been searching everywhere. Mother has been asking after you."

"The dog needed the exercise and I thought the slope would help strengthen his legs."

"Surely it gets enough exercise following you around."

"I can't help that. Anyway, I enjoy his company."

"Maybe so but not if it is preventing you from practising every day, as you should if you are to pass your entrance exam."

"That is ridiculous, this is much more important," Geoffrey said, turning down a corner of the page and snapping the encyclopaedia shut.

"That is no reason not to practise, whatever it is you are reading."

"It can wait for a while; there is not much likelihood of returning to England in the near future," he said. He decided against mentioning that he had also been put off by a nasty skin irritation that had erupted between his fingers and would undoubtedly interfere with his playing.

"Maybe not but Mother loves hearing you play. It would help lift her spirits if you could play something for her this evening."

"Another reason I have against practising is that I have no intention of attracting any unwanted attention," Geoffrey said, hoping his reasoning would satisfy his sister and she would leave him in peace.

"That is an absurd reason. Who could be listening? All we ever see are trees," Marguerite protested.

"There is always the chance of some unsavoury characters like those caiman hunters; or even worse, head-hunters."

"Head-hunters?" she repeated with alarm.

"That is what I have been reading up on. I can assure you that they do exist in the rainforest and that is why you should never come up here alone."

"There cannot be any such savages in these parts, surely?" she said, looking anxiously at the dog as it began to wake. "And what will you do with this animal when it has fully recovered, Geoffrey? You cannot keep it. We have barely enough food to feed ourselves, never mind a stray."

"What a rotten thing to say. There is a ton of tinned food in Father's store," Geoffrey snapped.

"We only have your word for that, Geoffrey," Marguerite grumbled.

"If you had bothered to come with me, we would not be having this conversation."

"So what are you going to do about this creature, Geoffrey?" she said, attempting to get some air through the top of her loosened gown.

"Nothing, since you ask. He is not going anywhere without me, not unless his owner comes to claim him." Geoffrey wished she would leave.

"There is not much likelihood of that happening in this wretched wilderness. And what makes you think this ferocious creature belongs to someone? It more than likely grew up in the wild."

"Someone must have cared about him if they gave him this amazing collar. The workmanship is incredible and have you noticed that the wire looks identical to that wrist band Churuma gave you?" Geoffrey said, fingering the mesh of the hound's collar.

Marguerite stooped to examine the copper mesh. "Can you remove it so we can make a comparison?"

"I have already looked and there's no clasp. It must have been woven around its neck."

"How could anyone do that?" she exclaimed.

"At least it proves that he was loved by someone. I have even wondered if this could be the same animal that was chasing after the priest and that naked savage."

"Geoffrey, mind your language!"

"Protest all you like, Maggs; all I am saying is that young man did not have a stitch on. I did at least see that much before I got something in my eye. Anyway, the evidence of what we saw that day is recorded in your journal. He could not have belonged to Father since he detested anything on four legs, except race horses."

"Whatever you say, once the animal has recovered you must allow it to go free. It is a monster compared to any ordinary dog and will need a lot more than just the odd piece of fish."

"If it bothers you that much, I will find meat for it; that way there will be no strain on our supplies," Geoffrey snapped.

"How on earth do you propose doing that, Geoffrey? You are no hunter."

"That is why I am learning how to make a properly balanced spear, one that will not break on impact." Geoffrey was not yet so angry as to blurt out what he had already been capable of but he wanted to shock her nevertheless.

"You could never construct a spear Geoffrey, or anything resembling one. You are not practical in any way... you are a musician!" she exclaimed.

"Then what better time to learn? There is evil out there and we need protection. If I had a weapon close at hand I would not flinch from using it."

"Geoffrey, you are barely eighteen. You could never kill anything."

"Actually I am nearly eighteen and a half," Geoffrey said, avoiding a response to her second comment.

"Do stop exaggerating, Geoffrey. You will be that age in three months," she retorted. "Please put an end to this talk of making spears and put those books away. Mother will be expecting you to play for her this evening. Do not let her down."

The following morning Geoffrey burned some more of the cots from the breezeway in the centre of the compound, well away from the buildings. When he returned the dog's agitated state told him instinctively that something was wrong.

"Do be careful, darling, you might cut yourself," his mother called out from the veranda as he returned with the machete.

"The dog seems restless and I think we need to remain on our guard. You and the girls must stay out of harm's way on the veranda. You will see more than I can from down here. And Mother… you might want to keep that pistol handy."

"If there are more of those head-hunters out there, then you must come up here with us," she called, which confirmed for the first time that she had indeed seen what had happened at the river when they arrived.

"I am safe enough, especially having the dog with me," Geoffrey said, rather more confidently than he actually felt.

Through the heat haze from the fire, from out of the undergrowth emerged a dark shape that eventually coalesced into the figure of a man, seated astride a hefty mule. Reining in the animal, the hunched figure began shouting orders into the dense foliage behind him, the sound of his voice distorted by the crackling of the bonfire.

With the machete clutched in one hand, Geoffrey slid Archie's hunting knife from its sheath with the other. His heart was racing in readiness to defend his family against anything that might appear, but he could never have anticipated the apparition that stumbled out of the bushes a moment later.

Through the haze it was difficult to determine the age of the bronzed figure, in a torn and ill-fitting shirt and with a mass of wild, untamed hair, which, caught by a strong shaft of sunlight, gave the impression of a radiating halo. Even though the stranger's spear was held only loosely in his hand, it was obvious he knew how to use it.

"You, sir, with the spear, lay that weapon on the ground before you dare take another step in this direction," Lady Claudia demanded, brandishing her revolver. "And you on the mule, if your companion attempts to lay one finger on my son, you will both be dead before you can dismount!"

"Madam, we mean you no harm," the mounted figure retorted in a tone that was somehow more like a threat. From what Geoffrey could make out through the haze the man wore a black robe. He now gestured urgently to the spear carrier behind him. "Lorenzo, do what she asks."

There was an instant reaction from the wolfhound, which rose to its feet and lurched forward with a throaty growl.

"Stay, damn it!" Geoffrey commanded as the animal brushed past his leg, gathering momentum towards the younger man before launching itself at him, the weight of the dog bringing the man crashing to the ground.

As Marguerite screamed with alarm, Geoffrey was already running towards the two men, clutching the machete in his right hand. He barely heard the crack of the bullwhip before he was yanked off his feet and dragged across the ground towards the mule. The last thing he heard was the sharp report of a gunshot before his head collided with a rock and everything went black.

When Geoffrey came to, his eyes ached and he found that his head was heavily bandaged over something damp packed tightly against his pounding temple that smelled like rotten eggs. The screech of parrots roosting in the tree outside was doing nothing to help ease the pain. He had a bitter, acrid taste in his mouth, like something used to clean drains. He tried to sit up and saw that he was lying on a chaise longue in the living room.

"Maggs… is that you?" Geoffrey asked, peering at his sister through bleary eyes.

"Finally you are awake," she said, laying aside her project on the table.

"How long have I been in here?"

"It has been a few hours. Mother asked me not to wake you after that nasty bang to your head. Rest seemed the best cure." She helped him stand.

322

"I feel sick," Geoffrey said, grabbing hold of the table to prevent him from falling, and becoming vaguely aware of a disassembled revolver.

"I will get you a bucket," Marguerite said, once they were outside and Geoffrey was seated in the recliner.

"There is no need. Being out here makes me feel a lot better. What were you doing with that gun?" He struggled to recall the recent events.

"Can you not remember?" she asked.

"Only bits. It's coming back slowly." Geoffrey remembered the echo of gunfire and the hound leaping at the man's throat, dreading the thought that his mother and sisters had been witness to the savagery.

"Why not begin by telling me why there is a revolver in pieces on the table?"

"It pulls to the right when fired. Mother asked me to fix it."

"Oh my God... Mother shot that brute on the mule," he said with alarm, surprised to see that this made her smile.

"Fortunately not; the second bullet jammed. Otherwise the old gentleman would have suffered more than a minor flesh wound."

"I cannot sympathise. At least that moron will be more careful with his bullwhip in future," Geoffrey said with some satisfaction.

"Geoffrey, please lower your voice!" she reprimanded. "This is a man of God."

"I will not. I am the one that idiot yanked over and not you, and it is I who is walking around with what feels like a cowpat strapped to my head because of him!"

Geoffrey lay back on the recliner, realising he couldn't blame everything on the intruder. He'd been feeling unwell all day, long before the incident. Within seconds he was sound asleep once more. When he woke, Marguerite was standing over him, shaking him gently.

"Geoffrey, I need you to sit up and drink this."

"What the devil is it?" Geoffrey asked suspiciously.

"A drink made from crushed fruit."

"Dear God, no… not more fruit."

"Drink it, for goodness' sake. This potion will help ward off any headaches you might have from that nasty fall." She handed him a horn beaker of green liquid.

"That was no fall. I was dragged across the ground by that idiot's bullwhip," Geoffrey downed the liquid without taking a breath, knowing instinctively it would taste foul. "Where is Mother?"

"She went to the burial site with Father Fitzgerald. They may be gone for some time."

"What were you thinking, allowing Mother to go up there with that barbarian? There is no need. The burial is done." Geoffrey struggled to his feet.

"Sit down and listen to me, Geoffrey. It is important for Mother that the priest will perform a Christian service." She helped him back onto the recliner. "Father Fitzgerald needed to know exactly where the burial site was, so that he could consecrate the ground."

"Well in my opinion that man is a charlatan; either that or completely bonkers. Priests do not go charging around on mules, deliberately injuring people. That bloody halfwit would do better as a gaucho."

"He is not what I would have expected from a missionary, I must say."

"Presumably that whip is how he gathers a congregation together." Geoffrey was already feeling remarkably better after drinking the syrupy, green liquid. "How did I get up here, Maggs? I don't remember any of that."

"That was Lorenzo, he carried you," Marguerite said with a smile.

"Lorenzo?" he repeated. "That was the name the priest called out, before I blacked out." He remembered how the wolfhound had tackled the other man and sent him crashing to the ground. "So he is still alive?"

"Of course he is."

"But the hound… I saw it leap for his throat."

"As we all did, Geoffrey. It turns out you were absolutely right in your assumption that the animal belonged to someone and that we actually saw them together on our way here. When the dog leapt at him, it was in greeting."

She had clearly not realised the mortifying effect this news would have.

"He should not be allowed to have him back. Not after leaving him in that state. If I hadn't been there that afternoon, the animal would have been dead; we both would."

"What do you mean, that you would both have died?"

"That is irrelevant now. What kind of rotter would leave a wounded creature alone in this damned wilderness, then have the nerve to turn up to claim it back?"

"There is no need to take a dislike to someone before you have even met them. I am convinced Lorenzo would never have willingly abandoned any animal, injured or otherwise. He is the sweetest young man imaginable."

"That is only because you never wanted the dog here in the first place," Geoffrey retorted angrily.

"You are being very unreasonable, Geoffrey."

"No I am not. That rotten swine took my dog!" Geoffrey yelled.

"Do stop overreacting, Geoffrey. I will go and get you something to drink."

"I do not want any more of that bloody green slime!" he called after her.

"Lorenzo made that for you. I am getting you something else."

"You see… you see what is happening? That bastard has already got my dog, now he is trying to finish the job that priest couldn't do, by poisoning me!"

It was a while before his head stopped spinning and he could lean back in the recliner, trying not to panic until he was able to breathe.

"Please go away, Maggs and leave me in peace," Geoffrey said when she returned, unable to escape the nauseating stench from the padding over his temple.

"I only want to help."

"Then get rid of this dressing. It stinks like cow dung! What the hell is it?"

"It was something Lorenzo came back with from the river. He assured Mother that if this was kept in place for a few hours it would stop the bleeding and seal the wound."

"I thought you were the expert on natural cures, not him?"

"I have no idea of the properties of these tropical plants. Lorenzo seems very knowledgeable and I trust him."

"But it's not your head caked in this revolting stuff, is it? What has happened to the dog?"

"Lorenzo has taken it downriver in search of a plant he says will speed up its recovery. Why are you scowling? I thought you would be pleased."

"I hope it's not the same stinking muck he put on my head," Geoffrey said, trying to loosen the bandage.

"For heaven's sake leave it alone, otherwise that handsome young face of yours might be scarred for life."

"My body is scarred anyway."

"If Lorenzo had been here he might have made a poultice to heal those dreadful cuts. I did not have the knowledge," she sighed

"You cannot blame yourself because you are not versed in the art of witchcraft the way he is. Did Rose go with them?"

"She went to collect some food from the cave, for our guests this evening."

"They are dining with us?"

"Mother invited them to stay on until the old man recovers, but he would not hear of it. They are leaving at dawn tomorrow. For a man of the cloth, his tone was bordering on incivility to Mother. I suppose it could be due to the pain but it may just be from living out here for the last thirty years."

"That does not excuse him behaving like that. Was she upset?"

"She did not show it. I suppose she feels obligated, being responsible for his gunshot wound."

"Well he can't be that badly hurt if he has gone with her to the burial ground. It's quite a climb."

"Anyone could see he was suffering but he went nevertheless."

"Then why not rest for a while if he is that badly hurt? Do you think he might have got the wind up about the virus?"

"I would not have thought so. Men of the cloth preach in all manner of conditions. Disgusting places that you and I would not go within a mile of. Apart from that, every inch of this place has been disinfected, we have been here for well over a week and none of us has been infected, so it cannot be that."

"Do you think he and Father were acquainted?" Geoffrey asked.

"I am convinced they were. Also, it may be no coincidence the priest has the same piercing blue eyes as the boy."

"That would make sense if he was a friend of Father's!" Geoffrey said churlishly. "And did this man of God have any idea what Father might have been working on to cause such a deadly outbreak?"

"None whatsoever. He and Lorenzo have not been here for eight months. Father's compound is the final call on his missionary circuit."

"What about the sleeping arrangements if they are staying overnight? I hope they are not expecting to bed down in the bungalow with you, Mother and Rose."

Although he had slept for an hour he still felt giddy when standing and the irritation between his fingers was getting worse. It also didn't help that the young boy was constantly skulking about in the shadows, chewing on handfuls of bulbous roots that were purple in colour and streaked with yellow. The sight and sound made Geoffrey feel even worse.

"Where on earth does he dig up that revolting stuff?" Geoffrey asked his sister.

"I have no idea. It must be a native delicacy," Marguerite said dismissively, resting her hand on his brow. "I came across a tin of Father's imported tea. I thought you might like some."

"Not a good idea at the moment," Geoffrey said, wishing she would leave so that he could lie down again. "And will you please ask that child to go somewhere else to chew on that damned thing? The smell is unbearable."

"Everything is so different out here. I do envy the priest leaving tomorrow. If Lorenzo had more than a one-man canoe, we could probably go too," Marguerite said, scribbling a note into her journal.

"This Lorenzo looks a lot younger than the priest," he observed, which made her smile.

"Yes, he is nearer my age."

"And he must be very strong to have carried me up here."

"I made a sketch of him while you were asleep," she said, opening a page of the journal for him to see.

"This cannot be accurate. No one could look like that."

"Let me assure you he does. I never embellish my work. You of all people should know that," she said crossly.

"Even if it is not deliberate, you have portrayed this Lorenzo like some mythical Greek God," Geoffrey scoffed.

"This is a true representation of him, whether you think so or not; and, quite frankly Geoffrey, I do not give a fig for your opinion!" She snapped the journal shut and stormed off into the bungalow.

Feeling much better that evening, Geoffrey still baulked at his mother's request that he give a short recital for their guests but finally relented as it was tipping down with rain and there was nowhere he could go to escape.

The constant pain in his head and irregular bouts of nausea gave Geoffrey no desire to spend more time in the company of the man he held responsible for his suffering than was absolutely necessary, so he ate alone on the veranda where he was delighted to be joined by the wolfhound, saying that he would return later.

Entering the dimly lit room, he could sense no goodwill in the brief exchange between the priest and his mother. The pressure from the rough, scarred palms as they shook hands seemed intended to crush his fingers but Geoffrey was determined not to give him the satisfaction of showing how much it hurt.

"You play then?" Harvey Fitzgerald said in a rasping voice, more a statement than a question. There was nothing friendly in the piercing stare of the blue eyes, only an intense, searching look. "I was hoping the Lady Rosamund would have entertained us with a musical interlude."

"Unfortunately, although my sister plays admirably, the piano my father imported has a wooden frame and it has long since warped in this climate. I doubt if Mozart himself could have produced anything recognisable on that, however grand. I would be perfectly happy not to perform for you and your companion if you so wish though I do have a slight headache."

"Unlike myself, Lorenzo enjoys any classical composition. Therefore I would urge you to go ahead with the recital."

"Then I would assume that you, like my father, are perhaps more familiar with the music that is popular at the Gaiety Theatre or in the music halls."

"Geoffrey, dear!" Lady Claudia reprimanded him in a hushed voice.

"That, Sir Geoffrey, would be termed as burlesque where I come from; but yes, although I do find a tuneful melody preferable, I am willing to make an exception for my companion's sake." He settled himself comfortably, if perhaps a little too close to Rosamund. It was only now that Geoffrey became fully aware of the other man in the dimly lit room. Lorenzo was standing in the shadows, where it was impossible to distinguish his features, so he could not see how accurate Marguerite's sketch of him was. What was apparent was his ill-fitting European clothes, items that must have been purchased before he had finished growing and his evident discomfort made it clear they were worn only for respectability.

Geoffrey had selected Brahms's Fourth Symphony in E Minor, Opus 98, music that he knew instinctively the priest would hate but would have to endure in order not to offend Geoffrey's mother. As he began playing, he was aware of Lorenzo moving into the light, not only to listen but also to watch the performance. As the final section came to an end he could barely control his fingers on the strings and was desperate to get outside to massage the inflamed irritation on his hands. He cursed Father Fitzgerald for his thumping head and watery eyes but, even more, he felt the need to get away from the unnerving, intense stare of his companion, who seemed mesmerised by the sound.

"Why you no stay?" Lorenzo asked, coming up silently behind Geoffrey as he headed for the door, making him jump with fright.

When Lorenzo did speak, which was rarely, it was in a strange combination of English mixed with fragments of Spanish and an unrecognisable dialect that had the sound of rushing water. His youthful appearance belied the unfathomable depth of ancient wisdom in those emerald-green eyes.

"Because I need to be on my own!" Geoffrey retorted, hoping he would leave.

At first glance Lorenzo appeared to be perhaps the same age as Archie but beyond that, any similarity ended. He was unlike anyone Geoffrey had ever encountered. In truth, the striking image Marguerite had sketched in her journal barely did justice to the raw charisma and sexuality with his hair and skin still damp from swimming in the river.

330

"I see much," Lorenzo said, as if needing to explain something important, his hand now resting lightly on the sleeping wolfhound.

"Oh really," Geoffrey muttered, wishing he would leave him alone with the dog and still angry that Lorenzo hadn't troubled to look for the animal when it was so badly injured.

"I know Perro, him come 'ere and you care for 'im." It was as if Lorenzo had been able to read Geoffrey's thoughts.

"I have no idea what you are talking about," he lied.

"You say you no comprende but this you do," Lorenzo responded with a fleeting smile.

"Bollocks, you know nothing!" Geoffrey exclaimed vehemently, hoping his mother was out of earshot.

"Why you no believe?"

"I am not some bloody halfwit off a banana boat. You could never have known that I would take care of this poor dog, no one could!"

In the final rays of sunlight, Lorenzo's damp auburn hair shone like burnished gold, the glow surrounding him like a saint in a stained-glass window.

"You have pain?" Lorenzo asked, resting his cool, damp hands on Geoffrey's temple.

"Yes, if you must know. My head is thumping like the blazes... as if I am being hit with a blasted sledgehammer, if you even know what that is. Now please go away and leave me in peace."

"Why you no want me stay?" Lorenzo persisted. "I take pain away."

"Piss off, you bloody heathen! I am only in pain because of that renegade priest of yours," Geoffrey hissed. "This stinking cowpat on my head is not helping either."

"I much sorry, I need get fresh from river make pain go away," Lorenzo said and, within moments he had melted into the shadows, just as Geoffrey's mother came out with two aspirin and a tumbler of water.

"I am so sorry I asked you to perform this evening when you were still in pain, my darling, but that was truly the most beautiful recital. Lorenzo seemed as captivated as we all were."

"You forget that obnoxious priest, Mother. I could have been playing 'Baa, Baa Black Sheep' for all he knew."

"Perhaps Brahms was not to his liking."

"Unlike Rose, I suspect… Mother, you should not have left them alone together."

"I am perfectly aware of the gentleman's attentions. Marguerite is with them now and will make sure that he keeps his distance." She peered into the shadows. " I was convinced Lorenzo was coming out here to compliment you."

"He was here, Mother but he went away. He understood that I need to be on my own for the rest of the evening."

"Your sisters also wish to congratulate you on your extraordinary performance this evening, Geoffrey."

"I honestly could not face it, Mother, not right now."

"Then I will make sure they understand you need rest. Tomorrow will be soon enough."

"And Mother, please make sure that awful priest stays inside too; he is the very last person I want to see tonight!"

"That will be no problem, I think, if Rosamund is remaining inside," she said with a wry smile.

When he awoke, Geoffrey was unsure if he had been asleep for a few moments or more than an hour. He rubbed his eyes in the hope of getting rid of an annoying blur that had recently begun to form over his eyes as he slept.

"This I need change," Lorenzo said, appearing as if from nowhere, shirtless and carrying a dripping lump of earthy material dripping with water.

"My sister can do that," Geoffrey exclaimed, startled. The annoying irritation between his fingers also seemed to be getting worse.

"This I make for you get better soon," Lorenzo began.

"What the hell is that? It stinks like a sewer. And for Pete's sake put your shirt on," Geoffrey cried, backing away.

"Why it trouble you? You no señorita," Lorenzo smiled, taking a tumbler from the table.

"No I am not but my sisters are, so cover yourself up before they see you!"

"It no possible," Lorenzo smiled. Tipping the water from the tumbler, Lorenzo scooped up most of the evil-looking mud, deftly removing two wriggling newts that he dropped over the edge of the veranda. Taking a bunch of green berries from a pouch on his belt, he crushed them between two flat stones, sprinkling the granules carefully into the mud. After adding two pinches of a yellow powder, then another of bright red, he stirred the mixture until it became a thick paste, then spread this on a pad of purple leaves. On the floor beside his leg was half a coconut shell filled with river water, beside which Lorenzo now knelt, directly in front of him.

"What the devil!" Geoffrey hissed, backing away.

"Make pain gone," Lorenzo said, carefully unwinding the bandage around Geoffrey's temple.

Dipping his shirt sleeve into the water, Lorenzo held it against the dried-out pad on Geoffrey's head for a short time until he could easily remove it, then replaced it with the fresh poultice that he gently bound over Geoffrey's temple. Sweat beaded on his chest as he moved back and forth, his muscular arms brushing gently against Geoffrey's face and body until it was all done.

"This much good… take away pain," Lorenzo said.

"Can you please leave now?" Geoffrey said, directly into the face now so uncomfortably close to against his. "Why are you doing this?"

"You have much care for mi Perro. Him much valiente… He brave," Lorenzo explained and Geoffrey finally understood how much he really cared for the animal.

"I would appreciate it if you would leave me now," Geoffrey said, increasingly intimidated by the close proximity of the naked torso. Curiously, in the evening light there appeared to be fine, scale-like blemishes on the otherwise perfect skin.

"Why you want me go?"

"Because I need to rest," Geoffrey lied, trying to look away but with no option than to stare at the naked chest.

Before dawn had broken the following morning, the loathsome priest was already astride the mule, their combined shape soon enveloped in the early mist like an angel from Hell. Having reined in the animal to glare back towards the bungalow, he sat tapping the bullwhip against his leg impatiently.

"Perro want say adios," Lorenzo whispered in Geoffrey's ear, having once again appeared beside him like a ghost.

"Where the hell did you come from?" Geoffrey responded angrily, alarmed but delighted to see that the wolfhound was with him, its condition much improved from the previous day, and walking more steadily than before.

"I no waken beautiful lady."

"What do you want with Rose?"

"It no she, I bring elixir for bella madre… for make well soon," Lorenzo said.

"What elixir?" Geoffrey asked moodily, desperate for his blurred vision to clear so that he could focus properly. To his delight the agonising pain in his head had all but gone, and he could only hope that his distorted eyesight would clear up as easily.

"This take away much of pain before I back," Lorenzo replied.

"You plan on returning then?"

"This I much hope," and with the hound close at heel, Lorenzo was gone almost as silently as he had appeared.

It was only then Geoffrey realised that Lorenzo was not only barefoot but, apart from a leather pouch protecting his genitals and a sheathed hunting knife attached to a narrow belt, he was naked and more perfect than any sculpture he had ever seen.

Geoffrey soon began to berate himself for not asking Lorenzo to make up some more paste to cool down the burning rash between his fingers. In places it was forming into open red sores, perhaps from scratching them in the night and seemed worse than ever that morning. He was just as angry with himself for not having been more amiable, as they could need the priest's help to find their way home.

Over the next few days, his mother and sisters moved out of the main bungalow and into the three smaller structures, allowing Geoffrey to remain in the main building with the privacy he needed to practise on the violin, although this was something he was finding increasingly difficult as the week progressed.

On the third morning after the move, Geoffrey woke to find Marguerite shaking him gently, the small boy peering at him nervously from behind her capacious skirts.

"Geoffrey, you must wake up. It is getting late and you have not eaten."

"I'm not hungry," he grumbled.

"But you must be. You barely ate yesterday."

"Just give me time to use the shower," Geoffrey said, expecting her to leave.

"You can do that once I have taken a look at that cut on your temple. It must have begun healing by now."

"I suppose." He flinched as she removed the bandage.

"I can hardly believe it! This was an awful mess yet there is barely a trace of any scarring. I cannot understand how this could have healed so quickly. I wish you could see this," she exclaimed.

"I will take your word for it. God alone knows what he put in it, to make it stink like that." He blinked hard until her features became clearer.

"Why are you blinking so much? Are you still getting those headaches from the fall?"

"If you mean when I was yanked off my feet, then no, not entirely." He wondered if he should mention the constant nausea too but decided against it.

"I can tell; it has been affecting your playing."

"How do you know that?" Geoffrey said suspiciously. "That is for me to judge and no one else. None of you is supposed to listen."

"It is unavoidable and we all enjoy listening when you play normally but, quite honestly, over these past few days it sounded as if someone else was playing."

"It is difficult to play well in this humidity; my hands get so clammy," he lied, not wanting to mention the worsening rash.

"Maybe after the rains it will get cooler. You do have the most wonderful talent."

"Until I got that crack on the head from that brute of a priest and had to wear that nauseating thing strapped to my head by his Adonis sidekick," Geoffrey snapped.

"I honestly cannot understand why you have such an unpleasant attitude towards genuinely nice people. As I recall, you were just as scathing about Archie Westbrook, even after he saved Rosamund's life and mine too."

"That is not fair. This is altogether different."

"It is nothing of the kind and you know it. You seem to have developed an inbuilt resentment to the good in everyone. Lorenzo has been wonderfully attentive to Mother, and also to this child that you constantly ignore. If you did not, you might have learnt that he is called the Otter, which is really sweet." She smiled at the child, who was now clinging to her skirts.

"That clearly relates to his eating habits, from a nearby swamp. I did not think they have otters in South America," Geoffrey said, trying not to scratch his itching hands.

"I doubt Lorenzo would have come up with that name if there were none. He knows more about wildlife than anyone I have ever met."

336

"Then maybe I should have asked him if he had another concoction to help get rid of this bloody irritation between my fingers. It is worse than the pain from any stinging nettle. The problem is, I can't remember how I did it."

"Let me see." She prised open his clenched fists and examined his hands with evident concern. "How long have you had this?"

"A few days, I suppose. If I could figure out how I got stung, I could have searched for the local equivalent of dock leaves."

"Mother has developed something very similar, Geoffrey, so whatever has stung you it must have been when you were together. I might find something to help this in father's laboratory."

Chapter Sixteen
Infection

By late evening, Marguerite had applied three different ointments to the irritation but only one – a particularly vile-smelling green-tinted cream – was effective in stopping the impulse to scratch and it was midnight before Geoffrey finally dropped off into a fitful sleep.

After a disturbed night crammed with nightmarish visions of demonic creatures scrabbling to drag him over the edge of a fathomless pit, he awoke to find Marguerite staring at him intently.

"Geoffrey… can you hear me?" she asked.

He tried to focus on her face.

"You were shouting so loudly that Mother asked me to come over." She handed him a dish with more of the green paste.

"Is this cream working for Mother too?" Geoffrey asked, gratefully smoothing the ointment over the inflamed area.

"I have not tried her with this yet. I needed to see how it affected you first. I decided not to give her anything else at the moment, not with the pills and Lorenzo's drink which she takes at hourly intervals, which helps ease the pain."

"Are you completely insane, allowing that Neolithic maniac to give Mother some mystery concoction to drink? There could be anything in the stuff."

"Whatever it contained she has slept well for the first time in weeks and was already dressed when I called in at her cabin."

"But why didn't you go through Father's medical books before subjecting her to God alone knows what he crushed into that mixture?"

"I have been through every reference book in Father's laboratory but found nothing that would ease Mother's pain, so I took a chance on this remedy. Lorenzo seems to know exactly what he is doing."

"How could anyone raised in this barbarous place know what medication to give someone when they have barely met?"

"Protest all you want, Geoffrey but you will not alter my opinion. Nothing Lorenzo has put together was haphazard. He meticulously checked and measured every amount. He may not be an English pharmacist but he has an instinctive knowledge. My initial concern was to ease Mother's suffering and, so far, that is exactly what it has achieved."

Thankfully she believed his lie that he had already eaten, so no food was forced upon him that morning but the odour of fried eggs drove him outside to rest in the shade. Twice he almost lost his balance, only just managing to avoid falling over on his way back to the bungalow. Mounting the steps to the veranda, his eyes began misting over once more and he fell heavily, cracking his elbow against the handrail.

Determined to find something to make him feel better, Geoffrey made his way to the laboratory. He stayed there most of the morning, scouring the books for anything relating to concussion or inflamed skin but found nothing for his symptoms.

As Geoffrey flicked through his father's worn notebooks he came across a list of the symptoms associated with the deadly virus. To his horror, he recognised the rapid deterioration of his own once-healthy skin, body and eyesight. In shock he stumbled out of the laboratory and made his way slowly up to the burial site where he could be alone.

Resting in the shade of a tree, Geoffrey could only stare blankly at the spearhead of tiny graves, fearing that very soon he too would be buried alongside his half-siblings. If his mother had similar symptoms then, she too must have fallen victim to the virus. He could do nothing but pray that, despite his reservations, Lorenzo would soon return. It would be too late to help Geoffrey, since he knew from his father's notes that he was now undoubtedly entering the second stage of the virus but he might just arrive back in time to save his mother and could perhaps prevent his sisters from becoming infected too.

Returning to the bungalow, Geoffrey stripped off his clothing to examine his body in a long mirror in his father's dressing room. From what he could make out, the eruptions on his skin appeared to be in the early stages and, except for the few lesions between his fingers, none had yet developed into the hideous sores that had covered his father's face and body in death.

"Geoffrey...? Are you there?" his mother called, about to enter.

"You cannot come in, Mother. I am undressed!" Geoffrey shouted.

"We were worried, my darling. No one knew where you were. If the oil lamp had not been lit, we would never have known you were back."

"I am sorry, Mother. It was not my intention to worry you."

"If you still have that headache, Geoffrey, you must try some of the mixture Lorenzo has made. I am feeling much better after taking a little each day."

"Tomorrow perhaps. I am just getting ready for bed."

"Goodnight, my precious boy," she called. The swishing sound of her skirt trailing along the veranda slowly faded away, her heels clicking down the steps until he was once again alone.

Engrossed in examining the eruptions on his body, he had no idea that anyone had entered the room the next morning until he heard a sharp intake of breath from the open doorway.

"Oh Jeffy... What have you done?" Rosamund cried anxiously.

"For pity's sake, Rose, do not come anywhere near me. Stay away from me, please," he begged, but in trying to pull on his trousers too quickly lost his balance and fell over.

"Jeffy!" she screamed, dashing over to help.

"Do not touch me, Rose."

"This is no time for modesty, Jeffy. You are hurt. You must allow me to help you." She came closer, but again he held up both hands, as if trying to fend her off.

"I am perfectly fine, Rose. I lost my balance. Just… go away and allow me to get some clothes on."

"I am not going anywhere until you tell me what you have done to injure yourself." She crouched down beside him.

"For Christ's sake, Rose, just stay away from me!" Geoffrey shouted, crawling away. "It is not what I have done. It is what I have caught. If you get any closer, you might get infected too."

For a short time Rosamund said nothing and came no closer as the realisation set in. "You have been infected with the virus?"

"It looks that way."

"You cannot be sure, Jeffy. It might be something else entirely."

"I only wish that was true. The symptoms are identical to what Father described in his notebook," Geoffrey said wearily, too tired to cover his nakedness.

"There must be something I can do, Jeffy. I cannot let you… let you…" She faltered, the tears running unheeded down her cheeks. "There must be something that I can find to calm the awful inflammation on your skin."

"There is nothing, Rose, honestly; I have already looked."

"Then we must look again in case you have missed anything."

"If there was, I could manage on my own." Geoffrey began scratching the rash under his armpit, his nudity forgotten.

"Not those open sores on your back, you could not," Rosamund said resolutely, getting to her feet.

"Where are you going? Promise me you will not tell Mother; not yet anyway."

"I am going to Papa's laboratory; and no, I will not tell anyone about this, not unless I know for certain there is no cure." She stumbled tearfully out of the room.

By the time Rosamund returned, Geoffrey had struggled into a pair of his father's baggy underpants and one of his shirts. "Did you find anything?" he asked, trying to focus on the blurred image of her face.

"I came across this jar of cream labelled for use on the children's sores."

"If you hand it over, I can apply it myself."

"There is no need," she said, pulling on a pair of rubber gloves that were at least two sizes too large. Papa told me about these things in one of his letters. He never said that he had actually bought any."

"Rubber... like they use in car tyres?" Geoffrey asked.

"It would appear so. I might make a mess putting this on because they are too big for my hands but it will prevent me making any contact with your skin if that makes you feel easier."

"You should not be doing this, Rose."

"You know you would do the same for me, Jeffy. Now take that shirt off and that ridiculous underwear," she ordered, "but keep perfectly still so I can get this done before Mother gets curious and comes back." She began gently applying the cream to the infected areas, which immediately eased the irritation.

That evening, after Rosamund had applied more of the cream, Geoffrey managed to fall into a more comfortable sleep. Waking briefly in the night, he was aware of a light burning in the laboratory. The following morning Rosamund came in carrying three of their father's research books and a dictionary.

"Was that you last night in the lab?" Geoffrey asked, struggling to sit up.

"I couldn't sleep and thought I would make myself useful," she said, sitting cross-legged beside him, and opening the first book at one of two marked pages. "Read this section, Jeffy and see if it makes any sense to you."

"I can't focus, Rose. The infection has gone into the second stage. This is why you should not be anywhere near me."

"I refuse to argue about this, Jeffy. I am not going anywhere until we can find a way to help get you better." She began going through the text meticulously. "This book uses so many technical words, it is almost impossible to make any sense of them." Soon after she looked up something in the dictionary, which she then snapped shut with frustration. "Well that was a useless exercise!"

"Rose, you have to accept that Father would have scanned through every one of these volumes to find a cure for his children."

"He might have given up but I will not. There must be something, somewhere, in one of these stupid books to help, otherwise why bother shipping them all out here? But I went through every single one last night and found nothing even remotely similar to what you have." Rosamund closed the third book.

"They came from the hospital in London?" Geoffrey asked.

"Yes. Each one is stamped as hospital property."

"That would have been Mr King's influence. I remember Father saying he was quite high up in that field of research."

"I am only surprised you and Maggie never picked up on this before."

"Picked up on what exactly?"

"Well, if these were compiled by so-called tropical disease experts based in England, what might seem plausible to them on paper is not necessarily going to work out here in South America, is it?"

"Presumably Mr King's name is listed?"

"He is one of the eight names. Why do Englishmen always presume to know what ailments there are in other parts of the world, when I suspect most of them have never even set foot on foreign soil. As far as I know, Papa travelled over from Dublin and worked in London. He knew nothing about this continent first-hand, not before he came out here, and yet he was allowed to carry out this research, concocting heaven knows what. Why not leave it to the people here to find their own cures, instead of interfering?"

"You are absolutely right, only someone local to a region would be aware of all the infections and cures," Geoffrey said, suddenly feeling more optimistic than he had all day. "Did you notice if there were there any books on the shelf written in Portuguese or Spanish?"

"But none of us can speak either of those languages."

"Then our only chance of finding something useful might be in one of those tattered old books Maggs brought out with her. Could you get hold of them without her becoming involved?"

"I will try my best but you know what she is like: always wanting to know why I do anything."

It was a short time later when Rosamund returned but this time she was not alone. "I am so sorry, Jeffy; I had to ask where she kept them and Maggie insisted on bringing the books herself."

"I suppose they were buried in that huge bag of hers," Geoffrey said.

"They would not have been safe anywhere else," Marguerite said, stepping into the room. "Why did you not call on me, Geoffrey, instead of Rose?"

"I had no choice… just like now!"

"Well I am here now, so can you please undress and allow me to see these sore places?"

"I am not taking everything off, no matter what you say," Geoffrey blustered. "They are pretty bad. Some are bleeding. It is not a pretty sight."

"Just take your clothes off, Geoffrey, so that I can examine you properly. I will not faint at the sight of a man's naked body."

"Very well but not do not touch any part of me with your bare hands and I am keeping my underpants on, whatever you say!"

"Geoffrey, please, you are being silly. I need to examine all of these sores properly." She repositioned the oil lamp as Geoffrey carefully removed his shirt.

"I know what this is… I have the virus," he said, as the full extent of the inflamed areas became evident.

"Please God, no!" Marguerite gasped, catching on to the back of a chair for support.

"I fear that Mother might also be infected, although not so advanced. That should allow you more time to find an antidote."

"There is no cure, otherwise Father and the children would still be alive."

"Maybe not, but maybe there is a chance of finding a clue in one of those books Violet Dobson gave you. There might be a tree bark or some sort of fungus that could prevent the virus from advancing any further."

"Jeffy is right, Maggie. There are so many bottles and jars on the shelves in Father's laboratory, labelled with names that we might find in one of these books." Rosamund began thumbing through Grifka's *Uncharted Tributaries of the Amazon* until she came to an illustrated, fold-out page.

There were eight such sections of the book in total. Six of them had information on unknown tributaries. The seventh had a detailed drawing of the author's discovery of a sacred temple, previously known only from legend. From its location on the map, it appeared to be situated close to the Jesuit mission. Finally, there was a page of detailed information on a collection of tree barks and leaf mould recommended as cures for various ailments.

The breakthrough, however, came from a section Rosamund found in the second book, *Lost Tribes of the*

Rainforest. "Take a look at this illustration," she said excitedly, indicating a drawing of a bulbous root. "Look here... this is what the the Otter is always chewing."

"It looks similar, I agree but I am not sure it is the same thing," Marguerite said, studying the image closely.

"Maybe not but the clue is here before us; otherwise, how could only that one child have survived such a deadly outbreak?" Geoffrey asked.

"The native mothers would surely have realised the potency of this root too. They were probably all from this region," Marguerite pointed out.

"Not necessarily. Maybe the boy tasted them without knowing what they were. This is what boys do. I did the same back home, with plants on our estate. If this strain of infection was created by Father, there can be no antidote in existence, otherwise he would have concocted something to combat that creeping paralysis in the final stage. Any ideas he might have had would have died with him."

"You must never give up hope, Jeffy," Rosamund pleaded.

"I am going back into the laboratory again," said Marguerite firmly. "There may be something we have missed. In the meantime, we must pray that Lorenzo will return soon. He could help us find a cure, I am convinced of it."

By the following morning, the paralysis that he had been dreading had begun to restrict Geoffrey's mobility and he could barely stagger outside to the toilet, grabbing on to anything within reach to stop him from falling. His breathing was increasingly laboured and any thoughts he may have had about getting the young Otter to take him to the source of the bulbous roots was abandoned.

Grasping the handrail on his return, Geoffrey managed to haul his unresponsive limbs halfway up the steps to the veranda before the strength in his hands finally gave out and he crashed headlong to the bottom, where he lay in a heap. Fortunately Marguerite had witnessed this and, despite his

346

protests, she helped him to his feet and assisted him up the steps and on to the cane lounger.

"You must never attempt that again without help, Geoffrey," she said, making him as comfortable as she could.

"I thought my limbs would loosen up again, if I made the effort."

"Perhaps after a good rest you might find it easier. Until then, I must see if I there is a commode, or find something adaptable. I cannot have you falling down those steps again."

"You are wasting your time. I will not use a commode, even if you find one!" Geoffrey retorted, a prisoner of his own body.

"And why not, might I ask? A commode is the most practical solution if you cannot get to a lavatory. Rose found one for Mother, so there may be another somewhere," Marguerite mused.

"Why does Mother need one?" Geoffrey asked, dreading the answer.

"You were right; it seems that she too has contracted the virus. Rosamund is with her now." Marguerite placed a small table beside the recliner and soon after brought up a jug of water and a plate with slices of fruit. "Do try and eat something, Geoffrey. I will be back as soon as I have checked on Mother."

Nothing that Geoffrey tried to get some flexibility back into his hands and legs during the rest of that day had any effect. By late evening, even though he dreaded falling asleep after his condition had worsened so much the night before, he eventually dozed off. The following morning he awoke with an agonising pain in all of his limbs, barely able to move.

From what little he could see of his body when Rosamund uncovered him, the sores on his skin had worsened and were fearsome even to look at, let alone touch.

"I can manage well enough on my own without any help," Geoffrey lied. Ignoring his protests, she helped him to his feet. Once Rosamund had set her mind on something, it was impossible to stop her.

"When you have used the commode, I will put more of that cream on these awful sores before you lie down again," she said.

"Why bother if it is not working?"

"Because… I need to do something, anything that might stop this from getting any worse," she said, fighting back the tears. "Did Maggie tell you that she has found out where the Otter gets those nasty-looking bulbs from?"

"No… Are they growing close by?"

"Unfortunately not. It seems they can only be found in an area of everglades, further up the river and the problem with that is that we have no way of getting there without a canoe." She helped to steady him back to the lounger.

"There was one close by here, hauled onto the bank, below the burial site, unless it has gone now," Geoffrey said, wondering if he should finally admit to what had actually happened that day.

"Surely the owners would have collected it by now, unless you are keeping secrets again?" Rosamund said. "So tell me… who did it belong to and why would it still be there?"

"They cannot collect it because they are dead."

"Dead… how would you know that?"

"There were two head-hunters. The dog killed one of them, trying to protect me."

"And what became of the other?"

"I killed him."

"You must take me for a fool, Jeffy, if you expect me to believe that?" Rosamund spoke lightly but her widened eyes said different.

"You wanted the truth, Rose, and now you have it," Geoffrey said, in no mood for an argument. "I ran the bastard through with a gardening fork before he could kill the dog and, before you ask, I threw his body over the cliff."

"You killed him... with a gardening fork?" she asked in shock and disbelief. "Why on earth would you do that?"

"It was the day I was digging the children's graves."

"I can't believe that you would take a human life to save a dog."

"Well… not only because of the dog," Geoffrey said, regretting it immediately.

"What could have made you do such a dreadful thing?" Rosamund steeled herself and gave him a look from which he knew there was no way to evade the issue. "What are you leaving out?"

"They were carrying a pole of trophies… heads, strung up by their hair. I recognised one of them. Now are you satisfied?"

"You knew one of them, Jeffy? Who was it?"

"It was Nia. Just don't tell Mother."

"Oh no... Nia was barely older than me."

"Now can you understand why I did it?"

"Yes, and I would have done exactly the same."

"Then you must take Archie's knife and keep it with you at all times."

"No, Jeffy, you might need it yourself," Rosamund said grimly.

"What use would that be? I can barely use my hands. Maggs can fire a gun and you need the knife." Geoffrey winced as she applied more cream to the sores.

"If the canoe is still there, then I will take it. This root needs to be found but first I must take this cream over to Mother. While I am gone, try and rest a while." Rosamund smiled and screwed the lid back onto the jar.

"Only when you have put on my belt with Archie's knife in its sheath," Geoffrey said.

"I couldn't wear that… this belt would go around my waist twice. But if it will make you happy, then I shall wear it as a bandolier," Rosamund declared. Angling the belt diagonally across her body the handle of the sheathed knife protruded just behind her right shoulder, where it could be easily reached with her left hand in an emergency and, after their recent conversation, Geoffrey was certain that she would not hesitate to use it.

The search for the root was further delayed the next day when his Mother, having made a supreme effort to attend to Geoffrey herself, collapsed on her way back. It was clear that she was in a considerable amount of pain and finding it impossible to disguise that her beautiful clear eyes were clouding over with the encroaching blindness, just like Geoffrey's own. Unable to help, Geoffrey could only watch as his sisters helped her to her feet, and supported her back to her cabin.

"Mother asked me to load the revolver for her," Marguerite said when she arrived in his room.

"Surely not in her condition," Geoffrey said, fearing his mother might be intending to take her own life.

"There was no alternative, Geoffrey. She insisted. You would have done exactly the same if it makes her feel safe. I will be sleeping there tonight anyway. Rosamund wants to be here with you."

"But what if the gun goes off and you are not there?"

"Mother does not have enough strength in her fingers to unlock the safety catch, so she will come to no harm," Marguerite reassured him.

That night, Geoffrey resisted Rosamund's attempts to get him into his bed, knowing, though not saying, that it was doubtful he would ever get up again.

"I want to spend one more night beneath a canopy of starlight, while I am still able. It can be Hell on earth during the day in all that humidity but at nightfall everything changes and becomes cool and serene."

"What a splendid idea. That way we can wait for the sunrise together, like in the nursery back home," Rosamund said, unconsciously taking his hand.

"How I loved that old nursery of ours. They were happy days."

350

"And they will be again, once you and Mother have recovered."

"I doubt that can happen at this late stage, Rose. You need to prepare yourself now for what lies ahead." From his father's notes he knew the virus would soon be entering its final stage, since he could now barely see anything and the creeping paralysis was badly affecting his breathing.

"I refuse to abandon hope of a cure, whatever you say. I am determined we will soon return home to the Dales as a complete family. I honestly believe that once the Otter has taken us to find those roots, this will happen," she said.

They spent a beautiful night together beneath an awesome canopy of stars and Geoffrey felt blessed to have spent it with his younger sister. As dawn broke, the glare of indirect sunlight on the river through the billowing mist was magical, as if they had been transported into another world.

"How wonderful this is, Jeffy. Just promise me that when you are better you will compose a piece of music we can dedicate to this moment. It is one that I shall treasure for the rest of my life."

"Then I will do as you ask, Rose, for the two of us," Geoffrey agreed. It was what she wanted to hear but in his heart he knew it would be impossible to live for much longer with the rapid acceleration of the virus.

"Is there anything I can do for you before I go to Mother?" Rosamund asked.

"There is only one thing I need and it is not something you can help me with," Geoffrey said.

"I might, if you tell me. Who else would understand what goes on in that mind of yours?"

"Very well then, I would like to make amends for some of the rotten things I have said and done in the past but that is impossible now."

"This is about Archie," she said.

"How did you know that?" he asked with surprise.

"Perhaps because I know you almost as well as I know myself, so tell me."

"I would like to have seen Archie once more, to apologise for the uncharitable way I behaved when he was being so kind."

"You will see him again yourself, Jeffy." Rosamund said, tears welling in her eyes as she busied herself to make him comfortable in the cane recliner.

"That is not possible," Geoffrey said.

"I cannot guarantee that he will hear anything you say but you will definitely see him again." She returned a short time later with the sketch of Archie Westbrook and carefully pinned it to the wall above where Geoffrey was now sleeping.

The first thing Geoffrey saw on waking was Archie's questioning smile, so perfectly captured by Marguerite and, for just a moment, he forgot the increasing pain in his stiffening limbs as the paralysis worsened and his breathing became more laboured.

Through the open doorway he could clearly see the landing stage. He watched as Rosamund returned with the boy in the head-hunters' canoe, noticeably not wearing the belt-bandolier with Archie's knife, which he now discovered she had left within reach on the nightstand close to his bed.

An hour later, Marguerite came in to report that their mother had requested Rosamund remain at the compound and allow Marguerite to go in her place.

"Mother feels that Rose would be safer if she stayed here and I agree."

"Either of you would be vulnerable away from here, Maggs. Rose is much smaller and she could run faster if need be," he said, though in truth he was relieved that it was Rosamund who would be staying behind.

"Mother reasons that she has a loaded revolver in her cabin."

"But she does not have the strength in her hands to release the safety catch," Geoffrey said. He could barely move his own fingers and, if they were taken by surprise, it would be impossible for his mother to have the weapon ready in time.

"I have already taken care of that. Rose knows how to release the catch for her."

"What about you, Maggs?"

"I have Father's old service revolver with me. It makes perfect sense that I should be the one to go with the Otter; and besides, he would not go with Rosamund, only me."

Chapter Seventeen
Execution

The dugout was much narrower than Geoffrey had thought and he remembered how hard it had been for his sister to squeeze into the canoe that had brought her here. It was only when she gathered her shapeless gown about her before stepping into the rocking vessel, that he became aware of the alteration in her size. Compared to Rosamund's slight frame as she steadied the canoe she was still rather overweight but now she easily fitted into the narrow space with plenty of room to paddle.

The dugout had barely moved away from the staging when the first drops of rain bounced off the veranda rail; heavy warm splashes spraying through the open doorway on Geoffrey's tortured skin. From where he lay he could see Rosamund continuing to untangle the fishing nets and smiled. As children they had loved nothing better than to be out in a downpour and his mind went back to the farewell garden party in Ashbourne. At that moment Geoffrey longed for nothing more than to be set free from the cursed virus, if only for an hour, so that he could be with her, reliving the glory of times past on their grand estate, free from parental intrusion.

As if she had the very same thought she now turned towards him, waving and lifting her face into the rain, twirling into the dance, just as she had done when they were children. It was an exhibition he knew was for his benefit alone. How truly blessed he had been, having this wonderful girl as a companion throughout his young life. Yet now his inevitable death would leave her in this wretched place without him and perhaps their beloved Mother too. He prayed that Archie would come to find her and take her back where she belonged.

Although the rain eased off after a time, there was still no chance for Rosamund to stay dry as she sloshed through the squelching mud between their mother's cabin and the bungalow.

"You must stay with Mother, Rose, not keep on going back and forth," Geoffrey urged.

"It will not be for long. Maggie will be back soon then I can stay here with you." Rosamund wrung out her sodden hair. "I can only pray they will be successful. How long have they been gone?"

"Maybe an hour or two, it is hard to say."

"I hope they are not too long. Nothing could be more important than this."

"Just promise me that when they return you will take some of this antidote yourself, and get Maggs to take some too as a precaution." Geoffrey made a supreme effort to regulate his breathing so his voice would sound normal.

"Of course but only after you and Mother have been treated. Maggie has already been nibbling on some of those roots to please the Otter."

"Did she not offer you any?"

"It was not hers to give and from what I saw, the Otter had almost none left." Rosamund made her way back across the compound.

That morning the humidity seemed to have increased tenfold with the damp rising from the forest floor, an airless moisture that intensified Geoffrey's laboured breathing. Every intake was agonising, as if he was inhaling shards of broken glass into his lungs. Only his hearing remained unaffected, which gave him little comfort.

Through the haze of his deteriorating eyesight, nothing looked the same, with the writhing mist off the river creating menacing shapes, making him fear for Marguerite's safe return. With so many unknown terrors lurking beneath the surface, the thought of the canoe colliding with an unseen obstacle and capsizing only magnified his fears.

Geoffrey had been alone for a while when he heard the chugging engine of a shallow-draught boat coming down the river and soon Rosamund came out from tending their mother and looked towards the sound.

"Jeffy… there is a steamer coming! Lorenzo must have come back to rescue us. If anyone can find an antidote for you and Mother it will be him, I know it." She hitched up her skirt as she ran towards the staging.

"Rose… Rose, come back. It could be anyone," Geoffrey croaked in desperation, barely able to move. "For pity's sake, stay out of sight until you know who it is."

Hearing none of this, Rosamund reached the staging and stood waving downriver to attract the steamer's attention as soon as it cleared the mist. Her hands lowered as the nightmarish image was revealed, the filthy vessel already close to the staging with its stinking cargo of caiman hides. Staring back at her were the grotesque faces of Valdez and his companions, beside them their scar-faced stoker and a pockmarked albino, all watching her every move.

Within moments Valdez had cut the engine and was screaming orders at his one-armed and one-eyed companions to moor up. Geoffrey could only stare with desperation as his sister backed away from the water's edge.

"There is nothing for you here," Rosamund called dismissively as the boat crunched to a stop along the staging.

"Get away as fast as you can, Rose, that bastard has a rifle," Geoffrey screamed as his vision cleared and he saw Valdez shoulder his weapon. As the bullet ripped into the bark of a tree just a few feet away from her head, Rosamund stooped to snatch up a weighted fishing net and a hefty piece of wood before racing back towards the compound.

"Arm yourself with the knife, Jeffy. I need to protect Mother," Rosamund called as Valdez fired off a second shot. She veered off the track, forcing her way into the dense undergrowth, by the pack of hunters close on her heels.

Even though he could barely move his limbs, he knew he must try. Desperately he rocked himself back and forth on the bed until he crashed to the floor, colliding with the nightstand, from which Archie's knife dropped and embedded itself in the floor. With a superhuman effort he forced open his stiffening fingers, tugged it free and began crawling along the veranda on his elbows.

Once he was able to focus through the railings, he could see three of the men approaching the compound cautiously; there was no sign of Valdez. Forcing his head to turn, he saw Rosamund close to the washing area, arranging the net in her hand before whirling it above her head and launching it at the one-armed hunter. It widened in flight before dropping like a winged predator over the startled man. Once he was ensnared, Rosamund yanked hard on the rope and tugged him down, thrashing, to the ground. With calculated deliberation, she now swung the lump of wood like a club and cracked him hard on the head.

"Run for your life, Rose!" Geoffrey cried through the railings, hoping to divert attention away from his sister and bring the enemy close enough to use the knife on at least one of them.

Rosamund turned instinctively to see the second hunter charging towards her as if a demented creature, his one good eye wild and staring, the other blinking with unseeing rage. He was almost upon her when, grabbing a weighty, enamelled bucket, she swung it as hard as she could, hitting him squarely in the face and felling him like a log. He squirmed about in the mud beside his struggling companion, clutching his bleeding face and screaming abuse.

"For God's sake, run for it Rose... he is behind you!" Geoffrey croaked. A short distance away Valdez was visible briefly among the bushes a short distance from her, while Scarface and the albino were making their way cautiously along the veranda of Lady Claudia's cabin.

"I will not leave you or Mother," Rosamund called back, dropping the pail and grabbing the wood before cautiously making her way back to the bungalow.

"Forget me... there are two men in Mother's cabin."

Now the nauseating stench of Valdez invaded his senses as the brute reappeared only a short distance away from the bungalow steps, upwind of the girl. Geoffrey could only watch as the bear-like figure grabbed her from behind and flung her into the mud close to the veranda, where he was soon joined by his two companions, fighting to be the first to abuse her. Neither was a match for Valdez.

Wrenching the wood from her hand, he pinioned the shaft hard across her throat and, yanking open the flap of his trousers, forced himself into her. Screaming with hatred, two of her fingernails were torn off as she raked deep gouges across his pockmarked face at the very moment of his vile penetration.

Rosamund screamed only once, the force of his weight crushing the breath out of her as she waited for her opportunity and grabbed the knife that hung from his loosened belt. As Valdez reared away from her, reaching his orgasm, he was oblivious to the vicious blade in her hand and its intended direction until she slashed hard across his gaping mouth, slicing through the exposed muscles of his tongue.

Showered in a fountain of spurting blood, Valdez lurched drunkenly to his feet, wrenching the knife from her hand and kicking Rosamund viciously on the side of the head before he staggered away. His tongue lolled out of his mouth, filled with gurgling blood and leaving him powerless to speak. He offered no resistance as the one-armed hunter pushed him aside before he and the other in turn straddled the now motionless girl.

Burning with hatred, Geoffrey forced his useless limbs into motion, powered by an intense fury that could be satisfied only by revenge. But as he crawled towards the steps his strength gave out, leaving him unable to move and barely able to draw breath as the first hunter mounted the steps and entered the bungalow, clearly intent on ransacking the interior for valuables.

It was the first crack of gunfire that revived Geoffrey, before a second that clearly came from his mother's cabin. He lifted his head in time to see Scarface stagger out screaming in agony, his hand pressed against the gaping section of his face that had been shot clean away, before he toppled into the rain-drenched slime. Moments later the albino dashed out of the cabin, clutching Lady Claudia's jewellery box and treading Scarface deeper into the slime as he made his escape followed by a third and fourth shot from the interior that splintered the doorframe, accompanied by scream of frustration.

Geoffrey dragged himself crablike along the rough boards of the veranda using his elbows, shoulders and even his chin but Archie's knife slipped from his hand as the intruder reappeared in the open doorway with an armful of loot. Grabbing the violin from the nearby table he slammed it viciously against Geoffrey's skull, the instrument shattering on impact, before hurling the twisted remains high over the veranda, the strings creating a wailing discord of death before it plunged into the mud.

Dazed but not unconscious, Geoffrey forced himself on to his knees and launched himself at Rodrigo. Grabbing him around the ankles, he bit hard and deep into his flesh like a wild animal, sending the two of them crashing down the steps where the hunter wrenched him up by the hair and dragged him back up the steps to where his companion was waiting.

Unarmed and barely able to move, Geoffrey realised he still had one weapon: he could contaminate both men with the virus. Now the one-eyed bruiser forced his paralysed fingers apart, holding down first one hand and then the other in a vicelike grip. He pinioned them on to the corner of the steps, where his accomplice now stamped down viciously with his hobnailed boots, crushing and splintering the bones.

Through sheer willpower, Geoffrey forced himself not to pass out but hung on grimly, waiting for the perfect opportunity. When the leering one-eyed face came close enough to his own he spat a mouthful of blood into the deep cut on the man's head where Rose had felled him with the bucket. With a final act of defiance, Geoffrey then forced his crushed and bleeding fingers into the savage bites on the other man's leg before the two hunters grabbed hold of him together and hurled him down the steps like a rag doll, where he landed, bleeding, in the mud and, thankfully, blacked out.

It had been barely two hours earlier when Marguerite, wearing one of her father's shirts over her gown, had embarked on the most improbable journey of her life, through narrow channels of evil-smelling water with unimaginable horrors lurking in the murky depths beneath her feet.

The Otter had made a primitive wooden paddle, its handle bound with reeds to afford some protection against blistering but, after an hour of intense paddling, Marguerite needed to rest brief and bind her hands with strips torn from the shirt.

As they set off again the boy motioned for silence. Here the tributary fanned out into a sinister area of gloomy everglades and the dank, stale air swarmed with mosquitoes every time their paddles plunged into the water.

Moving forward slowly, the Otter avoided the denser areas of overhanging trees where opaque, bagged nests of young spiders were being disgorged on fine silken threads. A short distance away, a flock of white birds took to the air, squawking with a flurry of beating wings as one of them was dragged beneath the surface by a partially submerged caiman. Several more of the reptiles, previously camouflaged amid the debris and rotted logs, writhed at speed towards this potential source of food.

Less than a mile beyond the swamp, the boy manoeuvred the dugout with uncanny accuracy to moor against a high bank of high ground. Eager to collect the roots and return as quickly as possible, Marguerite gave little thought to any danger on the bank, more relieved to get away from the hidden terrors beneath the water, quickly easing herself from the cramped space to set foot on dry land.

Stumbling awkwardly in her father's oversized boots, Marguerite made her way up the steep, rocky gradient, following closely behind the Otter along a narrow track until the ground levelled out. Ahead of them, beneath the spread of a substantial tree, was a large boulder, blocking the track and perched precariously at the edge of a projecting ledge, from where it appeared it could roll off at any moment.

Walking ahead, the Otter was about to pass through a gap to the left of the boulder when Marguerite cried out in warning. What had appeared to be a thick bough of the tree above him shifted position as the anaconda opened its gaping mouth, before pulling back into the dense foliage as the boy hurled a rock at its head.

Petrified by the size of the reptile, Marguerite moved off the path to avoid the tree and made her way across an area of open ground to the side of the rock face, leaving the boy on the track above. Her only thought was to bypass the boulder and the overhanging boughs, avoiding whatever other creatures might be lurking amid the foliage.

To begin with the ground felt soft and springy underfoot and she ignored the Otter's shouts of alarm. It was only when the squelching boots started to drag on the treacle-like surface that she understood the danger; all too late, as she began sinking into the mud. Struggling against the suction only made her sink faster, the black slime oozing over the top of her boots. Petrified, she realised that even if she stood perfectly still she was gradually sinking lower.

As the deadly suction of the mud squelched tightly around her calves, she felt a looped vine drop neatly over her shoulders as the Otter threw a lasso from the high shelf of rock above her. Needing no prompting, Marguerite secured it under her armpits. Once the Otter had passed the end of the vine around the tree, he threw the free end down to her and, after a few misses she was able to grab on to the end. She toppled over leaving the loose-fitting boots buried beneath the squelching surface. Spread-eagled across the mud, Marguerite yanked hard on the vine with a strength she would never have believed possible, and hauled herself clear until she could stand and scramble clear of the bog.

When she reached the Otter, he was sitting with his legs dangling over the edge of the rock face, clearly upset. She sat down next to him, examining his knife with interest.

"The carving on this handle is magnificent. Where did you get this?"

"Lollen… him make," the Otter stated proudly.

"Lollen... You mean Lorenzo?" she asked, handing it back.

"Si… him my Lollen," the Otter said, getting up and urging her to follow.

Now walking barefoot, Marguerite followed cautiously for a short distance until they came upon an area that was sheltered by a rocky outcrop. At the centre of this clearing was a dark pool, fed by a trickle of water through a fissure in a steep rock face. As they got closer, two red snakes basking near the pool slithered away into the undergrowth.

From his backpack, the Otter removed a flat tin and sprinkled some of the contents around the pool. He rubbed more of the powder onto his face, arms, hands and feet, and then, with great care, he dusted a quantity lightly over Marguerite's face and arms. Mixing the remainder into a paste with water from the pool he massaged this into her blistered hands, applying what was left to her grazed legs and bleeding feet.

"Estar aqui – here," he said, pointing with a short stick among the reeds and, miming chewing the root. "This comida."

Almost hidden between the thick clumps of dark leaves along the edge of the pool was a row of plants bearing clusters of brilliant, bell-shaped blooms in layers of red, yellow and orange, all attached to a single stem. Camouflaged among them was another flowering plant, with a solitary stem bearing a single, green flower, with a broad, tongue-like stamen of dark magenta.

Watching the Otter wade waist high into the water she could understand why he had dusted his skin with the white powder as a thick cloud of mosquitoes erupted from the reeds and begin swarming about him as he carefully dug out an entire plant with his knife. He then sliced off the stem and green flower, trimming everything back from the now recognisable tubers, repeating the process until there was a stack piled beside him. After Marguerite had washed off any clinging mud she handed them back to the boy, who skilfully continued to top and tail each one.

Working rapidly, Marguerite wrapped them in broad leaves to prevent them drying out, the way the Otter had shown her. She was working on the last of them when she heard a single rifle shot, way off in the distance.

Uncertain where the sound had come from, she continued packing the tubers into the Otter's bag until a second shot was fired. Now it was clear exactly what direction it came from. Scrambling to her feet and leaving the remaining tubers behind, she hobbled towards the canoe as fast as she could, calling for the Otter to follow as more gunfire was now heard from beyond the everglades. Stubbing her toe on a rock Marguerite went sprawling, her revolver skidded across the bank into the river.

Lying in a muddy, crumpled heap in the rain, Geoffrey was barely distinguishable from the pile of ransacked loot surrounding him. How long he had been like this was impossible to tell and his will to live was retreating into the darkness that was gradually alleviating the intense pain throughout his body. He was aware only that he was moments away from that fathomless pit, from which dark menacing creatures were clambering out in preparation to drag him to a place where he would no longer remember the nightmarish happenings of that day.

He was distantly aware of Marguerite's voice calling out his name but was unable to shout or move. Through partially closed lids Geoffrey saw a bedraggled Rosamund, hunched on the veranda steps, her torn and blood-sodden clothing pulled protectively around her but useless in the heavy rainfall.

Barely able to breathe through his nose and with his mouth half buried in the mud, he could only watch as his older sister staggered away from the horrific scene, stumbling through the mud until she fell, tripping over the shattered violin. Scrambling to her feet, Marguerite grabbed the instrument and hurled its remains high into the air. The taut strings of the violin, stretched to the limit, wailed like some avenging banshee, scattering the birds in the tree above. It was only then that she began to scream, high-pitched and almost demented. It was clear she had no idea the twisted heap was her brother until the Otter prodded him with a stick.

"Missy, missy… Massa, him aqui!" the Otter cried.

Perhaps it was because of the abusive beating Geoffrey had been submitted to, or that every other part of his body seemed to be shutting down but his sense of hearing seemed to have amplified, judging by the high-pitched scream his elder sister gave from inside the bungalow. When she reappeared on the veranda with her mother's revolver, with an icy deliberation, she fired four shots into Scarface's corpse, sprawled at the edge of the staging, obliterating what remained of the face.

Reloading mechanically, Marguerite fixed her gaze on the hunched figure of Valdez, slumped beside one of the mooring posts where he had been abandoned by the other marauders. With menacing calm, Marguerite made her way slowly towards him through the driving rain, ankle-deep in churned-up mud, the wind flapping her sodden gown against her bare ankles. The downpour was rebounding off the wooden planks as she came to a standstill opposite him.

Valdez made a feeble attempt to get away as she approached but fell back against the post. He was trying to speak but the gashed corners of his mouth and the severed tongue made it impossible. Instead, only gurgling noises came through the frothing blood in his gaping mouth as he tried to plead for mercy.

With deliberate slowness, Marguerite raised the revolver in line with the terrified face of Valdez, released the safety catch and took careful aim. The first bullet whistled across his scalp, splintering into the post above his head.

"This, I give you from my mother," she hissed, firing the second bullet as precisely as the first to remove most of his right ear. Blubbering, Valdez clasped his hand against the ragged space at the side of his head before she fired again, tearing off his left ear. With no hope of escape, Valdez slobbered blood as she aimed the revolver once more.

"These I give you for the brutal mutilation of my brother," she said, firing the fourth and fifth bullets in rapid succession. The first shattered his right wrist, held against the missing ear, while the second splintered the left. Like a grotesque living parody of Munch's *Scream*, his mouth gaped open and closed like a landed fish, gurgling wordlessly in a plea for the execution to end.

"And this, you animal, is what I give you in return for those unspeakable horrors you have inflicted upon my sister," she hissed with loathing, aiming the revolver at his groin and pulling the trigger.

Almost primly, Marguerite hitched up the hem of her dress to avoid dragging it through the blood, pressed her foot into the small of his back and pushed him off the edge of the staging and into the river. She stood for a moment, the revolver hanging limply at her side, as his body drifted away into open water.

"Rot in Hell, you evil bastard!" she screamed. Valdez was now partially submerged but somehow still alive and feebly struggling when the water erupted around him, boiling with savage piranha as they began tearing him apart.

The last thing Geoffrey remembered before blacking out was his sister collapsing into a heap like a deflated sail as Valdez was dragged out of sight beneath the surface.

"Missy..."the Otter cried a while later, crouching beside Marguerite where she lay in the mud.

"Leave me, I can manage," she said groggily, staring transfixed over the surface of the river as she crawled on her hands and knees to recover the revolver.

"Lollen, him come missy, take Holy Place," the Otter said, trailing after Marguerite as she squelched across the compound focused only on her sister, unaware that her distraught mother had staggered out of her cabin. She was aided by a snapped curtain pole as she sloshed through the mud to reach her, clutching the torn and bloody nightdress against her, oblivious to the deep gash on her temple that was bleeding profusely.

"Not now, Otter," Marguerite muttered hoarsely, ashen-faced and trembling, her eyes focused only on Rosamund's huddled form on the blood-splattered steps and unable even to glance at Geoffrey's body, half buried in the mud as she passed.

"I swear I will find a way to get you away from this dreadful place, Rosamund." She bent over her sister but staggered back as she was pushed away savagely,

"Take your hands off me!" Rosamund screeched, her ravaged body clearly exposed through the remnants of her sodden clothing as she scrambled to her feet. "I swear before God, I will kill anyone who dares to lay a hand on me... anyone!"

"Those men cannot harm you any more, Rosamund" said Marguerite gently.

"I will not go anywhere without him!" Rosamund screamed. "You can leave me out here to die. This Hell is where I belong. Save Jeffy, not me," she wailed, pointing at Geoffrey's crumpled shape.

"I would if I could but I cannot. I fear Geoffrey is no longer with us. He is with God."

"Liar. He has to be. I have no desire to live without him" Rosamund cried, stumbling past her to reach Geoffrey and lift his battered head clear of the mud. "You must save Jeffy... not a whore like me! SAVE HIM! Or I swear before God, I will kill you myself!" She howled, choking back her sobs, as Lady Claudia knelt in the mud against her, caressing Geoffrey's face on Rosamund's lap.

"Most precious boy, you cannot leave Rose and your mother here, not without you. You cannot." She pleaded, the bruising around her throat becoming more evident as the torn garment ripped, revealing more discolouration and deep cuts on her arms as she cradled him.

"Damn you Marguerite... Help him!" Rosamund shrieked wildly.

"Do as Rosamund asks Marguerite and help us get your brother inside. I do not have the strength to lift him. "The gash on her head was oozing more blood as she attempted to move Geoffrey in the mud.

"What am I supposed to do then?" Marguerite asked.

"Help me keep the boy alive until the priest and Lorenzo return."

"No one will come back for us, not now mother, not ever."

"The priest Fitzgerald might not but I have every confidence that Lorenzo will."

where with Noel Effingham once the liner has docked in Pernambuco?" Marguerite commented. "You are far too young to mix with any of that man's group. Who knows what they get up to?"

"It is an invitation to the opera, Maggs. I have not signed up for an expedition into the heart of the rainforest," Geoffrey said, doing his best to laugh it off, but wishing all the same that he hadn't agreed to be in Noel's party after all.

"It matters not who Geoffrey is seated with for the performance," said Lady Claudia. "For a musician such as him it has the promise of a spectacular event. Harriet is on the board of directors and assures me this is a show that should not be missed."

"But it would be so much better if Geoffrey sat with us," Marguerite said.

"Why would any young gentleman prefer spending the evening in the company of chattering ladies? Your brother is no longer a child and having male company will be good preparation for his introduction to London society, when he is accepted into the Royal Academy of Music."

"Why do you talk as if I am not here? I do have an opinion," Geoffrey complained.

"Oh do be quiet, Jeffy," Rosamund said, flushing with embarrassment and purposely turning her back on two men who were ogling her from a nearby table.

"I will inform Lady Drummond tomorrow that you are unable to attend," his mother said, her voice rising in alarm as Geoffrey got up and strode over to the men.

"If either of you gentlemen had an ounce of decency between you, then you would be concentrating on your food and NOT on my sister. She, like other ladies of refinement in this room, is here to dine and not be an object to be stared at by a pair of bloody halfwits! If you persist with this, I will demand the captain bars you from being seated anywhere near our table in future," Geoffrey snapped, glaring at the men. Embarrassed at the unwanted scrutiny they were now receiving from the other guests, they rose and left the salon with muted words of apology.

On the following afternoon, although the air conditioning appeared to be working well in other first-class areas of the liner, there was a problem with the units operating in the ballroom and Geoffrey was again granted permission to use it for his daily practice. Even so, the sweltering conditions made the session seem ten times harder, mainly because of the intricate finger changes required for each movement.

After playing for over three hours without a break, Geoffrey was both mentally and physically exhausted. His fingers ached unbearably and he'd forgotten to bring any oil to massage them, an omission that he fully intended to rectify on his return to the cabin.

After taking a short rest and returning the instrument to its case, Geoffrey unlocked the doors, only to be confronted by Noel Effingham, clapping his hands and beaming like the Cheshire cat.

"Well done… Bravo!" Noel gushed.

"What the hell are you doing here, Noel? I do not like anyone being around when I practise," Geoffrey grumbled.

"You should never keep such musical artistry from others. Practice or not, you should have an audience. Your playing was sublime."

"It was nothing of the kind. There were too many mistakes, way too many!" Geoffrey was embarrassed by this exuberant display from a man he barely knew and by comments which, in his own opinion, were completely unjustified.

"There were only mistakes no one else would have noticed."

"They were nevertheless and you should not have been there as they should," Geoffrey said, wanting to get clear of Noel and his fervent gestures.

"I have no longer Sir Geoffrey. I had to wait for your sister before I could get close enough to listen properly."

"Lady Marguerite was listening?" Geoffrey asked with surprise. "She is normally on deck, dabbling in her watercolours."

"Lady Rosamund. I have been back five or six times in the past three hours to get close enough but never could. She has been outside for most of that time."

For a moment Geoffrey was speechless, finding it difficult to take in the information. "That does not make sense at all. Rose loathes hearing me play. She always has."

"Then you are mistaken, Sir Geoffrey. I doubt if she even saw me here, not until she was leaving. She seemed to be hypnotised by those intricate melodies. I swear to you, there were tears in her eyes when we passed in the corridor."

"Then if you will excuse me, Noel, I really must dash." Geoffrey increased his pace as he strode purposefully away with the hope of shaking Noel off.

"You have a remarkable gift, Sir Geoffrey," Noel persisted, trying to keep up with the long legs of the younger man. "You must tell me the name of that piece you were playing. I am familiar with most classical works but cannot for the life of me place that work. It was truly exquisite."

"The composition was my own in preparation for my entrance exam to the Royal Academy of Music on our return," Geoffrey admitted reluctantly as they reached his cabin door. "Now if you will excuse me, Noel, I really must get inside to oil my hands."

"Then will you join me later on deck, after you have rested? I would like to learn more about your musical compositions."

"Not this evening, Noel; I have promised to read to Mother. The electric lighting in her cabin is too harsh and it reflects off the page and is affecting her vision."

In need of a bath and a lie down after the sweltering heat of the ballroom, Geoffrey came back on deck in the late afternoon to a mild and pleasant breeze, in mind to join his mother until he saw her in conversation with Lady Harriet Drummond. To avoid being noticed, he wandered to another section of the deck where Marguerite was leaning against the handrail, cautiously peering down on to a sheltered section of the lower deck.

"What's so fascinating down there, Maggs?" Geoffrey whispered, making her jump.

"How you startled me, Geoffrey. I do wish you would not creep up on me like that. You could have given me a heart attack," Marguerite retorted.

"If you were not so intent on being so bloody nosy, you might have seen me coming." He moved closer to the rail. "What were you watching anyway?"

"Do keep your voice down, otherwise they might hear you."

"Who might that be?"

"Agnes Hulme, the Effingham's maid. It is disgusting behaviour," she whispered, prompting him to look over the rail to catch the flash of red stockings, the woman still in the arms of a brutish sailor with a bull neck and tattooed arms like hairy tree trunks.

"They are only kissing. What is wrong with that?"

"Everything, if she is about to marry someone else," Marguerite said, urging him away from the rail. "Come away, Geoffrey, they might see you."

"Would it matter if they did?" Geoffrey complained.

Folding up her portable easel, she packed away her paints and brushes into the capacious bag she carried everywhere, allowing time for Geoffrey to examine her latest watercolour in the journal.

"I say, Maggs; this is a jolly good impression of the area with the palms and Mother lounging in that blue dress. I will never understand how you are able to breathe such life into these paintings with just a few strokes. Whenever I try, the damned things never resemble anything at all, except a nasty splodge of colour, yet yours look so real. How do you do it?"

"Practice I suppose, like you with the violin."

"When you come to think of it, we are a bit of an obsessive pair." Geoffrey smiled, massaging his fingers, before picking up the folding easel and paint box, leaving his sister to carry the artwork and the omni-present bag.
With every passing day it was becoming noticeably warmer but the cooling ocean breeze gave many unsuspecting passengers a false illusion of the oppressive humidity that would await them on arrival. Recently there had been sightings of other vessels on the horizon, sea birds circling in their wake. The dark shape of a cargo steamer, a dying breed of vessel with tall, spindly masts that, with sails furled, gave the impression of three crucifixes. It belched out black, acrid smoke from its twin chimney stacks as it ploughed its way through the water.
Later that afternoon, two graceful ships in full sail were seen on the horizon, the billowing canvas propelling the vessels across the ocean with the effortless elegance of swans. To Geoffrey, this was a sight as inspirational as a piece of music

and he gazed after the second one long after it had disappeared from sight. He came away from the rail saddened by the realisation that, all too soon, sailing under canvas across the Atlantic would become a thing the past. In need of some diversion, he found Marguerite on deck, reading.

"What are you reading? I have never seen you this absorbed, except when you are drawing or painting."

"Take a look," she said, handing over her battered copy of *Lost Tribes of the Rainforest.* "You should read this page. You might find it of interest."

Taking the book, Geoffrey skimmed over the page before finding the paragraph she had indicated. "'Therefore, based on all the relevant information, it is logical that an unidentified tribe of pale-skinned mystics, known as the River People, could actually exist,'" he read back to her. "Surely you do not believe this hokum?"

"There must be some foundation of truth in this mysterious sect. Otherwise, why bother writing about it?"

"Maybe sensationalism would be a start, otherwise why would anyone give the chapter such a bizarre heading?" he snorted. "'The White Rain Gods of the Cloud Forest'" He flicked through the volume. "Or what about this: 'The Mysterious Temple of Light'?" He chortled. "I swear, I have never read anything so outrageous. It reads like a Jules Verne novel."

"Unless you have read it, do not mock. Look through the information yourself and then offer your caustic opinion when I return."

"Where are you off to now?"

"To see if Mother is finished with Dr Beresford."

"Why… is she unwell again?"

"They are discussing the months of convalescence Florence will need before she can return to England and there is not much time to arrange it. The *Lugansa* docks in the port of Pernambuco for only ten days before it continues up the coast to Apalla. I would not imagine it will remain there for more than a few days before we set sail for England."

Once he was alone, Geoffrey was soon absorbed in the book reading of a lost geological site where in the year AD 420, a Peruvian mystic was said to have constructed the Temple of Light, a magnificent structure visible only by moonlight. The temple was reputed to provide a gateway into the afterlife protected by the spirit of the Moon, using a route identifiable solely by starlight when a pathway into the astral plain became clearly visible to the naked eye.

It was on the day the coastline of South America finally appeared on the horizon that Dr Beresford came up to Geoffrey on deck and handed him a bottle of pills.

"Please forgive me for this hasty exchange, Sir Geoffrey but unfortunately there has been an incident below deck which needs my urgent attention. Since I am unable to deliver these in person, I entrust Lady Claudia's medication into your capable hands. Please make sure Her Ladyship takes only one pill, four times a day as prescribed; taking any more than that could prove fatal."

"Fatal? What the hell are they and why does Mother need them?"

"These are the strongest painkillers we have on board for her condition, Sir Geoffrey. More than that, I am not at liberty to say."

"What condition? You cannot just say that and walk away, Beresford."

"Unfortunately I must. Forgive me, Sir, but there is an engineer being untangled from some equipment and he is in danger of losing his life if I do not amputate a leg to release him." He strode away, leaving Geoffrey to contemplate a bottle containing more red pills but much smaller than those he had previously seen.

Any thoughts of questioning his mother about her need for the pills went out of his head as he entered her cabin only to discover Agnes Hulme folding and packing gowns into one of the opened suitcases.

"What is that woman doing here, Mother?" Geoffrey asked suspiciously.

"Noel Effingham has very kindly offered Miss Hulme's services to assist with my packing since Florence cannot," Lady Claudia said, looking distinctly unwell herself. "Be a darling, Geoffrey and see if you can find Dr Beresford. He should have been here an hour ago."

"Are these what you wanted, Mother?" Geoffrey was frustrated that he could not question her further with Agnes busying herself about the room. "Beresford asked me to hand these to you. We met purely by chance on the deck. He apologised for not calling in person but he was on his way to deal with an emergency."

"Thank goodness you have them, darling, my head is splitting." She immediately swallowed two of the red pills with a tumbler of water.

"Beresford said they could be lethal if you take more than the prescribed dose. You should take one, four times a day. It is written here on the label."

"Do not fuss, darling. These are only to prevent the migraines from getting worse," she said lightly, although he wasn't convinced. "Has the steward provided someone to assist with your own packing, Geoffrey?"

"There is no need, Mother. I can manage it myself."

"Are you sure? You were never the tidiest boy. You must have your linen folded properly, or they will be dreadfully creased on arrival."

"If they are, then I will have someone at the hotel iron them."

"Then you must have them press every single item and have what you do not need for two days repacked."

"Repacked, why? The *Lugansa* will be in dock for more than a week."

"Please accept my apologies, darling. I have already informed your sisters about the change of plan."

"What plan? Is Father meeting us somewhere else instead?"

"This is not about your father, Geoffrey. It is important that we stay somewhere more socially acceptable than the

374

hotel. That is why I have accepted Lady Harriet's kind offer of some private accommodation at her plantation."

"What next? First a box at the opera and now we are invited to stay for a week with that old dragon? What about the meeting with Father? After all, he is the reason we have travelled out here and, as we have not laid eyes on him over the last four years, would a hotel not be a more appropriate place for us to become reacquainted?"

"Everything is arranged, Geoffrey. We will be staying at the Maximilian Hotel for the first two nights, by which time the business with your father at the solicitor's office will have been concluded."

"I see, and then we are expected to uproot and relocate somewhere else until the *Lugansa* sets sail, just because that old dragon snaps her fingers?"

"Mind your manners, Geoffrey. That is no way to speak about an offer of kindness. This is what comes of having an absentee father for the past four years. What Lady Harriet has so kindly offered is a separate wing of the main house and the reason I agreed to her generous offer is because, unlike hotel accommodation, there would be an uninterrupted space for your violin practice."

"I am truly sorry, Mother. I had no idea. The last thing I want is to upset you." Geoffrey turned and left abruptly before she could see the tears in his eyes.

Printed in Great Britain
by Amazon